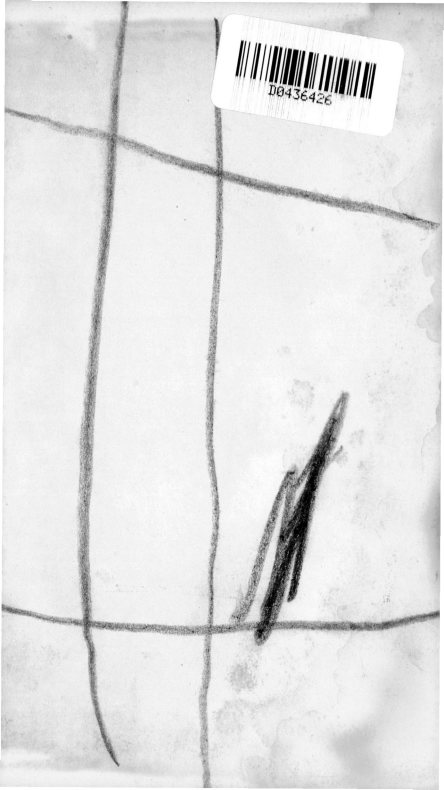

Never Dies the Dream

books by Margaret Landon

NEVER DIES THE DREAM

ANNA AND THE KING OF SIAM

NEVER DIES THE DREAM

Margaret Landon

Garden City, N.Y.

DOUBLEDAY & COMPANY, INC.

1949

The characters in this book exist only in the author's imagination. The background is presented with as much authenticity as the author, who knew it intimately for ten years, was able to convey.

For Kenneth Perry Landon

Who dreams shall live! And if we do not dream
Then we shall build no Temple into Time.
Yon dust cloud, whirling slow against the sun,
Was yesterday's cathedral, stirred to gold
By heedless footsteps of a passing world.
The faiths of stone and steel are failed of proof.
The King who made religion of a Sword
Passes, and is forgotten in a day.
The crown he wore rots at a lily's root,
The rose unfurls her banners o'er his dust.

The dreamer dies, but never dies the dream,
Though Death shall call the whirlwind to his aid,
Enlist men's passions, trick their hearts with hate,
Still shall the Vision live! Say nevermore
That dreams are fragile things. What else endures
Of all this broken world save only dreams!

—DANA BURNET

Never Dies the Dream

CHAPTER 1

THE GREAT HEAT OF THE DAY WAS OVER, AND BANGKOK HAD BEGUN to crawl out of its hovels and palaces for a breath of air. Austins, Fiats, and Chevrolets debouched from the narrow downtown streets and headed for the Sports Club. The men and women who rode in them had the pallid well-laundered appearance of people who stay long in the tropics. Now that the working day was over, they were hurrying out to the edge of the city to play golf and tennis, or drink ginger beers and whiskey *stingahs* on the club verandas.

In the canals that ran beside the streets naked brown children splashed, laughing and shouting. The sun glinted on their wet bodies. A Sikh watchman squatted cross-legged beside Sathorn Road polishing a brass bowl with ashes and dirt. His robes were loose, and his long frowzy hair was clubbed back carelessly. It would be several hours before he was required to stand, smartly turbaned, at the gate in the wall of whitewashed brick that lay behind him.

India Severn saw all this, as she had seen it a thousand times before, without observing it. She had lived in Bangkok twenty-five years, since 1905, and the kaleidoscopic streets, the nauseous odor of the markets, and the arabesque beauty of temples and palaces were more familiar now than her native Chicago.

She was absorbed within herself as the taxi rattled up Sathorn Road to the gates of the American Legation. Several motors with liveried chauffeurs pulled out of the drive as she turned in. There was a line of picture hats and afternoon dresses moving into the hall ahead of her, dresses of flowered georgette and chiffon that touched the ground and flowed around their wearers in soft ripples of color. Men in freshly donned whites, starched and immaculate, their faces already damp with perspiration, were signing the guest book.

India looked down at her old blue lace and wondered why she had come. She would rather have gone home to a bath and a nap before dinner. But even as she formed the question she knew the answer. Mr. Denniscort was the first American Minister since Hamilton King who had been friendly to the missionary community, and this made his invitation a command as surely as if he were royalty.

India Severn had long ago accepted the fact that to be a missionary was to be considered queer, to be herded into a kind of ghetto that was no less real for the circumstance that its walls existed only in people's minds. This was true in America even among church people, and it was true in Bangkok. Missionaries were regarded as *déclassé* not only by businessmen, whose instinct to profit found altruism suspect, but also by their country's official representatives.

India felt no rancor against them for this. Diplomacy was a quiet, ruthless game that left small time for other things. The prize was not money but power. Dinner with a prince, cocktails with the "right people"—these were important cards in a diplomat's hand. Missionaries were only troublesome compatriots, to whom time and attention were begrudged; or busybodies who should have stayed at home; or, at best, well-meaning eccentrics to be avoided.

When Mr. Denniscort arrived the year before, the missionaries had expected him to conform to the pattern of his predecessors. They had been more startled than gratified to see his long black car, with miniature flags on the fenders, draw up before the church on his first Sunday in Bangkok. They had gone to his lavish parties almost diffidently, and then, as they came to know him, with increasing pleasure. For the first time in twenty years the Americans in Bangkok were a national unit, loosely knit and heterogeneous, but still a community like the British with the Legation at its hub. It was the compulsion of his kindness that had brought India today.

The last of the men signing the guest book disappeared up the stairs, and she added her name to the list. The hall was deserted and for the moment still. She paused to straighten her old horsehair hat. Then, not yet satisfied, powdered her nose, but with the inattention of a woman whose face has never pleased her.

Yet in its way it was a charming face. The nose was delicately cut and faintly arched. The skin was a clear bisque, the eyes a deep sea blue. They had warmth and intelligence, and the mouth was kind. Gray hair fell in loose waves to a bun at the nape of the neck, enhancing the line of the bones. Time had etched humor and patience into the face, but India, looking quickly at herself in the mirror, was not aware of this. She had been told as a child that she was plain, and she still believed it.

The tea tables were on the veranda upstairs, and the Minister was receiving there. India waited while he talked to a fat and perspiring little count. She liked the Minister's height and leanness, and the look of controlled power that made him seem patrician and aloof as compared to the volatile European. For once, she decided, her country was adequately represented.

"Miss Severn," he said, turning to her, "I've been looking for you. I want to talk to you about Miss Kane."

India's face clouded. "I'm sorry she's annoying you, Mr. Denniscort. She promised to leave you alone."

His eyes were quizzical as they looked down at her. "I won't explain now if you can wait. I'd rather talk to you privately."

"Yes, of course," India agreed, "I'll be glad to wait," and left him to the next guest.

She threaded little knots of people, some sitting and some standing, to the tea tables, depressed by the knowledge that Dulcie had broken her promise. Apparently Dulcie still believed that someday, somehow, she would recover her father's property. And she had all the pertinacity of the wronged and helpless combined with the deviousness of the Eurasian. Not even the possibility that she might forfeit her livelihood seemed able to deflect her from the central passion of her life. "I ought to discharge her," India thought, knowing she would not, and wondered whether the inability to inflict pain was a sign of weakness or of strength.

Chinese boys in the livery of the Legation—white coats buttoned to the neck and wide white trousers gathered into black socks—were hurrying about replenishing the supply of elaborate cakes and sandwiches. A pretty woman India did not know poured her a cup of tea. There was a chair standing alone at the far end of the veranda beyond the talking groups of people. She went toward it, suddenly conscious that she was very tired.

The lawns of the Legation were green and beautifully kept, even at the end of the dry season. Hibiscus hedges hid the road, but beyond them India could see the canal lined on either side with great flame-of-the-forest trees. Their scarlet crowns were reflected in the water, and these reflections were stirred from time to time by laden boats being poled slowly upstream. India bit with pleasure into a small sandwich, and thought that Bangkok was never so lovely as when the flame-of-the-forest trees were in bloom.

A small puff of wind came in across the veranda, relieving the thickness of the heat. Sitting and looking at the trees, India could forget Dulcie for the moment. She could even put out of her mind the hovels in which she had been calling that afternoon, and all the tide of human problems that beat against her heart year in and year out. The beauty of the red flowers, the warmth of the tea filled her with a sensual pleasure that crept along her body, untying the knots of the day.

"Tea!" she thought gratefully. "What a wonderful institution!" and went on to play with the thought, blowing it up into a series of bubbles for her own amusement. She wondered if the world wouldn't be more livable if everyone stopped for tea at four-thirty in the afternoon.

"India Severn! What are you doing sitting off here?" Her rambling thoughts were interrupted by the boom of a familiar voice. "Haven't you any social instincts?"

The woman who spoke was tall and heavily built. Her thick chestnut hair was worn on top of her head in a style long outmoded. India thought irreverently that it looked as if it had been splashed there like a cow dropping. The woman was fanning herself with a mauve hat, and her vigorous middle-aged face was flushed.

"Grace, you startled me! Of course I have social instincts. They're full of holes from several hours of calling, that's all. I'm sitting here mending them."

Grace Rutherford found a chair and dusted it with her handkerchief. "I hate rattan chairs," she said. "You never know when they'll be full of bedbugs. Who did you see today?"

"Some members of Second Church," India answered evasively, unwilling to conjure up the long and tiring afternoon. "I wish drugstores sold wisdom in pills."

"The trouble with you, my dear, is that you try to do too much."

"No, the trouble with me is that I accomplish too little."

Grace settled back and took a sip of tea. "Everyone wanted money as usual, I suppose."

"Not everyone," India demurred, then added, "But Lamai's baby needs an operation for hernia."

Grace sat forward. "India, you're not to give that woman another *satang!*"

India's face closed. "I don't have it to give, but her need remains for all that."

"Mmmmmm, and who else?"

"The last person I saw before coming here was Major Rosenfeld. He grieves because none of his old friends come to see him, except Captain Swensen, who was there yesterday, incidentally. The Major was still chuckling over the Captain's troubles with his first mate on the run up from Singapore. I had to hear the story three times. 'An' they called the Captain to the mate's cabin, see? Said the mate was killing mosquitoes, see? So the Captain went down, and the mate was killing mosquitoes all right—he was shooting them with his revolver!' And he'd rock with laughter—— He's dying, Grace."

"Who's taking care of him? Marthe?"

"Yes, but Iner's helping financially. You ought to drop in and see him." The two women sat for a moment lost in thought. They both remembered the Major as he had been when they came to Siam, a big hearty man who entertained the great and near great, was intimate with princes and nobles. Now he had come to the end, with no one to care but the son and daughter of the Siamese wife he had never permitted to sit at his table.

Grace sighed. *"Sic transit gloria,"* she said heavily. Almost at once she regained her briskness, pulled a carved blackwood table toward her and set her plate on it. "India, I nearly forgot what I came over to say." Her voice took on the timbre of authority she used in the classroom. "My dear, it's twenty-five years since you and I came out together."

India laughed. "Why don't you omit the preamble, Grace, and get on with the scolding?"

The other woman frowned, and it was a moment before she

could rearrange her thoughts and start again. "Is it true that Mani Soderstrom is staying at Jasmine Hall?"

"And if it is, would it constitute a capital offense?" India mimicked Grace's portentousness, her eyes full of laughter.

"You shouldn't mix a woman of her sort in with your girls."

"I haven't 'mixed her in' with them. She has a room on my side of the house."

"So it *is* true! Did she run away again?"

"She came to Bangkok for medical treatment, and Mr. Soderstrom asked me to look after her."

"*You* look after *her!* That girl can smell a man for a mile!"

India chuckled. "What an inelegant expression, Grace."

The other woman shook her head impatiently. "You know as well as I do that appropriations are going to be cut after the Board delegation surveys the Mission. You ought to be more discreet."

"When I say 'look after her' I don't mean what you infer, Grace. Mr. Soderstrom wouldn't ask it." India's voice was sober, but it was unyielding. "All he wants is a respectable place for her to stay, and he's paying me two hundred and fifty ticals."

"You're begging the issue, as usual, India. You've got to stop turning your home into a warren for every waif and stray in the kingdom. The money you make out of it is beside the point."

"Not for me." The laughter was gone from India's eyes. "And if I avoid this subject it's only because we never agree."

In the florid expanse of Grace's face the hazel eyes blazed suddenly green. "India Severn," she said softly, "always the Good Samaritan."

India set her teacup down. The tea in it had grown cold anyway. "Grace, you're like the Red Queen in *Alice in Wonderland*. If anyone disobeys orders, you shout *Off with her head!*"

Grace Rutherford flushed deeply. The tropics had not drained her face of its natural ruddiness, and when her anger was kindled a strawberry mark, shaped roughly like the British Isles, flared along the left side of her neck. It was there now. India, seeing it, thought that Grace resented opposition increasingly with the years. She was the only woman member of the Executive Committee, and her position as principal of Wattana Wittaya Academy made her influential with the Siamese community as well. Perhaps it was natural that she expected deference.

"India, listen to me!" Grace's voice had moved up a key. "What do you accomplish sheltering derelicts like Mani? We both know that I could count the really useful graduates of your school on the fingers of my two hands. You ought to concentrate on the better type of girl, as we do at Wattana."

India's face went white. "You ignore the fact that no one sends me 'the better type of girl.' Not that I accept your valuation."

"No one will as long as you take in people like Mani. Upper-class Siamese don't want their daughters associating with women of doubtful morals. Not that there's ever been any doubt about Mani's."

"Mani has nothing to do with the school."

"She lives in the house that shelters it, she and a lot more like her."

"Not a lot, certainly."

"All right, India, tell me offhand how many people you have living in Jasmine Hall."

India laughed ruefully. "Just a minute until I count."

Grace's eyes gleamed. "That's what I mean!" she said.

When India did not answer, Grace lowered her voice and went on. "You seem to ignore the fact, India, that you can't afford to flout public opinion the way you do. After all, the Station pays your rent to provide you with a home and a place for your school. It never voted you the right to run a hostel for fallen women, and it never will!"

She stood up, brushing the crumbs from her lap with a firm white hand. India rose also. She stood very straight, but even so she hardly came above Grace Rutherford's shoulder.

Grace glanced briefly at India. "You're a rare and lovely person, my dear, but you need to remember the adage about casting pearls before swine." She patted India's shoulder and put on her hat.

India stood silent, her face still white, as the mauve figure under its load of violets moved off like a ship in full sail.

CHAPTER 2

THE PLEASANT REPOSE OF THE AFTERNOON WAS SHATTERED. THE veranda, the trees, the canal had lost their charm, and the heat was suddenly more than India could endure. Mr. Denniscort was still busy with his guests, who lingered laughing and talking over cocktails and tea, loath to go.

More than half of them, India saw, were Siamese. It was common knowledge in Bangkok that Mr. Denniscort was as popular among the Siamese as among his own countrymen, probably because he was what they thought an American ought to be. He was democratic, enterprising, and unconventional, and this they could understand. They were critical of Americans who seemed to them merely bad copies of Europeans.

Several more cars turned in at the gate while India waited, and she was tempted to postpone the interview until another time. Her argument with Grace had left her exhausted, and she wanted only to go home. Then she reminded herself that Mr. Denniscort was a busy man, and that there was really nothing to prevent her waiting a little longer. But not here. She was too tired to make conversation. She would go outdoors and find a quiet corner in which to sit until the Minister was free.

There was no one in the garden, but there were benches and a pleasant calm. The modulated cadence of voices floated from above. As she walked away from the house the sound became muted until it was only a murmur. She remembered a bench behind some hibiscus at the far end and was pleased to find that it was still there. It stood in a small separate garden where a statue of Pan with his pipes looked out from a niche in the leaves. The wife of a former Minister had planted the hedges to separate this corner from the whole, and had furnished it with tables and chairs. She had often used it as a place for serving tea to her friends.

India slipped through the narrow and seemingly unused opening with satisfaction, glad to have remembered this retreat. There was an air of privacy about it, as if it were a room walled away from the world but open to the sky. The lawn had been watered earlier in the afternoon, and there was a sweet smell of hay from a pile of freshly cut grass that the gardener had not yet removed.

The bench was long and backless, and so hidden from the house that India yielded to an overpowering temptation to slip off her shoes and stretch out full length. If she heard anyone coming she could get up quickly and retrieve them, and she was very tired! The stone of the bench was nicely warm from the sun. She felt guilty and a little abandoned as she lay down, but the relief was luxurious. After all though—one didn't really—at a party—and such a formal one—but just for a minute——

How long she slept she could not guess. She heard no one approach, and it was only gradually that words on the other side of the hedge penetrated her consciousness. At first they seemed part of a dream. Then slowly they separated on a sharp sound that might have been a gasp or a sob.

". . . go away! I tell you, go away! You've got to stop following me around like this. People are beginning to notice." It was a girl's voice speaking, low and intense.

"But look here, Angela, you make yourself so damned hard to get at." This was a man's voice, a confident voice. It was low, but it was laughing.

"Don't call me *Angela*. I'm not Angela to you."

"Yes, you are, darling. You run through my thoughts like a god-damned tune, *Angela, Angela, tum-te-tum, Angela, Angela, tum-te-tum*. You ought to be flattered."

"Please leave me alone, Benny, please, please!" The girl's voice was full of entreaty. "You're making me conspicuous."

"Listen, Angel darling"—the man's voice ignored the pleading—"God made you conspicuous. That's something you can't blame on me."

"Please go away, Benny. Please, please, go away!"

India Severn sat up on the bench and tucked her stockinged feet under her. She was nonplussed. Should she try to slip out through the hedge?

The man's voice was speaking again. "Look, Angel, I'm not going

away, and I'm not going to stop following you around until you
hear me out. If you try to run, I swear I'll run after you! I have a lot
to say to you, and it has to be soon. Promise you'll let me call for
you tonight and you can go back to the party."

There were tears in the girl's voice when she spoke. "Please let
go of my wrist, Benny. You don't understand. Charoon's family
would hold it against me. They're old-fashioned. It wouldn't matter
how innocent it was, they wouldn't like it."

"That's where you're wrong." The man's voice hardened. "They'd
like it very well, and the less innocent the better. You and I both
know they want to get rid of you. Why don't you come with me
to Java next week? I've got a month's vacation."

Angela gasped, and the sound was that of a terrified animal.
"No," she said, "no, no, no!" The pain in her voice implored him
to pity her, to hold back, to forego further pursuit. In some way not
clear to India she was defenseless and terrified, forsaken and at the
same time hunted, and the man knew this.

Into India's mind came a flash of that last horrible scene in Mary
Webb's *Gone to Earth*. She saw with physical intensity the terrified
figure of Hazel Woodus running from her pursuers with her pet
fox in her arms; saw the liver-and-white hounds come over the ridge
like water; saw the hunters with their ravening eyes and open cavernous mouths; saw Hazel small and dark against the sky as she fell
with Foxy into everlasting silence, and heard the cry go up, "Gone
to earth! Gone to earth!" Then the defenselessness of Hazel and the
defenselessness of Angela were fused in India's mind.

The deep anger that smoldered in her always against those who
prey upon the helpless, stalk and devour them without pity and
without shame, erupted now against the man beyond the hedge.
She had a crazy impulse to rush out and beat his face with her bare
fists. The ridiculousness of this idea sobered her. She lay back on
the bench and closed her eyes. If they blundered into her retreat
at least the girl need never know that she had been overheard. And
if not, one more secret could be added to the collection in the quiet
storehouse of her heart.

The girl was sobbing now. "I hate you!" she said in a passionate
whisper. "You've no right to say things like that to me."

"Yes, I have, Angela." The bravado was gone from the man's voice, and it was shaking. "I love you, and I'll do anything you say except leave you alone! I want you, damn you! Damn you! Damn you! And you can make your own terms, marriage and kids and all that. You ought to get rid of that stinking native husband of yours anyway. And I'm going to see you tonight if I have to knock him down to do it."

"Don't call Charoon a native!" The girl took hold of the word angrily. "He's a gentleman, and that's more than you are."

"He's a prince and I'm just a guy from Brooklyn, if that's what you mean, but he's a rotter, and we both know it."

He's trying to hurt her, India thought. *He's trying to crack her resistance to him with anger and pain.*

"No!" He had hurt her. "You're a beast to say it!"

"But I'm not a gentleman, as you pointed out a minute ago." There was no answer. "And here's something else a gentleman wouldn't say"—the words were coming from between his teeth— "being a gentleman doesn't keep your husband faithful to you, does it, darling?"

The girl did not reply, and after what seemed a long interval it was the man's voice that finally spoke. "It hurts, doesn't it, sweetheart?" Then almost angrily: "Why do you care so much? He isn't worth it. Don't cry, Angela!"

There was another long pause, and again the man's voice, uncomfortable now but persistent. "And you knew, didn't you? Everyone's been wondering." The girl still made no answer, and her silence seemed to goad him for when he spoke his voice was mocking. "You couldn't hold him, could you, Angel? Not against one of those succulent little brown girls?"

India was overcome with remorse to find herself listening avidly, eyes wide open, hoping against hope that the girl could fight back, could extricate herself from the mesh of words tightening around her. Then there was the sound of a loud slap and running feet.

"Great Caesar's ghost!" India said to herself, resorting in the poverty of her own vocabulary to an expression she had learned recently from the son of a friend. Then she unclenched her fists, breathed deeply, and sat up. The clear green air of late afternoon hovered around her like a mirage. Outside the hedge there was silence. She put on her shoes and waited, but nothing further disturbed the quiet of her garden.

Who was the girl—with an American voice? Married to a Siamese —and the marriage was crumbling . . . This Benny and how many others were stalking her? . . . She's afraid of him too—but why? Unless she has nowhere to turn . . . Someone ought to help her.

The word *help* tripped her thoughts in full course. *I'm as bad as that woman in Galsworthy with her lame ducks,* she thought ruefully. *What was her name? June Forsyte, wasn't it? Old Jolyon's daughter . . . I wonder what Grace would say if——* "Am I my brother's keeper?" probably. No, surely not! That was Cain's question. "Who is my neighbor?"—that was what they had asked Christ, tempting him. . . . Could Grace actually pass by on the other side, if she had heard? No, of course not. And what did people do when their lives disintegrated around them, unless someone helped? Those who couldn't pick up the pieces and fit them together again? The answer to that she knew, and the answer was stark.

"O God, I wasn't made to be indifferent!" she cried silently. "I can't let them do this to her without trying to help——" She whispered the words angrily, but they were a prayer.

No one disturbed her. On the far side of the garden she heard a succession of cars cough into life, and then leave. After twenty minutes she climbed the stairs again to the veranda. The Minister's guests were going now, many had gone. In spite of herself she looked around for the girl.

The woman over by the railing was young—yes, but she was too plain. That one? No, now that she turned she was middle-aged. Perhaps—yes, it must be—of course, it was! The girl in the yellow dress. And there was a Siamese with her. Why, it was Princess Sandhya's oldest son! Charoon Suksamran! The girl had said "Charoon," but there were so many Charoons.

How beautiful the girl was! Like something by Cellini in antique and very precious gold. Slender and yet ripe. That was the word that fitted her, ripe. In the last rays of the sun she seemed to have been carved of gold. What perfectly amazing hair! Like molten metal—too rich to be anything but natural—and her skin—it seemed to be lighted with candles. Her dress, almost amber, fell to her feet from a high young bosom. And her crownless hat was of a piece with her hair.

India found herself motionless, staring, absorbed in the breathtaking beauty of the girl. She felt a sense of outrage to think that anything so flawless could be violated by the sorrows of ordinary flesh. Or was such great beauty always too heavy a load to be carried?

"Oh, there you are, Miss Severn." Mr. Denniscort was beside her. "Won't you come into my office? I was afraid you'd gone."

India took a chair opposite his desk. He unlocked a drawer and drew out an envelope. "There, now about Miss Kane? Has she consulted you?"

"No, she hasn't. As a matter of fact, she promised to leave you alone, on pain of forfeiting her position with me. She's been hounding your predecessors for years."

He smiled. "So I've heard. She's convinced that the consul who acted as executor of her father's will disposed of the property contrary to the terms of the will, and she thinks that he profited from the transaction. In other words, she suspects fraud."

"Yes, I know."

"I'm rather more than half-persuaded that she's right."

"But it was all so long ago!" India exclaimed.

"True. On the other hand, her father was an American, and when he died American law applied. I've examined the will. According to its terms the property should not have been sold until the youngest child came of age. The executor was to rent the land and the three houses on it during the interval, and use the money for the education of the children. From what I've been able to learn about the mother she was an ignorant woman of the sort that attached themselves to white men in those days. I rather think she and her paramour murdered Captain Kane in the belief that she would inherit the property. You see, he had recently married her here at the Legation to legitimatize the children. Whatever happened to her, do you know?"

"The man who murdered Captain Kane was beheaded," India

answered. "Dulcie's mother got off with five or six years in prison. The two older children died of cholera, that same year, and one of our missionary families took Dulcie. She was educated in America with their own children, and then came back here to teach. I don't think she ever saw her mother. The woman disappeared upcountry somewhere after she was released from prison. And I'm certain Dulcie didn't know anything about the will until fifteen or twenty years ago. Surely there's nothing she can do now!"

"Ordinarily the statute of limitations would apply, of course," Mr. Denniscort agreed, "but this is a curious case. I'm going to talk it over with a lawyer. If she can prove fraud, and I think she can, she may be able to convince a court that there's a cloud on the title in spite of the lapse of time."

India leaned forward anxiously. "I think you'd better not encourage her, Mr. Denniscort."

The Minister's eyes glinted, and his bronzed face was transformed for an instant by a mischievous grin like a street gamin's. "Why, Miss Severn," he said severely, "I thought you'd want me to help your friend."

India smiled a little wanly. "Oh, I do, very much. If you can. Dulcie's sixty-two, and no one will give her work any more except me, and I'm not sure I can keep her if——"

"All right. I understand. She's coming to see me again tomorrow, and I'll promise to be circumspect."

India stood up to go, and then hesitated. "And please don't tell her that you've talked to me. If she doesn't know, I can wink at what she's done."

The Minister chuckled. "I understand," he said.

India Severn was one of the last of the guests to walk down the steps and out the drive. She was late to dinner. Dusk was gathering. Lights twinkled on the wheels of the red rickshas that stood waiting near the gates.

India walked toward them just as the golden girl climbed into a great blue car that looked as long as a locomotive. The girl leaned back against the blue leather of the seat and took off her hat. Even without the sun her hair glinted. Her eyes were on the flame-of-the-forest trees along the canal. She didn't see the slight gray-haired woman in the old lace dress who passed close to the car and turned into Sathorn Road. The car rolled out of the drive behind India and off down the street, scattering pedestrians and rickshas with the arrogance of its musical horns.

India looked after it thoughtfully, watching until it was out of sight. Then she seated herself in one of the rickshas and jogged off home.

CHAPTER 3

JASMINE HALL STOOD ON AN OLD STREET CALLED BAMRUNG MUANG Road, which in translation meant *Improve-the-City Road.* During the late nineteenth century the street had been fashionable. Now the good residential sections of Bangkok were several miles away on Sathorn Road and even farther out.

When it was new the house had stood well back in a garden of jasmine, roses, and flowering trees. Some years before, the owner had built a row of shops along Bamrung Muang Road, cutting Jasmine Hall off from the street. A narrow lane parted this row at the halfway point and ran back seventy-five feet to the high red gate by which the house was approached.

Like all the shops of Bangkok except the European-owned stores, these were the homes of their proprietors as well as places of business. The heavy wooden shutters that marked the end of the trading day rarely went up across them until midnight, and were down again by seven the next morning, Sunday included. The clatter and noise of bargaining, the raucous quarrels of the shop families, the wailing of babies in the night were objectionable to foreigners, who would no longer rent Jasmine Hall. That was how India managed to get it for the small sum she could pay.

The remnant of the original garden, at the center of which the house stood, was roughly circular and had a diameter of three hundred feet. There was still a profusion of jasmine and many old trees, tamarind, frangipani, and jacaranda. Half a dozen rain trees made lofty arches against the sky. They had the pleasing habit of folding their leaves at night to let in air and opening them every morning for shade. The roses were long since dead.

A wire fence and a canal, which was hardly more than a ditch, separated the semicircle of the front garden from the ebullient, wrangling life of the shop families, but gave little protection. Sometimes Chinese children, seeing India pottering around among the beds of amaryllis and plumbago, would chant derisively at her as she worked, *"Ang mau, ang mau, ang mau!"* (Devil with a red head, red head, red head!) It was their scornful epithet for all white-skinned people.

On other days when school children played hopscotch near the canal, clods of earth would come hurtling across it to scatter them. The Chinese children would shriek with pleasure to see them run and take up an alternate chant reserved for Siamese, "Barbarians, barbarians, barbarians!" Lined up on their side of the canal, they would vie with each other in throwing obscene maledictions and rotten fruit at the better world of Jasmine Hall, until a scolding woman exploded from the back of a shop and cuffed them indoors.

The house was a sprawling two-story building, painted gray, and encircled by verandas upstairs and down. Those on the second story jutted out beyond those on the first and were supported by wooden trusses. The resulting effect was vaguely reminiscent of a Swiss chalet. This illusion was enhanced by the steepness of the roof, which was made of red tiles imported from China. The tiles had weathered through the years to undulations of rose, with a froth of black mold across them, like the close conventional waves in a Chinese painting. Wide eaves overhung the house to keep out both sun and rain, and at the ceiling level of the verandas were fringes of lacy gingerbread to screen them further from the sun, for the house had once been very fine.

When India returned from Mr. Denniscort's party it was already dark. She dismissed her ricksha at the head of the lane and slipped through the postern gate without calling the watchman, whose name was Klee.

Sundown had brought no cooling wind, and the anomaly of heat and darkness was even more oppressive than the hot day had been.

As India walked toward the house, searching fingers of heat pulsed upward along her body from the bricks of the driveway. Just for a moment there was a stirring in the rain trees overhead. *Perhaps,* India thought, listening for some repetition of the sound, *the rain will come tonight.* It was the twelfth of May, and the change in monsoon was due.

She went upstairs quickly, intent on finishing her accounts before going to bed, but when she turned on the light all the confusion of her office leaped out of the darkness at her. She stood a moment bleak with despair. Ordinarily her apartment included the adjoining bedroom, as well as a kitchen and bathroom made from a section of the side veranda. Since she had let Mani Soderstrom have the bedroom, her possessions were crowded into the office.

"Things!" she thought wearily. "Things, things, things!"

She sighed and, turning to the table, cleared away several mounds of unsorted correspondence to make room for her account books. The table had been dragged into the middle of the floor where the unshaded bulb in the single fixture could shine on it.

As India set to work, Plo, her cook, brought in a tray. While India ate she sorted vouchers, pausing a moment to frown over the fact that rice had gone up a tical a sack since the beginning of the month. The food Plo had saved for her was tasteless from long standing, and she set it aside to concentrate on her work. She had hardly finished sorting when a puff of wind came through the veranda doors and whirled some of the carefully placed vouchers across the room.

"The monsoon!" she said half aloud, and gathered the flying papers under books, then stood silent, feeling the wind increase around her, alert to catch the first faraway rumble of the rain. The long dry season was breaking at last! Just this afternoon it had stretched into the future without boundaries or limits, like a shimmering expanse of dead ocean. Its unremitting fervor parched not only trees and grass but even people, until they rattled in the husks of themselves, or grew taut and brittle. It was the relentlessness of the heat, the conviction that this year it would prove eternal, which made it almost more than could be endured. Now it was over!

Listening intently, India heard in the distance the first premonitory roll of thunder, felt the hot rush of wind double its tempo. Then big drops fell like pebbles across the roof, and suddenly the whole school came alive. Children and teachers scampered. The house was full of wind and laughter. Every rule, every friction, every quarrel was blown away with the heat.

After the first scattered drops, there was a breathless interval of doubt before the storm broke. India did not move. She stood with her hand still on a pile of vouchers, waiting for what she knew would come.

In a few minutes the monsoon was upon them, thunderous torrents of rain that lashed the trees with sadistic fury and catapulted from the roof. It shot in along the verandas, drenching chairs and floor and several pieces of forgotten embroidery. The wide double doors that took the place of windows rattled and banged in a dance of their own. The endless clanging of trams on Bamrung Muang Road, the constantly blowing motor horns, the cries of hawkers, the shuffle of wooden clogs were cut off as if a switch had been pulled, and the monsoon was supreme.

India's first thought was for her Ali Baba jars. In the days before Bangkok had a modern pumping system, they had been used to store rain water, collected in the wet season, for use in the dry. India still preferred the taste of rain water to that of boiled city water, and every year she had the jars filled and stored under the house until the water lost its brackish flavor and could be drunk.

"Get the jars out, Det *cha*," she called to the coolie above the sound of the rain. He had just finished unrolling the *moolies*, flexible curtains of split bamboo lined with blue cotton cloth that were let down to protect the verandas from rain. The stale, dusty smell of them filled the house.

It was not necessary for India to supervise Det in the placing of the jars, since he had done it many times before, but it was part of the yearly ritual of the changing season, which she was unwilling to forego. Together they edged cautiously under the first-floor veranda, flashing torches around them for fear of snakes. Jasmine Hall had no basement. The ground floor rested on piles five feet high.

India took off the wooden covers of six jars, and Det rolled them out into the rain. As he put a jar under a downspout water roared into it. Each jar was emptied and set up again before he moved on to the next. Both of them were wet by the time they finished, but the violence of the rain felt good to India.

When the commotion had subsided, she had some of the soft water heated and carried to her bathroom. It was luxurious to plunge her head up and down in it, to feel the soap lather and froth, then to pour over herself dipper after dipper of the cool water gushing into her bathroom jar from the eaves, and overflowing voluptuously through the drain.

She went back to her accounts with her head turbaned in a towel. The house was relaxed and still. Outside the sweet and steady rhythm of the rain continued like music. Once more she arranged her vouchers along the table, and for an hour worked steadily, saying the figures aloud to rout the fumes of sleep. Then her mind slid away for the third or fourth time to the golden girl she had seen that afternoon at the Legation, and she thought again of Grace's accusation.

Was it true that her lifelong preoccupation with people in trouble was nothing more than a subtle form of self-gratification? She revolved the idea slowly, trying to gauge the measure of its accuracy. Could she, for instance, lay open the motive beneath her impulse to help the girl? The determination to do so had seized on her suddenly without any process of ratiocination. It had sprung completely formed from some hidden logic in which the sequence of thought was too swift to retrace. She had not seen Angela at the time, therefore the enchantment of her beauty had no relevance. It had been nothing more than an overwhelming awareness of the girl's need that had come to her through the hedge. Yet need was everywhere, and only certain needs had impelling force even for the most conscientious. She thought impatiently that questions of motive were hard to answer. In last analysis one had to admit that the ego was a slippery thing. One had to believe, in all humility—or would Grace find her humility false too?—that God spoke through the feeling of concern.

She dismissed the problem as insoluble and went back to her accounts. Twelve o'clock came and then twelve-thirty before the report was finally copied on the blank furnished by the treasurer's office. When she removed the towel from her head, her hair curled damply around her forehead. The rain had stopped, but there was a steady drip from the big trees onto the roof. Traffic had begun again on Bamrung Muang Road, and the muffled sound of it came blurred but persistent through the wet night air.

India was brushing her hair when stealthy footsteps echoed through the silence of the house. Her hand stopped, and she was instantly alert, then relaxed, hearing a familiar rhythm in the steps. There was a knock on her door, and a whisper asked, "Are you still up?"

"Come in, Dulcie," India called softly. "Did you get wet?"

The woman who entered was tall and spare. She was wearing a full black skirt that swept the floor and a white shirtwaist, long-sleeved, high-necked, delicately tucked and trimmed with lace. Above the foamy shirtwaist her face was dark, almost black, her nose hawklike, her hair a puffy mass, like spun sugar candy.

"I was at Khun Lian's for dinner," she said in a precise voice that carved each syllable to a forgotten standard of elegance. "Her son brought me home. Are you doing your accounts?"

"I've just finished."

Dulcie Kane sat down in a rocker, laying a rolled umbrella on the floor. She looked at India speculatively, and her jet eyes began to sparkle.

"I've been thinking all day that it's time we did something for the orphans of Siam," she said ingratiatingly.

"Orphans, Dulcie?" India blinked.

"We have a Biblical obligation to them, you know."

"I don't believe I understand," India answered slowly, but even as she said the words she had a premonition that she did.

"I was reading the Apostle James at devotions this morning and was struck with his command: *Succor the orphans and fatherless in their afflictions.*"

India put her brush down and took up the comb. "It's *VISIT the fatherless and widows*, isn't it?"

Petulance showed briefly in Dulcie's face, then she inclined her head. "You're probably right, but as I was saying, we're doing nothing for them."

"I have yet to see an unwanted orphan in Siam," India said, unimpressed.

"I know several," Dulcie retorted.

"In that case, let's *visit* them tomorrow."

"These children live in Ayuthia."

"That's not too difficult. I'm going up next month. I'll call on them for you." India spoke firmly.

Any question about Dulcie's purpose was gone. She had mounted another hobby and was bent on riding India down. Two years before it had been "a convent for Christian widows." India had allowed her to install five in the guest room at Jasmine Hall, but the project had died quickly in wrangling, and three of the widows had remarried. Last year it had been a Christian Women's Club for Chinese Relief. The Bible school girls had prepared refreshments for its monthly meetings, until it evaporated with Dulcie's interest. Evidently this year it was to be orphans.

Dulcie leaned away from her chair and looked at India suspiciously. "A social visit does nothing to improve the lot of a destitute child."

"It's what your verse enjoins on us," India parried. She was half-annoyed and half-amused at Dulcie's indirectness. Why didn't she say what she wanted?

Dulcie's face had frozen into disapproval. *"No verse of Scripture is of private interpretation apart from the whole,"* she quoted with her usual disregard for the exact text of the Bible. "You must compare it with other verses, like Christ's command to go the second mile."

This kind of game always ended badly, but India could not resist saying, "Ayuthia is more than forty miles from Bangkok."

Dulcie was outraged. "Holy Writ is not concerned with physical miles, India. Our Lord was speaking of spiritual values."

India was suddenly too tired to play hide-and-seek any longer. "Food and shelter are not spiritual values," she said shortly. "You can measure their cost in terms of money."

Dulcie sat back and interlaced her long black fingers with precision. "Three orphans wouldn't cost very much."

"Dulcie, you don't know what you ask." India pushed her account books across the table. "Look at these and see for yourself whether the school can squeeze in another penniless child."

"I'm not interested in figures," Dulcie said, refusing the books with a wave of her hand.

"I'm not myself, but they still have power to limit my benevolences."

Dulcie's mouth set stubbornly. "All I want you to do is help me get started. I've written Mr. Rockefeller for the rest."

"You've what?"

"I've written the philanthropist, Mr. John D. Rockefeller. It would be a small matter for him to send me four or five thousand dollars a year for an orphanage here."

India leaned back weakly, filled with a sudden irresistible desire to laugh. It was always like this, arguing with Dulcie. And yet there was something rather grand about the way she plowed through a discussion as a ship would ride the waves. But what would Grace say if Jasmine Hall took in three orphans to please Dulcie? There was really no question about the answer to that.

"Who are your orphans?" India asked curiously.

Dulcie warmed at once. "Two sisters named Ploy and Dang, whose father was killed on the railroad last year, and a little girl named Sanu, who's living with an aunt. I've planned the whole thing. They can sleep on mats in my room and work for their board."

India refused to be hurried. "If you press me for a decision tonight, Dulcie, I'll say *No*. I'm tired and I'm going to bed."

CHAPTER 4

LATE THE NEXT AFTERNOON INDIA STEPPED FROM A RICKSHA IN front of Princess Sandhya's palace. She had no plan of action. She had come to reconnoiter the situation of the golden girl. Darun Burananda, her head teacher, had accompanied her, since it would not have been correct even for a *farang* to make a visit of ceremony unattended.

The palace was located in the oldest quarter of the city, within what had been the confines of the city wall, but was not itself old. It had been built during the latter half of the previous century when the sumptuary laws reserving brick for monarch and church were revoked. The walls were plastered and whitewashed, the shutters and doors painted brown, the roof overweighted with tile. Although it was large it was nondescript, resembling in style the houses of Singapore that had served Siamese royalty as models.

A heavy gate in the high wall surrounding the palace stood open, unguarded in the drowsy cusp of the afternoon. India and Darun entered and crossed a paved courtyard toward the marble steps of the mansion. On either side were formal gardens with sanded paths, clipped trees growing in jardinieres of Chinese porcelain, and roses in tubs.

A servant girl, lying on a rug in the vestibule with her head hanging through the door, sat up drowsily at their approach and then crouched low in salute. Darun explained in quick Siamese that Miss Severn had come to pay her respects to the *Tan Ying*, and India gave the girl a faintly yellowed card. She ushered them into a reception room and crawled out backward on her hands and knees to announce them to her mistress.

The room was oval with niches along the walls where marble figures of Italian workmanship, modestly draped, had been set. On the floor was a thick carpet in a design of red and yellow roses. There were carved and gilded tables, and carved and gilded chairs, sofas covered with petit point that looked French, and a profusion of distended pillows richly embroidered in the Siamese style. Several bronze heads stood on marble pedestals, among them a likeness of Princess Sandhya's late husband. Twenty minutes passed, and no one came. The air in the room was fusty. India stood up and walked around, examining the pictures. There were several large prints in green velvet frames, one showing the Siamese Ambassadors sent to Louis XIV with their heads low and their rumps high. The supercilious courtiers behind the King seemed to be looking down on them with amusement. Another showed the Ambassadors sent to Queen Victoria. The chief Ambassador, with his chin propped on the lowest step of the throne, was reading the ceremonial address that King Mongkut had written.

Soft whispering from behind a screen hiding the door to the rest of the house told India that a clutch of servant girls was peering in at them. There was some scuffling, some giggling. Still no one came. After a tour of the room she sat down again. On the table in front of her was a copy of the *Lumbini Memorial Book* and a tiger's skull partially plated with gold to make a container, in which a few moldy cigarettes had been left standing. She picked up the book and turned the pages idly. She was accustomed to waiting for people of high rank. The delay was sometimes an assertion of superiority on their part and sometimes an indifference to time.

The *Memorial Book* was full of pictures of King Vajiravudh: the King as a student at Eton, the King in kimono during a visit to Japan, the King as king, the King in a field marshal's uniform. India wondered, as she had before when reduced to this occupation in calling on highborn Siamese, how he had climbed in and out of so many changes of costume in a single lifetime.

Then the soft whispering ceased. India replaced the book on the carved table. She stood up and Darun dropped to the floor. A moment later a Siamese noblewoman of the old school came through the door.

She was short and stout, dressed in a black *panung* and white sleeveless blouse, and her feet were bare. Her hair was cut in the even brush that had been the mode during the reign of King Chulalongkorn and was supposed to suggest the lotus. The only evidence of her rank was a long scarf worn around her blouse and over her left shoulder. It had been folded to form accordion pleats, and the mark of these could be seen horizontally across it. A diamond-studded pin fastened the scarf at her shoulder, and seemed to be the insignia of some order conferred on her by the King. She wore no rings nor other jewelry, but on her heavy-jowled face was the high look of one who is never crossed.

"Ah, mem," she said, limping over to India and shaking her hand, "I'm glad to see you. Sit down, please." She salaamed Darun carelessly, hardly raising her joined palms above her waist.

"How are you, Tan Ying?" India asked, resuming her seat.

The Siamese woman, intent on making herself comfortable in spite of a suppurating sore on her right ankle, did not reply. Two servant girls had crawled in behind her. One placed a stool and moved a gold spittoon to the side of her chair. The second carried a betel set on a gold tray.

"Will you have tea?" the Princess asked when she was settled. "No? Some aerated water then?" and without waiting for their reply called impatiently, "Cham, where are you?"

The servant who had admitted them slithered from behind the screen on her elbows and knees.

"Two glasses of cream soda and some biscuits," the Princess ordered.

From the wrought-gold tray her servant held she selected a slice of betel and rolled seri leaf. Carefully she waxed the inside of her lip and inserted a pinch of tobacco, opened a gold box from which she took lime to spread on the leaf, then put it and the nut into her mouth. Belatedly she offered the tray to India. The gesture was perfunctory for she knew that India would refuse.

"You should learn to chew, mem," she said, chuckling a little at the thought. "It's a great comfort as one grows older, better than smoking. And you?" She motioned toward Darun, who also declined.

"Oh yes, my health. I'm very well except for this abscess on—if you'll pardon the mention of it—my foot." She shifted to bring the well foot under her, and India thought that like all the women of her generation she was uncomfortable in a chair. "I never go out any more, my friends must come to me. It's the privilege of age. Of course on holy days I go to the temple when I can, but that isn't often. You never made a Christian of me, did you, mem?" And she chuckled again, amused by the memory of India's evangelistic efforts as they had applied to herself. "I haven't forgotten that you tried, but we of the royal family cling to what is our own. And how about you? Are you still trying to pry up our teak log with your sliver?"

The question, like those before it, was rhetorical, and the Princess did not wait for a reply. "All religions are the same, mem," she said, draining the laughter from her face and leaning forward. "I value the work of your Mission in teaching the poor and healing the sick, but we do not need your religion. You tell us, *Thou shalt*

not kill, and *Thou shalt not steal,* and we say that the Enlightened
One taught those same things four hundred years before Christ was
born. Why should we become Christians then?" She spat carefully
into the golden cuspidor, and looked at India.

It was an old argument between them and without heat. All the
things that might have been said formed themselves and rose to the
barrier of India's teeth, but the Princess had heard them before, and
neither was impressed with the other's reasoning. So India only
smiled. After an interval, during which the Princess waited courteously for a reply, she concluded that India had not come for religious discussion and returned to her own affairs.

The cream soda came and some English biscuits tasting of the
tinfoil in which they were wrapped. The Princess chattered with
animation, pleased to have an attentive audience now that she lived
in retirement, and India listened with interest. It was her spontaneous tribute to all people, but the Princess took it as a compliment to
herself. When a direct question was put to her, India answered.
For the most part she let the Tan Ying talk, asking only occasional
questions, hoping meanwhile for answers to those she did not wish
to put into words.

After an hour a small boy toddled into the room. He was naked
and dimpled, about two years old, and he leaned against the Tan
Ying's knee, looking shyly at India's hat. She removed it, then held
out her hand to him, but he drew back against the Princess, who
took the tinfoil from a biscuit for him without interrupting an
account she was giving of her one trip to Europe.

"I tell you, mem, I was so glad to get back I vowed I'd never leave
Siam again, and I never have," she concluded. "It wasn't the cold
that bothered me, as I'd expected. It was the food! I thought if I had
to eat another insipid farang meal I'd starve first. We Siamese can't
make automobiles, but we *can* cook."

India asked, "Is the little boy one of your grandchildren?"

"My only grandchild."

The Tan Ying gave him another biscuit, and he looked at the
stranger solemnly out of wondering eyes so large and dark that they
suggested Indian ancestry. India reflected that Charoon also had the
light skin and handsome features of a young Rajput, but then of

course there was Indian blood in the royal family. The little boy seemed to be debating the wisdom of examining her at closer range.

"He's Anotai's son," the Princess said.

"Anotai was a beautiful child, too," India answered.

The Princess was pleased. "Yes, really prettier than Du, as a matter of fact. He's a captain in the army, you know. I guess you heard that Ompai died the year before his father. He was in England studying to be an engineer. Sutai is the only one left in school now." A cloud moved across the pale moon of her face. "You know about Charoon's marriage, I suppose."

She looked at India keenly, and India tried to keep her face blank while she framed an evasive reply. She had begun to think that the Princess, who usually talked much of her sons, was avoiding the subject. Some hint of movement in her eyes must have betrayed her, for a rush of angry color stained the Siamese woman's throat.

"The girl is an American!" she said contemptuously with a sudden violence that was at variance with her previous manner.

She spat into the golden spittoon a stream of saliva as red as blood, then added in equally sudden contrition, or because she wished to make a distinction that India might miss, "I like Americans, mem, as you know, but such marriages are unsuitable."

She shifted in her chair, and the servant girl at her feet moved the spittoon closer.

"My brother married an Austrian," she remarked, as if that were conclusive, and looked at India briefly. "Yes, that was bad, very bad indeed."

She lapsed into silence, and India was silent also until the Princess should be ready to go on.

"You have a proverb I remember from school, 'Oil and water do not mix.' That is true, mem, very true." Her haughty face took on a brooding, unhappy look. "You know what we expect of our women. Our men can play, but our women must work. All our highborn girls learn the household arts because they are the marks of a woman of culture among us. I heard a farang say once that Siamese women made good wives because they knew how to wait on their husbands, and I think he was right. They're good businesswomen, too, but these farang girls know nothing except how to spend money. They can't speak our language, of course, or cook our food, and sometimes they can't even cook their own. If you ask them to clean raw shrimp they scream. All they want is to live in big houses and be waited on by Chinese servants like millionaires."

She still held the tinfoil from the little boy's biscuits in her hand. She had rolled it into a ball and was jabbing it with the long pointed nail of her forefinger. After a moment she tossed it into the spittoon and resumed her complaint.

At her time of life she had a right to expect the help of her son's wives in running the house, especially now that she could hardly walk. Her farang daughter-in-law was of no use in this, and Anotai's wife had had to work long and hard to make up the lack, although she had one child already and was expecting another soon. Still, someone must direct the servants. Someone must be alert to prevent thievery. Charoon's wife could do nothing useful, not even embroider or crochet. Her clothes had to be made for her by that Frenchwoman on New Road. All she did every day and all day was sit at the piano and sing farang songs. The Princess had grown weary of the sound of her voice going *oh, oh, oh,* and *ah, ah, ah.* When Charoon went out she expected to go with him, like a child who thought life was nothing but singing and dancing and playing games.

The flow of her discontent rolled on as the sunlight faded from the room. After a while the little boy came shyly to India's knee. First he put his chocolate-smeared hand on it lightly, and India did not move or show any sign that she was aware of his presence. Reassured, he leaned against her, and she felt the warmth of his body. Slowly and softly his eyes climbed to her face and then rested there until it lost its strangeness. Once he felt secure his hands went out to her purse. India slipped the catch, and with sudden decision he emptied the contents into her lap.

"The worst of it is, mem," the Princess was saying, "that Charoon was betrothed, so this marriage has hurt his career. I'm not old-fashioned. I wouldn't have chosen an old-fashioned girl for him, but Cheronai—you remember Chao Khun Aht's daughter—had lived in France. She drives a car and sings farang songs, and even dances in the farang manner that I find so unspeakably vulgar. I could overlook that. And if she wants to wear one of those indecent farang bathing suits when she goes swimming at Hua Hin, so that even respectable fishermen snicker, well, that too I could forgive. She has the natural filial regard of our girls for their elders. She never wears low-cut blouses that show her breasts, or short skirts, or tight clothes, or too much jewelry. But these farang girls flaunt their bodies as if they were for sale, and people come to the conclusion that they are."

As the Siamese woman talked the room darkened. Now a servant girl crept noiselessly around, turning on one light after another. India glanced surreptitiously at her watch, afraid that any sign of a desire to leave might rob her of what she wanted to know. It was almost seven o'clock. Beneath the tide of dissatisfaction and querulousness she heard the sweep of darker emotions, and it was to these that she was listening rather than to the words, hoping to guess the direction of the Princess' purpose.

A second girl had edged close to India and was trying to entice the little boy away. He resisted, clutching India's keys, then submitted but without relinquishing the keys. He made no sound as the girl urged him gently toward the screen, but India heard him cry out in the corridor a moment later, and shortly her keys were returned to her by the same silent girl.

The Princess was explaining that it was the marriage to which the family objected. An attachment they could have overlooked. In fact, they had taken something of the sort for granted. "One knows what young men are, mem, and a single woman is better than many." They would have paid to buy him free, if that had been necessary. The Princess blamed herself for not having sent Cheronai to him. It could have been arranged. Somehow it had never occurred to her that he would bring a farang woman home, and then demand a good house on Sathorn Road for her to live in! "She isn't used to living Siamese style," he had explained, and the Tan Ying had asked him if he too were a farang. And he had said to her, his mother, "After all, I've lived in America since I was a child, you know. Sometimes I forget that I'm not an American." Dark and angry color flushed the parchment smoothness of her face.

Perhaps she sensed a lack of assent in the quality of India's listening; perhaps, having intended to withhold what was to her most humiliating of all, the erosion of her own words now tore it loose and added it to the total.

"You'll never believe this, mem, but the girl was a waitress when Charoon met her. The Lord Buddha pity me, I live in terror all day and every day that my friends and relatives will find this out."

To India this fear was ironic in view of Darun and the servant girls on the floor. She knew from long experience that there were no secrets among the Siamese.

"If I could, mem, I'd cut Charoon out of his father's will, but it's too late for that. After the estate is settled in September he can do as he pleases, but until then he does as I please. When I upbraided him, do you know what he said? He insisted that in America many girls work to put themselves through school, and that it is not considered a disgrace. It's obvious, though, what kind of girls they must be if they work as waitresses. These things do not vary from country to country."

India had come to hear and not to tell. From some obscure instinct to caution she had refrained from explaining even to Darun the purpose of her visit. Throughout the conversation she had been careful not to betray herself by question or argument. Now to her surprise she heard her own voice saying, "It's true that many respectable girls in America wait table to put themselves through college."

The Tan Ying ignored the remark. "I should have known that a rich boy is fair game for a certain type of woman. That far I blame myself, but I *hate* her for taking advantage of him!" She stirred in her chair, ready now to end the interview.

There was one more thing that India wanted to know. "Where are your son and his wife living?" she asked, gathering her possessions into her purse.

The Princess shrugged. "I've given them a house that belonged to one of my husband's concubines." She motioned vaguely toward the back of the compound. "At least they haven't made me grandmother to any half-caste children yet."

India stood up and made her farewells. Darun, who had been sitting with her legs tucked behind her so that her feet would not offend the Princess, half rose and salaamed, then, still crouching, edged toward the door. India thought with a kind of irrelevant surprise that, if the Princess had been uncomfortable in her chair, Darun had been uncomfortable on the floor. It had not occurred to the Princess to offer her a chair. And it was odd, too, that Darun, who was fiercely democratic, should have reverted to the customs of her people so naturally in the presence of royalty.

The Princess sent a servant girl with them to the gate, which was closed now and guarded. It was quite dark. Lights had come on along the street. They walked several hundred yards before they could find a double ricksha. The seat smelled as if it had been used earlier in the day for hauling fish, but they did not want to hunt farther.

Both of them were silent. The ricksha rolled past the marble beauty of Wat Benjamabopit, outlined in the soft illumination of strings of lights. India regarded it absently. She was thinking of the beautiful Viennese girl the Princess had mentioned. It had somehow escaped her memory that the girl had been married to a half brother of the Tan Ying, but no one in Bangkok could ever forget the thrill of horror which swept the city that day twenty years before when her partially decomposed body was taken from the river. It had been whispered that there was a fragment of rope around her neck.

The position of the family had made them immune to ordinary processes of law, and only the most discreet inquiries were ever made. Still there had been muttering in the foreign community when the inquest returned a verdict of suicide. The ominous fact remained that the girl had not been reported missing.

CHAPTER 5

THE TABLE WAS SET FOR DINNER ON THE UPSTAIRS VERANDA, WHERE a small section adjoining India's office had been walled off from the rest with latticework to make a dining room.

Places for three were laid around the circular table, which was spread with a white cloth, and had a bowl of fruit and four Chinese altar candles at its center. The fat red candles, with good-luck characters of gold paper banding each at the base, lent a festal air to the coarseness of linen and willow-pattern china. These candles cost only fifty satangs a dozen at the market, and a dozen lasted a month. Besides, they cremated a great many insects during a meal.

A shockhaired servant girl, whose name was Dom, touched a match to the candles, and the table bloomed with light. When everything was ready, she went to the meat safe against the wall and took out the sugar. The legs of the safe had been placed in small bowls of kerosene to keep ants from crawling up them. Finally she rang a melodious small elephant bell with claw feet that a former house guest had sent India from Ceylon.

India herself came out first. She had bathed and put on an old white dress. She sat down abstractedly, and in a moment Dulcie appeared. She too was wordless. Dom placed a bowl of soup in front of each, and each bowed silently for grace. Mani Soderstrom's place remained empty.

The night air was sweet with the scent of jasmine rising from the garden below. A symphony of crickets tuned up with mounting enthusiasm. There was a sound of smothered laughter from a schoolroom on the first floor where the girls were doing their homework. One of the smaller children cried briefly. Beyond the great semicircle of the front garden lights shone through the trees in the shops that lined the street. A tram clanged on Bamrung Muang Road above the steady cacophony of motorcar horns and hawkers.

The dissonance formed only the familiar undertone to the thoughts of the two women eating their soup. India's mind was still busy with her visit of the afternoon. She had seen Siamese women handle the problem of a foreign daughter-in-law before and knew with almost prophetic clarity what could be expected to happen. The alien wife would be walled away from the communality of the Siamese family until she appeared an outsider, ridiculous, a little gauche. Eventually Charoon would miss the intimacy of the life to which he had been born, and would blame Angela, the foreigner, for this.

Then the Princess would try to absorb him once more into the family, gambling on the fact that his Siamese blood was her ally. She would dangle servant girls before him at first, probably, and later, more adroitly, the girl she wanted him to marry. It would be taken for granted that a man of his position would set up a multiple household like his father before him. The Princess was shrewd enough to know that Angela would probably leave before she would accept her servants as her husband's concubines, especially if they lived in her little house. India had a strong conviction that the campaign was farther advanced than the Princess would care to have her know.

After several mouthfuls of soup she laid down her spoon with distaste. There was too much pepper in it tonight. Then she looked more closely at her bowl. Ants! Infinitesimal red ants floated in small rafts on the surface. The dishes had not been properly washed, and the ants had been at work on the greasy plates when Plo served the soup. Ignore it or reprimand Dom? Neither did any good. What would it be like to have a maid who washed dishes clean? India glanced at Dulcie eating methodically, oblivious of the ants. Well, after all, they weren't poisonous.

In the candlelight Dulcie's face sagged, and the vertical lines in her cheeks were cavernous. India was startled by the bitterness in the older woman's eyes as she looked up briefly. It was this afternoon that Dulcie had been going to see Mr. Denniscort. He had discouraged her, and all her air castles were in ruins.

Dom took the soup plates away and brought meat loaf, soggy yellow potatoes that had come from Java, and string beans. A moth fluttered into Dulcie's glass. She snatched it up savagely and held it out at arm's length. Some of the water slopped onto the floor.

"Ugh, how disgusting! Dom, take it away!" When Dom had removed the glass Dulcie turned to India.

"I wish we could screen this veranda where we're obliged to eat," she said, and her voice was full of self-pity.

"We can, Dulcie," India said, glad to have at hand so convenient a means of deflecting the sour course of Dulcie's thoughts. "I forgot to tell you. When I took my report to Mr. Mellis this morning he told me that the station had voted us screening for *three* porches."

"Hmmmmmph."

"He says he'll put it on during mid-term vacation in September. He has a whole consignment of copper screening coming from New York."

"We don't need copper screening." Dulcie cut a slice of bread into fourths with quick spiteful movements. "Ordinary screening would be quite good enough. We could use the money better in a dozen other ways."

"Copper screening isn't an extravagance, Dulcie. It costs more in the beginning, but it lasts much longer."

The older woman's back was stiff. "It's not as good an investment in eternity as a child," she flung back.

"Now, Dulcie!" India was placating. "You know as well as I do that Mission money is divided into classes. Class V is for repairs and Class VII is for evangelism, and never the twain shall meet. If we don't accept this screening, it will be given to somebody else. Besides, Grace tells me that our appropriation is more likely to be cut than increased after the Board delegation surveys the Mission."

Dulcie's eyes were sharp points. "Why do you even hesitate over my three orphans then? Are a few paltry ticals so much more important than human souls?"

"Not 'a few paltry ticals,' Dulcie, the lack of them. I wish you'd try to understand the difference."

"I don't believe it's a matter of money."

"Dulcie, it is, essentially at least."

The black eyes lost their fire and resumed their expression of hopelessness. "You don't share my concern for these orphans, India."

"Dulcie, you're unfair. I feel the pull of human misery no less than you, but I'm limited in my desire to serve mankind by the amount of money the Station gives me to do it with."

Dulcie sat looking out into the dark garden as if she did not hear. "I wish I could get my hands on——" She broke the sentence in two, having said more than she intended. *"Strain at a gnat, and swallow a camel,"* she added bitterly. "Deny food to three hungry children, but by all means have the best screening."

India felt a strong urge to answer sharply and close the subject once and for all, but the sadness in the dark face was real if the arguments were specious. Under the self-righteousness and ill temper lay a morass of dead hopes, frustrations, and despair. *If our places were reversed, would my head still be unbowed as Dulcie's is?* India wondered. *I doubt it. I'd have stopped trying long ago.*

The thought softened her answer, and she merely reiterated, "We can't stretch our resources further or they'll snap."

"But if we took in these three girls it would be our act of faith, our stepping out into the future relying on God."

Dom removed the dinner plates and brought dishes of stewed prunes topped with custard. She replenished the water in the glasses and put finger bowls beside each plate.

Dulcie extracted a pit with quick dissatisfied movements of her spoon. When India said nothing she darted a glance in her direction and spoke again. "Dom's leaving the end of the month. Did she tell you?"

"Dom's leaving?" India felt consternation out of all proportion to the loss. "She hasn't said anything to me about it."

Dulcie looked smug. "No, and she won't until the last day of the month. Her family's arranged a marriage."

A little earlier India had deprecated Dom's shortcomings. Now she was upset because the maid was leaving. Inadequate as she was, she had learned to set a table, wash dishes after a fashion, and serve meals without commotion. A new girl would be awkward and noisy, and months would pass before meals were served satisfactorily.

Dulcie saw that the news had breached India's defenses. "If I brought Ploy down this week end she'd be ready to take over the first of June. I'd train her myself."

All the weariness of the day washed over India. "Dulcie, how many times do I have to repeat? I should like to let your orphans come to Jasmine Hall, since it means so much to you, but I cannot, cannot, cannot afford it."

A gleam showed in Dulcie's eyes, but her voice was meek. "I'm sorry. I didn't mean to annoy you. I just want to ask one more question, and then I won't bother you further. Do you mean that your only objection to my plan is a lack of money?"

India sighed. "As for starting an orphanage, that's out of the question. But because you're so interested in these three girls I'd be willing to let you have them here if it wasn't for the expense. How old is Ploy?"

"Seventeen."

"By Siamese reckoning, or by ours?"

"By Siamese, sixteen by ours."

"And you'd undertake to train her yourself?"

"Certainly."

India hesitated. "I suppose you could train her in a month, if she's reasonably intelligent. But will you be satisfied to have just this one girl?"

Dulcie reached down into the pocket of her voluminous skirt and extracted a purse. Slowly under India's eyes she opened it and counted out fifty ticals. "That will take care of the two little ones for a term," she said dryly. "Under the circumstances, you won't ask more than the minimum of six ticals a month, will you?"

India studied the money curiously. "Where did it come from, Dulcie?"

"It was a gift," Dulcie replied with hauteur.

"Not from Mr. Rockefeller, I suppose."

"No, of course not. I just wrote him yesterday." Then, unable to resist preening herself a little, she added: "I mentioned these girls to someone with whom I happened to be talking this afternoon. You wouldn't expect a man in his position to be sympathetic, but he was. He volunteered the money. I didn't ask him for it."

Surely Mr. Denniscort didn't think he could buy himself immunity from Dulcie for fifty ticals! India thought incredulously. *No, it couldn't be that. He was, as Dulcie said, a sympathetic man. This was a gesture of some kind, but it was also a mistake. Now he would never see the last of her!*

"Will you be satisfied to take the girls back when the money runs out?" India said aloud.

"I won't ask any salary for Ploy until the end of June, but when she's trained you'll be willing to give her sixteen ticals a month and her keep, won't you?" India nodded. "After that, she can pay for her sister Dang. I'll find the money for the third child myself. I guess my faith in God is equal to six ticals a month. I think I'll go up after them tomorrow."

"Not tomorrow. You'll have to wait until Saturday."

Now that Dulcie had won her battle, she was ready to be agreeable. "Where were you this afternoon?" she inquired graciously.

That was something India had little desire to discuss. Then it occurred to her that the other woman might supplement her limited knowledge, if she cared to do so. In her ceaseless wanderings about the city Dulcie garnered all the news and most of the gossip, hoarding it carefully to her own ends. She liked to display nuggets of startling information calculated to astonish her audiences, but was chary of giving information when she suspected that it was wanted.

So now India asked nothing. She merely said, "Darun and I called on Princess Sandhya, and she told us something that will surprise you."

"No, it won't," Dulcie answered shortly. "You mean that the Tan Ying hates her American daughter-in-law, and wants to get rid of her. She tells everyone that. The girl's pretty, too, and well behaved. But not pretty enough, though I don't suppose the Tan Ying told you *that*."

She saw from India's expression that this was true, and dropped her voice confidentially.

"Do you remember Cheronai? He has her in a house on Bush Lane. She's expecting a child in October. Her family made a terrible fuss when they found out, but that's what comes of letting young people run around in cars without chaperones."

Dulcie saw the shocked look on India's face with something like satisfaction. "That isn't the worst of it either," she continued, almost in a whisper. "One of his servants is pregnant, too, right in the house with his wife. You'd think Madame Suksamran would leave, wouldn't you? Why do you suppose she stays?"

CHAPTER 6

INDIA AWOKE THE NEXT MORNING TIRED AND UNREFRESHED. DUL-cie's news, added to the Princess' invective, had churned through her mind for most of the night. The sense of impending tragedy had grown, as had her feeling of urgency. She must forestall the thing she saw coming. The problem was how.

She lay motionless on her wide bed, pressed down by a sense of inertia. There was so much that needed doing, and so little time and strength with which to do it. Thin gray light had begun to trickle into her room. Two mosquitoes swollen with blood were silhouetted against the net that curtained the bed. India stretched out her hand to kill them, envisaged the smears, and thought better of it.

It had rained during the early hours of the morning, but without clearing the air, which seemed freighted with a million unborn sorrows. Her Buddhist friends believed in the endless wheel of birth and rebirth. How long was the interval between death and reincarnation supposed to be? Did the souls of the dead—or whatever the Buddhist equivalent was called—find immediate shelter? Or was there a lapse of time? Perhaps her friends thought that these mornings were heavy with a load of souls who had died in the night, and who were waiting sadly and eagerly to be born again, wondering whether they were to have the bodies of worms or cats, elephants or men.

The house was not yet astir. It was just five-fifteen. There would be three-quarters of an hour for prayer before the rising bell. She sat up, pulled the edge of the net from under the mattress, and thrust her feet out.

India rarely mentioned her habit of getting up early to pray, although it was the core of her life. She took literally the injunction: . . . *When thou hast shut thy door, pray to thy Father which is in secret; and thy Father which seeth in secret shall reward thee openly.*

There were fashions in religious practice, and the present emphasis was on "the social aspects of Christianity" rather than on the *sin* and *repentance* and *conversion* of her youth. Yet people were the same, and their problems the same. Childhood still had its unearthly beauty and cleanness. The same tarnishing came with the years. There were the same tragedies, the same glittering sins, the same disillusionment and sadness. It was this ancient continuity of the human heart that gave the Bible its day-by-day freshness for India. The old words, except for their grace, could have been written yesterday. Here in Bangkok she had known the Woman of Samaria, and the Magdalene, Joseph and Absalom, Peter and James, and John, only by other names.

She turned on the light and picked up her Bible, which was worn and underlined from use. For twenty minutes she read quietly, then snapped off the light and knelt by the bed.

O Lord, we beseech thee mercifully to receive the prayers of thy people who call upon thee; and grant that they may both perceive and know what things they ought to do, and also may have grace and power faithfully to fulfil the same; through Jesus Christ our Lord. Amen.

As she prayed the day unrolled. Her prayers were always on two levels, the practical and the spiritual, so chorded as to make one refrain. Classes this morning—talk to Darun about the coming of Dulcie's orphans—Mae Suan had a new baby—she must call there—and on Major Rosenfeld—and try to prepare Marthe for the ordeal of her father's death.

"O Lord, give Thy servant more wisdom and more patience," she prayed. "Help her to understand those around her with Thy own compassionate understanding. Put Thy words in her mouth that through her they may know Thee better, whom to know aright is life eternal." She must send letters to the parents of her paying pupils and ask them to be more prompt in their remittances. And then Angela. She must find some way to help Angela. "O Father, have mercy upon her. Pity her youth and inexperience. Shield her from the storm that has gathered about her head."

Somewhere in the night she had abandoned the last vestige of her concern over Grace's reaction to the way she ran Jasmine Hall.

There were things Grace could never understand. "And bless Grace, too, O Lord, in the work she does at Wattana. Temper her efficiency with mercy, for *The sacrifices of God are a broken spirit: a broken and a contrite heart, O God, thou wilt not despise.*"

"Here, here!" she said, speaking to herself, struck by the patronizing sound of her petition on Grace's behalf. In her prayer she had accused Grace of self-righteousness, and now found it in herself. Self-righteousness was an easy sin, easy to overlook in oneself, and as easy for others to detect, and by any absolute standard of love it was as corrosive as adultery. Was it because David was free of self-righteousness that he had been a "man after God's own heart"?

The mood of prayer broken, India got stiffly to her feet. Slipping her toes into native sandals, she went to the kitchen, where the cook had left a teakettle on a carefully banked charcoal brazier. The fire had smoldered throughout the night, and the water was steaming. India emptied it into a brown earthenware jar she kept on a stool in her bathroom. A low wall enclosed the six-foot square that was tinned for bathing. To the hot water she added several dipperfuls of cold from the big green *ong* that stood against the wall. It was the same size as her Ali Baba jars but glazed, and could be filled from a faucet when there was no rain. This morning several green leaves floated on the surface of the water.

Slipping out of her nightgown, she put on the wooden clogs she always wore for bathing to keep from getting Hong Kong foot. An old missionary had warned her when she first arrived: "Never put your bare foot to the floor! Never touch your eyes without washing your hands first! Never eat uncooked food!" It had been good advice.

She stepped over the low wall to the bathing area and scrubbed herself down with mildly antiseptic soap. She was careful not to put her washcloth into the clean water of the brown jar. Rather she dipped cold water from the ong and rinsed the cloth free of soap. Then with the dipper, she sloshed warm water over herself and after that cold. She could feel the depression of the humid morning roll away with the soap.

While she was drying herself the rising bell rang, and the house came alive. There was the soft pattering of many bare feet, laughter, and the tinkle of Siamese spoken quickly. From the section of veranda adjoining her room came the clink of dishes being laid. She paused a moment to listen, interpreting the tuneless music of the house note by note and phrase by phrase. Its rhythm was familiar, and she loved it.

She had not been able to tell Grace offhand how many people lived in Jasmine Hall, but she counted them now to herself. The teachers—Kru Darun, Kru Tawin, Kru Suwon—fourteen Bible school girls, six small boarders, and Eng Siow, twenty-four; Dulcie, Mani, and herself, twenty-seven; Det and Klee, Doe and Chu, Dom and Plo. That was thirty-three people actually living on the compound. Then the three teachers who came by day, and the pupils of the primary school. Almost a hundred and seventy people were in the house every day except Saturday and Sunday, and on Sunday there were the church people instead.

Dulcie was already seated when India stepped out onto the veranda for breakfast. In the morning light she looked very dark and aquiline, more as if her father had been a Sikh than an American. India, remembering the tarnished reputation of Dulcie's mother, wondered briefly if that could be.

The older woman did not rise to greet her employer, but went on meticulously removing every vestige of skin from a piece of pomelo, with long prehensile fingers.

"Good morning," she said, looking up. "Mani didn't get in until one-thirty. I suppose she'll sleep all morning. Don't you think we might take ice again? Fruit needs to be chilled."

India took a sip of coffee, unwilling to let Dulcie batter down her feeling of content. The morning had cleared and freshened. Sunlight came through the trees and dappled the deep green of the garden with flecks of gold.

"Ice?" she asked inattentively. "Don't you think we can get along without that?"

"I suppose so," Dulcie replied tartly, "but ice costs only a little, while those taxis you and Darun are always using cost the school a lot."

India sighed, unable to maintain her mood under continued assault. It would be easier to deal with Dulcie, she thought, if she could rid herself of the conviction that the older woman was pathetic.

Whenever sharp words took shape on India's tongue, the tragic panorama that had been Dulcie's life floated before her eyes and deprived her of the power to utter them. Dulcie's father had been murdered with a machete less than three months before she was born, and the murderer had been her mother's paramour. The court had placed the child in a missionary family, who had educated her in America with their own children.

Later she had come back to teach at Wang Lang. India could imagine what it had meant to the slender girl with dark skin to find herself, on returning to Bangkok, excluded from the white community to which she felt akin. Each snub would have been a rock cast at her self-respect. She must have been hit and hit again, until she was battered into something hardly recognizable, something at once assertive and servile, teetering unhappily between the two.

As she had grown older, Dulcie had grown more difficult, losing one position after another, either because she was irresponsible or because she refused to conform.

Jasmine Hall was a place of last resort, and it was obvious that Dulcie considered it a little beneath her. This was not only because the building was shabby and the pupils recruited from the middle and lower classes, but also because India's way of life was too unpretentious to please her. And yet where else could she go?

India had asked her once whether she ever wanted to return to America. The irritability had died out of Dulcie's eyes to be replaced with a sadness so profound that India felt as if she had fallen through a crevasse in the other woman's soul. "There is never a day and never an hour that I don't long to go back," she said in a low voice that held nothing of her usual petulance, but the same infinite sadness.

So now, instead of rebuking her, India explained: "Using taxis isn't really extravagant, Dulcie. It costs less than trams when two or three of us go. And it certainly isn't a matter of pride. Those baby Austins don't leave any room for it. By the way, Mae Suan has a new baby."

Dulcie was diverted. "Girl or boy?"

"A girl."

"Is this her third girl?" Dulcie put down her coffee cup to consider. "No. Let me see. The first was a girl, then a boy, then two girls, then two boys. This is her fourth girl."

Dom removed the fruit dishes and placed bowls of cereal in front of the two women. Her black hair was neatly brushed. Her bare feet made almost no sound as she moved about the table. She was wearing a fresh white blouse and a well-laundered panung in an old-fashioned pattern of tiny stars.

India poured evaporated milk over her cereal. "I'm calling on Major Rosenfeld again this afternoon. He won't live through the rainy season, you know. Would you like to come with me?"

"I may not have time." Dulcie was evasive. "I have to go to Pahurat to get some thread for the girls' crocheting. Of course I can come if you insist."

"Not at all," India answered equably.

The two women were silent through the rest of the breakfast. When the chapel bell rang they rose together and went downstairs.

The inside design of Jasmine Hall was basically simple. It was one of the "wagon-run-and-haymow" houses common to Siam. The rectangle formed by the exterior walls was divided upstairs and down into three sections by wooden paneling a single board thick. The top thirty inches of this were an elaborate scrollwork designed to permit free passage of air. Spiders claimed this region as their own. Once a month, Det, the school coolie, warred on them with a long broom of twigs, but they quickly re-formed, and festooned the wooden combers with lavender lace.

The central sections of the rectangle were the wagon runs and went across the width of the house, uninterrupted with walls. The sides were divided to make the haymows. Verandas encircled the whole. Segments of the upstairs veranda at the back and sides had become sleeping porches, bathrooms, and a kitchen for India, while a part of the veranda downstairs, farthest from the entrance, had been walled and screened to make an apartment for Darun.

The wagon run on the first floor was the chapel. Upstairs it was the church, which meant that the bedrooms opened off it. The reverse of this arrangement would have been more convenient, but was not feasible. Tradition imbued the upper story of a house with honor, so that until the church could afford to buy or build, the members would consent to worship nowhere else.

A hundred years before, the Ambassador of the Governor-General of India, John Crawfurd, had watched with amusement while the Minister of Foreign Affairs, a very fat man, had climbed precariously up a shaky ladder to the second story of the warehouse in which Crawfurd was staying, rather than allow his head to be defiled by entering below the level of the Ambassador's feet. Siamese no longer refused to enter the first story of a house, but the residue of this prejudice was deeply embedded in their thinking, and made it impossible to install the church downstairs.

The chapel was a plain room, painted cream. When it was not in use as a place of worship it served as the first grade classroom. The furnishings were simple wooden benches in two ranks, a piano, and a table on a low dais for the leader of the meeting. The singing had started as India came down the stairs. She could hear the children's voices in their favorite hymn:

> "When He cometh, when He cometh,
> To make up His jewels,
> All His jewels, precious jewels,
> His loved and His own."

Kru Darun was leading the singing, and Kru Suwon was at the piano. Only the front benches were filled, for the day pupils were not due until nine o'clock. This was the school's private devotions.

In the front row sat six small children that the school was sheltering more or less temporarily. Howard and Jeannie Ansel had an English father who thought them too young for regular boarding school, but would not trust them to their Siamese mother during his furlough. Mo Tek and Mo Kiang were there because their parents were in China for a year. Riap, a little boy of seven, was a hunchback. He had been left on the doorstep of Jasmine Hall one rainy night four years earlier. Tui Sanchai, a girl of eight, was feeble-minded. Her mother, who had ten other children, had found her an almost intolerable burden, and had begged India to take the child for a while.

Then there was Eng Siow. She was older than the other boarders —fourteen, in fact—and went with Pastor Rasami's children to Jane Hayes School. Her father was a Christian Chinese. Her mother was a low-class Siamese and an inveterate gambler. Eng Siow was at the school for a year, while her father was on business in China, because he refused to leave the girl, his only child, in the care of her mother.

Back of the children, on the second and third benches, were the fourteen girls who made up the student body of the Bible Training School. India thought of Grace's condescending insistence on the superiority of Wattana, where they accepted only "the better type of girl." What was "the better type of girl"? Did Grace mean money or social position? India looked at the row of black heads and the long glossy bobs, enjoying the smooth café-au-lait of their skins, the suppleness of their young bodies, and the neatness of their blue *pasins* and white blouses. They scorned the *panung* of the servants, as they scorned the cropped hair of the previous generation. They wore the tubular *pasin* of the northern Thai with its triple fold in front, held in place by a silver belt. School regulations would not permit them to wear jewelry or gold belts, or even belts of the alloy called *nak*. Experience had proved that these were liable to theft.

Kru Darun read the morning Scripture lesson. There was a brief prayer, a second hymn, and the service was over. The day's duties were assigned, straightening the dormitory, sweeping, dishwashing, the care of the small children, office duty, practice teaching.

On her way back upstairs India paused to look out over the garden. The morning was clear now. Under the angsana tree at the far end of the lawn was a pool of gold. As she watched she could see fresh flowers falling from its branches, slowly and steadily like golden rain. The air under the tree seemed to be illuminated with them.

It was early, but the day pupils were already streaming through the red gates. The little boys wore black knee-length trousers and white shirts with short sleeves. Some of them had tennis shoes, but most were barefoot. The little girls wore dark blue pasins and white blouses, the school uniform. They all looked clean and combed at the start of the day, and some of the smallest girls had roses in their hair.

CHAPTER 7

INDIA SAW ANGELA ONLY ONCE IN THE THREE WEEKS BETWEEN MR. Denniscort's tea and Major Rosenfeld's funeral. It was a mere glimpse, which did nothing to forward a solution of the problem she had set herself.

Dulcie had not returned from Ayuthia on Sunday evening as agreed. Apparently she could not resist the temptation to see everyone she knew in the old capital. Monday passed and Tuesday, and still she did not appear. India stayed home both days to be on hand for the arrival of the orphans. When Wednesday came, she gave up and went on with her usual routine.

About three o'clock that afternoon she was walking down New Road toward the Karachi Store. She saw Angela come out of a smart little shop that specialized in custom-made clothes and French importations. Remembering the Princess' complaint about her daughter-in-law's extravagance, India smiled. She had bought a dress there once, and it had cost half a month's salary.

The girl was not tall, but she was erect and graceful. She set her feet down as she walked with lightness and precision. She was wearing a dress of heavy white silk and a cartwheel hat. The Karachi Store into which she turned was one of several run by Indian merchants, who had almost a monopoly on the sale of yard goods in Bangkok. Some of their shops were hardly more than holes in the wall with bolts of cloth piled to the ceiling. The Karachi Store was spacious and catered to the foreign trade. It offered for sale many things hard to find elsewhere: embroidery cotton, silk hose, English linens and voiles. There were also brass trays, rugs, carved ivories, and ebony elephants for tourists.

One of the sleek Indian clerks greeted the girl with an obsequious flourish as if he knew her well. "Ah, madame, and what will it be today?"

"Some blue linen if you have it," India heard her say.

She was as beautiful in daylight as India had remembered her, but rather paler. Her skin, even in the hot glare of afternoon, was translucent, but it had nothing of the golden look India had observed at the Legation. Rather, it seemed incandescent, like an alabaster lamp, and the hair under the wide hat was silver gilt.

What a model she would have made for Botticelli! India thought. Glancing around, she saw that six or seven women shopping in the store were covertly examining Angela from beneath their topees. *She does exact that tribute,* she concluded, *even from women.*

A clerk had spoken twice before India became aware of him. She bought a pair of hose and left the shop. She had felt an impulse to wait for the girl and try to talk to her, but had rejected it. Some more natural approach must be found. It would accomplish nothing but to discompose Angela if a dowdy woman she had never met began to probe the intimate difficulties of her private life, without even the preamble of an introduction.

As India walked on down the street, the episode invoked a succession of pictures that she was powerless to suppress. She could imagine the back compound of the Tan Ying's palace in all its squalor. In her mind's eye she could visualize the dingy little houses with two or three rooms apiece. And no bathroom of course. Or perhaps Angela's house was one of a row with thin partitions between that strained out none of the sounds passing back and forth. She could feel the servants watching her all day with eyes like pebbles, denying her privacy, doing as little for her as possible, pretending not to understand what she wanted, making insulting remarks about her in Siamese. She could see the face of the family calcified against her, and Anotai's wife moving about the compound in her new importance as the Tan Ying's favorite, affecting a martyred air because she was carrying the foreigner's load as well as her own, a little insolent, letting Angela know that they all looked down on her. And Charoon's friends, envious of his possession of so beautiful a girl, telling him that he had made a mistake, looking at her with eyes that measured her insultingly, making ribald remarks.

How did she know that Angela was vulnerable to all this? Because we are all vulnerable to those around us, having no immutable dimensions in our own minds but only the stature we see reflected in their eyes. Struggle against it as we will, the image of ourselves we all carry is without constancy, nine feet tall one minute and six inches the next, like Alice in Wonderland. Granted, but how did she know that Angela was not able to outwait and outmaneuver her opponents, until Charoon should come into his money and break away from his family? *That* was what he could never do. They were flesh of his flesh, and bone of his bone. It was Angela who was the alien. She would be lucky if she escaped before they had stripped away the total of her self-respect, for in their ignorance they were pitiless. Did she know yet about Cheronai? She could not shut her mind to the condition of her maid. Why then did she stay? Had her family perhaps disowned her because of the marriage? Or was it some kind of inverted pride that kept her from admitting defeat and asking their help?

As India turned into Suriwong Road, Mr. Denniscort came out of Badman's and crossed the sidewalk to the curb where his car was waiting.

"Hello there," he called. "Can I give you a lift?" And when she was seated in the car he remarked, "You look worried. Has the world been unkind to you today?"

It occurred to India that she was concerned about a problem that others more able to help might already have solved. She decided to use the opportunity chance had presented to find out.

"I've heard something that troubles me about a young American girl I don't even know," she said. "Perhaps you're the proper person to talk to."

He looked at her sharply.

"Do you know a girl called Angela who's married to a Siamese?" she asked.

"Angela Suksamran? Yes, I know her quite well."

"Has she ever come to you with her troubles?"

"No," he replied, "she never has."

"You'd have to say that, of course, even if she had, and I shouldn't have asked, but——"

"No, she never has," he repeated, "and I wish she would. I've heard the rumors too."

"What can be done to help her?"

"Well, what is there to do?"

"I suppose she still has her citizenship?" India queried.

"Oh yes, of course."

"That's something anyway." And there she let the matter rest.

It was four o'clock when India reached Jasmine Hall. The compound was empty of primary pupils. Four or five of the younger boarders were absorbed in a game of jackstones under a big rain tree on the lawn, while several of the Bible school girls played badminton near by.

She went directly to her room to bathe before tea. She had put on fresh underclothes and was standing in front of the mirror brushing her hair when she heard a faint titter behind her. The inside doors of Jasmine Hall swung on hinges and were set into wide frames in pairs. There were two feet of space top and bottom to permit free circulation of air. Turning quickly, India was jarred by the impact of a row of eyes watching her every move with bright animal interest. Three children were lying on their stomachs just outside the door that led to the church, although the one in the middle was not, properly speaking, a child. She was large, with a stubble of black hair, and a round, flat, empty face.

India's whole body tingled with a sensation she had almost forgotten. Years ago, when she first came to Siam, she had felt the same creeping of the nerves under her skin whenever she encountered the impersonal scrutiny of eyes like these that found her fair coloring abnormal, grotesque, even a little repulsive. As she walked along a street, they had seemed to pelt her like stones, but through the years she had become inured to them. Now she knew again that old sensation, and it was the more abhorrent for the violation of her privacy involved.

"The orphans!" she thought, with a sinking awareness of what lay ahead.

Was it possible they had never seen a white person before? Where was Dulcie? Anger coursed through her tired body. She fought it down, unwilling to make her first contact with them a lash of words, then started across the room. As she did so, they scrambled to their feet and ran.

"Dom!" she called. "Dom *cha!*" and when the maid appeared, told her to summon Dulcie.

"She's not in, mem *kha.*"

"You mean she's left the compound?"

"Yes, she went out an hour ago."

"Who did she leave in charge of them?"

"No one, mem *kha.* She locked them in her room, but they got out and ate all the coconut custard cook had made for supper. Then they went swimming in the canal."

"Not the canal!" India was incensed. The outbuildings at the back—kitchen, storeroom, and servants' quarters—were separated from the main house by a length of sluggish canal. Here pink sacred lotus floated among their great round pads like ladies of quality, ignoring the reduced circumstances in which they found themselves. But even they could not redeem the canal. It was polluted by neighboring privies, and at low tide nothing could disguise its odor. One of the strictest rules of Jasmine Hall was that no child was ever to swim in the canal. "Why didn't someone tell them it isn't allowed?"

Dom looked aggrieved. "We did tell them. Auntie Doe said she'd go in after them if they didn't come out, and they trailed water all up the stairs to Miss Dulcie's room. Auntie Doe made *me* wipe it up."

It was so like Dulcie to create a problem and leave it for others to solve that India hardly bothered to acknowledge her exasperation. "Ask the teacher on duty to come here," she said.

Only three of the school's six teachers lived at Jasmine Hall. The girl who came in answer to Dom's summons was named Tawin. She was slender and lively with wavy hair that she had considered a handicap until permanent waves became the fashion.

"Did you send for me, mem *kha?*"

"Yes, Kru. You'll have to take charge of Miss Dulcie's orphans until she comes back. I turned around a few minutes ago to find them peeping under my door."

Kru Tawin giggled. "Oh, mem, how terrible! And their heads are full of lice."

This too? And Dulcie was no doubt sitting somewhere having a cup of tea and regaling one of her friends with all the gossip from Ayuthia.

"Get them cleaned up then, Kru. Doe can help you."

The school maid was a powerful woman who had been a vendor on the river when she was younger. She had a fund of profanity that she leashed only with difficulty. India had threatened to dismiss her unless she modified her language, but it seemed unlikely to Doe's simple mind that the school could exist without her, so she took the threat lightly. As a matter of fact she was a cheerful person, and her outbreaks were rare, for she loved the children, even the most obstinate of whom obeyed her.

"I suppose we'd better kerosene their heads?" Tawin asked.

"By all means! Mix some coconut oil with the kerosene for their bodies. Have Doe bathe them in the washtubs with hot water and plenty of soap. Oh yes, have Det take their bundles out into the sun. They'll be full of bedbugs."

Kru Tawin looked uncertain. "They won't like it, mem *kha*," she said. Siamese girls over six rarely bathed without sarongs.

"Well, we can't let them give everyone else lice."

"The big one, too?"

"Explain what you want her to do, and if she refuses let Doe go ahead. Here, take this talcum!" It was violet-scented and very strong. It had been a Christmas gift. "Tell her she can have it when she's clean."

India's nerves were still jangling five minutes later when Dom knocked on her door to announce "Mem Rutafawt."

No, India thought, *not today!* It was Wednesday, and Grace should have been at prayer meeting. "Make us some tea and bring it to the *mook*, Dom."

"No tea for me," Grace called through the door. "I've already had mine."

"A cold drink then?"

"Thank you. A ginger ale, if you have it."

India remembered too late her lack of ice. She stepped to her dresser for money. "Run down to the corner and get some ice," she whispered to Dom, "and be quick about it."

Grace was already seated on the mook when India joined her. While the rest of the veranda was ten feet wide, the mook, which projected over the porte-cochere, was twenty. It was the place in Siamese homes where guests were usually received, and served that purpose at Jasmine Hall also. Grace was looking around appraisingly, and India's eyes followed, seeing every cobweb, every rumpled cushion, every misplaced magazine. During twenty-five years of school life Grace had developed a faculty for seeing instantly all that had been left undone. Teachers and school children respected this skill, and were in fact proud of the perceptiveness that made it impossible for them to deceive her. Grace made the inspection unconsciously wherever she went, and was unaware of her own rudeness.

"I came this noon, India, but you were out."

Before or after the orphans? India wondered, but did not ask.

"I thought you'd want to know that the Board delegation won't get here until Christmas after all."

"How momentous will their report be?"

"No one seems to know. But what I really came to see you about was Suwon. I've gotten her an appointment to Singapore Hospital for the first of June."

"Grace!" India wailed. "You can't do this to me! The term has just opened and we have a hundred and thirty children in the primary school. Besides, she signed up for the whole year."

"It's too good a chance for her to miss, India. Her mother came to me several months ago and asked me to get her into the hospital."

"And nobody thought it necessary to tell me?"

"It wasn't intentional discourtesy, I'm sure. It never occurred to me Suwon hadn't spoken to you until today."

"And then she persuaded you to speak for her." India sighed.

"These girls always leave things of importance to their elders."

"They manage to get what they want, though." India felt tired and defeated. Suwon had been one of her resident teachers for five years, but she knew it would be futile to try to hold the girl against her will. Still, she resented having Grace justify Suwon.

"Could you use Maria?" Grace asked.

"I could not. I need someone to play the piano."

"Linchee then?"

"Well——" India hesitated.

"I'll have her transferred from Jane Hayes to you, and I'll send Maria there. I was wondering——"

A bellow from the downstairs veranda interrupted them. The stairs opened close to the wall, just at the first of the double doors leading to the church. A little girl of about nine, completely naked and glistening with oil, appeared at the head of them and raced across the mook. There her way was blocked by the lattice wall beyond which was the private section of veranda where Dulcie and India ate. She did not try the lattice door but veered into the church and plunged through the swinging doors to India's room. Twenty feet behind her pounded Doe, shouting, "Come back, you dropping of an ape, you child of a pariah, spawned in a gutter——"

India started to her feet, but before she could move Mani Soderstrom flashed onto the mook. "My gold belt's gone and my pearl eardrops!" She did not bother to speak to Grace, her enemy of old, but stood wringing her hands and looking at India.

She was a pretty Eurasian, with the soft beauty that sometimes follows the mixing of East and West. Her face was a delicate oval, her skin a dusky off-white. She had large eyes, and a heavy sweet mouth, which she painted coral. Her high-heeled shoes were foreign, and the style of her blouse, but she clung to the Siamese pasin, worn tight around her hips, which gave her height.

Grace looked at her with open distaste. Mani was one of her failures. Wattana had dropped Mani after she ran away with the brother of a classmate, and Grace had never forgiven her the disgrace that had touched the school because of the incident. Mani had returned at the end of the week moderately penitent, but Grace had delivered her to her mother with a stinging rebuke. Later the mother had arranged a temporary match with a German businessman for, it was said, two thousand ticals. When he left Bangkok, she arranged another with a Dane, who was Mani's present husband. He was a kindly man and had grown fond of her. Two years before he had married her.

India decided that Doe could take care of the commotion in her room and asked Mani, "Where did you leave them?"

"In my trunk, but I left the keys on my dresser when I went out, and the trunk's been opened." She began to cry. "The earrings cost a thousand ticals," she sobbed.

India thought quickly. "Go down to Kru Darun and report your loss, Mani. I'll join you as soon as I've said good-by to Miss Rutherford."

The girl turned sulkily away, wiping her eyes, but India saw that the ruse was not going to work. Grace was halfway across the porch toward the bedroom from which the sounds of Doe's swearing still came strongly. The child had taken refuge under the big double bed. Doe was on her stomach poking beneath it with India's best silk umbrella. "Come out, you breeding ground for lice, you abortion of a black pig," she was shouting, "or I'll spear you like a fish!"

India laughed; she couldn't help it. Grace was kneeling at the foot of the bed with that automatic comprehension of what was needed which made her formidable, even when, as now, she did not fully understand what was going on.

The child had crouched in the farthest corner against the wall. Doe's rump heaved as she wielded the umbrella, cursing and grunting. Suddenly the child crawled rapidly out Grace's end and tried to wriggle past her. The large white woman pounced, Doe backed out and lunged, and it was over. She carried the kicking girl away as easily as if she had been a baby. They heard the sound of a broad hand on bare flesh and the child's screams.

Grace looked at her soiled dress. "Who was that?" she asked with distaste.

As if in answer, Mani Soderstrom burst through the door without the formality of a knock. India caught a glimpse of Dom standing outside, too polite to follow.

"It was those orphans Miss Dulcie brought from Ayuthia," Mani said angrily. "Dom saw them in my room."

India felt like a child caught with her hand in the cookie jar.

"All right," she said resignedly, "we'll search their things. They haven't been off the compound."

"Was that one of them?" Grace asked.

India nodded. "Yes, that was one of them," she admitted.

Grace turned toward the door. "Whom the gods would destroy they first make mad," she said, and went out to the mook to collect her things.

CHAPTER 8

IF INDIA HAD NOT PROMISED DULCIE THE ORPHANS COULD STAY through the first term, she would have sent them back almost immediately. The word *orphans* had conjured in her mind a picture of cringing, unwanted, submissive children. There was nothing cringing about these orphans, certainly, but then she ought to have known that people rarely fitted their categories.

Dang and Sanu were nine and ten, respectively. They were put into first grade. Dom refused to coach Ploy in the duties she was to assume at the end of the month. For lack of anything better to do with her that first morning, India set her to weeding the brick driveway. Ploy did not object, as India had rather thought she might, since it was coolie work. When India looked out an hour later she was still weeding, but Dang, her sister, was helping her.

India hurried downstairs. "Dang," she said to the child, "why aren't you in class?"

Dang looked at Ploy, looked down, then without answering walked away. Thirty minutes later she was back, weeding as before. This time India spoke to the older girl.

"Your little sister is supposed to be in school, Ploy. This is *your* job. *Hers* is learning to read."

Ploy had been squatting on her haunches like a toad, with the complete ease that comes from never having used a chair. She looked up at India without apology. In her dark eyes was an expression that was not so much defiant as simple.

"Mem *cha*," she said in her broad country voice, "I do not mind hard work. I do not even mind the sun on my head. There is only one thing I cannot do. I cannot work alone. If you won't let Nu Dang stay with me, I must work with someone else."

India bowed to the inevitability of this. She knew the communal spirit of the country Thai. "Tomorrow, Ploy," she agreed, "but today you must work here by yourself."

At eleven-thirty, while India was teaching her class in New Testament history, the first-grade teacher, Kru Prapai, came hurrying to say that Dang and Sanu had not appeared after recess, and that neither they nor Ploy was on the compound. A quick check confirmed this and revealed that Dulcie had also disappeared, leaving her fourth-grade class to hemstitch a side of their handkerchiefs in her absence. The presumption was that the four noncomformists had set out together, but at noon Dulcie returned alone.

"I've told you not to leave your classes like that," India scolded her. "And where are your orphans?"

Dulcie had no idea. "They'll be all right," she said. "Ploy's with them."

"We can't just sit here and let three country children lose themselves in the city." India was indignant. "After lunch you must come with me to the police."

Dulcie shrugged. "If you insist, of course."

The police had not seen the children but promised to look for them. India found a taxi and gave the chauffeur orders to drive slowly through the streets in the neighborhood, while Dulcie protested the waste of time and money. After two hours of going up and down lanes, and looking in shops, India gave up.

About five o'clock, a police private appeared with all three orphans in tow. Ploy was carrying on a lively conversation with him. He turned the truants over to India, suddenly tongue-tied in her presence. His bare feet were sticking out of khaki puttees, and he rubbed one against the other as he explained where he had found the children.

Two days later they ran away again, and once again India went to the police station. The same police private returned them several hours later, having discovered them emerging from a moving-picture theater.

The orphans had no sense of discipline, and certainly no sense of private property. They looted with abandon. The schoolgirls complained daily of their depredations. India found them in her room, trying on her hats and giggling. When they were hungry, they raided the school kitchen, or India's. Once she discovered Ploy sucking an orange from the bowl of fruit on her table, and scolded the girl with a vehemence she rarely used to Siamese. Ploy threw the orange over the railing into the garden.

"Go get it, Ploy!" India ordered, but the girl would not.

For an hour she stood in the corner of Darun's office sulking, before she capitulated. She was equally stubborn about the school showers. Unless she were watched, she slipped into the canal every evening to bathe. After this happened five or six times, India had all three orphans inoculated against typhoid fever.

They ran away for the third time on the morning of Major Rosenfeld's funeral. The Major had died the afternoon of June 4, and India spent the night with Marthe, as she sat beside her father for the last time.

About ten o'clock the next morning, India was waiting on the veranda of Jasmine Hall for Grace's car, which was to take her to the funeral, when Kru Prapai came to tell her that the orphans were gone. India went at once to the office in search of Darun. It was unfair to add the orphans to the head teacher's load, but for today it was unavoidable. Dulcie's sense of responsibility for them had ceased to operate. The problem was clearly, so far as she was concerned, no longer hers but the school's.

Darun stood, frowning a little, while India explained the situation. The teacher was only thirty-six, but looked older. Her shoulders were stooped, as if she had carried young, burdens beyond their strength. The planes of her face fell away rather too quickly from the cheekbones toward a pointed chin, so that in repose her face seemed a triangle, with freckles like cinnamon shaken across it. This natural angularity was emphasized by her hair, which was drawn back into a knot from a central part. It was only when she smiled that the sharp-cornered look disappeared, and one noticed her eyes, which were brown, fathomless, and very beautiful. She had been with India during the whole lifetime of the school, and even more than the missionary was the functional center of it.

"Don't worry, mem *kha*," she said. "I will send word to the police. And if the children come back, I'll talk to them myself."

There were fewer than twenty people in the church for the service. India was surprised to see Angela among them.

"Did you notice Madame Suksamran?" Grace asked on the way to the cemetery.

"What did you say?" India answered abstractedly, her mind also on Angela.

"Didn't you notice the woman in black across the aisle from us? She's Charoon Suksamran's wife. He came out to Wattana last week to see our little canal school. He has a high position in the Department of Education, you know, and he's working on a plan to reduce illiteracy. I must say he's charming."

"I wonder how she happened to attend the funeral," India remarked.

"Oh, she's a friend of Marthe's. Weren't you at the Club concert last month? Marthe accompanied her solo."

"No, I wasn't." India was chagrined. "And I never heard Marthe mention her, either."

"They've gotten quite intimate lately," Grace said. "I suppose the fact they're both musicians drew them together."

India thought of her efforts to find a natural approach to Angela, and was annoyed with herself for having missed this one. She had been at the Rosenfeld house frequently in recent months. Hardly a week passed without Marthe's coming to Jasmine Hall to play badminton with the Bible school girls. Yet somehow her friendship for Angela had escaped India's knowledge.

By the time the car turned into the school lane once more, India had the outline of a plan.

The three orphans and their now familiar escort passed through the red gates just ahead of the car. India was glad that Grace had declined her invitation to lunch. She let the culprits stand under the porte-cochere until the chauffeur had turned the car. Then she sent Doe for Darun.

Both Grace and the policeman were gone before Darun came. She studied the orphans a moment without speaking, and then said, "Come here!"

They climbed the stairs and knelt on the veranda before her, disheveled but unrepentant.

"Where have you been?" she demanded.

Ploy answered for the three of them. They had boarded a tram at the head of the lane and ridden downtown to see a movie. Since none of the theaters was open so early in the day, they had wandered up and down streets, names of which they had forgotten, buying cakes from vendors and looking into shops. After their money ran out, they started for home and had almost reached it when their friend the policeman found them.

India listened as Darun scolded them with a deftness that deflated them. Their heads drooped. They admitted their fault. They promised never to leave the compound again without her permission. When Darun sent them to Miss Dulcie's room, they dragged penitently away.

"Not that they cared about missing lunch." Darun flashed an amused smile at India. "They were bulging with cakes."

"Where did they get the money?" India asked.

"Stole it, probably. The two little ones will be all right if we can only keep Ploy away from them."

India considered. "Perhaps she could work with Doe."

"I'm afraid not. Pa Doe dislikes her. But Pa Chu might use her."

This seemed a solution, since Chu, the school cook, was a settled woman of middle age not to be trifled with by any girl of sixteen. Ploy was still expected to assume the duties of India's maid at the end of the month, so the arrangement was not permanent, but it set a guard over her for part of the time and separated her from the little girls.

When Marthe called two days after the funeral to thank India for all she had done, India inquired about Angela.

"Is she a friend of yours, Marthe?"

"Yes, she is." Marthe's face lighted up at the mention of Angela. "She came to the house every morning to practice until Papa was too ill to have her."

"Won't you bring her to tea sometime? I'd like to meet her."

Marthe sat jabbing the toe of her shoe with her umbrella, as if she did not know how to answer. She was small and fine-boned, but the bones of her face and especially those of her nose had the clear configuration of the European. Brown hair fell softly to her shoulders. She was wearing a tight black dress and a large hat, and she looked very young and forlorn, sitting in the big wicker chair with its bright cretonne pillows, her shoulders hunched forward in thought.

Twenty years before, when India first remembered her, she had been a familiar sight in Bangkok, clinging to her father's great hand, with a nurse walking behind. She was a tiny child, exquisitely dressed in clothes imported from Paris. As soon as she was twelve her father sent her to Denmark, and she had returned two years previously, a pretty girl, but dark with the blood of her Siamese mother.

By that time her mother was dead, and the Major had set himself to guard her fiercely, with all the protection his proud will and shrinking fortune could provide. His son he left free. Iner had a good position with a Danish firm and was engaged to marry a Danish girl. Marthe he cloistered, driving young men away indiscriminately, unable to believe that their intentions were honorable. She had always been timid. Now there was a congelation over the surface of her being that did not speak of peace, but of the suspension of life. It hurt India to see it there. *I wonder what I can do about it,* she thought to herself.

Something moved indeterminately in Marthe's hazel eyes as she raised them from her shoe. "I'd love to bring Angela here," she said, ending the debate with herself. "I want you to know her."

India did not press her to set a day, but asked: "Now that you have so much time on your hands, won't you come and teach music for me? Suwon has left, you know."

This was the first favor India had ever asked of Marthe, and she saw consternation on the girl's face.

"Oh, I *do* wish I could! But part of what I came to tell you is that Iner's taking me to Denmark almost right away. What's left of Papa's money is there, and Iner thinks we should settle the estate together."

"When you come back then, Marthe?"

The girl's eyes flickered. "Iner wants me to stay in Denmark."

And marry, too, India thought, *with a dowry provided from the estate.* Iner was going to look after Marthe, and that was good. There was no happiness for her here.

With sudden animation Marthe leaned forward. "Why couldn't Angela teach for you? She has every morning free."

India's imagination leaped at the suggestion, and then faltered. "I wasn't planning to pay you, Marthe."

"She might be willing to do it for nothing. Let me ask her, anyway."

India considered the idea. Was this what she had been looking for?

"It's almost too much to ask of a stranger," she said slowly.

"I think she'd enjoy it, really I do! Please let me ask her." Marthe leaned forward eagerly, with a greater enthusiasm than the occasion seemed to warrant. India wondered if their minds were not running parallel, even though each supposed that the initiative was hers.

Seeing India hesitate, Marthe went on: "She has a degree in music. She was planning to teach until she met Charoon. I'll see her tomorrow and ask her."

But when tomorrow came Charoon Suksamran was dead.

There were two English-language newspapers in Bangkok, one the Bangkok *Times,* a dignified English paper, the whole first page of which was devoted to advertisements in small type; the other, the Bangkok *Chronicle,* which in the American pattern used banner headlines and pictures on the front page. India took the *Chronicle* because it was cheaper. It was an afternoon paper, but often she did not find time to read it until the next morning.

She had it in her hand Sunday as she came out to breakfast. Dulcie was already seated, looking green with fatigue. "I've been at the palace all night," she said, glancing up from her fruit. "I thought maybe you'd come too."

India was startled. "What happened, Dulcie?"

"Didn't you read the paper? Didn't anyone tell you?"

"I have it here now."

Dulcie got up from her place and, taking the newspaper from India, spread it across the table. On the front page was the picture of a car lying bottom up in a canal, with little more than two wheels showing. The headline read: PRINCE KILLED IN FREAK AC-CIDENT. India's hands shook as she picked it up to read.

Mom Chao Charoon Suksamran, son of Princess Sandhya and H.R.H. the late Prince of Udon, was killed at 10:30 this morning when his car was overturned into the Talat Canal by the charge of a royal elephant.

The story went on to explain that the elephant was being taken to the river to bathe. Twice previously it had charged motorcars, but without unfortunate results. Seemingly the elephant became enraged at the approach of the blue Cadillac driven by the Prince and trumpeted for the attack. The mahout was unable to control the animal, but escaped unharmed by sliding to the ground. Passers-by said that the Prince had been unaware of the elephant's intention until warned by their shouts. He had tried to swing to the left around the enraged animal, but the elephant was moving at too great a speed and rammed the car head on.

"Cheronai was with him," Dulcie said. "They're both dead."

India sat back in her chair, faint with shock. The bowl of cereal on the table before her swam outward in a dozen concentric circles. She felt a deep wave of pity for the Princess, who had lost her favorite son—two sons and her husband in less than three years. It did not comfort her to know Angela's problem solved. This was one more horror to add to those that had gone before. When the bowl swam back into focus she stood up.

"Aren't you going to eat?" Dulcie asked sharply.

India shook her head and turned away.

The bell had rung for Sunday school when Marthe knocked on her door.

"Will you come with me to see Angela?" she asked, and India saw that she had been crying.

India drew the girl through the door and shoved her gently down on a chair. "Of course I will. Do you want to go now?"

Marthe put her head in her arms and began to cry. The church was filling with the patter of feet. Benches scraped. The piano played a prelude, and then the first chords of *Holy, holy, holy, Lord God Almighty*. Marthe took the handkerchief from her eyes and wadded it into a ball.

"I'm afraid for her, mem. The Tan Ying hates her."

"Perhaps she'll leave the palace as soon as the bathing ceremony is over."

Marthe's eyes pleaded for something, but all she said was, "Where could she go?"

India thought she understood, but she wished Marthe would be explicit.

"Do you want me to ask her?"

"Would you?" Marthe asked tremulously. "Would you? I'd ask her to stay with me, but we're selling our furniture Wednesday and going to the hotel."

"Why don't you come here too? Would Iner let you?"

"Oh yes, of course."

"Then suppose you invite her to stay here with you as your guest until you sail, and once she's here we can make plans for the future."

Marthe wanted more than this. She wanted a note to reinforce her verbal invitation. Or, if by any chance she could not see Angela, she wanted a note to leave with one of her own.

When India sat down to write it was some time before words came. *Dear Madame Suksamran,* she began, and for twenty minutes could think of nothing further to say. Then she wrote:

I have read of the sudden death of your husband and should like to express my deepest sympathy. I hope that you will pardon me if I do this in an unconventional way. I do not know you, but have known Marthe, who brings this note, since she was a little girl.

She is distressed because she cannot invite you to her home during the period of your mourning, but, as she will tell you, she and Iner are going to Denmark. She hopes you will consent to stay with her here until she sails, and I hope too that you will feel you can accept our joint invitation.

If you and Princess Sandhya had been deeply attached to each other this letter would be an impertinence, as perhaps it is. Recently she told me that your relationship with her was not happy. It has seemed to me that this might add unbearably to your grief, and that you might prefer to live elsewhere until the cremation. If I am right, and if you would care to share a room with Marthe here at

Jasmine Hall, where nothing will intrude upon you but the noise of this busy school, we shall be happy to place our guest room at your disposal. There will be no obligation on your part, either social or financial. You may eat in your room if you prefer.

Do not trouble to answer this letter. If you decide to accept this invitation, let Marthe bring you at your convenience. She will carry the letter to you herself.

Sincerely yours,
India Severn

Jasmine Hall,
Bamrung Muang Road beyond the Black Bridge,
June 8, 1930.

CHAPTER 9

CARPENTERS WERE BUSY IN THE WALLED GARDEN OF PRINCESS Sandhya's palace, putting up a wooden pavilion to house the coffin of the young Prince until the cremation. After the ceremonies were completed—the seventh-day rites, the fiftieth-day rites, the hundredth-day rites, and the cremation itself—this pavilion would be given to a temple, as was the custom with wealthy Siamese.

The carpenters were Chinese. They chattered shrilly as they worked. They had set uprights in place where before had been a garden of rosebushes in tubs. The tubs were lined up irregularly against the compound wall. A truckload of sawed boards turned in through the gate just ahead of India and Marthe. The driver shouted to the head carpenter, who shouted back in a perfect frenzy of annoyance.

There were many people coming and going, older women in black, girls and younger women in white, men in the usual dress of government officials, white tunics and dark blue panungs, with black mourning bands on their arms. India and Marthe followed several groups of these toward the mansion, and entered behind them. The Princess, dressed in black, was sitting in the reception room surrounded by relatives. She did not rise. Other people moved about the room taking care of the guests, their heads and backs bent respectfully below the level of the Tan Ying's own.

While India waited to speak to her she looked about. Angela was nowhere in the room. When India's turn came and she stood before the Princess, the Siamese woman regarded her out of dull eyes, and India fumbled in her effort to express something of the sympathy she felt.

"I am so sorry," she said, and again, when no more adequate words came, "I am so very sorry."

One of the other women in the room, also dressed in black, took India and Marthe in charge. "Come this way, mem," she said in a low voice. "The Tan Ying will want you to bathe the corpse."

India drew back. "It isn't necessary. I didn't expect it."

"Oh yes, of course you must. You're a friend of the family."

They were led through a series of rooms to one larger than the rest. Here a knot of people squatted respectfully outside in the hall, and others were seated on the floor inside with their hands folded before their faces. The shutters were closed. A man in official dress and a black arm band was in charge. Bending at the waist, so that his head was lower than theirs, he conducted them to the dais on which the body lay. Flowers were banked along the lower tiers, and many candles also.

The body had been covered with a fine Persian rug of silk. Only a hand was visible, extended over a golden bowl, lying on palm leaves as if it rested there. The hand was yellow from the turmeric with which the body had been rubbed after the ritual bathing with hot water and kaffir lime. There was something terribly poignant about the yellow hand. Outside the shouting and pounding of the carpenters continued. Here in the still room was the heavy odor of flowers and incense, rich furnishings and the drone of monks, and at the center of it was the outstretched hand of a young man. It was lying palm up, empty and unseeking. It had relinquished, after so short a span, the functions of life, the holding and the grasping and the getting.

The man in charge offered India a bottle of scented water. She shook it over the hand, and the water splashed into the golden

bowl. Then she returned it to him. Marthe, who was kneeling behind India, demurred when the bottle was offered to her, as if the
honor were too great, but he insisted.

As he started to lead them out, India shook her head and motioned that she would sit for a while with the mourners. Pleased
with her punctiliousness, he led her to a chair. Everyone else in the
room was seated on the floor, so India refused it and sat instead on a
mat. Her eyes were accustomed to the dimness now and she
searched covertly for Angela.

A chapter of monks was seated in the opposite corner of the
room on a low platform. Their yellow robes shone dully. Their
voices rose in the monotonous chant of the *Abhidharma*:

". . . *As mountains are made of great rocks as high as the sky, which,
rolling down, crush creatures in all four directions around them, so old
age and death bear down upon all creatures whether kings or Brahmans
or householders, whether common citizens or people of mixed blood or
the coolie who carries out the refuse.*

"The Great Refuge of the world is filled with great mercy,
filled with all grace for the benefit of all creatures. He
reached supreme enlightenment. With this true declaration
may all misfortunes be prevented from coming.

"*There are no exceptions, all suffer under this burden. An army with
elephants is not able to fight against old age and death, or an army of
chariots or of infantry. No one is able to conquer old age or death,
whether by fighting or by incantations or by wealth.*

"The Great Refuge of the world is filled with great mercy,
filled with all grace for the help of all creatures. He reached
supreme enlightenment. With this true declaration may all
misfortunes be prevented from coming.

"*Therefore people who are wise, when they see what is useful for
them, ought to use their wisdom to put their faith in Buddha, the
Dharma, and the Sangha. Whoever keeps the Dharma with body,
speech and heart, such a man is praised by pundits in this world, and
when he leaves this world he enjoys happiness in heaven.*

"The Great Refuge of the world is filled with great mercy,
filled with all grace for the happiness of all creatures. He
reached supreme enlightenment. With this true declaration
may all misfortunes be prevented from coming. . . ."

Not far from the monks was a pile of new robes, blankets, cartons of cigarettes, betel nuts and seri leaves, ready for presentation. As the service drew to a close there was a stirring among the mourners. They shifted to more comfortable positions and brought their hands down from the attitude of reverence. Several stood up and lighted cigarettes. Relatives began to place the various offerings and trays of food before the monks.

India turned to Marthe and, speaking in a low voice, said in English, "Have you seen her anywhere?"

Marthe shook her head.

"Hadn't you better look for her?"

Marthe's face took on a frightened expression, as if her determination had buckled under the demands of the actual situation. "What if someone stops me?"

"No one will," India assured her, "and if anyone does, just say you're looking for her. There's no reason why you shouldn't, you know."

The same older woman who had brought them to the funeral chamber was waiting for them at the door. "Now come and have something to eat," she said, starting off briskly. Before she had reached the end of the corridor she stopped. "Maybe you'd like to see the coffin first. It just came."

The coffin had been placed in an anteroom, and a group of people were admiring it respectfully. It was plated with gold and resembled a Chinese coffin in shape, being narrower at the bottom than at the top, with sloping sides like a boat. The base was finely carved with symbolic figures and set with bits of colored glass.

"His Majesty sent it," their guide explained with satisfaction. "I think when the Tan Ying herself dies His Majesty will send one of the state urns. She's always been his favorite, you know, but of course this coffin is a great honor," she added, lest they deprecate it because it was not an urn.

Tables had been set with food in one of the larger salons. Forty or fifty people were standing around talking and laughing, or were sitting at small tables against the wall, eating. Chinese waiters in shorts and singlets hurried in and out with roast fowls and tureens of steaming soup. Their guide found plates and served them rice from a covered dish.

"That curry is full of chilies, mem," she warned, "but this one is quite flat. Try these fried prawns, and some of those cakes."

She chose a table and, after helping herself, sat down with them. Nor did she leave them. She seemed to know India well and think that India knew her. She chattered of Mem Cole and Wang Lang as if she had been a pupil there, but India could not place her. She listened for clues, names she could recognize, incidents that would identify the girl lost now in the woman, but without success. Her thoughts were divided anyway. Their guide's assiduity had posed a problem.

Marthe sat quietly eating. When they had finished there would be no further excuse for staying. Surely, having gone this far, Marthe wasn't giving up? Or was she? She had always been timid, and she seemed to find something ominous in Angela's failure to attend the ceremonies in the big house. Yet if Angela had been up all night, as other members of the family certainly had, she might well be sleeping now.

When they finished, their guide looked about for a servant to remove the plates, but India forestalled her.

"Marthe will take them out," she said, and gave the girl a commanding look. Then, turning back to the woman opposite, she asked, "Is there anything at all I can do for the Tan Ying?"

The woman in black settled comfortably into her chair and lit a cigarette. "No, nothing, thank you very much. Everything is being taken care of." She sighed. "He was her favorite son, you know."

Marthe had stood up and was removing the plates. India did not glance at her. "I remember," she said. "It must have been a great shock to her."

"To all of us," the woman agreed. "When the chief of the gendarmerie came yesterday morning, the Tan Ying wasn't even up. She was sitting on her bed talking to me while she ate her breakfast. We had been discussing Charoon, and she had just said that he was growing more like his father every day, when the man was announced. Wasn't that a strange coincidence? She sent Khun Lop and me down to find out what he wanted. At first he only said that there'd been an accident.

"Even when we knew that Charoon was dead we couldn't believe it. Neither of us dared tell the Tan Ying, so we sent for her oldest brother."

She lowered her voice to explain that if Charoon hadn't married a farang wife it might never have happened. Dissatisfaction had driven him to Cheronai, and now they were both dead. She described the consternation and grief of the household, all the preparations that had had to be made, told how the Tan Ying had lost two sons and her husband in less than three years. It was her karma. And one of her sons was in England and couldn't get back for the cremation.

Ten minutes passed, fifteen, twenty, before Marthe slipped quietly into her chair. When their guide had finished her third cigarette they stood up to go. People were still coming, many with flowers, some with candles and sticks of incense.

Neither India nor Marthe said anything until they were seated in a taxi, then Marthe buried her face in her hands and began to cry.

"I found her, mem," she sobbed. "I *did* find her."

She swallowed her tears and began to tell India what she had done. She had gone through the mansion toward the kitchen and down the stairs into the back compound. No one had stopped her. Angela's house was a dingy cottage with an atap roof. Marthe had been there twice before and had little trouble finding it.

The door was shut, and no one answered her knock. After several minutes, she had gone in, thinking to leave her notes on the living-room table. The cottage had two rooms, one behind the other, and a separate kitchen. Through the doorway connecting the rooms Marthe could see Angela lying on the bed, apparently asleep.

Marthe had tiptoed to the bedroom door and called softly. A ray of light coming through the closed shutters had fallen across Angela's face, and Marthe had seen that Angela's eyes were open and sightless. The look of the staring eyes had frightened her. She had thought with horror that Angela was dead.

Marthe began to cry again, remembering the moment of terror that had overwhelmed her at the sight of her friend.

India put her hand on the girl's shoulder. "Try to control yourself, Marthe," she said, sharply enough to interrupt the sobs. "You can tell me the rest when we get home. Angela had probably taken a sleeping pill."

Then she was struck with the thought that there might be some reason other than hysteria for Marthe's panic. She knew that the young, who expect happiness around every corner, are ill prepared to cope with despair. It suddenly occurred to her that Angela might have taken an overdose of sleeping pills.

"She was breathing normally, wasn't she?" India asked Marthe, and was reassured by Marthe's nod.

They got down from the taxi at the head of the lane and walked to a bench in the garden. Dinner was over and the children were having their naps. The Bible school girls were nowhere about. Watery sunlight seeped through the trees in patches of pale yellow.

"Now tell me what you did, Marthe," India ordered.

Marthe dabbed her eyes with a wet handkerchief. She had gone to the bed and taken hold of Angela's hand to rouse her. A servant girl who had been sitting unnoticed on the floor told her sharply to leave her mistress alone. It was Din. The Tan Ying had given her to them the year before, and she had hated Angela from the first. She had waited on Charoon hand and foot, fastening his panung for him, polishing his shoes, and ironing his tunics. After a while Angela awoke one night—and heard them in the kitchen—and then —many nights it was like that, while Din grew more and more insolent to her every day. Now Charoon was dead, and there sat Din on the floor, large with child, staring at Angela, and hating her, hating her, hating her. Marthe was convinced that Din had drugged Angela and was waiting to see her die.

"She wouldn't do that!" India said, and was instantly less sure, although she went on to say: "You know the Siamese superstition about the spirit's being absent from the body during sleep. That's why she told you not to wake her."

Marthe rejected the explanation. Din hated Angela. Probably she blamed Angela for the fact that her child's father was dead. Siamese were often vengeful. Charoon wasn't there to protect Angela any more, and the Tan Ying wouldn't care what happened to her.

Marthe had been unable to think what to do when Angela did

not rouse, but she had done the best she could. She had interposed her body between Angela and the servant. Then, leaning down, had slipped the two notes into her friend's dress, hoping Din had not seen what she did.

To quiet Marthe's fears, India promised to see Mr. Denniscort that afternoon and ask him to throw the protection of his official interest around Angela. Somewhat reassured, Marthe went home.

India felt uncomfortable and a little foolish as she turned into the Legation compound. She wanted to attribute Marthe's fears to her native timorousness, but she could not discount them entirely.

Mr. Denniscort was sitting on his upstairs veranda, reading a magazine.

"Hello there," he called. "Come right up, won't you?"

She told him the story briefly, without embellishments, and asked if it would be possible for him to call at the palace and see Angela before evening. He did not ridicule her mission, as she had feared he would.

"I'd intended to, anyway," he said, frowning a little. "It's too bad it happened like this, but at least she's free of them again for whatever it's worth. You and I can stop worrying about her soon."

"If freedom is as superficial as all that."

He cocked an eyebrow at her. *"Stone walls do not a prison make, nor iron bars a cage,"* he quoted, and there were traces of mockery in his voice. "I suppose you mean that freedom is also a state of mind."

"Well, isn't it?" India persisted. "It's surely more than the absence of fetters."

"Yes, of course," he said soberly, "but then our past clips the wings of us all."

"That doesn't rule out hope for the future," India argued. "Birds sometimes fly again after their clipped wings grow."

"We like to think they do," he agreed.

CHAPTER 10

THERE WAS A LIGHT RAIN THE MORNING ANGELA SUKSAMRAN CAME to Jasmine Hall. A week of dry weather had just ended, one of those pleasant intervals in the monsoon.

The rainy season was now well advanced, and the storms had lost much of their early violence. Sometimes a downpour continued for days, and the canal at the back of the house overflowed its banks. At other times soaking showers fell briefly and with predictable regularity. If the rain had fallen at nine yesterday, it would come at ten today, and eleven tomorrow. Before and after, the sun shone. It lacked power to dry the air, however, which was often so thick with moisture that shoes turned green, and clothes soured before they dried.

On this morning the rain was fine and soft, falling with a kind of gentle melancholy. The moolies were down on the upstairs veranda, and the smell of mildew from the blue cloth that lined them filled the house.

Ploy came to find India during her class in Old Testament history. "Mem *kha*," she said, kneeling courteously, "there's a mem come to see you."

India looked at her watch and saw that there were only ten minutes before the end of class.

"Ask her to wait a little, and I'll be up," she said. "You can take her a glass of orange crush while I finish."

It did not occur to India that it was Angela. Three weeks had passed since the Sunday morning she and Marthe had gone to the palace. For the first few days after that, India never left the compound without wondering whether Angela would come while she was out. But the girl did not appear, nor did she send any reply to the letters that had been tucked into her dress.

Marthe went to the palace twice before she sailed, but was not admitted either time.

Mr. Denniscort succeeded better. He called the afternoon of the bathing ceremony and expressed his sympathy to the Princess. Then he asked to see Angela, explaining that he was deeply concerned for the young American girl, bereaved and far from her family. When he was told that she was indisposed, he said that he would call again in a day or so.

On Tuesday, Angela came to him in the reception room, looking ill and sad. Not much was said beyond the conventional expression of sympathy from Mr. Denniscort. He offered to notify her family, if she had not already done so, and she told him that her only living relatives were some middle-aged cousins with whom she had lost touch.

"I don't believe she's in any danger," he reported to India on his way back to the Legation. "She looks dazed and sick, but that's natural."

Marthe's ship was sailing on the morning of the seventh-day rites. She came to say good-by to India the afternoon before. Her soft brown hair was carefully coiffed under a new hat. She wore a traveling dress of black crepe and high-heeled slippers that matched a large patent-leather purse. Her nervous fingers kept opening and closing the catch on the purse.

She described her efforts to see Angela, and enlisted India's further concern for her friend. "I have the feeling that she needs help, mem, even though she hasn't written. And I don't know of anyone else to ask. For one thing, the only money she has is what the Tan Ying gives her."

India agreed to do what she could, if Angela showed any sign of a willingness to accept help.

There had been no word in the two weeks that followed. This silence had seemed to India an answer in itself, and she had stopped expecting any other.

When India came upstairs from class, one of the moolies had been raised to let in air.

A girl stood up from the corner of the mook where she was sitting.

"Miss Severn?" she asked uncertainly, fumbling in her handbag. "I'm Angela Suksamran."

"Oh yes, of course." India shook her hand warmly. "Do sit down. Has Ploy brought you anything to drink?"

The girl went on as if she had not heard. "I received your kind letter several weeks ago and intended to answer at once, but—well, as you know—I didn't. So this morning I thought I'd come and thank you personally."

India felt vibrations of tension beneath the modulated tones of the girl's voice. "You didn't need to do either," she said easily. "It wasn't my purpose to add to the number of your obligations. Please sit down, won't you? I'll pull up the rest of these moolies."

She turned away so that the girl might have time to regain her composure.

There was no wind. The rain was falling straight down. In the pale silvery light that came in, once the moolies were up, Angela's face looked fine-drawn. Clearly the effort of coming had been very great. She laid her bag on the table, and India saw her hands flutter as she returned them to her lap. It was the fear in Angela's hands that gave India her cue.

"My invitation is still good," she said. "Perhaps I ought to explain that I've known the Tan Ying a long time and realize that she can be—shall we say, difficult? Then, too, the customs of a Siamese household are not our customs. I thought it might be easier for you to accept hospitality from a stranger than to stay where you are. By the way, Marthe left for Denmark on the fourteenth. She tried to see you twice the week before she sailed."

The girl looked distressed. "No one told me she called. I'm so sorry I missed her."

"She thought it was that."

"Is she coming back?"

"Probably not. But to return to what I was saying—I want you to feel that whether you accept my invitation or not you have a choice."

"It's very kind of you." The girl smiled wanly.

"So I'm leaving the invitation open," India went on. "You can avail yourself of it any time."

There was silence on the mook except for the soft and steady whisper of the rain. Angela's hands were pleating the white linen of her dress. After a minute she looked directly at India, drawing no screen across the pain and bewilderment and fear and unhappiness in her eyes. The effort cost her a great deal, and the oval of her face was pinched.

"That's really why I came," she said simply.

As a little girl, India had brought home a procession of stray animals, fed them, bound up their wounds, nursed them back to faith in mankind. She had known a wild and special joy whenever one of them crawled to her for the first time, rubbed against her, licked her hand. She knew it now.

"I'm glad you could trust me," she answered quietly, careful to throttle the emotion that rose in her, for she was deeply touched. "Did you bring your trunks?"

Angela looked away, but not before India had seen relief in her eyes, and a kind of shame.

"I could hardly do that, could I? Not until I'd talked to you. I'll go for them now," she said.

Her hands left her dress and began to twist a handkerchief round and round in a disembodied agony of their own.

"That's fine," India agreed. "It will give us time to clean your room before you move in."

Then she had another thought. Everything was difficult for this girl worn down by grief and abuse. The effort of collecting her things, the necessity for telling the Tan Ying that she was leaving would require a decisiveness that seemed beyond her.

"Would you like me to come with you and help you pack?" India asked.

Angela shook her head. "No, thank you very much."

She dismissed the suggestion as if it had no bearing on her problem and the special concern underlying it.

"I must explain something first," she said. "You see, I haven't any very clear plans, except that I want to find work and eventually go back to America. I'd like to stay in Bangkok, though, until after— well, until after the cremation, if I can. And the difficulty is that

—well . . ." Her voice almost failed her. "You see, I have very little money."

"I said in my letter there'd be no financial obligation," India reminded her gently.

"I'd have to reimburse you sometime!" The girl's answer was hurried and emphatic. "I couldn't let you provide shelter and food, and not pay for it. I couldn't do that, you know. But I might need credit for a while."

Tears of nervousness and fatigue were close to the surface. India heard the sound of them through the words.

"And I'm terribly sorry," Angela concluded, "but I can't ask the Tan Ying for any of Charoon's money."

"Some of it belongs to you," India protested mildly. "If you stayed on with her, she'd provide for you as a matter of course."

"Yes," the girl said, acknowledging her inconsistency and her powerlessness to act against it, "but then I can't stay with her any longer."

"I understand." India was matter-of-fact. "And I understand your feeling about wishing to contribute. What I'd really like much better than money is your help in the school music."

"But——"

"No, please. I'm not inventing this on the spur of the moment to take the sting out of what seems to you like charity. Marthe and I talked about it before your husband's death. From the financial point of view I'd have the better of the bargain, you know, but I think you may prefer it that way for the time being. Then later, if you want to, you can look around for a position that pays more nearly what you ought to have."

The girl did not answer immediately. She sat with her hands clenched, deeply sunk within herself. The effort of appraising India's plan seemed physical.

Then there was a slight lifting of her expression.

Quick to sense it, India said, "Come and see your room."

Angela stood up. "No, thank you very much. Now that I've made up my mind I'll go for my things." She smiled faintly. "Before I have another attack of indecision."

"You're sure you don't want any help?"

The eyes in which pain was so deeply embedded looked straight at India, scorning evasion.

"That won't be necessary," Angela said. "They'll be glad to see me go."

It was eight o'clock in the evening before Angela returned. When she had unpacked and put away her clothes, India suggested that she spend her first week at Jasmine Hall resting.

"You're more tired than you realize," India urged. "Grief is an exhausting experience. Don't get up for breakfast tomorrow. Ploy will bring you a tray."

"Oh, Miss Severn, I'd rather get up. I want to begin work right away. And please call me Angela."

The next morning she was on the mook when India came out of her room for breakfast.

"We eat in here," India said, opening the lattice door that made a courtesy separation between the mook and the section of veranda where the table was set.

The girl looked white and listless, as if she had slept badly. There were dark circles under her eyes.

Dulcie appeared a moment later, walking quickly. She acknowledged the introduction to Angela with a slight tilting of her head and a sharp look. Throughout the meal she continued to dart speculative glances at the girl. Mani's place remained empty.

Conversation was desultory. No one made any attempt to keep it going. Angela swallowed a mouthful of oatmeal and laid her spoon on her plate. She peeled a section of pomelo and took a few sips of coffee. India guessed that she was eating from courtesy rather than hunger.

"Now what may I do first?" the girl asked when breakfast was over.

"Can you type?" India led the way across the mook.

"A little."

"I have a file that needs reorganizing," she explained as they went downstairs to the school office. "Darun will be in sometime this morning to make out your application papers for the Ministry of Education. If you brought your diploma, will you please let her have it? This afternoon, though, you must rest. I really do insist on that."

Angela set to work with quick comprehension. By noon she had sorted and rearranged the correspondence in two drawers of the five-drawer file. She did not protest when India sent her to bed after lunch. "Just for this one day, though," she said.

India had errands in town, but she made a special effort to be back in time for tea. Angela came out of her room looking white and tired.

"Did you sleep?" India asked.

"I did, yes, but I feel worse for it."

"So do I, when I sleep in the afternoon. What you need is a cup of tea. I wonder sometimes why tea is more important in the tropics than it ever was at home. Maybe it's because four o'clock is a lower point here than it was there. Cream and sugar, or lime?"

"Cream and sugar, please."

A moment later Mani Soderstrom appeared. She was wearing a periwinkle pasin tight around her hips. A blouse of the same glowing color brought out the warm opalescence of her skin. She scarcely glanced at India. Her attention was focused on Angela.

"Madame Suksamran," India said, "this is Madame Soderstrom, who's also staying at Jasmine Hall for a while."

"How do you do?" Angela smiled politely.

Mani's eyes completed their avid survey of the American girl before she acknowledged the introduction. "We've met before," she said.

Angela flushed. "Have we? I don't seem to remember where, I'm sorry to say."

"At the Sports Club."

"Oh yes, of course."

"Won't you have a cup of tea with us, Mani?" India invited. "Or are you going somewhere?"

"Thank you."

Mani sat down next to Angela and accepted a cup of tea from India. She stirred it with inattention while she studied Angela's dress.

"Where do you buy your clothes?" she asked.

"At Femina usually," Angela replied.

"Did she make that dress?"

"Yes, she did." There was a slight stiffening in Angela's voice. If Mani heard it, she paid no attention to it. "How much did she charge you?" she asked next.

"I don't remember."

"She's expensive, though, isn't she?" Mani was persistent.

"She is, rather."

At that point the conversation crumpled of its own weight. Mani set her cup on the table and her hand strayed to the diamond clip that held her sleek black hair in place. She continued to examine Angela with frank interest.

Angela kept her eyes on the tea she was sipping. She seemed to have withdrawn into some private retreat of her own. If she resented Mani's half-admiring, half-envious stare, she took no other means of showing it. *Perhaps it's her usual defense against the jealous scrutiny of other women,* India thought.

She made several attempts to start a conversation, but each languished for want of response. She could find no subject to act as catalytic for the interests of three such diverse people as they were. In the end she was content to drink her tea while it was hot and let the girls find something in common when they were ready to make the further effort.

They were an interesting picture sitting side by side in the two big wicker chairs. The contrast went deeper than the color of eyes, skin, and hair, India thought. It was a matter of temperament also. Mani was sultry like an August day. One felt in her the possibility of passion, and of storms, too, violent storms, but soon over. Angela was controlled, almost too controlled. There was about her, at least now in her grief, a stillness that suggested one of those snowy mornings in January with hemlocks standing white and motionless in a silent world. Yet *If Winter comes, can Spring be far behind?* India wondered, incurably hopeful, as always.

From the garden below came the laughter of children at play. "*Li-li-kao-san,*" they were chanting in unison. One of the Bible school girls practiced her scales on the chapel piano with uninspired repetition. From the office downstairs came the point and counterpoint of Siamese conversation, as some parent argued with Darun.

"Hello! Cheerio! Pip-pip!" It was a man's voice. "May I come in?"

He was standing on the next to the top step, a stocky young man with a square jaw and conscious good looks. He had spoken to them all, but he was smiling at Angela.

"Benny darling!" Mani jumped to her feet and ran across the mook to take his hand. "Come in, come in!"

So this was Benny! He had black hair, and blue eyes in a red-and-white face. It was a turbulent face, India saw, full of perverse humor. What it lacked in strength, it made up in the wildness of the eyes.

India had a trick of applying a word to people when she first met them. She gave Benny one now—*insouciant*. He was the very personification of insouciance. He was wearing fresh whites, very stiff, and a blue tie. There was even a blue handkerchief folded into the pocket of his coat.

"Hello, Mani. Long time no see." He dropped her hand and turned toward Angela, who was regarding him without expression.

"Hi ya, Angel," he said, ignoring the absence of welcome. "I had the devil's own time finding you. The old dowager's maid wouldn't tell me where you'd gone."

He sat down in the chair Mani had vacated, and exerted the entire force of his personality against the surface Angela presented. "I combed the whole damned town before I ran you to earth. I hope you're flattered. I just got back from Java yesterday."

Angela did not offer him her hand. Instead she turned and introduced him to India. "Miss Severn, Mr. O'Hanlon."

He nodded briefly in India's direction and turned back to Angela with a quick movement that shut India and Mani away as effectively as a wall.

"What made you come here?" he demanded, his voice engagingly intimate.

His manner evoked no response from Angela. "I'm staying here," she said, and took another sip of tea.

He shrugged, apparently reserving further comment on that subject. "Well, what'n'ell have you done to yourself since I last saw you?" he asked next. "You look sick."

"I'm all right, thank you."

India offered him a cup of tea, but he declined.

"I had a drink before I came, thank you." He turned back to Angela.

"Look, Angel, my car's downstairs. Come out for a little drive. It'll do you good."

The girl's hand trembled as she set her cup down, but her voice was steady. "No, thank you, Benny."

"Oh, come on, darling. You need fresh air." His voice was persuasive. When she did not look at him or answer, he leaned over and took her hand between both of his.

"Angel, I'm terribly sorry about what happened, really. I just didn't want to talk about it. But it's over now, and you've got to go on living. I won't make any passes at you. I just want you to come out in the air."

"No, Benny. Thank you just the same." Angela pulled her hand free.

"But why not, Angel? You might at least give me a reason."

"I don't want to go, Benny. That's the reason. I don't want to go anywhere with you, now or ever. I've told you that before."

The black eyes flashed. "You don't need to be so goddamned rude," he said roughly.

Mani sat down on the arm of his chair with a quick movement that was feline in its fluid directness. She slid her hand around his neck. "I'll go with you, Benny, if you'll let me. Won't I do? Please, pretty please. I'd love a ride in your nice car." She laid her cheek against the top of his head.

He paid no attention to her. He was looking at Angela, and his eyes were hot. A muscle twitched under the skin of his cheek.

Angela had turned her head away and was staring out at the green of the rain trees. There was so little expression in her face that it looked serene in the late afternoon sunlight. It was a counterfeit peace coined from numbness, India thought, and yet the security that made it possible was real. She was glad that Jasmine Hall had provided Angela with refuge and the prerogative of the shut door. There was no fear of Benny in the girl now as there had been that afternoon at the Legation.

Before the detachment in her face, Benny surrendered.

He glanced briefly at Mani. "O.K., baby. Collect your valuables and let's roll."

Mani jumped up at once. "I already have them here."

Her coral mouth opened in a delighted smile, and she held out her hand. "Come on, come on," she urged.

Benny came slowly to his feet, still frowning at Angela's averted head. Then suddenly he leaned down, cupped his free hand under her chin, and turned her face toward him.

"I'll be back, Angel," he said softly. "Some other time."

CHAPTER 11

ON HER THIRD MORNING AT JASMINE HALL ANGELA BEGAN MUSIC lessons for the girls of the Bible school. Three of them came to her before lunch, and three in the afternoon. India planned to give each girl two lessons a week. From then on the tinkly old pianos in church and chapel were busy from dawn to dark.

The girls were enchanted with Angela.

"I didn't know mems were ever pretty," India heard Salee say to Bua Kham as they sat outside her door waiting for their lessons.

Bua Kham was superior. "Haven't you ever been to the movies?"

"Yes, but actresses are different."

"It's more that they're young," Bua Kham insisted. "All the mems we know are old."

By the end of the first week Angela had fitted herself smoothly into the routine of Jasmine Hall. The forces tearing and clawing below the surface produced no visible effect upon her, except one. She came to breakfast every morning white from lack of sleep. Her weariness was so apparent that India continued to insist on a daily siesta.

"Oh, Miss Severn," Angela protested, "everyone else is working. I don't need it, really I don't."

"Yes, you do, Angela." India was firm.

One day in passing, she laid her hand on the girl's forehead. "Your cheeks are flushed," she said. "Do you have a fever?"

"No, really I don't." Angela moved from under India's hand.

"Let's take your temperature and see."

"No, please, Miss Severn. It's just that I don't sleep well."

"Have you ever had malaria?"

"No, never. I'll be all right in a week or so."

"Won't you let Dr. Crane look at you? Malaria is so insidious, you can have it for a while without knowing it."

This Angela refused, almost impatiently.

Benny was only one of a score of men who found their way to Jasmine Hall the first two weeks that Angela was there. If she was giving a music lesson, she asked to be excused. If she was caught on the mook at teatime, she was polite but unresponsive.

India had not known there were so many unattached men in Bangkok—tall, short, thin, fat, British, Danish, French, American. Ostensibly they came to express their sympathy. If they had expected to do more, they were disappointed. Angela replied to their questions in monosyllables. After a few uncomfortable minutes they left, as it were, on tiptoe, abashed by the withdrawal in her face.

When women came it was hardly different. "Darling, we're all terribly shocked and sorry, but you can't hide away like this. Come to cocktails on Tuesday. It's not a party, of course. Everyone just wants to see you again."

"No, please. I'm not going anywhere."

"But, darling, Charoon wouldn't expect you to immolate yourself. This is worse than suttee! You've got to face up to life, you know. Now, please. Be a good girl and come."

At that Angela would raise her great dark eyes, as if she were too weary to hunt further for words. Before the gutted look in them, her tormentors left with the disconcerted abruptness of people who have strayed into a hallowed place.

Not all the visitors were Angela's friends. Many were India's. She was able to gauge the extent of gossip from the spate of people who inundated Jasmine Hall. Some of them she had not seen in years and knew only casually.

Almost the entire membership of Bangkok Station came. It was like a procession. One afternoon it was Dr. and Mrs. Llewellyn from Bangkok Christian College, with their young contract teacher, Howard Timmans, looking so clean he reminded India of a freshly scrubbed puppy. The next, it was Mr. Mellis and his wife—Mr. Mellis needed to measure the verandas that were to be screened. After that came Dr. and Mrs. Baker—they invited India to dinner— as did Peter and Alix Brentwood, and the Wilsons, and the Desmonds. She could have called the roll of Bangkok Station those first ten days that Angela was with her.

"Bring Madame Suksamran along," they all said, a little too casually, as if it were an afterthought. India was puzzled to understand the reason for the various elaborate subterfuges. Perhaps they were ashamed of being curious. Or perhaps they imagined she was deceived as to where their interest really lay.

Perversely she did not mention Angela unless they did, and Angela avoided the mook.

The Howards, when they came, were frank.

"India, we want to have a peek at her," Anne whispered, laughing. She was plump and pretty in a green voile dress that made her red hair look burnished. "The whole town's buzzing, you know. Everyone's trying to find out how she happened to come to you. Is she as pretty as they say? Jim's dying for a look, and so am I."

"If you can wait twenty minutes, I'll ask her to come out," India said. "She's just started a lesson, so she won't come now. That's your reward for not pretending you came to see me. Sit down, won't you? Ploy, bring two more cups."

The Howards had been Jasmine Hall's most loyal friends from its inception. They were new to the Mission when the school opened.

As soon as the building was in order they called, bringing thirty books from their own library. Jim was a big dark man who seemed to be always laughing, and yet there was in him a deep and continuing earnestness. Sitting on the mook that first afternoon as now, with a cup of tea held carefully between two large fingers, he had looked across at India quizzically.

"What will you have, Miss Severn?" he had asked. "I marry and bury, baptize, and teach, excoriate and exhort."

India had been pleased with their interest.

"No marrying for a while!" she protested in mock horror.

They had asked to see the building, and she had shown them over it from chapel to kitchen. When they came back to the mook, they were full of enthusiasm.

"What does Mr. Hillow think of it now?" Anne wanted to know.

"He hasn't been here yet," India replied.

Anne's mobile face drew into a frown.

"That's rude of him," she said, wrinkling her nose in disapproval. "I knew the first time I saw him he was a poor loser."

"Oh, he'll come." India was embarrassed by Anne's directness. "He's busy, you know."

"Not so busy as all that," Anne insisted. "You'll have to keep an eye on him, if you don't want trouble." Then she added in a rush, "I might as well be frank, Miss Severn. I don't like him, and you don't either, do you?"

"Anne!" Jim warned her.

"Jim, don't *Anne* me! I'm intuitive where people are concerned. We all know why he hasn't come."

She turned to India. "But don't let it worry you, Miss Severn. Just remember that if Mr. Hillow gets in *your* hair, Jim's big enough to pull *his*."

India laughed at the vehemence of Anne's partisanship. "Why should he, Mrs. Howard?" she asked, amused.

"Anne's seeing ghosts," Jim interposed. "It's the Irish in her."

"Jim, that's unfair!" Anne was indignant. "Why all this beating about the bush? Mr. Hillow's opposed to Jasmine Hall. He said so at Station Meeting. He said it diverted too much money from the evangelistic fund, and ought to be part of Wattana, anyway. He didn't like having the vote go against him, either. Have you forgotten?"

This was true, and yet the event itself had seemed less sinister than Anne's retelling of it.

"Perhaps he'll change his mind, if he can be shown that the money's well spent," India said doubtfully.

"Of course he will." Jim was reassuring. "Don't let Anne frighten you, Miss Severn. She's always setting up straw men for the pleasure of knocking them down. It's her fighting hair. She just means that she's your friend. Besides, when your school's a success, Mr. Hillow will think it was his own idea."

Well, Jim had been wrong about that, India thought. Every year at Mission Meeting she had tried to have her school changed from a Station to a Mission institution. She had coveted the endorsement of the whole group this changed status would have implied.

Amery continued to argue that the school should be a department of Wattana, and there were several who agreed with him.

Three or four others were as firmly convinced that it ought to be transferred to Chiengmai, nearer the rural churches of the north, which were the most numerous in the Mission. Because of these conflicting points of view, it was never possible to get a decisive vote in favor of the change.

"It's Amery's fault entirely!" Anne said after one such defeat. "He keeps the opposition alive." She tossed her red head angrily. "I believe he does it to spite you, India. Was he in love with you, and did you turn him down?"

India laughed in spite of her discouragement. "I'm afraid that's an oversimplification, Anne. Things like this are matters of policy."

"But matters of policy are always personal matters to Amery. Don't you realize that?"

The disbelief in India's face made Anne only more emphatic. "Yes, they are, India. Really! His friends are the hope of the world, and his enemies are 'visionary and impractical,' so he squashes them. Don't pretend it's not true."

"You're too hard on him, Anne."

"Well, he's a hypocrite."

"Oh, Anne, he's not that!"

But Anne was unmoved. "The trouble with Amery is that he's never accomplished a single piece of constructive work, something that other people could see and admire. He's a person of small ability with a sense of failure to exorcise. No, India, be still until I finish!" She laid her hand lightly across India's mouth. "Other Executive Secretaries kept on with their regular jobs after they were elected. I know, because I've asked. But Amery gave up even the pretext of teaching. Haven't you ever wondered why? Because he has a Jehovah complex, and the position gave him power at last. He loves to manipulate people, putting this one up and that one down. It compensates him for his own inadequacies."

Her anger was a catharsis for India's own. "I think I'll forget the whole question of Mission status for a while," she said, returning to her own problem. "I'll try to put first things first."

That had been three years ago, and nothing had changed during the interval, except that India was now reconciled to going on as she was.

Angela was reluctant to leave Bua Kham when India invited her to come to the mook for a cup of tea. This one time India was insistent.

"The Howards are two of my best friends," she urged. "I want you to know them."

Angela complied like a dutiful child. She sat in one of the big wicker chairs and said, "Yes, perhaps you're right," to Jim, and, "No, I don't think so," to Anne. In fifteen minutes, with a murmured apology, she went back to the chapel.

Anne sighed. "I didn't believe the gossip, India, but she's really as lovely as people say. The Princess with the Golden Hair! Of course, we never see a young girl out here, so perhaps she's more devastating in Bangkok than she would be at home. Jim, did you have to ogle her? I thought you belonged to me."

Jim reached over and rumpled her hair. "Jealous?" he asked.

Anne shook her head impatiently. "But, India, she's so still! Do you think you can bring her to life again?"

India did not answer, and Anne sighed for the second time. "May I have another piece of cake? I'm not going to worry about my figure any longer. I might as well enjoy myself. Now, India, tell us about it. Last time we saw you, we didn't so much as know that you had your net out."

Even Amery Hillow made one of his rare visits to Jasmine Hall. He brought with him the tentative itinerary of the Board delegation. Since it was only July, and the delegation was not due until December, India surmised that he could find no better excuse. He said nothing about Angela, nor did India mention her.

She spent the hour he was there going back over their association in her mind, to see if she could discover the seeds of his opposition to Jasmine Hall. Was it really a personal matter, as Anne insisted? And if so, why did Amery dislike her? She had never disliked him. In any case, they were no longer children, to be governed by their likes and dislikes.

A slight feeling of guilt crept into her thoughts at this point. Strictly speaking, it was true that she didn't dislike Amery. On the other hand, there was something else, something she had supposed a secret. Amery was perceptive. Perhaps he had guessed it. If so, was it that which he resented? But surely not! It was too small a thing.

Still, the fact was that she had never given him the full measure of her respect. It was an involuntary withholding. There was a kind of spontaneous admiration she felt for those of her associates who were creative in their work or in their relations with other people that she could not feel for Amery. He was too concerned with little things. Was this the nub of the matter?

Even on first meeting, she remembered, she had thought him, if not inconsequential, at least unimpressive. He had been a little too eager to please, a little too ready with his smile. His too-brown hair had looked like a wig, and his too-light eyes had reminded her unkindly of turquoises, without depth or warmth. He had seemed to India's younger self a little too short, a little too dapper, and entirely too facile. Superficial observations, all of them, she reflected. How critical she had been in those days!

Looking back, she could not decide to what extent her attitude had been formed by the older teachers at Wang Lang. Amery was something of a joke there, largely because he had courted each of the teachers in succession, among them India and later Grace. India had never taken him seriously, but Grace had been attracted to him, even though she was three inches taller than he and thirty pounds heavier. Grace would probably have married him, if the other teachers hadn't teased her so unmercifully.

He had been considered less able than other young men of his generation in the Mission. Twenty-five years ago who could have foreseen that he would one day be Executive Secretary? Perhaps that was exactly it. Abler men preferred their own work, disliked administrative detail, and therefore avoided the position.

"Amery has the soul of a clerk," India remarked to Grace once, years before, and Grace had retorted, "Maybe so, but he gets his reports in on time, which is more than can be said for you."

He was very pleasant this afternoon, very suave. It was as if he sensed the import of her thoughts and would breach with charm the barrier they raised against him in her mind. She doubted for a moment her own fairness. It was hardly right to question Amery's intentions. Perhaps she had allowed Anne's dislike of him to warp her judgment. Surely he meant the school no harm.

Then the cold trickle of experience quenched the flare of hope which his manner had inspired. Amery coveted applause. It meant no more than that. He would exert himself to charm even those he disliked, so long as he was with them, craving from everyone the bagatelle of approval.

Grace brought up the rear of the procession. She had waited longer than was usual with her to censure India's newest undertaking.

"I don't see how you got involved in this latest scandal," she said tartly when she was seated. "A few weeks ago you didn't even know the principals. But that's neither here nor there. Can't you see, India, the time has come to be discreet?"

"By which you mean, I suppose, that I should keep one eye on my work and the other on my associates to see whether they approve of my actions. I'd accomplish very little that way."

"You can't disregard your associates in a small organization like this."

India was patient. "I don't disregard them, Grace. I count on them. There's a difference. As I see it, the group of us form a hollow square facing outward in the direction of our work, with our undefended backs toward each other."

The explanation gave Grace pause, but not for long. "That's all right when you keep within the limits of your assignment. But running a rescue home is a far cry from what you're supposed to be doing. The Station never gave you an appropriation so you could shelter Mani and this widow of Charoon Suksamran's. I heard an influential person say yesterday it would be hard to justify Jasmine Hall to the Board delegation in the light of what you're doing."

"Who is your 'influential person,' Grace?"

"You don't expect me to tell you, do you?"

"It couldn't be anyone but Amery."

"Then why ask?"

"Because there was a time when he wasn't an 'influential person' where your friendship for me was concerned. I just wanted to make the shift in loyalty clear."

"You're trying to obscure the issue, India. I never at any time would have approved of having Mani or this other woman here."

"Well, don't bracket Angela with Mani, Grace. They have nothing in common except my mutual interest."

"You might have trouble proving that. At least from what the Tan Ying says."

India was exasperated. "The Tan Ying tried to tell me what she's obviously told you. She reasoned that because Angela had been a waitress she must also have been a prostitute. I'm surprised that you accepted her *non sequitur*. Angela's father died during her junior year in college. She worked her way through her senior year by waiting tables. I can vouch for her character."

In argument Grace's normally full contralto climbed the scale. "You've made some notable mistakes in judgment, India," she said, almost shrilly.

"Who hasn't?" India's voice was cold. "Except, perhaps, the people who never attempt anything for fear they'll make mistakes. Besides, Grace, there's a difference between being deceived and giving someone a second chance. I believe that people *can* be transformed by the power of God. It's perfectly true that I've tried to help some who have sinned grossly. That has nothing to do with my powers of perception. What business would I have being a missionary if I didn't? But Angela doesn't belong in this category."

"You don't know anything about her character or past actions." Grace's wide mouth set stubbornly.

"I know she has integrity. It doesn't take two weeks to find out that much about someone who lives in the house with you. And I know she's considerate and intelligent and industrious. I've seen her repel the advances of one importunate male. Let me put it like this, Grace: If I'd ever had a daughter, and if she'd been caught in a web of circumstances beyond her control, I'd hope and pray that someone would help her in spite of the fact that she happened to be beautiful. Can't you understand that?"

"I can understand that the circumstances were of her own making."

"Perhaps so," India conceded, "but most of our troubles are of our own making. That alters nothing."

Grace rose to go, pulling her dress down over her hips with an impatient twitch. "Well, my dear, all I can say is that there are none so blind as those who will not see."

India stood at the head of the stairs watching Grace descend, with a feeling of bafflement that escaped definition. Grace was kind and intelligent and helpful and hard-working. And certainly, in the conventional sense of the word, she was good. And yet there was something in her that had changed with success.

India remembered the words of a Catholic sister from the Philippines she had met once on shipboard. They had discovered that they had much in common—their schools, their wayward children, their spiritual problems. One day as they were discussing these, the sister, who had a lively sense of humor, remarked with a twinkle that she understood perfectly Christ's preference for publicans and sinners. In her experience, religious people were often thorny with spiritual pride.

CHAPTER 12

THE USUAL ROUND OF PROBLEMS TOOK THEIR USUAL TOLL OF India's attention. She saw Angela at meals and for a few minutes after breakfast, when she gave the girl her instructions for the day. The rest of the time, both of them, like everyone else at Jasmine Hall, were caught up in the routine of the institution.

India taught her classes, was available to parents who called, acted as judge in disciplinary cases that Darun could not settle alone, and wrestled with the problems which were her special concern. Of these, money to meet the relentless bills was both chronic and acute. The two hundred and fifty ticals Mr. Soderstorm paid for Mani every month hardly alleviated the pressure.

One of the teachers claimed that Darun had promised her a raise of five ticals a month, and hinted that she would leave if it was not forthcoming. A quarrel had broken out between two of the church elders over a business deal to which they were both party. Pastor Rasami and India were struggling to reconcile them before dissension split the congregation.

More disturbing than any of these things was an eruption of India's perennial difficulty with the mother of Sawang, a pupil in the Bible school.

A few days after Angela's arrival at Jasmine Hall, India returned from a long session of arguing with Elder Plon to find Darun waiting for her.

The teacher stepped quickly out of the school office at the sound of India's step and called, "Mem *kha?*"

It was eight o'clock and she was exhausted with the effort, and hungry besides. "Yes, Kru?" Her voice was reluctant.

"Will you come to the office a moment, please?"

Protest rose in India, but only weakly. Darun would not have asked for help on anything but a serious problem.

One of the students was sitting on the floor in the shadow, her legs folded politely under her. She slipped to her knees as India entered, and salaamed without raising her eyes.

"Sawang!" India thought with an access of discouragement. "Again!"

Sawang was one of her favorite pupils, in fact she was everybody's favorite. Her disposition was naturally happy, and of all the girls she alone seemed immune to the quarrels that periodically ravaged the school.

Most of the Bible school pupils had come to India from the provinces, but Sawang was a Bangkok girl whom Pastor Rasami had found. Her father had been a Chinese merchant, her mother was a Siamese. She was the youngest of five children. Her two brothers were in the Buddhist priesthood, her two sisters married to Chinese shopkeepers. The younger of these was a Christian and a member of Second Church. It was in the course of his pastoral calling that Pastor Rasami had found Sawang living with her sister, Boon Chui. He had been deeply concerned for the safety of the two girls, sleeping unprotected in a tiny apartment on the ground floor of an old building.

At his urging India had called, and the next week Pastor Rasami called again. He was a dignified man in the starched white tunic and blue panung of the upper classes. The Panama hat he wore, the black shoes and knee-length socks, the Malacca cane, all looked imposing to the simple market people among whom the girls lived. It needed nothing more to warn the neighborhood that they had a protector.

After Boon Chui's husband returned from China, Pastor Rasami had persuaded Mae Tam, who was a widow, that she could not properly care for Sawang. He argued that the girl would have a better chance in life if she was presented to the foreign mem to educate. That was six years before.

Sawang was bright and eager, with a gentleness that won everyone.

"God gave her a loving heart as well as a pretty face," Darun remarked approvingly to India, when Sawang had been with them a month. "Already she has taken charge of the little children as if they were her sisters and brothers."

She had not been a Christian when she came, but she had joined the others at church and prayer meeting. After a year she had asked to be taken into the church, explaining to Pastor Rasami: "I see now that it was well I lost my old home. God had prepared this new home for me so that I might learn about Him."

Her mother had not objected except on one count: "How will I find her a husband? We're poor already, and no one will marry a Christian."

Pastor Rasami had reassured her. "Don't worry, auntie. I'll promise to attend to it myself when Sawang is old enough."

With that she had been satisfied. Nevertheless, the problem continued to worry her, and now that Sawang was seventeen she fretted about it continually. Pastor Rasami had been hard pressed to keep her from taking Sawang out of school.

"You gave her to the mem," he argued. "You can't take her back unless you pay for the schooling she's had. I promise you, auntie, that I'll take care of it if you'll only leave her alone until she finishes school."

In April one of the country pastors, whose wife had recently died, came to Bangkok and called several times at Jasmine Hall. Before returning to his village he tendered a formal proposal of marriage to Sawang through Kru Darun. Sawang's mother gave her consent with delight. It was the girl herself who surprised them by refusing to consider the proposal. She was ordinarily obedient to the point of docility, and it had occurred to no one to consult her in advance of her mother. She had a great simplicity, however, that could be reached by pity but could not be flattered or deceived. She knew that the pastor had been less than kind to his first wife, and nothing would persuade her to marry him.

Her mother was bitterly disappointed. "If you won't marry this Christian, I'll have to look around myself," she told her. "You're seventeen, and nothing is settled."

Darun had been working at the flat-topped desk when she heard India's step on the veranda. She offered this seat of authority now, but India refused it for a chair near Sawang. The room was quiet. A single bulb under a green shade, hanging on a cord from the ceiling, illuminated it. Darun sat working over her papers. India waited for Sawang to speak, but without impatience. She had grown used to the slow and ceremonious way the Siamese approached problems of importance and found it peaceful. She glanced at Sawang, but the girl's eyes were on the mat. She had sunk back to the position in which India had first seen her, feet folded on her right side and covered with her pasin. Her soft round face was framed in black hair. Thick lashes lay against her cheeks.

After the clock had ticked out several slow minutes, Darun spoke. "Sawang's mother has found a husband for her and wants to take her out of school." India looked questioning, and Darun went on. "She was here this afternoon and would have taken Sawang away with her, if I hadn't prevented it."

India looked at Sawang and found the girl watching her out of the corners of her eyes. "Well, Sawang?"

The girl cast her eyes down again in the gesture of modesty that Siamese etiquette found polite. She waited several moments, as if too shy to speak, then said in a small voice, "This time it's all right, mem *kha*, Mother and I agree."

"Who is the man, child?"

Sawang looked up for a fraction of a second. India could not identify the emotion that made her eyes shine. "Not a stranger as I feared, mem *kha*, but my older sister's husband."

India's heart dropped. She knew now why Darun had wanted help. "Is this your mother's idea or your brother-in-law's?" she asked, careful to keep what she felt out of her voice, for fear of arousing the stubbornness that lay under the silken docility of any Siamese girl.

"Mother's really, but Brother is pleased too. You see, he has a store in China where his Chinese wife was in charge, and a branch here with Boon Sri in charge. Now his Chinese wife is dead, and he is going to promote Boon Sri to the China store. She'll take charge of his Chinese family, and I'll take charge of her children and the Bangkok store. Then Mother can stay with me."

India considered this carefully. "You mean that if he took a wife from outside the family your mother would have to go?"

"The new wife might not let her stay, and then, too, she might be unkind to Boon Sri's children."

"Why can't your mother live with Boon Chui?"

"Boon Chui and her husband are Christians."

India looked at Sawang in surprise. "But so are you."

"Boon Chui's husband says it isn't fitting for Mother to make offerings of food to the priests from a Christian shop, so she won't live with him. She says he's stingy."

"And Boon Sri's husband doesn't mind?"

"No, Pi Lum is very generous."

India looked at the girl in wonder. She had not said that she loved her brother-in-law. That factor had not entered into anyone's considerations. What quirk of filial feeling made her willing to do this without regard for her own future? India had often pondered the strains and stresses, the compulsions and pressures that formed the actions of her Siamese friends, but after twenty-five years she was still taken by surprise on occasion, as now.

"And do you think you'd be happy?" she asked.

"Yes, of course. I love the children and they love me, and I'm good at business."

India sighed. "I suppose you are, child, but I can't let you sacrifice yourself like this. You couldn't do it and go on being a Christian."

"Oh yes, I can." The girl's voice was eager. "Pi Lum follows the path of no religion himself, but he lets Mother make offerings to the priests out of his kitchen, and sometimes even gives her boxes of cigars for them. He has agreed that if I marry him he'll pay for Mother's cremation, and I'm to be allowed to come to church every Sunday."

Sawang looked down again at the floor, waiting for India's approval. India did not speak immediately. She knew that Sawang had a passion for service and that she would sacrifice herself for her mother without any thought of self-pity. It would not be possible to appeal to her on the basis of her own interests. India could have appealed to Sawang's sense of obligation to herself, as teacher and benefactor, but she was afraid to risk it. The bond might snap under the pull of her mother's demands. Yet she must somehow hold Sawang for a wider service, and there was only one other appeal possible.

"Didn't you mean your pledges to the church, Sawang?" she asked.

"But of course, mem *kha*."

"The church forbids plural marriage," India went on. "Surely if you meant your promise to abide by the laws of the church, you wouldn't be planning to go against them. Your mother entrusted you to me to educate, and I can't believe that it's right for you to leave Jasmine Hall when you'll graduate in less than two years. But even if I did agree to release your mother from her promise, I couldn't give my consent to a marriage that is contrary to everything the church teaches."

Sawang did not look up, but her whole figure drooped. She was always distressed by the smallest quarrel among the girls in the school, and to find her mother and her teacher on opposite sides in so important a question as her marriage was catastrophic.

When Sawang said nothing India went on. "I bitterly regret that you are forced to choose between your mother and your church, but you must remember that it's your mother who has forced the issue. She had agreed to let you finish school, and she had also agreed to let Pastor Rasami find a Christian husband for you. In a few years you'll be able to make her comfortable in a home of your own if you wait, but the decision will have to be yours."

The girl sat quietly, and the clock ticked its somnolent, slow, hypnotic tick. Darun had stopped working, and her hands were lying in her lap. Through the door drifted the sweetness of angsana flowers. Outside on Bamrung Muang Road a tram passed with a steady clanging of the bell, as the motorman kept his foot working to clear the tracks of pedestrians and rickshas. Nothing in the limp figure of the girl gave any hint of the conflict within her.

India prayed in a kind of quiet desperation: "O God, don't let the generosity of her nature betray her. Please hold her for the happiness she ought to have and for the wider service of which she is capable——"

Tears began to slide down Sawang's cheeks, one, then another, then faster and faster. Her breast moved up and down. She turned around suddenly and, getting to her knees, laid her head in India's lap.

"Oh, mem *kha*, mem *kha*. I am a Christian. I will always be a Christian. Only, only——"

India did not touch her head, for the head is sacred to the Siamese, but she laid her hand lightly on the girl's shoulder. When the sobbing ended she slipped her handkerchief into Sawang's hand.

After Sawang had gone back to the dormitory India spoke to Darun. "Tomorrow you'd better talk to Mae Tam yourself."

"I'd thought of that. She'll be very angry."

"Why doesn't she leave Sawang alone until she finishes school?"

"She believes it's her duty to find a husband for her daughter."

"Yes, of course," India said, and stopped.

Among the Siamese the selection of a suitable husband for a daughter was a mother's primary obligation. The old woman's distrust of Jasmine Hall in this regard was not unjustified. Neither India nor Darun was married. Why should Mae Tam believe that they could do for her child what they had not been able to do for themselves?

Before the week was out Darun told India that Sawang was asking to visit her mother.

"Oh no, not so soon," India protested, but that night Sawang was kneeling at her door when she came upstairs to bed. The girl had been crying, and when she spoke her voice hardly rose above a whisper.

In the few days since her mother's visit she seemed to have wilted. She had overheard what was said between Kru Darun and her mother from the classroom next door, where she had been leaning against the wall, listening. Her mother's unwillingness to understand had hurt her deeply. She was sure that if she could see her mother and talk with her they could be reconciled.

"It would be better to wait a month at least," India told her.

"Please, mem *kha,* please, please, please take me," she wept, and before India knew what she was doing had slid to the floor and laid her forehead on India's shoes.

India knelt quickly beside the prostrate girl. Across the darkened church in the dormitory there was silence, a rare silence, as the other girls listened.

"I'll take you tomorrow afternoon if you insist," she promised, "but I must tell you that you're making a mistake. You ought to wait until you've had some sign from your mother."

The next afternoon Sawang was ready when school was over. She was dressed in the school uniform of long blue pasin and white blouse, and she looked very young and woebegone. India was touched by the sadness in the round face, the more because it was usually full of laughter.

"Where do you want me to take you?" India asked.

"To Boon Chui's shop first," Sawang said.

Boon Chui and her husband lived over his family's store in Sampeng Lane, only a five-minute walk from the shop of the older sister, Boon Sri, where Mae Tam stayed. Both shops were in the congested Chinese quarter of the city. India and Sawang left their ricksha in Worachak Road, which was broad, tree-lined, shady.

There were some Chinese shops on it, but the street was Siamese in mood, leisurely in pace, with many Siamese moving along it at their unruffled gait, and with the pungent odors of Siamese cooking in the air.

Sampeng was China. It was narrow and cobbled and full of the quick and ceaseless clatter of wooden clogs. Overhead pieces of matting and cloth shut out the sun so that the lane was in perpetual twilight. The shops were side by side in an unbroken row with their fronts open to the lane. Ancient and lecherous-looking dogs prowled the gutters. On chairs in front of the stores old men nodded, some thin and yellow with sparse beards, others round and fat with faces as blank as the full moon. Long pipes with tiny bowls were in their mouths.

The lane had many secrets. They hung in the air like the musky odor of spices and dried fruit and the sickly sweetness of opium. Here at the Christmas season India came to buy grapes from Italy, and apples from Washington State wrapped individually in tissue paper, and even lemons from California. There were shops that sold birds'-nests and sharks' fins for special feasts, rare teas that cost forty and fifty American dollars a pound, watermelon seeds toasted, bean sprouts and water chestnuts, and dried lichee nuts. There were also tubs of pickled cabbage, piles of bean-curd cakes, Chinese molasses, and the liquid salt that Siamese call "fish oil."

Boon Chui's shop was a cheerful place, full of things from all over the world. There were great piles of snowy enamelware from Sweden, and a cupboard of cheap earthenware from England. In one glass case were dozens of flashlights from America, toothbrushes, tooth paste, and baby powder. In another there were tennis shoes from Japan, lacquered boxes and trays from China, and hundreds of other small articles. Hanging from the ceiling was a collection of assorted objects for sale.

Boon Chui herself, a plump and older edition of Sawang, was waiting on a customer at the front of the shop. She smiled as they entered, and after the transaction was finished came over to them. When she had greeted India, invited them to sit down, and offered them soda water, she turned to Sawang.

"What brings you today, little sister?"

"Haven't you heard?"

"Yes, Boon Sri was here yesterday."

Tears came to Sawang's eyes. Boon Chui with quick sympathy motioned India to follow and, taking Sawang by the hand, drew her to the back of the shop, where there was a table and four wire-backed chairs, away from the curious glances of customers. "Tell me about it, little sister."

"There's nothing to tell if Boon Sri's been here. I want to see the honorable mother and talk to her myself. I want to tell her that in another year I'll be working and will give her money, and as soon as I'm married she can live with me and I'll take care of her the rest of my life."

Boon Chui's face was sober. "You were right to refuse Pi Lum, little sister. It is important for you to finish school. Our honorable mother is not really in need. Both Boon Sri and I are looking after her, and you know that she can come here to live if Boon Sri goes to China. But you mustn't try to see her yet. She has told the neighbors that you have deserted her in her old age. Ever since she came back she has done nothing but go from shop to shop and tell them that you are cruel and disobedient and willful. If you went to Boon Sri's house, the neighbors would stone you."

Sawang began to cry. Boon Chui patted her shoulder and smiled a little at India across the bowed head. "It will be all right in time," she urged, but Sawang refused to be comforted.

"Please, Boon Chui," she sobbed, "at least send Bo to the honorable mother and see if she will not receive me."

Her sister was reluctant. "I'm afraid it won't do any good." In the end she yielded to the misery in Sawang's eyes and called, "Bo, Bo *cha*."

A small boy in black shorts detached himself from a group of his playmates at the front of the store and came to her. He bobbed his head stiffly at India and waited while his mother told him in detail what he was to say.

In twenty minutes he was back with Mae Tam on his heels. He gave his mother a frightened glance and bolted for the interior of the shop.

Mae Tam was a small, thin Siamese in a white sacque and faded black panung. Her legs were bare, her feet in flat heelless babouches.

She was moving rapidly and her face was livid. Boon Chui touched Sawang on the shoulder, and the girl, turning, saw her mother. In an instant she had crossed the shop and knelt at Mae Tam's feet.

The old woman raised her hand to strike, then let it drop. "So you order your honorable mother to come to you, do you, child of the cold heart? You have not even so much courtesy as it takes to come to me. That's what the farang religion has done to you, made you despise your mother's gray head. Now in my old age I must humble myself and come to you like a dog."

She stormed across the front of the store and back, and Sawang cowered on the floor. All business stopped in the shop, as clerks and customers turned to watch. The shrilling voice had penetrated neighboring shops also, and people from them began to collect around the open front of Boon Chui's store.

The older daughter hurried to her mother and put her hand on Mae Tam's arm, but she shook it off impatiently. "If I had known that you were coming, O honorable daughter, I should have spent the day making cakes with which to receive you, delicate little cakes of rice flour and coconut milk that melt on the tongue and have the sweetness of honey. If you had only informed me in advance of the hour at which I was to be honored, I should have been waiting at the head of the lane to receive you. It would have been my greatest pleasure to conduct one of your high station and attainments to my humble dwelling. I can only apologize for the long wait you have had by saying that I had no idea my unworthy self was to be so overwhelmed with the generosity of your sublime nature. *Wah!*"

The crowd sniggered. Sawang covered her face with her hands. India stood up to intervene, but Boon Chui motioned her to sit down. It was just possible that when the old woman had vented the whole vial of her wrath she would be satisfied.

For fifteen minutes, twenty minutes, half an hour, she ranted, walking up and down across the front of the shop. The crowd listened respectfully. The art of vituperation was a woman's field, and this was a consummate performance. At the end she turned to her audience, making them witness to her words and to all that had gone before.

"This my daughter with the face of a doe has in reality a heart like a tiger's. She has forgotten the maxims of our people: *Honor thy elders; bend low before the will of thy family.* Her backbone no longer bends at all. It is made of clay, baked hard in a furnace, that can break but cannot bend. Her heart is a stone seven times harder than a diamond. Her mouth is a sword, and her words are knives that cut and wound and slash. Her ears are stumps of wood that will not hear her mother's teaching. Her feet are the feet of a pig that carry it grubbing, grubbing, grubbing, only where there is rich food to be got. Her hands are kittens that play and play and will not work even to care for the mother that bore her. I, who nursed her at my breasts and rocked her in the cradle and stuffed her small belly with good things, now that I am old, she has left me for a rich farang who will make a lady of her, so she thinks. What is it to her whether I have a place to lay my head? Or food for my mouth? Or clothes to cover my nakedness? I am old, and if I die, I die. My body is only a carrion to her. She will not give it a proper cremation. 'Throw it to the dogs,' she will say, 'let the vultures eat it.'

"My other daughters are married and have children of their own. They must work for their husbands and their children, and that is right. My two sons are priests. Only this one is left to me, but will she help me? No. *She* is a Christian. She has left me for the Christian school," and seeming to catch sight of India for the first time, added, "and for that farang over there in the corner at that table." She paused, as if the force of her anger had emptied itself.

She stood glaring at India, her thin chest heaving. The crowd shuffled and stared at the foreigner. Sawang still knelt with her head in her hands. Suddenly the tide of Mae Tam's anger rose again.

"Do you think you can steal my child from me?" she screamed at India. "She is mine, not yours! You cannot keep her from me if I wish to take her back."

Again she paced the floor, backward and forward, shouting at India. The crowd listened intently. Her anger had not abated, but her language was more restrained.

India sat quietly. There was nothing else to do. She detached her mind from the stream of foul words Mae Tam hurled in her direction and looked around. The street had begun to darken. A ray of light from the setting sun came through a slit in the matting that was stretched from shop to shop across the street. It danced along one of the showcases. Suddenly the woman stopped.

"I'll get her away from you now! Tonight!" She said in almost a normal tone of voice, "I'll go home and get three hundred ticals and pay you back for her schooling. Then you must let me have her, you farang bitch. And if you don't I'll go to the police, and then we'll see who owns her, you or me."

She whirled and left the shop, running jerkily on her thin legs. Boon Chui came quickly across to India.

"Mem *kha*," she whispered, leaning close, "take Sawang away at once. I shall go into the back of the shop so that I cannot see you leave. Hide her somewhere for several nights, not at Jasmine Hall, until I tell you it is safe. I shall explain to the honorable mother that the police will be of no use to her because you are a farang, but she may not believe me." She turned and walked toward the door that led to the living quarters. "Bo," she called, "Bo, where are you hiding?"

India stood up and glanced at the door through which she had gone, as if speculating on Boon Chui's return. Then she hurried to Sawang and, leaning down, took one of her hands.

"Get up, Sawang, quick!"

The girl was dazed and slow. When she stood up she seemed to totter. India tensed herself against the possibility of restraining hands as she dragged Sawang through the gawking crowd, but no one stopped them.

"They wouldn't though," she said to herself, calming her overwrought nerves, "it's just a show to them."

She pulled Sawang after her down the lane and almost boosted her into a ricksha.

"To the Black Bridge on Bamrung Muang Road," she ordered the puller. "There'll be something extra for you if you run."

He set out with a burst of speed. India looked back through the tattered hood, but no one took up the chase. In a few seconds the head of the lane was out of sight.

Halfway home she changed her mind, paid off the ricksha, and found a taxi. "Sathorn Road," she said, "I'll tell you where to stop."

She and Sawang got out at the corner of Bangrak. It was dark now, and she did not think that Mae Tam was astute enough to trace them, but she was taking no chances.

"We'll walk from here," she told Sawang, and the girl followed dully.

Anne was home! For that India was profoundly glad. She saw a light burning on the veranda and Anne's red head bent over a book.

The watchman saluted smartly as they came across the bridge. "Good evening," he said to India in English, and she replied, "Good evening."

Anne heard the exchange and jumped to her feet. "Who is it?" she called.

"It's India. May I come up? Don't come down."

Anne had climbed out of her mosquito bag when they reached the top of the stairs.

"India!" she said. "What's the matter? What's happened?"

India told Anne quickly while Sawang knelt on the floor.

"And you want to leave her with me, is that it? But will she stay?"

"I don't know. I think so, but if she doesn't, you're not to worry. I'll talk to Pastor Rasami about her and try to make some plan. I don't know the law, but he will."

She turned to go.

"Stay for dinner," Anne urged. "Jim's late, but he'll be here any minute, and afterward he can drive you home."

India refused. "If Mae Tam comes tonight I want to be there," she said.

CHAPTER 13

THE MAELSTROM OF EXCITEMENT THAT HAD DISRUPTED JASMINE Hall with Angela's arrival subsided quickly into routine. Angela seemed to welcome this comparative oblivion gratefully. She completed the reorganization of India's files and began to sort and answer current correspondence from notes she took in longhand. The music lessons were going well. The girls vied among themselves to see who could please her with the most rapid progress. By the time the influx of visitors receded, Angela was part of Jasmine Hall.

Few of her friends came to see her a second time. The death of her husband, and the events before and after it, had worked a change that disengaged her from them. There was a withdrawal in her almost monastic.

This preternatural aloofness did not surprise India. Illness of the spirit was hardly new to her. She had improvised remedies before, and did so again. Pain, bewilderment, grief—for these time alone was adequate, but there were palliatives that had value during the interim. Work was one of these.

The whiteness of Angela's skin was so crystalline, India was troubled by a persistent illusion that the bones of the girl's skull would soon become visible. Still she let Angela go on with her work. Once or twice India suggested tentatively that the girl take the day off and rest, but Angela clung to her schedule as if it alone, of all she thought and did, had significance.

India was careful in her daily contacts with Angela to avoid personal questions or other approaches to intimacy. Such things were abrasives. She wanted to give Angela the assurance that there would be no prying into the past. Her emphasis was on the details of the immediate present. She was careful also not to offer much of her own companionship, fearing that the very offer would engender in Angela an instinctive necessity to reject it. And since Angela felt herself indebted to India, this in turn would be accompanied by a feeling of guilt.

In the meantime, Jasmime Hall was able to supply such casual human contacts as Angela could assimilate. The fullness of the days was in itself therapeutic. The current of interrelated lives neither ignored her nor avoided her, but caught her up and swept her along, and this was good for her.

If the Bible school girls in their cooking class made sponge cake, they shyly presented her with some, carefully arranged in slices on a small tray. Or, just at dusk, several of the small boarders would bring her a saucer of jasmine buds floating in water to perfume her room during the night, or they would lay a small wreath of jasmine on her pillow.

The Bible school girls tried in their stilted, uncertain English to persuade her to eat curry and rice with them. "Is goot, mem *kha,* what you say 'speschal.' Many spice, not many chili. Please, mem *kha.* You try." If she took a few spoonfuls and praised the curry, they were delighted. Some of the bolder ones began to teach her the Siamese names of things.

Angela had seen one side of the Siamese at the palace. Now she was seeing the other face of the coin, their gaiety, their kindness, their grace and charm, and all the delicate little courtesies with which they made life sweet.

India had known many Siamese women who steeped flowers in a silver bowl at night so that their husbands might have scented water with which to wash in the morning. She had seen the girls carry food to Dulcie when Dulcie came in late, and then, seating themselves on the floor around her, listen with flattering attention while she told them where she had been and what she had learned.

They did not really like Dulcie with her mincing ways and her scolding manner. It was simply their natural impulse to enrich the lives of their elders with such small amenities. Even the starched contentiousness of Dulcie could not hold out against them. Sometimes she would slip to the floor and sit relaxed, with the little dishes of food around her, talking cheerfully. For that short while she was her better self.

It was too soon for any of this to have a noticeable effect on Angela, but at least the school had induced the first natural laugh India heard from her. This occurred on the afternoon when she caught sight of a child in the garden below running around on all fours.

"What's the matter with that little girl?" she asked India. "She seems too big to play at being an animal."

India set her teacup down to come over and look.

"Oh, that's Chawee," she said. "Didn't you hear Dulcie and me talking about her last night? She's one of our third graders, and on Monday she took some other child's artgum eraser and refused to give it back. Kru Sawai told her to stand in the corner, but Chawee turned and called the teacher a dog instead. I don't know whether you realize the seriousness of that or not. If you've seen the pariahs scavenging in the streets, you probably do. It's a deadly insult. Kru Sawai didn't even try to do anything about it, she was so upset. She brought Chawee to Kru Darun."

India chuckled. "Have you heard us speak of Miss Edna Cole yet?"

"I don't think so."

"She took Wang Lang when it was a feeble little school and built it into what it is now—that is, what Wattana is. She was really the founder of women's education in Siam, and she was as famous for her wisdom as Solomon. Once years ago something like this happened at Wang Lang, and Darun remembered what Miss Cole did then. So she told Chawee that only dogs would go to school to a dog, and that as a pupil of a dog she must herself be a dog, and could act accordingly. Chawee was condemned to walk on all fours for a week. Of course the children thought the punishment fitted the crime to perfection, so if Chawee forgets they all shout at her, 'Down, doggy, down,' and back down she goes."

Benny was the only one of Angela's former friends who continued to ignore her desire to be left alone. She would go nowhere with him, but still he came to Jasmine Hall at least every other day. Sometimes, when Angela excused herself to give a music lesson, he followed her into the church and sat beside her while she gave the lesson. If he felt the force of her dislike he disregarded it and covered her silence with chatter.

"I say, Angel, do you remember old Dobbs out on Wireless Road? Well, the other day——" And he was off on a long, involved, and often amusing story.

Several times, watching Angela's still face, India was tempted to ask whether she wanted the servants instructed to turn him away. This was difficult at Jasmine Hall. The open doors, the outside staircases, the wide verandas meant that any determined person could go where he pleased. Then, too, she hesitated to interfere unless Angela asked her to do so. In the end the only protection she gave was the tacit one of her presence. For the time being she discontinued her practice of late afternoon calling.

Whenever Benny appeared, India went back to work after tea instead of going out. She would leave Benny and Angela on the mook, Benny in animated conversation. Mani, who had been like a phantom in the house until now, was much in evidence on these days also. Several times India saw her leave the house with Benny.

The lattice wall between the mook and India's section of veranda was no barrier to sound. Sometimes Benny's words would carry to India working in her room, sometimes only his laugh. Eventually his voice would cease, there would be the sound of a motor starting below the porte-cochere, and India would know that Angela had extricated herself.

One afternoon as India sat writing letters, she had heard neither Benny's laugh nor his voice for ten minutes. Subconsciously she was waiting to hear the motor of his car start, when she heard instead the crash of a chair on the mook. She was up and across her room before she had time to analyze the sound.

It was Angela's chair that had gone over. Benny's back was to India, but he seemed to have his arms around Angela, who was fighting furiously. India saw her raised fist strike, and then Benny pinioned her arms and picked her up, throwing her across his shoulder like a sack of rice. Neither had said a word. Only now Benny was laughing.

He started quickly for the staircase, but India was there before him.

"What are you doing?" she demanded, stretching her arms from wall to railing.

"Look," he said, turning the full power of his charm on India, as if it could not fail him with a woman, "she hasn't been out of this goddamned hole in almost three weeks. She needs a change, and she's too stubborn to admit it. I'm not going to hurt her, honestly. I just want to give her a little ride in my car. I'll bring her right back."

He advanced a step toward the stairs and smiled winningly, keeping his eyes on India, but India did not respond.

"Put her down at once and leave the house!" she ordered coldly.

The smile left his face, and the brutal squareness of his jaw came forward. The sparks in his eyes were red with anger.

Deftly he took the arm holding Angela's legs and struck India's hand from the wall with a swift hard blow, then shouldered past her on the stairs. India whirled, but her arm hung numb and useless.

At the foot of the long flight of stairs Mae Doe was just starting up with two small children, one on either hand.

"Doe!" India called as Benny reached the landing. "Stop him! Doe!"

The big servant girl had only a second, but she was proud of her agility. "I'm as strong as any man alive," she had often boasted, "and there isn't a child in school can run as fast as me."

Now she dropped the hands of her charges and jumped backward down the two steps she had mounted, crouching a little like a cat. Benny's hands were engaged with Angela, and if he anticipated trouble he thought himself adequate to handle it.

As he reached the bottom step Doe leaped at him. Her fist caught him on the chin and jarred his head back. Then her bare foot and knee came up in the terrible kick to the groin of the Siamese boxer. Before he could move she had struck him again on the nose. Blood spurted, and he doubled forward in pain.

Angela was catapulted to the floor. Like a fiend, Doe was back at him, kicking and flailing. Unable to stand, the best he could do was ward off her blows with a hand. As soon as he could he ran limping toward the steps that went from the veranda to the porte-cochere where his car was parked. Doe was beside him, behind him, around him, her feet moving with precision and force—kick, bounce back, kick, jump, kick. With one final swing of her leg she sent him stumbling down the steps, shouting after him in waterfront Siamese:

"And don't you dare come back here, you bastard son of a bastard, unless you want more of the same! I'll kick the hell out of you, you dropping of a black dog, you excrement of a pig, you seven-day spawn of a turtle! Your presence fouls the air! May your entrails turn to worms——"

He leaned against his car for a moment, then crawled into it. India began to come down the stairs, shaken and in pain, holding the railing with her good arm. As she leaned over Angela she heard the car start. The girl was lying in a limp heap where she had fallen, moaning to herself, a little whimpering sound.

"Doe!" India called. "Stop that cursing and get Chu."

Doe paused. Several Bible school girls had appeared on the veranda and were watching at a discreet distance. The smaller children who had been playing in the garden were collected round-eyed at the edge of the porte-cochere. Det appeared running, followed by Plo, India's personal cook.

"What's going on? What's going on?" Det was shouting.

Doe stood a conscious moment in triumph before her whispering audience, then turned and swaggered toward the kitchen to fetch Mae Chu. She ignored Det, who hurried to India.

"Shall I pick her up, mem *krop?*" he asked in a worried voice.

"No, Det, don't touch her. Let her lie where she is until Chu examines her."

Then she saw the collected children. "Go back to your play, children," she ordered.

Reluctantly they withdrew a few feet and stood whispering together, with their backs to the veranda. The Bible school girls disappeared into the office, from where India could hear their low, excited voices. The two little children Doe had abandoned on the stairs stood where she had left them. No one had told them to go away, and they watched in stupefaction the drama below.

Very shortly Chu came walking onto the veranda with her usual measured dignity. In addition to being the school cook she was an accomplished masseuse. She was a settled woman of middle age, a woman of property but too thrifty not to work. Her clipped hair was parted in the middle. Small old-fashioned glasses with silver rims were perched halfway down her nose. Her white blouse was starched, her panung black and a little shabby, as befitted a woman who no longer desired to attract men.

She knelt and went expertly over Angela's body. The girl had not opened her eyes. She still lay crumpled as she had fallen, her body moving slowly with low sobs.

"There's nothing broken," Chu announced. "We'll carry her upstairs, and I'll massage her."

"Det, we'll take care of this, thank you," India said, dismissing him.

Her hand still tingled, and there was a puffy place on her arm that would be black and blue before night, but she could use her arm and her hand, so there was nothing broken.

Doe and Chu leaned over to pick the girl up, but when she felt their hands on her she pushed them away and climbed shakily to her feet. As she started to mount the stairs, the two little girls squatted on the second step and brought their hands together in salaam. They were looking at her with round, wondering eyes, but she did not seem to know that they were there.

Blindly she avoided them and climbed slowly on. The three women mounted behind her, India, Chu, and Doe, who was still strutting a little.

When Angela reached her bed she threw herself across it. Chu took an arm and began to massage it. The girl tried to pull away.

"No, no, no," she whimpered.

India was firm. "That was a bad fall, Angela. I want you to let Mae Chu massage you. Sit up first, and we'll take your dress off. Point to the places that hurt, and Mae Chu will take the soreness out for you. Or tell me, and I'll tell her. There now, just lie down and relax."

Angela lay with her eyes closed, barricading herself against them. Mae Chu worked methodically over her body with an impersonal and kindly efficiency. Gradually under the skilled fingers Angela's body lost its tension. Several big bruises were blackening on her arms and legs. Otherwise she seemed unhurt.

India sent Doe for a cup of hot cocoa. When the massage was finished, she insisted that Angela drink it. Nothing was said by anyone about what had occurred. Angela sat looking down, holding the cup in both hands. India and Chu watched her from the side of the bed. Behind them Doe stirred restlessly, eager to get away and talk about her share in what had happened.

When the cocoa had disappeared India said, "Now lie down and rest. Ploy will bring your dinner on a tray."

The girl obeyed. She looked very slight and young with her eyes closed. India pulled the sheet up to her chin, and the three women went out.

The next day Angela spent in bed. India had her breakfast sent in, and went herself when chapel was over. The girl was lying with her head pillowed on her arms, looking into space. When she brought her eyes around to India they seemed dull, as if some last spark had burned out.

"Miss Severn, I'll have to go."

"Because of what happened yesterday?" India asked. "No one blames you for that."

Tears welled up in Angela's eyes. "I'm like Jonah. Wherever I go something terrible happens."

"This wasn't very terrible, really," India said, discounting the incident. "Someday we'll all think it was funny. Besides, by that reasoning we're all Jonahs, my dear."

"But suppose he came again."

"I don't think he will. Last evening I went to see one of Jasmine Hall's good friends. Perhaps you know Dr. Crane?"

Angela nodded, and India went on: "He's not in our Mission, but he's often helped me. I told him what had happened and asked his advice. I didn't know whether Mr. O'Hanlon had been injured or not, but I felt it was my responsibility to find out. Dr. Crane knows him well, and he went to see him. Everything's all right. There's nothing to worry about. The doctor talked to him while he was there. I don't think he'll ever bother you again."

For several days after that India noticed with amusement that Doe had assumed the defense of Jasmine Hall as her own. Every afternoon at teatime she could be seen patrolling the front lawn, sitting with the smaller children at their games, or squatting near the steps.

Benny never rewarded her with so much as another glimpse of himself.

CHAPTER 14

THE MORNING OF JULY 16 WAS HOT AND STILL. RAIN WAS TANTA-lizingly close but did not fall. Angela came to the breakfast table listless and white-faced, as if she had not slept. She drank a cup of coffee and asked to be excused. Dulcie sent out word that her stomach was upset. Would Ploy please bring her tea and toast?

India was sitting alone when Pastor Rasami arrived to tell her that Pa Tim had died during the night at Central Hospital. Her death was not unexpected, since she was eighty-five and had been ill for months. She was Jasmine Hall's oldest retainer.

"Sit down, Kru," India urged, "and let Ploy bring you some coffee."

He bowed from the waist and sat down to give her the details of Pa Tim's passing and make plans for the funeral, which would be that day. He was a man of medium height, with a slanting forehead from which the hair was receding, and the beardless face of the Siamese. His body sloped toward the middle under the white duck tunic he wore, reminding India unkindly of a seal. She was very fond of him, actually. He had been pastor of Second Church for seven years, ever since the members had grown weary of hearing missionaries garble their language and had persuaded him to give up his position at Bangkok Christian College for the more precarious life of the ministry.

Ploy brought coffee, toast, and marmalade, and he began to tell India that Pa Tim had asked the hospital to call him the previous evening, but that he had delayed sending for India and Darun because the doctors were not convinced the end was near. As he knelt beside Pa Tim's hospital cot to pray, the old woman had laid her frail hand on his shoulder and smiled. Later she rallied and fell asleep. He had gone home about two o'clock. Then an hour later Pa Tim had died alone, the nurse said, without waking.

Eight years before, when the primary school was newly opened, she had attached herself to it more by sufferance than consent. In her thinking, formed on the old feudal pattern, it had seemed natural to assimilate her life to that of the school without asking whether she might or not. She had been a cake seller at the time. Every morning just before recess she would come hustling through the gate with a basket of Siamese confections to sell to the school children. There were half a dozen cake women, and Pa Tim was the oldest of them. There was nothing else to distinguish her. She was neat and spare, barefoot and bareheaded, as they all were. The teachers checked them daily, to be sure the food they sold was clean. That was all.

One morning she knelt before India and asked if she might rent the unused loft over the kitchen in which to live. India asked about her family, but she was vague. She was a native of Surat, she said. She had left there in the Year of the Monkey, four cycles ago, when her husband came with his *nai* to Bangkok. Her children and her husband had all died the year of the big cholera epidemic—she must have been a great sinner in a former life. The nai had moved away with his family, and she no longer knew where they were. Did she have any relatives living in Surat? She thought they were all dead. She couldn't read or write, and her husband had never kept in touch with them.

India let her have the loft, a hot little space under the roof over the kitchen. She paid her rent for a year, and after that it was never mentioned between them. For five years she continued to support herself, going out each morning to buy cakes from a store on Worachak Road, and coming back to sell them to the school children at recess. Then for days at a time she was not well enough to work.

Darun assumed charge of her in the same unobtrusive way she had picked up the load of other responsibilities she carried. Days when the old woman was not in her place at recess, Darun would climb to the loft to see if she was ill and would have her carried to the main building where she could nurse her. As soon as Pa Tim could totter about, she would return to the loft.

"I think she imagines her husband and children are there," Darun told India. "Sometimes I hear her talking to them. She says she lights a candle for them every night so they won't stumble on the stairs."

"Don't let her do that, Darun," India urged. "It's too dangerous."

The previous year the schoolgirls had arranged a celebration for her. It had been the Year of the Little Serpent, and she had completed seven cycles of twelve animal years since the day she was born. This had seemed an extraordinary thing to everyone, including Pa Tim.

On the afternoon of the celebration Det carried her down from the loft and set her in a wicker chair twined with flowers. The youngest child in school knelt before her to present a garland of jasmine with a tassel of rose petals at the end of it. Pa Tim put the garland around her neck, pleased and excited by the attention. She watched out of rheumy old eyes, for she was almost blind, as each grade in the school performed some little play or dance in her honor.

She nodded and smiled, her head with the thin fringe of white hair on it bobbed back and forth, her toothless gums widened. One of the girls squatted beside her, pounding betel to powder, in a kind of tubular mortar, for her to chew. She dozed off to sleep before the performance was over, but wakened to eat some cakes and sip a little hot Chinese tea before the coolie carried her back upstairs.

She had grown very childish, and the care of her was a heavy burden, too heavy a burden for Darun, in addition to her school duties, India thought. Darun argued that she did not find it so, that someone else had cared for her own mother during her last illness, and that she would perform this final service for Auntie Tim instead.

There was no electricity in the loft, and every night Pa Tim continued to light her candle, in spite of India's remonstrances. "You mustn't use candles up here, Auntie," she warned. "It's dangerous. I'll have Det bring you a kerosene lantern, if you like."

The old woman was stubborn, or forgetful. One night toward the end of April they heard her scream. The watchman Klee was up the loft stairs before Darun and India reached them. Pa Tim's clothing was on fire. He beat it out quickly, but she was badly burned. The doctors at Central Hospital told them she could not live. Still she had clung to life for three months.

Twice they had been called in the middle of the night by news that the old woman was dying. Each time at Pa Tim's request Pastor Rasami had administered the communion.

Pa Tim had joined the church the year after she began to live in the loft. Pastor Rasami had been doubtful of the wisdom of allowing this, since it seemed unlikely that she understood what she was doing. She could not join the communicants' class because she could not read. Nor, for that matter, could she keep her attention fixed for more than a few minutes on what was said to her.

Pa Tim had been persistent. Every Sunday she came to church

and sat in the front row. Every Sunday she went to sleep, even before the sermon, and the children tittered as her head nodded. But next Sunday she was back again. Finally Pastor Rasami gave in. "Who am I to keep her out if she wants to join?" he had asked. "I don't know whether she's doing it out of gratitude or faith. I'll leave the decision to God."

Both times as he administered the sacrament he had knelt by her bed to pray, and the old woman had laid her bandaged hand on his shoulder and smiled. The sunken eyes and wrinkled mask of a face had taken on a look of peace. Then, in the end, she had died in her sleep alone.

It was decided that only Darun, India, and Pastor Rasami should attend the funeral. The school children made wreaths of gold and silver leaves from the garden and tuberoses Plo bought in the market.

It was noon and very hot when they reached the cemetery. The sky was still lowering, but no rain had fallen. The coolies from the hospital were late, and India began to be anxious for fear the storm would break before the funeral was completed. One o'clock came and one-thirty. Then at last they arrived with the rough wooden box and lowered it into the grave.

As Pastor Rasami opened his *Order of Service* and began to read, the coolies squatted down, smoking straw cigarettes, to watch the novelty of a Christian burial. There was no impertinence in their curiosity. This was something they had not seen before, and rather than return to their duties at the hospital they chose to sit on their heels and watch.

India was disturbed by the unfeeling stares they turned on the little group beside the grave, but neither Darun nor Pastor Rasami seemed to mind. She wanted the last rites for the old woman to be dignified. She felt a pathetic loneliness in the thought that Pa Tim went to her final resting place unmourned by any of her own family. This was the more poignant for the fact that Siamese held such rites to be of the highest importance. There was nothing so sumptuous in the average life as the cremation accorded the body when it was over.

Pastor Rasami began to read the simple and beautiful words of the service. He had removed his hat, and there was a red line across his forehead. Overhead the leaves of a pipal tree rubbed against each other in a soft whisper of lament. The scent of frangipani and tuberoses in the wreaths came on a lift of air to India's nostrils, overpoweringly sweet. Far away, beyond the walls of the cemetery, the world rolled by like flowing water. The shrill sudden note of a bird cut through the humid air with painful precision.

As Pastor Rasami reached the end of the service he knelt to pray. It was at this point that he spoke several times of "the body of this old woman."

One of the coolies interrupted him, taking the straw cigarette out of his mouth and placing it behind his ear.

"She's young," he said laconically. "The one in the box is young. We left the old one at the hospital."

The service stopped with a jolt.

They all looked at the coolies as if they hoped they had misunderstood, and India felt her mouth go dry.

"Pa Tim was eighty-five," she made herself say, and in the oppressive heat of the cemetery among the lichen-covered stones the words sounded accusing.

The other coolie took his cigarette out of his mouth to think. Both of them, as if in unison, removed their broad-brimmed hats and wiped their heads with the scarves they had tied around their waists. The first one spoke again.

"This is the young one," he said with finality.

Darun, after a glance at India's shocked white face, took over. "There's been a mistake then," she said firmly. "We were expecting the body of an old, old woman who died last night in the hospital. If you've brought us a young woman, you'll have to take her back and get the proper body."

The two coolies looked gloomily at the box lying in the shallow grave. They made no move. Overhead the leaves of the tree rustled with a puff of wind. The first coolie put his cigarette back in his mouth and puffed it to the end.

"Wouldn't she do?" he asked.

Darun spoke coldly. "Get the coffin out of the grave at once, and hurry before Pa Tim's body is taken to the wrong cemetery."

India made a motion toward her purse, and the coolies' eyes brightened, but Darun restrained her. "Not until they come back, mem *kha.*"

The men resigned themselves to the inevitable and got busy with their ropes. India turned away with a sickness in her throat. Pastor Rasami touched her lightly on the elbow.

"There's an interesting old tombstone over here, mem *krop,*" he said. "It seems to have been put up seventy or eighty years ago by the crew of a ship for one of their members who fell overboard. They composed a verse in his honor. I wonder if you've ever seen it?"

The device was transparent, but India followed obediently and listened as he talked, until the coolies had left the cemetery. Then he took them to a Chinese cookshop around the corner and ordered bowls of congee and a pot of tea.

"No congee for me, Kru," India objected. "I've had my lunch."

He was insistent. He stood over the proprietor, making him plunge each bowl and spoon into the great kettle of boiling water at the front of the shop, and restrained him from wiping the dishes with the towel he had used on the tables and, even a second before, on his perspiring face. When the congee came it tasted wonderfully good, although none of them had felt hungry.

They sat talking together in the lich-gate of the cemetery for an hour before the coolies returned. As the body was lowered into the grave and the second service began, the whole occasion assumed the mocking image of travesty for India. She felt around her a subtle slipping of the real and good, until all the world was distorted to her eyes. The pipal trees writhed, the green light sifting through their leaves was sick, and even the song of the bird was harsh. And India wept for the pitiableness of life that could end so with indignity.

The rain did not fall until they were leaving the cemetery. Then it came in great sheets that swept the street clean of traffic and forced them to take refuge in a shop. They were all drenched to the skin in the few seconds it took them to find shelter, but in some obscure way the vehemence of the storm was a relief to India.

CHAPTER 15

WHEN THE FORCE OF THE STORM WAS SPENT AND TRAFFIC BEGAN to move again, Pastor Rasami found them a taxi. It was after four o'clock before India and Darun climbed wearily to the veranda of Jasmine Hall. They both went directly to their rooms to change.

The final macabre jest that life had played on Pa Tim had left India depressed. It had brought her back from her preoccupation with life to consciousness of the immanence of death, everywhere in everyone, old and young alike. Across the reaches of her mind the intoning of solemn words came like the sound of bells:

Lord, make me to know mine end, and the measure of my days, what it is . . . we spend our years as a tale that is told . . . and if by reason of strength they be fourscore years, yet is their strength labour and sorrow . . . verily every man at his best state is altogether vanity. . . . He cometh forth like a flower, and is cut down . . . yea, man giveth up the ghost, and where is he?

The words still echoed in her thoughts as she sat down to tea with Dulcie.

"Have you noticed how well Sanu is doing?" Dulcie asked brightly. "She's already fifth in her class. Kru Prapai tells me she stays after school every day to sweep floors and wash blackboards."

Since Ploy was not doing well at all, and Dang had been caught the day before with a handful of coins that did not belong to her, Dulcie's strategy was plain. Nevertheless, what she said was true. The smallest and saddest of the orphans was doing very well. She had quietly deserted her former associates and aligned herself with Jasmine Hall.

"Where's Angela?" India asked, noticing for the first time that Ploy had brought the tea tray.

It was quarter of five, and there was no sound of a music lesson in the chapel.

"She may have gone out."

"She never goes out."

"Well, I haven't seen her today."

India set her cup down and went through the church to Angela's room. The girl was lying across the bed, still dressed, her face flushed with fever.

"I thought last week you had a temperature," India said accusingly, "but you denied it."

"I'm terribly sorry," Angela answered weakly. Two tears slipped from under her eyelids.

India, looking down at her, could see how hard it was for her to admit illness. A cloud of despair rose from her at this new helplessness and the humiliation of needing care. India responded to the psychological need, reserving the physical.

"Angela, don't be silly," she scolded, her voice light as to a child. "Everyone has malaria sooner or later."

The girl on the bed did not answer.

India felt her hand. The skin was hot and dry. "I'll take your temperature and then send for Dr. Crane."

More painful tears followed the first down Angela's temples. "You know I haven't any money."

"If I were paying you the salary you deserve you'd have plenty, so don't even think about that. Besides, trouble never comes when you can afford it." India was rueful with something she knew too well. "Does your head ache?"

Angela nodded.

"I could give you an aspirin, but I'd rather wait for the doctor. Do you think you can?"

The girl nodded again.

Her temperature was 102°. India sent Det for Dr. Crane with a note giving Angela's symptoms as she had observed them and a brief explanation. The doctor knew Jasmine Hall well, and he probably knew more about Angela than India did. At any rate, he would be kind.

While she waited she washed Angela's face and combed her hair. It was the first time she had touched it, and the feel of it was lovely in her hands, like a skein of silk, thick and soft. Then she found fresh pajamas, helped Angela into them, changed the sheets, got some orange juice, and left the girl dozing.

India had been cheerful as long as she worked around Angela, but sitting on the mook waiting for the doctor, she gave way to discouragement. If Angela had only admitted she was ill when the fever began! Now it had fastened its tentacles upon her. And a long illness would be a strain on India's overtaxed resources. This had to be faced. Yet Angela must never guess that she was a burden. In her despondent state of mind such knowledge would be the final humiliation, and she had had enough of humiliation.

The disheartening sensations that dragged at the pit of India's stomach came from more than the multiplication of her problems which illness brought. They came also from an awareness that Angela was very ill indeed. There was about her the look of one who has slipped across an invisible border into the land of shadows. India had seen that look often in other faces and was shaken to find it in Angela's. She was shaken as well by the conviction that the girl was too spent to make a good fight. She wondered why she had accepted Angela's easy explanation. It should have been obvious that the girl was more than tired.

As India sat with her hands folded, the spreading shadow settled across her also, and she experienced a surging renewal of the dark and bitter knowledge that the end of all flesh is decay.

"The darkness is at its worst before the dawn," she reminded herself, trying to stiffen her will, but it hung limp as before.

"Help me, O God, *for the waters are come in unto my soul,*" she prayed in the words of the Psalmist. *"I sink in deep mire, where there is no standing: I am come into deep waters, where the floods overflow me."*

The doctor arrived shortly after seven. He was a big man, and his white suit was rumpled. Gray hair pitched forward over light eyes that were keen, almost mocking, in a leathery face. Something in his personality was astringent, like an antiseptic. India had watched him enter sickrooms on many occasions, and each time had felt a lift of spirit as she did now.

She took him over to the bed. "This is your patient, Doctor. Angela, this is Dr. Crane."

He set his bag on a chair. All his movements were deliberate.

Angela opened her eyes and looked at him. Her face was troubled and uncertain, as if the dream she now encountered were no better than the one she had left. Her pupils were dilated. She seemed to have difficulty bringing the doctor into focus in the dusk-filled room. Fear contorted her face for a second. Then her will ironed it out.

"How do you do, Doctor?" she said faintly.

He took her temperature and pulse, listened to her heart through his stethoscope, asked her how long she'd had a headache.

"Felt tired for the last week or so?"

"Yes," she said, her eyes trying to retain their hold on him.

He examined her chest, then prodded her abdomen with big skillful fingers. "Haven't wanted to eat?"

She shook her head.

"But you're thirsty?"

"Yes."

"Nauseated?"

"Yes."

"How about sleep?"

"I dream—and then I wake up—and then I dream——"

He stood looking at her thoughtfully. She coughed, a dry hacking cough.

He took a hypodermic from his bag and handed it to India. "Have this sterilized for me, please."

When she returned with it held carefully in a saucepan he went at once to work taking a sample of blood from the vein at the elbow. India shut her eyes as he inserted the needle. She had a childish hate of hypodermics. Angela made no complaint.

As soon as the doctor had shaken the sample he returned the hypodermic to his bag and stood up. "You're going to be all right," he said, patting her on the shoulder.

She asked him nothing. Her wavering eyes seemed to plead for a light sentence, but that was all.

"Thank you, Doctor," she whispered, and brought her arm up across her face to cover the fact that her lips were trembling.

The doctor followed India to the mook before he spoke. "We'll have to take her to the Nursing Home in the morning. Shall I make the arrangements?"

"She hasn't any money, and neither have I, Doctor."

"We have no choice, Miss Severn."

"Why? I've managed before."

"I think she has typhoid."

India felt the weight of his words crushing the air out of her. Typhoid fever! Not typhoid fever!

For several seconds she could say nothing nor feel anything but the load of helplessness that bore her down. Then consciously, with great expenditure of will, she fought upward against it, and as she struggled her mind revolved with that economical use of time which expands moments of crisis to the width of days.

The doctor was standing by the railing looking down into the garden, where darkness was gathering over the jasmine bushes. Several of the children were playing on the lawn until Doe should call them to get ready for bed. Their laughter floated upward with the scent of the flowers.

"Doctor"—India spoke hesitantly—"across the canal at the back of this house there's a brick cottage where the watchman and coolie live. If I moved Angela there, would it be possible to care for her here?"

"You'd still have to have a nurse."

India thought with longing of her friend Catherine Darrow, who was taking eighteen months' leave for advanced study in obstetrics. Catherine would have loaned her a nurse.

She hunted for words to make clear their dilemma, the tautness of her own resources and Angela's desperate sickness of spirit. She had long ago sold the last of her bonds. Grace accused her of squandering her inheritance, but she could regret nothing of what it had made possible, only that it was gone. She still owned a small farm in southern Wisconsin to which she would retire someday. Given time, she could borrow on that, but there was no time.

When she became aware of the lengthening silence she spoke quickly, unable to find a better way of presenting her plan than the simple statement of it.

"Doctor, I'm a good practical nurse myself," she said, and braced herself to counter his disapproval.

He turned from the railing, and she could feel his eyes on her in the dusk. "It's hard work, you know."

She exhaled in relief. "I know."

"Can you leave your school?"

Yes, her school. It was futile to deny that there would be loss if she took six weeks from it to nurse Angela, but the loss would be less now than in either the second or third terms. Besides, the problem of the school was not insuperable. Anne would teach her classes, and Darun could assume the administration, as she had done during India's last furlough. Her critics might accuse her of neglect, but to offset that possibility there was an equally impelling fact. Angela was ill with more than typhoid, deeply endangered by defeat. And for diseases of the spirit there was no specific.

No one else cared what happened to the girl, India reasoned, therefore the obligation was her own. Actually there was no argument, only the rationalization of the thing she had to do. A few words from a hymn floated through her consciousness as she stood sunk in thought. *Keep thou my feet; I do not ask to see the distant scene; one step enough for me.* Well, there had been other times when the next step was as far as she could see and, having taken it, the step beyond had become clear.

"You'll have to tell me exactly what to do," she said to Dr. Crane.

The watchman's cottage was well suited to India's purpose. It was the remnant of an older house than Jasmine Hall and had heavy brick walls with barred windows set into them like embrasures. There were two rooms fifteen feet square with twelve-foot ceilings, and a bathroom between them. She had the whole cottage thoroughly scrubbed and the walls whitewashed. Klee took his possessions to the loft over the kitchen, and Det decided to go back and forth to his home in the city while the cottage was in use as a hospital.

A bed, table, and chair were moved into the room nearer the main house, where India would stay. The other was prepared for Angela. It was all done very quietly. India had been afraid that there might be panic among the teachers and children, but there was none. They were accustomed to the widespread incidence of dysentery and typhoid and did not seem alarmed. Dr. Crane suggested that the staff and boarding pupils be inoculated. India herself had had a series of inoculations the month before.

The only unpleasant note in the hurried preparations came from Dulcie, who objected to Darun's being made her superior.

"I take it as a personal insult, India," she protested resentfully. "I'm her senior. Then, too, things like this ought to be decided on their merits. Of course, she dances attendance on you all the time, and I don't, but even so——"

It would have been wasted effort to argue that the issue *had* been decided on its merits, so India tried to pacify her obliquely. "I'm counting on you to take over my share of the church calling. Surely you don't consider the school more important than the church, Dulcie." And Dulcie emphatically denied that she did.

"If you have any free time you can tutor the girls evenings," India added to complete the rout. "I've always counted that one of the most important things I do."

"Yes, of course," Dulcie replied evasively, for she did not like to commit herself to any kind of evening duty.

The task of telling Angela about the move to the cottage was left until all preparations were complete. Dr. Crane had sent word in the morning that the report was positive. India shrank from transmitting the news as much as if it were a physical blow. When the cottage was ready about four o'clock in the afternoon there was no further excuse for delay.

Angela was lying on her bed staring at the ceiling, where a dozen colorless lizards no longer than a finger, called *chingchoks*, moved back and forth in search of mosquitoes. Her face was stained with fever, and her eyes burned with it.

India had learned to tell bad news in one swift summation, leaving nothing further to come.

"Angela." The girl focused her wandering attention and tried to smile. "The doctor has sent the result of your blood test, and you have typhoid fever, not malaria."

The moment India said *doctor* Angela shut her eyes. As the older woman watched anxiously, alert to shore up any break in courage, the girl let go of a long shuddering sigh. Several seconds later, when she opened her eyes, India was amazed to see behind the burning of the fever a look of intense relief. Angela groped for her hand, and India took both of Angela's between her own.

"I was afraid," Angela said, and shuddered again. "I vomited—and kept vomiting—and I thought I was pregnant."

She shut her eyes for the second time, as if she were at peace. "It would have been so much better to die than to——"

Tears sprang to India's own eyes and rolled down her face. Anger billowed within her against the Tan Ying and Charoon at the thought of the indecencies worked upon this girl to make her prefer death to her husband's child.

India hunched her shoulders under the force of her own emotion and wiped her eyes on her sleeve without releasing Angela's hands. For the first time she had looked into the girl's shuttered mind and seen clearly the shame and revulsion secreted there.

When India was sure of her voice she spoke again.

"We're moving you to a cottage back of the house, and all you have to do is rest and follow the doctor's orders. Is there anyone in America you'd like me to cable?"

"There's no one," Angela said with disinterest, and sank out of sight within herself.

She was docile, almost torpid. When India and the coolies shifted her from her bed to a cot spring and pad they were using as a stretcher, she said nothing, permitting herself to be moved like a bundle of clothes. India sat with her while her bed was taken down and transferred to the cottage. Presently the coolies came back for the stretcher. Angela's eyes were still closed as they carried her down the back stairs, out across the canal with the big pink lotus flowers, and into the room prepared for her. When India tucked her under the sheet in the freshly made bed she opened them heavily and smiled, then closed them again.

The bed was a high one made of wood, with four straight posters holding a frame on which a net was stretched. India had it placed in the middle of the room, facing the windows to the south. She had debated turning it so that Angela would look at the blank wall between her room and the bathroom, but the dead white of this seemed less pleasing than the two barred windows and the bamboo beyond.

The thicket of bamboo was close enough to the windows to screen the afternoon sun, and the gently waving branches of fine-leafed green were beautiful. India had always intended to have that thicket cleaned out, for it certainly harbored snakes. Now she was glad she had never found the time. There were often advantages to inefficiency.

Washtubs had been brought into the bathroom, which was large, and Det was busy constructing a crude stove of bricks at the back door, onto which he could set a copper wash boiler. Food would be sent down from India's kitchen, but India had Klee place a charcoal brazier in her room on which she could make cocoa or boil an egg. She had a small meat safe installed as well, with its legs in bowls of kerosene. It would hold fruit, tea, sugar, soup. The icebox was carried from upstairs, and Det went for ice so that Angela's orange juice could be chilled and an ice pack kept on her head if she wished it.

When Dr. Crane came about five he approved of the arrangement. Angela's temperature was 104°, and she was restless and uncomfortable.

"It's usual with typhoid," he explained. "Just keep her clean and try to get her to eat. Don't urge her to take what she doesn't want. Find things she likes."

"I already know that she won't drink milk but will take chilled orange juice."

"Good. Try cocoa and coffee too. And if she won't take anything else we can always resort to Scotch." His blue eyes twinkled. "You'd be surprised how many patients would starve if I didn't keep them going on Scotch."

CHAPTER 16

GRACE AND INDIA HAD DISAGREED MANY TIMES IN THE TWENTY-FIVE years they had been members of the Mission, without in any way disrupting their friendship. They had come to Siam together and taught at Wang Lang for seven years. They had then gone home together on furlough and returned together for a second term.

It was not until they had been in Siam fifteen years that their lives diverged. Wang Lang School was being sold to the government for a hospital, and a new site had been chosen across the river in the suburbs of modern Bangkok. As reconstituted, the school was to be called Wattana Wittaya Academy (The-fostering-of-knowledge Academy), so the break with the past would be complete.

All the farang mems except India were moving with the school as a matter of course. She had decided that this was the appropriate time to put into effect a plan which had been dormant in her mind for several years. She wanted very much to organize a Bible school, where she could train lay workers for service in the Siamese church. As soon as the sale of Wang Lang became a certainty, she applied to the Mission for authorization and for an appropriation with which to begin.

Grace alone of all her friends opposed the plan. She urged India to incorporate her training program into the framework of Wattana, but this India refused to consider. She was convinced that her school would be overshadowed there, unable to put down roots and grow. The half-educated village girls she wanted to train would feel out of place among the sleek and pretty daughters of the wealthiest families in the kingdom. Nor could she expect the few Wattana girls who were Christians to undertake the ill-paid work village churches needed.

"Isn't your true reason for insisting on a separate school your unwillingness to work under *me*?" Grace flung at her one afternoon, referring to her own recent appointment as principal of Wang Lang, soon to be Wattana.

India was stretched out on Grace's bed in the little room that Grace was about to leave for the principal's suite, while Grace manicured her nails. Now she sat up quickly.

"Did you think I wanted to be principal?"

"Well, didn't you?"

India laughed in sudden comprehension. "No, a thousand times no!" she said with relief. "Besides, you're the logical one for it."

Grace continued to buff her nails without looking up.

"Don't you see how much better it will be if I go now," India said persuasively, "when the school's making all kinds of changes anyway?"

"Not when everyone thinks you're leaving because of me!"

"But they don't, goosy! Everyone knows I didn't want to be principal." India jumped to her feet and shook Grace's heavy shoulders affectionately. "I'm not jealous of your advancement. Really! I couldn't be."

Grace brought her eyes up slowly, unable to believe that what meant a great deal to her could have no meaning for India. Something she saw—the amusement, the mockery, the earnestness—convinced her. Awkward color suffused her face, and she turned away, but from then on she gave India her ungrudging support.

She began that same afternoon by promising India the furniture from Wang Lang. Wattana was installing modern equipment and had no further use for the old. When the Mission refused an appropriation from the general budget, Grace persuaded Bangkok Station to divert part of its evangelistic fund to the new school. She accomplished this against the opposition of Amery Hillow, who, as Chairman of the Station and Executive Secretary of the Mission, was the most powerful individual in both Station and Mission. In the end it was she, also, who discovered Jasmine Hall.

At that time the house had long been unoccupied. The roof leaked, termites were in the flooring, the paint was gone, and there was no plumbing or electric wiring. Weeds, briars, quick-growing bamboo had appropriated the garden where roses once grew.

"It's not so discouraging as it looks," Grace insisted as they stood together just inside the sagging gate from which most of the red paint had disappeared. "The Privy Purse will repair the floors and roof, and we can get money for plumbing from the Station. It's a well-built house, you know. All its faults are superficial. A coat of paint would change its appearance completely."

India was unconvinced, and Grace went on: "I wouldn't hesitate, if I were you. Where are you going to find another house this big and this cheap? You can have your classrooms downstairs. Then you can put the girls' dormitory upstairs and still have room for an apartment of your own."

It was Grace's special magic to move swiftly from thought to action, carrying everyone else with her. As she talked, the school emerged from the mists and shadows of the dream world and assumed corporeal reality. Suddenly India's imagination kindled.

"You're right, Grace," she said. "I can see it now. I'll throw the bedrooms on the west into one for the dormitory and build a screened room behind it for the teachers. Then I can take two of the east bedrooms for myself and keep the third as a guest room."

Grace nodded absently, already planning the next step. "You have those two center rooms upstairs and down," she told India. "They must be forty feet long, at least. Use the downstairs one as a chapel and invite Second Church to use the upstairs one. After all, they'll have to move when we do. Then your girls can do their practice teaching in the Sunday school." She smiled at India triumphantly.

India had one qualm. "A hundred a month is a lot to pay, though, don't you think?"

"We can get it for sixty."

"But the Privy Purse said a hundred."

"I'll talk them down for you," Grace said confidently, and did.

Grace had continued to take a proprietary interest in Jasmine Hall during the intervening years. This had been advantageous in many ways, but it had one disadvantage. Grace was strong-willed and assertive, impatient of opposition, and not averse to contending for what she believed right even with her closest friends.

India sometimes suspected that Grace experienced a feeling of release from quarreling, like the sweetness in the air after a thunderstorm. She herself felt defiled and made it a policy to avoid controversy where possible.

With Grace tact availed little. She was unable to leave an issue alone once it was raised between herself and India, but worried it as a hound a quarry. Her persistence was limitless and her antagonisms inflexible. Only when the issue lay dead could she abandon it, and only then did peace return to their friendship.

These periods of dissension were very trying to India, who hoped fervently after each one that there would never be another.

The hope was futile, however, since each new thing she attempted involved a clash with Grace.

When India started the primary school, Grace disapproved on the grounds that it would detract from the main purpose of the Bible school. If she realized she had been wrong about this, she had never admitted it. On another occasion India's decision to accept a few small boarders in need of temporary shelter had precipitated a quarrel. Their most recent disagreement had been over a Chinese evangelist who had come to Bangkok two years previously for a series of meetings.

"I don't believe in emotionalism in religion," Grace had argued. "I believe in the quiet day-by-day effect of teaching."

"Both have their place," India countered. "There isn't any either/or between them. Besides, aren't you ignoring the fact that all the deep experiences of life are emotional?"

Grace had kept the evangelist out of Wattana. Jasmine Hall had co-operated with him. Amery Hillow had supported Grace. It had been the beginning of a nebulous alliance between them. This was the only one of Grace's and India's quarrels that had not ended with the occasion for it, perhaps because it had spread from them to the Mission until there was no one who had not taken sides.

India had realized that the old round was starting again the afternoon at the Legation, when Grace reproached her for sheltering Mani. In spite of this fact, the rhythm of these quarrels was so familiar that she did not recognize a difference of quality in the newest one until after Angela was taken ill.

One morning during the first week of her illness, India heard Grace calling from the bridge. She glanced at Angela, who was asleep, and slipped out, closing the door quietly. Grace was waiting where the bridge joined the veranda of the cottage. She was wearing a blue voile dress from Manila, smocked around neck and hips, which made her look even bigger than usual. She had taken off her topee and was fanning herself. Her chestnut hair was crushed, her large red face damp, and her expression ill-humored.

"I just caught that oldest orphan of Dulcie's flirting with a policeman out by the gate," she began.

"Oh no!"

"Oh yes! When the cat's away the mice will play."

"What did you do?"

"Found Dulcie. She fluttered off like a distracted hen. You know her morbid fear of sex."

"Thank you, Grace."

"And while we're on the subject, I have news for you about Mani."

Mani too! Grace could be very irritating! India was not to be permitted any ignoring of the fact that she was sheltering Mani and the orphans against Grace's advice. She stood silent in protest of this interference, but Grace had no understanding of passive resistance. She had always assumed that their friendship gave her the right to censure what she did not approve at Jasmine Hall. If she knew that India sometimes resented her criticisms, it did not deter her from making them.

"Aren't you even interested?" she asked, tapping her foot on the planking of the bridge. "You should be. The reputation of your school's involved."

"Frankly, I'm not, but I can see you're determined to tell me anyway."

"You remember Mr. Norbert whose wife left for Australia a month ago to have their baby? Well, Mani's being seen all over town with him. How can you let a woman like that stay in a Mission school. *I* couldn't!"

India hesitated between explaining that Mani was going home in September and challenging the source of Grace's information. In the end she decided on a *démarche*. "Wouldn't it be more logical to blame Mr. Norbert?"

"India, you're not condoning Mani, are you?"

"No, but I'm disavowing responsibility for your friend Mr. Norbert."

"He's not my friend!" Grace was indignant. "You don't imagine I have any special interest in *him*, do you? I hardly know him. My interest is in *your* reputation!" Her voice in argument would have filled a lecture hall.

"Please lower your voice, Grace!" India was urgent. "You'll disturb Angela."

"I came here to disturb Angela. I'm going to tell her that she's imposing on you. There are hospitals for sick people, and sick people belong in them."

"Grace, I insist! Lower your voice! Angela isn't imposing on me, and I don't intend to let you or anyone else tell her that she is. I'm nursing her because I choose to."

"India, have you lost your mind? You abandon your school as if you had no responsibility for it, and then resent my protest. How do you rationalize your actions? I could understand how a man might fling his cap over the windmill for a pretty girl, but not how a woman like you can jeopardize the future of her life work in this ridiculous way."

She stopped short, apparently finding what she had said more perspicacious than she had intended. A wheel rolled over in her eyes, and exasperation gave place to a crude look of comprehension. "I guess I do understand after all, but *you* of all people! And at *your age!*" She laughed, and the sound was full of innuendo. "No fool like an old fool, of course."

India flushed angrily. "If that's what you came to say, Grace, you should have left it unsaid."

She turned back toward the cottage, but Grace reached out and took hold of her arm.

"We've both taught in girls' schools, India, and we know that these things happen. I just didn't realize before what was wrong. And I should have, of course, the day you flared up like a Roman candle when I tried to tell you what the Tan Ying said. You've applied the remedy to girls often enough. Now it's a case of *Physician, heal thyself!* Why don't you send her to the hospital this afternoon?"

India's voice was coldly quiet, her eyes a flinty blue. "And will you lend me the twenty ticals a day it will cost?"

"Let her go as a charity patient."

"The Nursing Home doesn't take charity patients. Foreigners are never indigent in the Far East. It's one of the things that isn't done. Hadn't you heard?"

"Ask the Tan Ying for money, then. The girl's entitled to a third of Charoon's estate."

"That I cannot and will not do."

"I'll do it for you."

"You certainly will not!"

"And why not?"

"Because Angela has a right to the few tatters of self-respect the Tan Ying left her."

"India, be sensible. Orientals are uncanny when it comes to reading character."

"They're no more infallible than dogs or children. You're too easily impressed by clichés, Grace."

"It seems quite possible to me that the Princess knows more about her daughter-in-law after three years than you do after three weeks."

"Grace, you ignore the fact that prejudice warps her vision."

The other woman shrugged. "That means, I suppose, you're keeping the girl here at any cost."

"It's because the cost will be negligible, Grace, that she's here and not in the hospital."

"I wasn't speaking of money. People will talk, you know."

"Not unless you talk first. They'll pass along anything you choose to say, of course."

Several of the Bible school girls, who were sauntering along the lower veranda of the Hall, cast sidelong glances at them. It must be time for recess. One of the teachers passed, walking quickly.

India was aware that not even the English words could disguise the fact that she and Grace were quarreling. How had it happened? She was humiliated by her own inability to prevent the argument. And yet what was the answer? Certainly not to concur in Grace's wretched allegations, even to the extent of silence.

India hoped no one had caught the mention of Angela's name but realized that there was little chance of concealing the occasion for the quarrel. Siamese were very acute about these things, and in spite of the fact that she always denied it, Grace talked a good deal.

She denied it now, annoyed at the implication of India's remark. "I never gossip," she protested vehemently.

"Call it what you like. I'm just warning you that I'll not sit tamely by and let you destroy the reputation of a young girl."

"Is that a threat?"

"It's an expression of desperation, Grace. *Even the worm*, you know."

"It's you that's bent on destroying your own reputation."

"Don't be silly, Grace. I'm merely trying to help a young girl *who fell among thieves*."

"Many people need help."

"So you frequently say, as if the fact that you can't help everyone absolved you from the responsibility to help anyone. Even the Good Samaritan is remembered for his kindness to a single man, you know."

"But the Samaritan's motives don't come into question. The man was a stranger to him. You're enamored of this girl, India. That's why you won't listen to reason."

India abandoned the argument in sudden loathing. "You have a perverted mind, Grace. I wonder why I ever valued your friendship. Believe me, if there's any feeling other than pity at the bottom of my relationship with Angela it's the protective feeling of a mother for a child—someone else's child."

"Freud would think otherwise."

"Even that doesn't impress me," India said quietly.

"You know what he'd say then?" Grace was persistent.

"Matthew, Mark, Luke, John, and Freud. Is that your Bible, Grace? As for me, I stop with John."

Grace shrugged angrily and turned away. "Well, don't say I haven't warned you."

All through the quarrel India had had the sensation of slipping, of snatching at twigs to slow her fall, seeking a toehold that did not exist. She could find no place to stop even now.

"I'll never say that, Grace." Her voice was very quiet. "On the other hand, there's one more thing I'm going to say, since we've gotten down to these raw basic emotions. Angela has no morbid attachment for me, nor I for her—we're hardly more than strangers —but your feeling for me has always included a large element of jealousy. You're very possessive, you know. Isn't that what's wrong with you now?"

Grace turned slowly back. Her eyes glowed like a cat's. "How dare you say that to me after all the hundreds of things I've done for you these many years?"

"Because there's nothing you feel you can't say to me."

"Why should *I* be jealous of *you?*"

"It's curious, really, that you should be, considering your more important position in the relative scale of things in the Mission. And yet it comes to me now that you always have been. Perhaps it's your nature. Or perhaps there's something in me that you resent. Certainly there's something you can't control, isn't there? I don't know what to call it, but I can see that it challenges everything you've become. And with you it's rule or ruin, isn't it, Grace?"

CHAPTER 17

WHEN INDIA RE-ENTERED THE COTTAGE ANGELA WAS STILL ASLEEP. She went through the bathroom to her own bedroom and lay down. In a moment she was up again, unable to contain the seething pressures within her. She felt an overpowering need to walk but could not leave Angela, so took off her shoes and paced back and forth, nauseated with what had happened and sicker as revulsion was added to the ferment of other emotions.

She went back over the quarrel again and again, trying to discover how it had started, trying to affix the blame. Would it have been better to remain silent? But that would not have satisfied the juggernaut in Grace. Why pretend otherwise?

For an hour India walked, getting what relief was possible in motion. Then Angela called for the bedpan. India fetched it, took it away, washed Angela's face, squeezed some orange juice, iced it, held the glass to Angela's mouth. India was surprised to see her hands and feet doing these things. The connection between them and her mind had gone dead, and they seemed to move in response to an intelligence outside herself.

All that day her anger burned against Grace, and her mind protracted the argument, admitting and denying, finding reasons and forming answers. It was true that any association of human beings held within it the bacteria of soft rot. The normal could degenerate into the abnormal, the decent into the vile, but that was only to say that all things human were capable of abuse, which was obvious. And because there was abuse, could there be no use? And because there was wrong, could there be no right? Surely to see only the putrescible was to prove nothing more than one's own outlook was twisted.

Her dinner came, and she could not eat it. She pushed the two yellow potatoes around with her fork in the puddle of gravy. She cut a piece of meat from the slab on her plate and took it out of her mouth again. The watery custard repelled her. She drank the tea and set the tray outside her door.

It was the next morning before the fire was reduced to embers. Looking down as from a great height on herself, she saw where the flames had swept across the whole fruitful valley of her soul, revealing under what it had consumed blackened gullies of hate. The words of Jeremiah, prophet of doom, echoed accusingly through her thoughts: *The heart is deceitful above all things, and desperately wicked: who can know it?* Who indeed?

She felt dull and dispirited. Before she went in to Angela she knelt for a while beside her bed. Words came with difficulty.

"*Almighty and most merciful Father,*" she began, bowing her head upon her hands as tears escaped her eyelids and fell hot along her fingers. "*We have erred, and strayed from thy ways like lost sheep.—We have followed too much the devices and desires of our own hearts.—We have offended against thy holy laws. . . . Lord, have mercy upon us. . . .*"

The tears fell faster and, unwilling to get up for a handkerchief, she wiped them away with a corner of the sheet. Her head rested on her hands until they grew numb, but no more words came. Nevertheless, when she stood up some of the burden had rolled away. She felt humble and uncertain, but able to go on.

All through the week that followed she found herself examining her thoughts, everything she did, her motives, her impulses, the slightest stirring of emotion, for possible taint. Her resentment against Grace still smoldered, even when she admitted to herself that she was always too headlong and that Grace's words had forced her to realign her purposes with God's. She reminded herself that the Christian life was in essence a daily truing up of every thought and action against a standard that was absolute. Considered in this light, she owed Grace a debt of gratitude for recalling the fact to her attention, but it was a wry thought and did nothing to diminish her bitterness.

One thing this self-examination made clear: her feeling for Angela had gone deeper than she would have believed possible in so short a time. But then time was not an element in the emotion she dredged up and examined, almost against her will, under the prodding of Grace's accusation. Perhaps the attack had stirred her protective instincts. Or did the explanation matter? In some strange way Angela was *bone of her bone, and flesh of her flesh,* as none of the Siamese children she had loved and cared for had ever been, not even Darun. With the most exacting honesty of which she was capable she could analyze her feelings no further than that.

Angela's deepening illness removed her finally from the round of anger, recrimination, self-examination, and self-doubt which the quarrel had set in motion. The hacking cough had persisted, and on the day after Grace's call, rose spots appeared across Angela's chest and abdomen, flat and bright and about half an inch wide. She no longer complained of headache, but she refused to eat.

Every morning as soon as her temperature had been taken and her face washed, India would bring a cup of coffee into which, on the doctor's suggestion, she had stirred a generous teaspoonful of lactose and some evaporated milk. There was no fresh milk in Bangkok. Angela would reach for the cup, her hands shaking eagerly. Some mornings she drank half of it. Usually she gave up after a few sips and lay back fretfully. An hour later the breakfast tray appeared from the big house—farina, a soft-boiled egg, toast, and cocoa. Angela would open her mouth obediently for two or three spoonfuls, then shake her head.

"Thank you very much, but I can't."

Dr. Crane had said that India could go up into Jasmine Hall when she needed to, if she was careful about washing first and changing her clothes. She had borrowed some of Catherine Darrow's uniforms from the Maternity Home, and these Det boiled and Doe starched and ironed for her. Actually there was little time left from the routine of nursing. Except for a hurried conference in late afternoon with Darun, she spent her time at the cottage. So far as she could see that first week the school moved ahead without loss of momentum, and this reassured her.

During the second week Angela began to be delirious at night. The first time it happened India was aroused by the sound of a fall and found Angela lying on the floor mumbling, "Jerry, Jerry, Jerry." Who was Jerry? It must have been her name for Charoon.

"Jerry doesn't need you any more," India said firmly as she helped the girl back into bed. Reaching under the net, she held Angela's hot hand until she drifted off into troubled sleep.

The next night almost the same thing happened. Fears crowded close around Angela, and she tried constantly to flee from them. Dr. Crane suggested that boards be attached to the sides of the bed, and after a little experimenting Det devised a fence of bamboo with a gate on one side hung from hooks screwed into the bedposts.

Angela talked a great deal now in a low monotone, as if the stream of her consciousness flowed along the surface rather than under it. Most of the time what she said was unintelligible, a soft unhappy complaining. Over and over in the night she would call, "India, India," and India would get up and go to her, taking the slender fingers that plucked at the sheet into her own hands to calm them. She would wash the girl's face, make a fresh ice pack, change the pajamas that seemed always wet with perspiration, get the bedpan, some chilled orange juice. After she was through, Angela would be quiet for a little and then would resume her talking.

She was fretful in the day also, and then, too, India's presence was a bulwark against the shadows haunting her. For a while her mind was partially clear and India would read to her, but by the end of the second week she had moved out into the world of phantoms and could no longer listen.

The work was very hard, and the lack of sleep was exhausting. Dishes and utensils had to be sterilized after each use. Bedding and clothes were soaked in a solution of chlorine bleach and then boiled. It was Det's job to keep the fires going in the outdoor stove, and

Doe's to dry and iron the clean clothes, but even with this help India scarcely managed to keep up with the endless sterilizing. Her hands grew rough from chlorine, and her back ached continually.

These things she could endure. What troubled her was that Angela was growing noticeably thinner. The doctor had prescribed a quart and a half of milk daily, three eggs, lactose, sugar, bread, butter, orange and lime juices. Angela could not seem to eat. She would take a few bites and then refuse more. India tried potatoes. She tried soup. She tried cocoa. She tried soft-boiled rice. It was a bitter and futile fight.

One day in the third week India asked the question that had lain unspoken in her mind from the beginning. Up to this point Angela had reacted to orders spoken sharply and close to her ear. As her body became more emaciated her deafness increased, and although Dr. Crane insisted that this was characteristic of the disease and not anatomical, India was more than ever troubled by the question in her mind. The accretion of fear incasing it grew a layer for each day it was unacknowledged, until only a colossal effort of will could dislodge it. Yet in the end she needed to hear Dr. Crane deny it.

After his morning examination she asked, "Do you think she's getting worse because she doesn't want to live, Doctor?"

He answered brusquely, "Her body wants to live," and as India fumbled to explain, added impatiently, "I know, she's had a bad time, but she isn't thinking about that any more."

India wasn't sure, and the next day the doctor came with a bottle of Scotch in his hand. "I knew you'd refuse to buy whiskey," he said.

India wondered if he was aware that she could hardly have afforded it, and then thought with annoyance at her own slowness of mind that of course he knew.

Angela made a face when the tube was placed between her lips. The doctor spoke sharply. "Drink it, Angela, or I'll spank you!" Obediently she drank it down, making a face with each swallow.

"Imagine wasting good Scotch on anyone who makes a face like that," he said in disgust, but when the bottle was empty he brought another, and the struggle to get Angela to swallow something went on.

CHAPTER 18

IN SPITE OF DR. CRANE'S ENCOURAGING WORDS IT SEEMED TO INDIA that the battle ran against them.

Gradually Angela's delirium became constant. She was no longer able to sleep, but lay picking at the sheet and talking aimlessly to herself, as flotsam and jetsam from the breakup of her mind floated along the surface like bits of driftwood. She did not have the strength to get out of bed, so the bamboo fence was taken down. Almost imperceptibly she passed into somnolence and from that into stupor, lying on her back with her eyes open and sightless, her mouth agape. The muscles in her arms and trunk twitched occasionally, then she was still.

India cared for her with a kind of frantic tenderness. She kept Angela's hair carefully brushed, and washed out her mouth several times a day with a mild dentifrice. When it proved difficult to keep her lips and tongue from cracking, she discovered that by slipping a small piece of ice into Angela's mouth on a spoon she could achieve moderate success. The girl's clothing and the bed had to be changed many times a day, for she had lost control of her bodily functions.

As Angela grew steadily worse India's conferences with Darun became perfunctory. Even when she willed herself to concentrate on school problems her mind wandered. Several times she caught a look of resentment on Darun's face. This stimulated her to closer attention for a few minutes until the fog of worry and fatigue closed in again. She did not seem to care as much as she should that Dulcie had almost abandoned her pretense of teaching in favor of church calling. India knew that she ought to summon Dulcie and reprimand her, but she could not, and let the matter drift.

Darun complained that Ploy was surly and unco-operative. Sometimes she sat all day on the veranda outside India's room, ignoring Darun's every command. Dulcie evaded responsibility for her ward by the expedient of declining to admit the existence of the problem.

"You can't expect obedience when you aren't fair," she told Darun. "The child shouldn't be asked to do all the work in the house. You're too hard on her."

A young medical student and member of Second Church had fallen in love with Sawang and she with him.

"Thank goodness for that," India said, grateful for a bit of good news. Darun wanted someone besides herself to act as go-between with Mae Tam. Whom should she ask?

"Why, Pastor Rasami, of course." India was surprised that there should be any question.

Darun looked at her obliquely. "I'd rather ask *Ajan* Hillow, if you don't mind."

The title *Ajan* or *Acharya* meant *Reverend Teacher* and was infinitely more respectful than *kru*, which applied to all who taught. India did not find it strange that Darun should use it of the missionary when she denied it to the Siamese pastor, since many Siamese did this, but she was amazed at Darun's decision. Why Amery? Of all the men in Bangkok, he was least willing to help Jasmine Hall. Little bells of warning jangled along her overtaxed nerves, but after a barely perceptible interval she said, "Anyone you like, Kru." She was too tired to cope with mystery.

"Ajan Hillow has invited me to represent Bangkok at the conference of Christian workers in Petchaburi next week," Darun said tentatively.

"Oh, Darun, that's impossible. Angela won't be well enough to leave until September, and I can't do without you until then."

India spoke sharply, annoyed that Darun should even suggest leaving Jasmine Hall at this time. Considering her own involvement, the teacher might have spared her the necessity of denying a request. Then she checked her impatience, remembering that Darun was under a strain running the school. There was a flicker of disappointment in her eyes, and it moved India to regret. Darun rarely asked anything for herself. Later some way must be found to compensate her for everything.

"I'm sorry, Kru," India said. "I'm too dependent on you now to let you go, but when Angela's well you may have a month if you like."

It seemed to India that eternity had intervened since the afternoon in July when she had found Angela lying across the bed with what she had thought was malaria. The calendar disproved this. It was only the middle of August.

Angela's temperature began to moderate during the fourth week of her illness, and India hoped that the worst was over. One morning it was 101° with a rise of less than a degree in the afternoon; then it was 100°, 99°, and a few days later it was normal. India felt a great lifting sense of relief. As she went about her work she hummed scraps of old songs and hymns.

She was not disturbed when the next morning Angela's temperature had dropped to 96°. She knew that subnormal temperatures often followed serious illness. Late in the afternoon Dr. Crane took it again. It had risen only to 97.5°.

"What was it this morning?" he asked. When India told him, he stood for some time studying the chart, and then examined Angela with more than ordinary care.

"Has she shown any signs of abdominal pain?" he asked.

"No, Doctor." India's mind raced to intercept the direction of his thoughts.

When he had finished she followed him to the veranda before he spoke. "I want you to take her temperature every hour until she goes to sleep and once during the night. Watch her for signs of abdominal pain, and if there are any send for me."

"What is it, Doctor?"

He was abrupt and impatient. "Perhaps nothing at all."

India's spirits plummeted. She was like a runner who has miscalculated the length of a race and has nothing in reserve for the final lap. Fear revived and was unbearable after the interval of hope. Wearily she resumed her watch. There was no change in Angela's temperature during the night, but in the morning it dropped suddenly to 94°. Her breathing became hurried and shallow, her face pallid, her hands and feet icy. India sent for Dr. Crane with the sodden conviction that he would arrive too late.

In half an hour he was there. "Has there been any evidence of pain?"

"No, Doctor."

He felt Angela's abdomen with expert fingers. She did not wince, but lay dully as before.

"Has she passed blood?"

"Yes, a lot."

He frowned and went on with the examination. India was suddenly quite faint. The long weeks of nursing had sapped her vitality, and all at once the will to fight left her. She felt the sunshine in the room turn to a brown mist. Deep in her throat was a lump of congealed fear that she could not swallow. She stumbled outside and leaned against the wall until the mist lifted. The thought filling her mind was that if it was a perforation Angela would not have the strength to rally from an operation.

Dr. Crane came out presently and stood beside her, his forehead creased into lines of concentration. Several times he pulled at the thatch of gray hair that pitched forward over his eyes. It was an absent-minded gesture which sought by physical force to elicit something from the brain under the hair. India waited for him to speak and, when he did not, drew on her slackened will to ask the thing she did not want to know. "Is it a perforation?"

He came out of himself slowly and shook his head.

"What is it then?" Couldn't he tell her without waiting to have information pried from him?

"Intestinal hemorrhage."

Go on! Go on! her mind implored, but he stood looking at the canal and frowning to himself, oblivious of her until rising panic expelled from her the question she hated most to ask. "Does she have a chance?"

"As long as she's alive she has a chance."

India hardly noticed the testiness of his voice. Something more important had taken possession of her thoughts. It was evident that she could whip herself no further. The whole apparatus of feeling had ceased to function except for that one indigestible lump in her throat. She could no longer counter the rebellion of her hands and feet. That meant only one thing.

"Can you get me a nurse, Doctor?"

He was looking absently at the plump buds of lotus floating on the surface of the canal. He had taken a cigarette from a pack and was about to light it, but stopped and turned to her curiously with the match still burning between his fingers.

"I think so," he said. "At least I know the right person. I'll try to have her here by noon."

He lighted the cigarette and lapsed again into thought. When it was finished he picked up his bag.

"Don't disturb Angela unless you have to. Nothing to eat. Nothing to drink. A little ice in small pieces. I've given her morphine. Put a flannel on her abdomen and keep an ice bag on it, but don't make it heavy. If it annoys her take it off. I'll be in at eleven."

India followed the doctor's routine woodenly. The strange emptiness which filled her made it necessary to work out the mechanics of each simple and familiar action as if she had never done it before. Occasionally Angela stirred, then lay still again. India slipped small pieces of ice between her lips every ten minutes and changed the ice packs once an hour. The rest of the time she sat with her hands in her lap, watching Angela's uneven breathing and the waxy whiteness of her face. The golden hair was lusterless, cut in a short irregular halo. The body was paper thin beneath the sheet.

Vina Stout arrived at ten-thirty, even before India had let herself begin to hope. She was brisk, square, middle-aged. Det carried her suitcase into what had been India's room, and she changed to a white silk uniform from the smart Liberty print she was wearing. Her gray hair was cut short and waved tightly to her head. Her brown eyes were like agate marbles. When she had washed her hands she came back to the sickroom and gave it a practiced appraisal before taking Angela's temperature.

She hardly needed India's faltering explanations. "We sterilize the sheets in the wash boiler at the back door."

Vina looked up absently from the chart. "What do you use to sterilize the bath water?"

"There's a big pail in the bathroom and a large jar of chlorine bleach."

India had thought she was beyond feeling. Now suddenly, irrationally, she was feeling too much. Doubts of this cool impersonal woman assailed her. There were a thousand questions that needed answers before she surrendered Angela to a stranger.

Does this mean anything to you? she wanted to ask. *Or are you one of those nurses to whom a job is good or bad depending on the amount of trouble it causes you? Will you burn something of yourself on the altar of Angela's tiny chance for life, or do you hoard yourself for yourself? O God, I'm so afraid of parsimonious people! Make this woman care what happens to Angela!*

India offered a few more explanations, but Vina was impatient of them, as if she knew where to find what she wanted under all circumstances. India felt no response to her unspoken pleading, and her spirits sagged. She tried to prop them up by chiding herself.

Vina has never seen Angela before—weariness has made me unreasonable—nursing is her life—she knows all the holds, all the dodges, all the tricks—and that's what matters now—to her Angela is THE PATIENT—and if she's no more she's no less—this professionalism is what we need—emotion like mine is a handicap—I know this—but I want more—I want an ally in the war, not a mercenary.

Vina's eyes were on her with something of comprehension shining through the brown glass surface. "You need sleep. Go along now."

"I am tired."

"Go right to bed. I'll be all right here."

"You'll call me if there's a change for the worse?"

"I will, of course."

It was evening when India awoke. The air in her mosquito net was thick and gray. As she lay with her eyes half-closed her mind was blank until memory pricked her consciousness. Then all the nerves along the back of her neck tightened, and she started up quickly. She found Vina sitting on the railing of the narrow veranda smoking a cigarette.

"Pretty things, aren't they?" she asked, gesturing toward the lotus. "Someone told me they close at night. I've been watching to see."

"How is she?"

Vina turned and studied her keenly, as if aware for the first time of India's feeling for *THE PATIENT*. "Her temperature came up another degree. The doctor's been back twice. She's still under morphine."

India wanted to ask more, but did not. Vina Stout would probably have returned an easy *Yes* to the question gnawing at her heart. And besides, it seemed less dangerous immured there than set free in words. She had the illogical conviction that, once released, it would feed upon them all with a power for evil it did not yet possess.

So she sat quietly on the railing and watched the shadows deepen until they closed in around the cottage. Imperceptibly the lotus had closed. Lights showed one after another in Jasmine Hall.

Vina got up and went into Angela's room, where India could hear her walking about with quick, sure movements. She had turned on a night light. Angela groaned a little and mumbled. Vina spoke firmly. The fireflies came on along the shrubs bordering the canal like tiny electric candles blinking together on a series of Christmas trees. A giant bullfrog croaked at the edge of the water.

As India sat there Dr. Crane came over the bridge, grumbling at her. "You ought to have a light on this damned thing. I don't know why all your children haven't drowned."

The doctor's acrid criticisms usually prodded India to explanation, but tonight she merely recorded his words with a mild surprise that there had been no serious accidents in these ten years, in spite of the fact that the bridge had neither lights nor railing.

The doctor went into the cottage, and she heard his lowered voice in conversation with Vina. Like the coolness of the evening wind against her face had come the knowledge that these two were good. They would do all that could be done for Angela in response to the only impulsion that mattered—because they were people who permitted themselves no carelessness or indifference, but fought illness with a wary skill that squandered little on emotion. Whether or not Angela herself meant anything to them was irrelevant. India said that over to herself with a profound feeling of discovery.

Presently they came out to her. In the peace of her new understanding she asked them nothing. She would harry them no more with her fears. Dr. Crane reached out suddenly and tipped her chin up so that the faint light from Angela's window could fall across her face.

"Sleep any today?"

"All day."

"Go back to bed. There's been no more hemorrhaging, and there's no evidence of perforation."

India turned to Vina. "You'll call me if——"

The doctor propelled her toward the bridge. "Vina will call you *if*, but there isn't going to be any *if*. Go on now."

India obeyed, forgetting that she had eaten nothing since morning. She sank at once into a pit of insensibility that the evening sounds of Jasmine Hall could not disturb.

Long before her craving for sleep was satisfied hunger dragged her back toward sensibility. She seemed to come up through layer on layer of consciousness as limitless as infinity, black first, dark gray, then gray, lighter gray, and finally awareness. For the moment she had no feeling of place or past events and wondered resentfully what had aroused her. Then she felt the drawing of her stomach.

The night was very still. A mosquito buzzed drunkenly around inside the net, coming close to her and then droning off to the far end of the bed. Torpor immobilized her limbs, and sleep was closing in once more, when she heard from the dim reaches of her consciousness the echo of her name.

She lurched upward to a sitting position and waited. There was no sound. With her flashlight she picked out the face of her watch. It was four o'clock. The conviction that something was wrong grew. Had Vina called her? She listened intently. There was no sound. Or was it Angela? *Has she regained consciousness at the end? And is she calling for me?*

India tore aside the net and snatched an old blue kimono. Without stopping to find her slippers she started quickly through the silent house. To reach the stairs on the back veranda she had to open the bolts on one of the double doors at the choir end of the church. The sound reverberated through the empty room but seemed no more thunderous than the pounding of her heart. She hurried down the stairs, oblivious of scorpions and snakes.

Her bare feet made no sound on the bridge. Every hinge of the cottage had been oiled early in Angela's illness, and she entered without noise. She could hear Vina Stout's regular breathing in the next room, punctuated by a tooting little snore, and knew a moment's anger that Vina could sleep on this crucial night.

A dim light burned on a stand behind the bed, which stood in the middle of the room. Angela lay as before, inert, unmoving. Her hands were at her sides, palms up. Her eyes were half-open and unseeing. As India watched she could see quick, shallow breathing lift and lower the sheet. Her own swiftly drawn breath of relief was so loud she thought it would wake Vina, but there was nothing except after a minute another truncated snore. India's sense of the nearness of death had not abated. She knelt beside the bed and began to pray, feeling its presence behind her in the room, relentless, impassive, unhurried, sure.

"*Our Father which art in heaven* . . . in Thy infinite grace spare this young girl who is so close to the end of life without having known anything of its fullness. Thou who hast made the helpless of the world Thine own have mercy upon her and heal her. O Lord, I thank Thee for the help that medicine has given. Now the issue has moved into the no man's land of the soul where only Thou canst reach. Gracious and omnipotent Father, pity her and heal her of this mortal illness and of that other illness which has consumed her spirit. Guide us whose human hands minister to her need that we may proceed in Thy wisdom and with Thy power . . ."

The prayer gaining momentum flowed out of the dimly lit room and up toward the sky, where already the morning star shone unobserved. India lost all consciousness of time in the rise and fall of her petition. When she was through her heart was at rest. She leaned away from the bed.

Vina was standing a few feet behind her, making no move to interrupt her until she had finished. India stood up, and Vina lifted the net to put a thermometer into Angela's mouth. They waited together quietly. Outside, high in one of the rain trees, a bulbul began to sing with assertive cheerfulness, and his song announced that the dawn earthbound people could not see was visible to him. Presently Vina withdrew the thermometer and bent to the light.

"Ninety-eight," she said.

They went out to the veranda and sat side by side on the railing. A cock in the Siamese village behind them crowed sleepily. The gong at Wat Tepsirindra began an insistent tolling that would arouse the monks to their morning devotions. In a little while they would be passing on Bamrung Muang Road with their yellow robes drawn tightly to their bodies and their begging bowls held before them.

Vina lit a cigarette. "You believe in prayer, don't you?"

"Yes."

"So do I." She puffed abstractedly. There was no breeze. As she inhaled and exhaled smoke rose in the graying air and hovered around her head. "Do you believe she'll live because you prayed she would?"

"I couldn't know that, could I?"

"But when you pray do you feel that God hears you?"

"I have a sense of communion. I'm not always sure He will return a *Yes*."

"Are you ever sure?"

"Sometimes."

"But this time you're not?"

"No. I want her to get well, and it's hard to pray *Thy will be done*."

"I think she will," Vina said. They sat quietly until she had finished her cigarette. "Let's get ourselves some coffee, shall we?"

CHAPTER 19

WHEN DR. CRANE CAME IN LATER ANGELA'S TEMPERATURE HAD risen another degree. By night it had passed a hundred, and there was no longer any doubt that the crisis was over.

"So you have your answer," Vina said as she finished telling India the news. "That was quite a prayer."

"It's too soon to be sure."

"Well, I'm sure."

India's spirits soared. She tried to rein them in, but in spite of her they mounted higher and higher like a child's balloon escaped from its string. The next morning Angela drank half a cup of milk without protest. The day after, she ate her breakfast egg as if she were hungry. On the morning of the third day, when India went in to see her, intelligence was in her eyes. She lay weak and spent, but she smiled. It was different from any smile India had seen on her face. It wavered, but there were no reservations in it.

India returned to her office in the big house, free of concern for the first time. She was tired, but she gritted her teeth and attacked the accounts and the most urgent of her correspondence. As she worked she picked up again the many strands from which life at Jasmine Hall was woven. Dulcie was still giving Darun trouble. She insisted that her commission from India canceled any obligation to her regular classes in English and sewing, and she had indulged in an orgy of wandering around the city.

There was an epidemic of mumps in the second grade, and a curious disease had appeared in the fourth. It had affected the hair of several children, causing nodules to appear along the individual filaments so that the hair could not be combed. There was no cure but shaving, and three little girls in that grade were now completely bald.

The most startling development had not been reported to India at all. As she was working she heard a baby cry. The sound persisted until she realized that it was closer than the shops, somewhere in the house.

Ploy was dusting the office with languid thrusts of a large cloth. Her broad lackluster face was framed in a bristling bob. She was growing her hair in imitation of the Bible school girls.

"Where's the baby, Ploy?" India asked her.

"In Kru Darun's room, *kha*."

"Whose baby is it?"

It had occurred to India that one of the teachers must have brought her youngest child to school. This had to be permitted under certain conditions, but it always made trouble.

"It doesn't belong to anyone, *kha*," Ploy answered indifferently.

"Babies always belong to someone," India reproved her.

"Well, to the head teacher then," the girl said with laconic impertinence.

"What!"

Having gone as far as she dared in evasion, Ploy answered fully. "Someone threw it away on the rubbish heap by the canal, and Kru Darun found it."

Darun confirmed the story. The watchman had heard a baby's faint cry in the night about a week before. He had called Darun, and together they had hunted with flashlights until they found a newborn child wrapped in newspaper. In spite of his experience the baby was strong and well. Darun had named him David.

"Why didn't you tell me?" India asked.

"It was when the Mem Thewada was very ill."

India caught the Siamese designation for Angela with interest— *Mem Thewada*—the angel lady. All foreigners were given such designations, usually uncomplimentary. India had never succeeded in learning her own, although she knew that Grace was *The Maharaja*.

"What are we going to do with him?" India asked. "Perhaps the Maternity Home will take him until we can find someone to adopt him."

Darun's face set. "I'm going to adopt him myself."

There was a stubborn finality about her mouth that defied India to take the child from her.

India thought of her refusal to let Darun go to Petchaburi. She must walk softly. "Who's taking care of him?" she asked, postponing argument.

"I've hired a nurse."

While India was considering the ramifications of this unexpected happening a child screamed, not the baby, but an older child outraged by pain. Both of them jumped to their feet, and by the time it came again they were running, for the sound was laced with agony.

Darun was in the lead when they entered the third *pratome*, from which the screaming came. There was a taut and frightened silence over the thirty children cowering in their seats. Kru Sawai stood behind her desk, clutching the edges of it with stiff fingers. Her ashen face was so distorted that India first thought she was having an epileptic seizure, then knew a chilling conjecture that she had gone insane. Her bloodless lips were drawn back from her teeth, and her eyes were rolled up into her head. Their shining whites gave her a crazed look that halted India and Darun just inside the door.

Sawai was ordinarily an inconspicuous girl, small-featured, plain, not very able, who brought her disciplinary problems to Darun. The one unusual thing in her appearance was her teeth, which had been filed along the edges and rimmed with gold in a pathetic bid for beauty.

The screams subsided into sobbing through which the note of pain was authentic. A little girl at the front of the room, with her hands covering her face, was crying between sobs, "I can't, I can't, I can't." It was Chawee, the same child who had been condemned to go on all fours as punishment for calling her teacher a dog. It was obvious that she was being punished again, and now they saw how. A box of thumbtacks had been scattered on the floor, and Chawee was being forced to walk across them in her bare feet.

"Stop this at once!" India's voice was peremptory, although the words were superfluous.

Chawee had not moved since they entered the room. Now she backed toward the wall, screaming again as she stepped on a tack. Her feet left a row of small bloody marks. A little boy in a front seat whimpered and wet on the floor.

"What's the explanation of this?" India demanded in outrage, deliberately ignoring the tenet of Siamese school etiquette that said no teacher was to be humiliated before her pupils.

The children's eyes were large with fright. No one answered, neither Kru Sawai nor any of the children. The teacher stood motionless, still clutching her desk. She made no sign that she had heard or even that she knew anyone had come into the room. India wanted to rush at her and shake her, but she did not. There was a strong prejudice among the Siamese against violation of the person. So she waited, as did Darun and the children, for the catalepsy to pass. Minutes dragged by. The school, which had been deathly still, listening, resumed its normal life. A welter of confused sounds walled in the silent third grade.

Slowly Kru Sawai's lips came down over her teeth, and her

mouth closed. The lids of her eyes lowered themselves. Her body heaved forward slightly, and her hands relaxed their hold on the desk. Something of the shuddering aversion in the room abated. Slowly, as in a trance, Kru Sawai began to pull out the drawers of her desk and empty the contents.

Chawee's crying had ended and she, too, was watching, pressed against the front wall out of the teacher's line of vision.

India shook herself free of the hypnosis that immobilized the room. "Kru, I demand to know why you were punishing Chawee in this way."

The teacher went on emptying her desk, as if no sound had penetrated her ears. A muscle twitched in her cheek, and the movement of her hands seemed uncertain as she gathered things into her purse. She did not shut the drawers of the desk or replace the jumble of things, some of them her own, on its top. Without a glance at anyone she walked across the room toward the door.

India stepped in front of her. "Where are you going, Kru?"

Sawai looked through India almost dreamily. There was a vacant moment, as if the words took a long time to pass from India to Sawai. Then a single word came from her.

"Home," she said. So unadorned with *cha* or *kha*, it was shockingly bare.

Sawai stood listening to it fill the room and then merge into the strained silence of the children. When it was gone she roused and, moving like an automaton, walked around India, through the door, and out onto the veranda.

India followed her. "You mustn't abandon your class, Kru. Come upstairs, and I'll give you a cup of tea."

The girl stood at the head of the steps, waiting for India to finish. It was not so much that the words spoken to her conveyed significance as that their sound had power to halt her forward motion.

"We all know that Chawee is a difficult child," India persisted. "Please tell me what happened."

"I can't."

"Will you tell Kru Darun?"

"I can't."

"Please come upstairs and let me get you some tea."

"I can't. I can't." Her hysteria began to mount again. "I've talked to Chawee! I've kept her after school! I've sent her to the head teacher! I've tried everything, and now this happened! I'm going home."

"Try to tell me how it happened."

The moment of hysteria passed. Sawai began to sink into lethargy. Instead of answering she repeated as to herself and with something of wonder, "I've tried everything, and now this happened."

The words and the manner in which they were spoken denied responsibility for what she had done. They said that she had been the unwitting agent of an evil force larger than herself. It was her karma. It had taken possession of her. She was not at fault. It was inevitable. India's concern and indignation did not impinge upon the circle of her thoughts. They were faraway things belonging to another orbit.

India admitted defeat. She had encountered this fatalism before in Siamese and knew it unanswerable. Sawai was disassociated from her sadism now, as if agent and deed had existed separately and crossed paths only by unfortunate chance, which eliminated all reason for guilt. The girl moved down the steps without speaking further.

"Come back tomorrow, Kru, and we'll talk it over," India said to her retreating back, knowing the words futile as she spoke them.

The teacher walked across the yard toward the gate with the disjointed movements of a walking doll. She had taught at Jasmine Hall more than five years, but India, watching her go, knew that she would not see Sawai again.

The next afternoon, working in the school office, India looked up in surprise to see Mr. Denniscort smiling down at her. He was followed by a Chinese boy with a large basket.

"It's not a picnic," he said, "so stop looking greedy."

"Do I look greedy?"

"As if you were waiting to snatch the biggest banana. Where shall Lai put these things?"

"Upstairs, I think."

They climbed to the mook while Mr. Denniscort asked about Angela. He took the napkin from the basket with a flourish.

"The manager at the B.M.C. helped me pick the things out," he explained. "I bought a leg of lamb for broth."

India melted with suppressed laughter. "Goodness!" she said weakly, thinking of the extravagance of lamb from Australia at five or six dollars for broth!

"And here's lettuce and celery. It came from San Francisco, so it's perfectly safe. The manager said if you'd wrap it in a damp cloth and keep it in the refrigerator it would stay crisp a week." India felt her amusement tempered with awe. She had seen neither lettuce nor celery in three years. "And here's a roast of beef. I'll allow you and Vina Stout a slice or two from this, if you like."

There were apples from Washington State, the cost of which India computed at fifteen cents apiece, lemons from California at twenty, and big navel oranges whose price she could not even guess. There was fresh butter from Australia, tinned soup from England, and cocoa from Holland. Mr. Denniscort set the last tin down and smiled at her.

"It's the most beautiful bouquet I ever saw," India said, "and exactly what we need to tempt Angela's appetite."

He was pleased by her praise, pleased and a little amused. His eyes were laughing at her for some reason she could not guess. Since only the moment before it had been she who was amused by his naïveté in the matter of the lamb, his laughter disconcerted her. It gave her the uncertain feeling of a child in the presence of a too-clever adult. She had an impulse to ask him what she had said that was funny, but doubted that he would tell her. She asked instead, "Did Dulcie Kane ever report on what she did with your fifty ticals?"

"She shouldn't have told on me."

"I guessed."

He looked a little rueful. "I suppose I shouldn't have done it, but she kept saying that she needed her father's money for charity, some 'worthy cause' that she was interested in, and I gave her a little to soften her disappointment. I hope she used it on herself."

"There's part of her 'worthy cause' peeking at you from under my bedroom door."

He looked quickly and saw Ploy scrabble backward out of sight. They both laughed.

"Dulcie wants to start an orphanage, and she used your money to bring three orphans from Ayuthia. The other two are in school, one stupid, one bright, and this one is my maid. She's also stupid, I may as well add. Dulcie's sense of duty was satisfied by getting them here. She's left the rest to us."

"Three for fifty ticals!" Mr. Denniscort exclaimed. "Trouble comes cheap in this country. I thought she'd buy herself a hat. I'll be more discreet next time. I'm sorry I did that to you." He stood up. "Incidentally, I'm optimistic about getting her money. If I succeed, it won't be long before she can take her orphans elsewhere."

"I don't think I'll count on it."

"No, don't. And let me know what I can do for Angela. If she needs help in collecting her share of her husband's estate, let me know."

Vina cut the leg of lamb in half. "If we had an electric refrigerator we could keep it all for her, but we can't, so we'll roast some of it for ourselves." She was unwilling to trust their share to Plo or Chu. "These cooks ruin good meat. Now I'll rub it with a little garlic and roast it slowly."

Angela's half they boiled. Vina washed the celery tops and put them into the broth with onion and a touch of garlic. It had a delicious and almost forgotten flavor.

Angela was eating ravenously. They collaborated to devise dishes that would please her. Vina was a master of the art of making soft custards. "You have to know the exact point at which to take them off the fire. That's the trick, and you mustn't let the water boil hard."

They were working together in India's kitchen, using the charcoal braziers rather than the small wood stove. "I've gotten to like these things," Vina explained. "What are you going to do with Angela when she gets well, India?"

"I haven't planned that far."

"You ought to begin."

"There's more than her body to get well."

"That's what I'm talking about." Vina poured the custard into cups.

"She told me before that she wanted to stay in Bangkok until Charoon's cremation. I have a feeling the Princess will outwait her on that if she can."

"Isn't there any legal limit on the time you can keep a corpse?" Vina asked.

"None, so far as I know. A hundred days is usual for people of their class, but I know a family that kept a body in the house six years."

"Horrible! Don't let Angela wait, then. She'll never get really well out here. The air's full of moral bacteria." The timbre of Vina's voice had changed. Ordinarily it was a brisk contralto. Now it vibrated with an intensity foreign to it. "The only women who ought to stay out here are women like you with something to do. The rest of us rot."

"I don't see any signs of deterioration in you."

Vina did not answer immediately. She was washing out the custard pan, and when she spoke her voice was tinged with bitterness. "Nevertheless, they're there. You never get over some things, and that's a fact. You think people have forgotten, and then you bump into curiosity in someone's eyes and the old wounds start bleeding. If you go home where people don't know anything about you, and don't care, it's easier. You can forget—a little. But—well—out here you can't."

"Who was he, Vina?"

"You wouldn't know. A Chinese. He deserted me a week before our baby was born. In Shanghai. They took me out of the river. The baby was dead. It was a long time ago." The pain memory had evoked died in her face as if the route she traveled were an old one, the landmarks quickly recognized and left behind. "I stayed on nursing in the hospital. That's where I met Miles. He had dysentery. His wife was dead. He thought I pulled him through. He's older than I." She set the custard cups carefully on a tray.

"I'm sorry, Vina. I didn't know."

"I don't know why I burden you with it except that I want you to send Angela home. The whispers will ripple behind her the rest of her life. I know. They're all bitches out here. At home they'd have to do laundry and wash dishes and cook for their children and clean their houses, and the work would keep them decent, but out here they just sit on their backsides, call *Boy* when they want a cigarette, and rot. I don't want Angela left to their mercies. She's too good for them. Now, India, what about a fluffy omelet for her supper? Do you think the oven is up to it?"

CHAPTER 20

VINA LEFT AT THE END OF TEN DAYS, AND INDIA RESUMED HER nursing. Angela had been eating ravenously, with the result that her skeleton was once more veiled in flesh. She sat up in bed to feed herself and had been promised that she could sit in a chair soon.

India deposited her salary check and shut her eyes to the bills on her desk. They could wait another month.

"Can you manage without me?" Vina asked over coffee as they had a late breakfast together.

Angela was fed, bathed, and asleep, and Vina was dressed to go. India's cook left for market at nine, so they had prepared their own breakfast. Vina had scrambled eggs and made the coffee on her own insistence.

"You're not very good at coffee, India," she said. "I don't know what you do to it, but it always tastes bitter."

"That's true," India agreed. "I'll do the toast and fruit."

They set the table themselves, dispensing with Ploy. It was a dark morning with occasional showers, and the sound of rain on the roof obscured noises from the school. Every so often gusts of wind blew a spray in across the veranda, but they did not lower the moolies. The fresh odor of wet trees mingled pleasantly with the smell of coffee and Vina's cigarette. Below them the garden was a lush and humid green.

"I can manage unless Angela has another relapse."

"She won't. She's convalescent now."

"It's wonderful how the body responds when the crisis is past. I'm so grateful for your help, Vina, I can't find words to express it. And I've enjoyed having you here on my own account."

"I'm not going to Timbuctoo."

India laughed. "That did sound like 'farewell forever,' but then I never go anywhere, so I don't expect people to bother with me. How long have you lived in Bangkok?"

"Two years."

"You see what I mean."

"But we did meet, so we can again. You need to get away from your work once in a while, anyway."

India offered Vina the toast, which she refused. "I have to watch my figure. You're lucky, you know. I'll just have some more black coffee. Can I get you a cup?"

After breakfast India produced her checkbook. "How much do I owe you, Vina?"

The other woman's eyes sparkled with amusement. "Alvin Crane must have told you something, surely."

"He didn't explain the financial arrangements."

"And you really don't know anything about me?"

"All the important things."

"Well, India, one of the less important is that I don't need your money or want it."

"But you must let me pay you for your services."

"Haven't you ever heard of Miles or any of his activities?"

"I've heard his name, I suppose, but the fact is I don't know more than five or six Americans outside the Mission. I haven't time."

"Don't apologize. I like the idea. India, listen! Miles has more money than he and I can spend in ten lifetimes. Put your checkbook away!"

India was confused. She laid the checkbook on the table, still open, and looked at Vina. "Why are you working, then?"

"I'm not, darling, I'm not. Alvin bludgeoned me into helping you."

"Didn't your husband object?"

"He was in Shanghai making another million. He won't be back until next week."

India felt unexpected tears perilously close to the surface. "I don't know how to say this, but, Vina, will you let me buy you something —as a token—of my gratitude?"

"Definitely not!" Vina spoke sharply, her voice roughened, but not with anger. "You know why I did it, and that's enough. Do you think God gave you a monopoly on kindness? Look, these things aren't decent if you talk about them. Let's talk about having dinner together some night next week. I'll make a lemon cream pie, and damn the calories!"

The first few days after Vina left Angela slept most of the time. During the second week she was awake for longer periods. All kinds of food tasted good to her, milk, eggs, custard, soup, farina, cocoa.

Anne Howard brought her a mold of ice cream in the shape of a rabbit, and she was charmed with it. Her body was filling out, and her color had improved. She looked fragile still, and her hair was dull, but a suggestion of Dresden beauty had returned.

There was a spiritual change also. In some indefinable way Angela had made peace with herself. The change showed in her eyes, which looked out at the world clearly. India speculated much about this. Had the defeat of illness been so overwhelming that it encompassed all previous defeats?

Whatever the process, the tide of fever had flushed out with it the debris of the past. Angela was weak but not unhappy, content to be cared for like a child. She was like a child also in her preoccupation with the present. She spoke neither of what had been nor of the future, but was engrossed with all the variegated details that comprised the immediate. She seemed to be rediscovering the taste, the feel, the smell of life.

Flowers entranced her. Det brought her a fresh lotus every morning, which India placed in a green glass bowl beside her bed. Angela found each one a fresh revelation of beauty. The school children sent her saucers of jasmine buds, and Kru Tawin appeared shyly at the door with a bouquet of roses. They engaged Angela's interest for most of a morning.

"Did you know you could actually see a rosebud open?" she asked India.

The bamboo outside her window gave her constant pleasure. She called India one afternoon to watch the lashing of the slender branches in a storm.

"Doesn't it seem to be moving to the 'Danse Macabre'?" she asked.

When it was clear, the play of sunlight along the leaves and the quivering shadows captivated her. "I see why Chinese artists painted bamboo," she told India. "It has a special quality like no other tree."

After a few days India brought down *The Man of Property* and began to read it to her. Sometimes Angela fell asleep, and India put the marker into the book and went on about other work. When she suggested borrowing something newer from Vina, Angela refused. "No, I like it very much even if I do fall asleep."

After the book was half finished she remarked to India that she felt a kind of sadness in Galsworthy's writing and wondered if he hadn't believed he was recording a way of life that was passing forever.

"I'll find something more amusing," India offered.

"No, it doesn't depress me. I didn't mean that. But there's an odor of decay coming up from the words, don't you think? It reminds me of a windless day in fall when the leaves are burning."

"What are you reading now?" she asked a few mornings later as India sat beside her, thinking her asleep.

"My Bible."

"Read it aloud, please."

So India read the Psalm for the day, a chapter from First Samuel, and one from Luke.

"Do you pray every day too?"

"Whenever I have something to pray about."

"How often is that?"

"Many times a day."

Angela looked at India wonderingly. "Do you kneel every time?"

"Oh no, hardly. I'd never get my work done."

"How do you do it then?"

How did she? The habit was so well established she had difficulty analyzing it for someone else. "I just send my thoughts up. Sometimes in a quick little sentence. Sometimes with a puff like a breath of wind. Not always asking, you know. Sometimes being grateful, and sometimes"—this was the hardest to explain—"sometimes just talking, you might say, talking things over with God. Prayer can be an obbligato to thought, you know."

"I guess I've always taken it for granted that it was presumptuous to bother God with any but important things."

"And which are they?"

Angela smiled with sudden sweetness. "Who knows what will turn out to be important? Is that what you mean? You don't think He minds, then, the little matters of every day? How can He hear them all?"

"I don't know whether there's a celestial switchboard with angels taking the calls or what there is, Angela, but I do believe that He hears us and welcomes our prayers as an earthly father does his children's confidences."

Angela considered this. "I pray when I'm frightened," she concluded, and went on reflectively, "But maybe it's a bad idea to wait until you're drowning to learn to swim." She looked at India, hesitated, and then asked, "Would you mind very much praying aloud?"

India knelt by her chair and began to pray. She was self-conscious at first, but after a little her thoughts carried her forward and she became part of them, not disregarding Angela, but drawing her into the stream of petition, feeling in the girl a groping toward the kind of living faith that sustained herself.

Toward the end of August, Dr. Crane let Angela sit in a chair for the first time. India steadied her as they walked the few steps from the bed. Angela laughed all the way. When she sank into the chair, she examined the altered aspect of her room with surprise.

"It looks smaller," she said.

"Wouldn't you like to see the newspaper?" India asked, but Angela refused.

She recoiled from the outside world and limited her thoughts to Jasmine Hall. Within the confines that began at the high red gate nothing was too inconsequential to interest her. She explored with

questions every detail of the school's history and ponderous operation.

"Tell me how you began your work here," she would ask when
India had a moment of leisure. And another day, "Tell me about
Miss Cole and Wang Lang."

India ransacked her memory for details to satisfy Angela's curiosity and told the story as she had heard it and observed it.

"So you see," she concluded after an hour, "both Wattana and
Jasmine Hall are descendants of Wang Lang, but we're the poor
relation."

"Do they turn up their noses at you?"

"Maybe a little."

Satisfied on that score, she began to ask about the people who
lived and worked at the school. "What's Kru Darun's story?" she
wanted to know, and later, "What's Miss Kane's story?" or, "Tell me
again about the day the orphans arrived," or, "Tell me more about
Kru Tawin."

One morning as India picked up *The Man of Property* she asked
about Mani, and India laid down the book in favor of a slightly
expurgated version of the living tale. Each of the girls in the Bible
school and each small boarder interested her. How was Sawang's
love affair coming? What would Bua Kham do after graduation?

One morning as India gave her a bath she wanted to know:
"What's the name of the big woman with chestnut hair who doesn't
like me? I met so many people those first weeks I can't remember."

"Do you mean Grace Rutherford? She's principal of Wattana.
Why do you say she doesn't like you?"

"She made it perfectly clear."

India laughed. "You probably felt the crosscurrents of our present
quarrel. Grace disapproves of much that I do at Jasmine Hall." A
faint look of distress showed on Angela's face. "She was angry with
me before you came for letting Mani stay here," India explained.

"She doesn't like my being here either, then. But isn't that a
trivial reason for a quarrel between friends? After all, it's your
school."

"Only an occasion, really. Grace thinks I dissipate my energies."

"You don't run things as she would, I suppose."

"No, I consider myself a better judge of people and usually ignore her advice."

"She doesn't look as if she'd like that. What happens next?"

"Oh, she just leaves me alone for a while."

Angela sensed an evasion basic to herself. "She's a very determined-looking woman. Doesn't she ever carry the matter to the bishop?"

"We don't have a bishop, only an Executive Committee chosen from the Mission. Grace is a member, incidentally."

"Who are they responsible to?"

"There's a Board in New York over all the Missions. The Committee corresponds with them, and they send out a delegation once in a while, as they're doing this fall. Otherwise they leave us pretty much to ourselves."

Angela still tried to catch in the net of words some significance that eluded her. "Doesn't she ever take your quarrels with her to the Executive Committee?"

"Oh no, Grace isn't vindictive. She's one of my oldest friends, in spite of the fact that we often disagree."

"I hope my being here isn't going to make trouble," Angela said doubtfully.

India disclaimed this possibility. "The trouble between Grace and me, if it deserves that name, is inherent in ourselves. It flares up every year or so, and then it's over until the next time."

Rather diffidently as the days went on, Angela began to ask questions that concerned India herself, where she had grown up, where she had gone to school, what her childish interests had been. Like her other questions, it seemed more than a device to fill empty hours. She was piecing together the pattern of Jasmine Hall to satisfy some need within herself.

India, who rarely thought about her childhood, obligingly brought out of her memory incidents she had not called to mind in years. What had she worn to dancing school? Well, high-buttoned shoes, of course, and a red velvet dress with a lace collar, and an ermine coat her father had given her. How foolish for a child of ten to have an ermine coat, but her father had been like that.

Had she been an only child? Yes. Her one brother died in infancy. Was her mother pretty? Very beautiful and very gay, the despair of her plainer daughter. Everyone had loved her mother. She always remembered her as surrounded by people. When her father made money they gave dinner parties for twenty or more. She could see her mother now, dressed in satins and velvets and jewels. Then, when things went badly, the jewels disappeared, and there were small suppers, but people seemed to come just the same.

What had her father been like? A big man who tumbled and teased her and bought her expensive gifts. Once she had had a doll from Paris with a trunkful of clothes, and another time he had given her a dollhouse like a mansion, furnished throughout, with a family of dolls to live in it. He had made and lost several fortunes on the grain exchange. The family was always up or down. Perhaps that was why she never worried about money.

Had she been a good child? Not too difficult, except for her habit of bringing home all the cats and dogs in the neighborhood. The only time she remembered causing a scandal was when the boy sitting behind her in school dipped the ends of her curls into his inkwell. The ink had dripped onto her favorite dress of gray nun's veiling with a white embroidered collar that her mother had brought her from New York. She had stood up and hit him over the head with her geography until the teacher pulled her away. Then she had wept for the dress until the school sent her home. Ralph, that was his name. A horrid boy! He'd grown up to be president of a large bank in Chicago.

Had her family objected when she decided to become a missionary? Not really objected. They were a religious family. Her mother was an Episcopalian and her father a Presbyterian. She thought they were more troubled when she told them that she had broken her engagement to the boy who had been her constant companion since she was fifteen. But they had always let her have her own way. They hadn't been happy about her determination to go to college either, but they had yielded, and in the end she thought they understood.

"And so you never married?"

"And so I never married." India repeated the words noncommittally.

Angela felt the closing of a door and changed the subject. "How did you happen to choose Siam?"

"When I was a junior in college I heard Dr. Eugene Dunlap speak at chapel. He'd been a missionary in Siam since shortly after the Civil War. He was a very great and simple man, and what he said impressed me."

"There must have been more to it than that."

"Yes, of course there was. I'd always had a longing to be of use, but that isn't the whole story either. My religious experience had deepened in college until sharing it seemed the most important thing in life."

Angela pondered this for a moment. "Isn't it almost impertinent to try to win other races to our religion?"

"Not unless you believe that truth and beauty have national boundaries."

"But what is truth?"

India looked at her strangely, hearing Pilate's question on her lips, then answered by quotation: *"Jesus saith unto him, I am the way, the truth, and the life: no man cometh unto the Father, but by me."*

"You believe Christianity true, then, and all other religions false?"

"Perhaps not so much false as shadows, and God the substance."

Then feeling the explanation inadequate, India went on, after a search for words: "I suppose the basic problem in all life is the problem of good and evil. The knowledge of what constitutes good and what constitutes evil is a universal possession, at least in some degree. It isn't the knowing that's difficult, it's the doing. *For the good that I would I do not: but the evil which I would not, that I do.* We of the Christian communion believe that the conflict can be resolved only when man is reconciled to God through Christ. It's the possibility of reconciliation and the resulting power for good that we try to share with all mankind, not just the knowledge of what is good and what is evil. Put that way, does it still seem an impertinence?"

"No," Angela said slowly, but India could not be sure whether she spoke from conviction or courtesy. "But how can you prove anything like that to people who don't believe in God?"

"How many things can be proved, outside of mathematical equations and some physical facts? I can testify to my own experience of the power of God in the human heart. I wouldn't try to do more. Most people believe in a Supreme Being anyway."

Angela hesitated. "What about modern science and the Bible?"

"Well, what about it?"

"Doesn't it disprove the Old Testament stories like the creation?"

"That can be argued, but it's not a particularly profitable argument. So I'll beg the question and answer with the words of—wasn't it Mark Twain?—who said: It isn't the parts of the Bible I can't understand that trouble me, but the parts I understand too well. *Love thy neighbor as thyself. Pray for them which despitefully use you, and persecute you. Forgive us our trespasses, As we forgive those who trespass against us.*"

"Yes, but look at the way some Christians behave."

"Granted. Those commands are often honored in the breach, and yet outside of the Christian church where do you find the stubborn conviction that the poor, the sick, the filthy, and the leper are worthy of reverence in the form of care because man was made in the image of God? Hospitals, schools, all the attempts of our imperfect civilization to solve the problems of the individual come out of the concept of man's importance as something more than an animal. For if God so loved the world that He sent His only begotten Son into the world for us, then we must be worth something in His sight. And by that measure we're worth something to men who follow His teachings. Strip us of this valuation and what is left? Besides, not all men fail to live up to the standards of their faith. I know many whom I honor for their service to mankind, and their lives are a testimony to me of the truth of what they believe."

It was Angela who spoke next, and the simplicity of her words silenced India.

"As yours is to me," she said.

CHAPTER 21

WHEN SCHOOL CLOSED FOR THE FIRST TERM ON SEPTEMBER 10, Angela was strong enough to go with India to Nong Khae. This was a seaside resort five hours by train south of Bangkok, where the Mission had several cottages. India felt sure that salt air and a change would complete the cure. The rainy season was not over, but she decided to take a chance that the number of sunny days would be sufficient to make the trip worth while.

She invited Darun to accompany them, but Darun had made plans to spend her vacation in Chiengmai, leaving David at the Maternity Home. The party included five of the Bible school girls, all the small boarders, three servants, and Sanu, the most tractable of the orphans. Dulcie was left with Ploy and Dang, the remaining servants, and a list of things that she was to do or supervise during the two weeks they were to be gone.

There was little food to be bought at Nong Khae except fish, so the servants were busy for several days collecting provisions. A sack of rice was shipped ahead with Det.

India bought second-class tickets for herself and Angela, third-class tickets for the children and servants. The third-class benches were too crowded and hard for Angela after her illness. There were dozens of frail baskets called *chalom* filled with fruit, boxes, bales, and packages to be stacked around them in the train, even a few suitcases. When it was all in, no one could move more than a few inches.

The train was a local, stopping at many country stations where the children bargained for rice baked in lengths of bamboo, fruit, and sweetmeats. At Petchaburi the servants bought a chalom of palm sugar in cakes, for which the town was famous, and quantities of a thin wafer that kept for weeks and could be baked over the coals to a delicious crispness.

It was one-thirty before they reached the Nong Khae stop, where

Det met them. By four they had settled themselves into a large double cottage, and the children under Doe's supervision were in the water. The beach in front of the cottage was wide and white, and beyond it the blue of the gulf stretched off limitlessly toward the east.

Angela was very tired from the trip. Her cot was set on the front veranda, and she lay there with the salt wind blowing over her. Two of the children brought her a handful of sea shells, which she turned over and over in her hands as they knelt beside her.

After a few days she was able to go down to the sand for an hour in the early morning and another in the late afternoon. By nine o'clock the sun was so hot that India would not let her stay in it. The rest of the day she dozed on her bed or read the books they had brought with them. The children formed the habit of bringing her the curious things they found, and she talked with them in her halting Siamese. India often heard their soft little voices busy about her.

One morning she announced her intention of beginning a dress for India. She measured and cut and fitted, and then sewed the long seams on a portable machine they had brought with them, while one of the children turned the crank. India, after a first protest, had not objected.

"Haven't you anything to sew?" Angela had asked when they were getting ready for the trip. "I don't want to read all the time."

India had hunted through her drawers for lengths of material that had been given her at Christmas by pupils and friends, and Angela selected three. She refused to sew for herself. "I'm going to make you two silk prints, and then I'll figure out how to get a dress from that piece of blue grass linen."

"I guess I do need them," India said doubtfully.

"You certainly do," Angela answered, and they both laughed at her disdaining of pretense.

It was one afternoon as they lay on the beach with the children frolicking around them that Angela began for the first time to talk about herself. The sky was a hot blue, and the combers were rolling in topped with ridges of foam. Several little girls with their black hair in strings and their wet sarongs flapping about them were running back and forth chasing crayfish. Hundreds of crayfish had made a lacy pattern of tracks on the wet sand near the water's edge, but no matter how quickly the little girls darted the crayfish were always quicker. With a shriek one of them would dive toward a cautious claw emerging from a hole, and the claw would be withdrawn.

The doctor did not allow Angela to go into the water, but she enjoyed the beach and sometimes walked along the edge where the tide lapped her bare toes. Her shoulders were red from the sun and her nose was peeling. Even her long slender legs were tinted with color. She had been playing with the little girls for an hour until she was tired.

India lay on a blanket with an umbrella over her head, dozing in the warmth and listening to the beat of the waves. Their steady pulsing was soporific and slow. High overhead she could hear the occasional shrilling of gulls. A silken wind wrapped her around like a sheet. Bangkok seemed a long way off, the clattering streets, the pressing people, the weariness and tension.

After a while Angela came and stretched herself on the blanket. India blinked, then shut her eyes again, drowsy and relaxed. They lay for perhaps half an hour soaking in the sun and air. The children, with the innate courtesy of Siamese, were careful not to play too close.

India was almost asleep when Angela spoke. "Do mixed marriages ever work, India?"

The older woman did not open her eyes, but she was instantly alert, groping through the barriers of age and differing experience, past her own instinct to protect by equivocation, toward the need that prompted the question. "O Lord," she prayed, "help her to find healing in comprehension." She had the illusion that Angela's spirit stood like a doe at the edge of a dim wood, on the point of emerging, yet ready to draw back.

When India spoke it was slowly, and her voice was quiet. Yet the words she chose were frank, because she could offer Angela nothing less than honesty.

"Not very often, Angela," she said. "I think perhaps they ask too much of the human heart."

She could detect neither falseness in her words nor too great emotion in her voice, but she waited apprehensively, afraid that her own unease might have communicated itself to the girl and repelled this first timid advance. It was a relief to hear Angela speak in her natural voice, a little diffident, a little hesitant, but not retreating.

"Why do you say they ask too much?"

"They're human associations, Angela, so they don't occur in a void, but in a society that's hostile to them. It's that hostility which proves the one thing too much."

India stopped to arrange her thoughts and then went on.

"Any association of two people involves the sacrifice of self by one or both in hundreds of specific instances, and marriage more than most. But the heart is a wild free thing, Angela. It can be prodigal and parsimonious by turns. Look at the husbands and wives who quarrel about tooth-paste tubes or towels left on the bathroom floor. It takes flexibility as well as love to make a marriage work. When there are dissimilarities of background the number of adjustments increases. All of us act on a code that's so much a part of us we can't define it. To someone with another code it may seem lacking in any sort of logic except selfishness."

India paused, then resumed.

"That makes enough of a problem, but in a mixed marriage it doesn't end there. Society enters the lists against the marriage. The young couple have to contend with disapproval and open criticism. Dissimilarities become harder to reconcile, and betrayal easier with the conflict of loyalties. Then hurt pride and resentment come along to finish the wrecking."

"We were happy for a while."

"I'm glad you have that to remember."

"I'd like to tell you about it, if you don't mind."

"Of course I don't mind."

India still lay with her head pillowed in her arms and her eyes closed. Angela sat up and hugged her knees.

"What you say about racial differences and hurt pride is true, but it's not the whole truth. We were happy until we came here, and I believe we'd have gone on being happy if we hadn't come. I didn't have any near relatives to object to my marriage, and we had our own friends. Maybe young people are more tolerant, I don't know. It seems to me, looking back, that it didn't matter to any of them that Jerry had been born a Siamese. They liked him because he was a nice person. He never even used his title, you know."

She stopped abruptly. India was silent, leaving the way open for Angela to continue or not as she pleased. After a while the girl's voice began again, hesitantly now.

Jerry and she had met during her senior year at the university. She was very much alone that year for the first time in her life. Perhaps that had something to do with the way things turned out.

She had been an only child. Her mother died when she was two, and she was raised by her father's sister. Aunt Susan's own sons were grown and her husband dead. Angela had adored her father, a tall, gray, withdrawn man, already fifty years old when she was born. She was the only person with whom he ever unbent.

It was Aunt Susan, though, who was the core of her childhood. Aunt Susan was gay and companionable. Angela remembered the big house as always full of sunshine. Aunt Susan started her on music lessons when she was five, sat with her while she practiced, took her to dancing school, gave her birthday parties, marvelous parties with a magician to entertain the guests and limitless supplies of ice cream. Aunt Susan installed a sandbox, teeterboard, and swings in the back yard. All the neighborhood children played there, running into the kitchen for cookies and lemonade.

Aunt Susan had kept a cook and maid, and a butler who doubled as chauffeur, the same three as far back as she could remember. Like her father and aunt, they had revolved around Angela. No doubt she had been a spoiled little girl. At any rate, her childhood had been full of happiness, and her adolescence also. When she outgrew the sandbox and swings, Aunt Susan had a tennis court built, and lemonade gave way to cokes in the refrigerator. There were always chicken and ham sandwiches, and cookies in a big jar for anyone who was hungry. If she had ever been unhappy for more than a day or an hour, memory had dropped those times out.

Then within the period of a year everything changed. Her home was in Lake Forest, and she entered Northwestern to be near it. During her junior year Aunt Susan died very suddenly. She was seventy-six at the time, but she had seemed to be in perfect health. It broke up their home. Her father took an apartment in Evanston. A few months later a building and loan company of which he was president failed. There were veiled suggestions in the newspapers that dishonest management was responsible.

Her father had tried to lessen her distress by telling her that in affairs of this kind there was always a shout of fraud from people who had lost money, and that the courts would vindicate his integrity. Nevertheless, what had happened worried him, and he became more than ever withdrawn and gray. Two days before the end of the school year he died of a heart attack.

She turned over his insurance and other assets to his creditors, keeping only her piano and car, some jewels she had inherited from her mother, and the pearls her father had given her on her eighteenth birthday. That summer she taught in a girls' camp, and the next fall transferred to the University of Chicago. She decided to prepare herself to teach public school music. She had had a thousand dollars in her checking account, but it was frightening the way money disappeared. Her voice lessons were fifteen dollars an hour, and her piano lessons twenty. She sold her car, but she couldn't sell the few things that had come to her from her mother, nor the pearls.

She came to the conclusion that she could stretch her money far enough to complete her training if she could earn her meals. It wasn't as hard as she had expected. She found a job in a drugstore only three blocks from the rooming house in which she was staying. The work had not seemed humiliating to her. Rather she had been proud of her ingenuity, proud to find herself fighting circumstances as her father would have wished her to fight.

At first she had trouble with boys and men, but it hadn't been too difficult to discourage them. There were several pretty girls at the counter, anyway. That was where she had met Jerry. He came in one night late in February.

"Hello," he had said, smiling at her, but casually, not as if he were interested in her personally. He ordered a sandwich and coffee, and she served him and gave him his check. She was through for the evening, and when she came out of the building he was standing on the corner reading a newspaper under the street light, but not as if he had been waiting for her, although several months later he told her that he had been.

Looking up and seeing her, he said, still sounding casual, "Can I take you anywhere?"

She had hesitated, but she knew he was a university student, and she didn't feel any threat in him. He had a Cadillac convertible with red upholstery, and she had enjoyed the feeling of a big car again. It was one of those false spring days that come sometimes in February, wet underfoot, but clear and almost warm.

"Are you in a hurry?" he asked, and even when he said that it was not as if it mattered much to him, but as if he were naturally amiable—as indeed he had been.

"Not particularly," she had said, and without saying anything else he swung the car out along the Midway to the Drive and went north.

"I like to go up along the lake when the weather's like this," he explained.

He didn't talk to her, and she didn't talk to him. It was peaceful rolling along with the dark water on one side and lights twinkling in the tall buildings on the other. Angela sat there and felt the cool wind on her face and enjoyed watching a boat, with its lights sparkling like a necklace of diamonds, setting out across the lake.

It was two weeks before she saw him again, and then he was at the counter, eating. He smiled at her but made no effort to talk to her. He never tugged at her as some of the others did. There was a quality about him that she liked, something easy and friendly and undemanding. Several times he drove her out along the lake, and then one night, as he was turning around to go down the steps after he'd brought her back to the rooming house, he asked very diffidently whether she'd care to go to a movie with him the next night. It was his look of expecting a rebuff that made her accept. And then, too, it was Friday night, and she was restless and lonely. She had not tried to make friends in the university. She had even avoided her old friends and concentrated on her music and her school work.

Jerry had been studying for his doctorate in education. They had talked about their interests, and a few days later he had come into the drugstore with some concert tickets. The next week he had taken her to dinner at the Blackstone on her night off. It was the best dinner she had eaten in months.

When spring came they were in love. Neither of them knew how it had happened, and neither of them cared.

Jerry had been a handsome man, tall and well built, more like a Spaniard in appearance than the conventional idea of an Oriental. But that had had little to do with it. They both liked good music from Bach to Gershwin, and football games, and Chinese food, and Hemingway's style, and hundreds of other things.

The day after her graduation they had been married. She had no family left, and he never talked about his as if it meant anything to him. They spent that first summer traveling over the United States in his car. Jerry wanted to see every one of the forty-eight states before he returned to Siam.

In the fall they took an apartment near the university and Jerry went on with his thesis. After he received his degree the following June they sailed for Europe, taking the car with them. They spent a year in England, France, Switzerland, Germany, then the Scandinavian countries, and finally Italy and Egypt. It was an idyllic time. They were very happy. Apparently Jerry had inexhaustible funds. He never talked about money. He bought Angela beautiful clothes, and everywhere they stayed in the best hotels.

When they talked it was of themselves, their interests, what they had seen and wanted to see. Jerry scarcely mentioned his family. He made a few casual references to them, but that was all. He didn't even carry their pictures. He had been in Siam only twice since he was ten, for no longer than a month either time. He had lived with an American family in Ohio until he graduated from college and transferred to the university. He talked about them a great deal, never about his own father and mother and brothers. He had no Siamese friends, as far as she knew. In fact, he seemed no different to her from any American boy, except that she loved him.

When they reached Siam his father was dead, and the force of their reception from his mother was terrible for them both. Angela expected Jerry's mother to be like him. She expected to be loved and welcomed, was prepared to love in return. To be hated and shunned was a shock that went very deep. The younger people in both the Siamese and foreign communities were kind enough, but that did not help much because Jerry was dependent financially on his mother until his father's estate was settled.

This was hard, but not so hard as what was to come. With time Angela felt a change in Jerry that frightened her. Imperceptibly he became a Siamese. In America he had been one of her own kind, and she had loved him deeply. Now among his own people he took on their coloration of thought and action until to Angela he seemed almost alien. He adopted the blue panung and white tunic of the official as a matter of course. It startled her the first time she saw him dressed so.

Perhaps if he had understood something of her difficulty, he could have done more to protect her. She had been too proud at first to ask for his help, and he had never understood his mother's purpose where his wife was concerned. He kept urging Angela to try to please her, explaining that she was old-fashioned in her prejudices, but that in time they could win her over if they were only discreet. When Angela tried rather hesitantly to suggest that this was impossible, he refused to believe that his mother could hate his wife and want to be rid of her.

At this point the Princess sent them a maid who was not only a spy, as all their servants were, but who quite openly expected to become Jerry's concubine. Angela tried again and again to send Din away, but Jerry would not let her. He said that his mother had given Din to them and he saw no reason to offend her in a matter of small consequence. Even after Din began to swell proudly with his child he would not send her away. In the meantime the Princess sent them a second maid, named Samai, who was also young and pretty. Both of them waited on Jerry with abject devotion, quarreled over his favors, and were rude to Angela. It was agony to be made a stranger in her own house.

She knew, of course, that he was living with Samai as well as Din, and she was deeply revolted and frightened. Then sometimes he did not come home, and she heard rumors that he was being seen with the girl to whom he had been betrothed by his family several years before. If Angela had had only a little money, she would have left, but she had nothing. She decided to wait until Jerry came into his inheritance and then sue him for divorce. There was a core of something in her, hardened by what had happened, that would not let her run away before she had achieved a solution of some dignity.

When Jerry saw she had ceased to protest he was pleased. He had been afraid she would leave him when she knew that Din was to bear him a child. With her seeming acceptance, he began to plan what he would do when he came into his money. He even chided Angela for letting the servant beat her in doing her duty, and then assured her that Din and Samai meant nothing to him. They were merely passionate and responsive. He would buy or build a house for Angela, and leave the servants and any children they bore him to his mother.

Angela had said nothing. Even when he told her that he had taken Cheronai as his second wife she said nothing. He explained that he was doing it secretly so far as his mother was concerned, although Angela was aware that his mother had planned it so. He told her he had installed Cheronai in a house on Windmill Road that was part of his inheritance, and he promised to write a will giving Angela's children precedence over Cheronai's.

The strange thing to Angela had been that in his way Jerry still loved her and was blind to the fact that her feeling for him had turned to hate. He saw that men admired her and that she refused their attentions, and this flattered him. Benny gave her trouble, even coming to the palace to ask for her, but she refused to see him. Jerry had seemed proud to possess a woman whom other men desired, and more than a little proud that he had been able to fit her into his pattern of life.

She gritted her teeth and waited, counting the months, holding her head high, pretending and pretending and pretending. She was scrupulously careful of her good name. She confided in no one, not even Marthe, the only real friend she allowed herself to make. She tried to convince everyone that she was happy and that she knew nothing of what was going on, except that once in a moment of weakness she had told Marthe about Din. But she never let anyone talk about Jerry to her even when they tried.

Then Jerry died. At first she felt more tightly caught in the trap than before. She was penniless, and over and around and below her there was hate. The servants hated her, the family hated her, Din and Samai hated her, her mother-in-law hated her and willed her dead.

"I actually thought for a little while that maybe she was right. Maybe there was nothing to live for. I had nowhere to go. I have three cousins in America, but they're men in their fifties, and I wouldn't know them if I met them on the street. When I found your letter I didn't plan to do anything about it. I only thought that with Marthe going there would be no one in Bangkok to whom I could turn for help. But for some reason I didn't throw the letter away, and after a week I read it again. It seemed just a little straw, but something made me hold onto it and come and see you. You know the rest."

India sat up. She had only one concern. She wanted to forestall the sense of shame that comes after self-revelation.

"Now I must tell you something strange, Angela," she said, and went back to the day at the Legation, relating her own experience, the conversation she had overheard, and the concern that had grown in her for a girl she did not know. "Many times I thought I must be wrong, that you couldn't possibly need my help, and yet I wasn't able to shake myself free from the conviction that you did. Strange and wonderful, isn't it, the leading of God?"

"Very strange and very wonderful." Angela's voice, which had been steady until now, broke, and tears flushed her face. She leaned her head on her arms and wept.

India did not touch her. She continued to look out over the gulf. Long shadows were creeping up on them from behind, and the waves were slowing toward stillness.

"None of us can escape the past, Angela, but gradually we accept it and turn toward what is still to be. It's futile to push it down out of sight, as it's morbid to dwell on it. Somewhere between there's a middle way. Then finally the time comes when we can lay what has happened, all the failure and sordidness, at God's feet like a burden carried too long. Do you know the verse that says *Come unto me, all ye that labour and are heavy laden, and I will give you rest?* I love that verse. There is a rest for the soul, Angela, and you're close to finding it. Please believe that. Now come along, child. It's teatime. We can talk again tomorrow."

CHAPTER 22

SCHOOL OPENED FOR THE SECOND TERM ON SEPTEMBER 25. A FEW
days later Mani Soderstrom went back north with her husband. In
a moment of weakness, India agreed to let her return for three
months after Christmas.

"I feel guilty taking your money," India protested the afternoon
Mr. Soderstrom came for his wife. "Mani rarely eats here, you
know."

He brushed the protest aside. He was a small weather-beaten man
with kind eyes, possessed of a queer faith in the goodness of Jasmine
Hall that was more than a preference for having his wife in an
establishment of women.

India could find no way of telling him that the teachings of
Jasmine Hall never impinged on Mani for a moment. It was doubtful, India believed, that Mani would stay in a Mission school except
as a condition to being in Bangkok. Well, perhaps next time there
would be some opening, some way to help her. No heart was impervious to God. There must be an approach, if only it could be
found.

October was a pleasant month in Bangkok. The yearly processions
that marked the end of Buddhist Lent gave the city a carnival appearance. The northeast monsoon began, and the rains ended, except
for occasional showers. Already the air held the first hint of that
golden sparkle, like champagne, which would pervade it later.

It was to India the best of all seasons, finding its climax in the
excitement of Christmas. The clear weather had the mellowness
of Indian summer and approaching harvest. Knowledge that another
year ebbed toward its close was without sadness. Rather, there was
a feeling of the great sweep of time. Days were fat with accomplishment. Months were a broad river of minutes and hours. Everything
seemed possible. The school did its best work. The church was
active. People quarreled less, co-operated more. Good will burgeoned.

When Grace, meeting India after prayer meeting, remarked sourly, "I hear Mani has gone," India refused to take offense.

She answered impulsively, "It's a long time since I've seen you. Why don't you come in for tea tomorrow?"

She half expected Grace to refuse, but Grace accepted. It was not quite as it had been between them, however. Neither Dulcie nor Angela had much to say. Grace talked about Wattana and the coming visit of the Board Secretaries. India made conversation.

Outwardly it was a casual and pleasant occasion. Underneath there was a hard residuum from their quarrel that did not yield, either then or later, when India had dinner at Wattana. It remained, like a hidden reef, below the surface on which they had resumed their old friendly intercourse.

India felt guilty about this. She tried consciously to re-establish the bond between them, even after she admitted to herself that it was a relief to see less of Grace than formerly.

With the opening of the second term, Angela had begun teaching again on a part-time schedule. Dr. Crane insisted that she rest afternoons for at least two hours, but she was glad to be permitted this limited activity and did not complain. India often heard her singing in her room. The sound of her clear soprano filtered through the wooden lace at the top of the intervening walls.

When school was over for the day, the girls flocked about her, teasing her to come out and watch a game of badminton, or play the piano for them while they sang, or help them cut out blouses. The teachers, Tawin and Linchee, frequently joined them.

India did not remark the fact that Darun was never part of the group. Even if she had, it would have meant no more to her at the time than that Darun was busy. She had a nurse for David, but she liked to take care of him herself when she had a few minutes left over from school activities.

Angela still refused every invitation to leave the compound. India did not urge her when she saw that the girl was not ready for the step. It would come soon, in any case. There was enough evidence of Angela's return to mental as well as physical health to make concern unnecessary.

India spent several afternoons a week calling on members of

Second Church and parents of school children, as she had before Angela's illness.

Angela always waited for her return to have tea. She would detach herself from the bench where the schoolgirls sat watching a badminton game, or come skimming through the house at the sound of India's footsteps.

She had assumed the task of setting the tea tray, which Ploy relinquished without protest. The tray was always attractively laid with a fresh cloth and India's best rice china. Angela wheedled Plo into making small sandwiches and cookies, and herself prepared the tea.

"Here, India," she would say after India had washed her hands and emerged to sink wearily into a chair. "What you need is a cup of hot tea laced with rum."

This was a joke between them, since India was a complete and practicing teetotaler. Angela's thoughtfulness was in any case as heady as rum. India had been for so many years the one who served that she was embarrassed at first to accept service. She had to remind herself that it was important for Angela to give it.

The girl found other ways of being useful. At Nong Khae she had made two dresses for India, and from that time forward took an interest in her wardrobe.

"India, that dress isn't becoming to you," Angela scolded one afternoon when India appeared in an old brown gingham she had bought on her previous furlough.

She had a dozen similar wash dresses, which she had purchased at the same time in late summer sales. None of them had cost more than five dollars, and all had been so frequently laundered that they were somewhat faded, but they still seemed good enough for school. Not to Angela, however.

"Let's throw that one into the rag bag," she said persuasively. "I'll make another from some of the material you have put away in your drawers."

"It would be a waste of your time and strength," India objected. "My clothes aren't important enough for that."

"Oh, but they are." Angela was earnest. "Becoming clothes do something for a woman. I know *you* don't have time to think about them, but I do, really, and I want to."

When the dress was finished India liked it very much.

"Now we'll dispose of the rest of them," Angela said with satisfaction. "I can't endure seeing you in those Mother Hubbards you affect any longer."

"They're not Mother Hubbards," India protested, laughing.

"Well, they might as well be."

Before the middle of November she had dispensed with India's collection of old hats also.

India came home one afternoon to find Angela directing Det in the cleaning of her room. It was a chore she had postponed from month to month since spring. When Mani arrived, India had hastily moved her things from the bedroom to the office, and there they had remained while the accretion of the new school year collected over and about them. It had hardly seemed worth while to put them back into the bedroom as long as Mani was returning after Christmas. And yet there was no escaping the fact that the room was more and more reminiscent of Miss Havisham's in *Great Expectations*. After the school year ended, probably sometime in April, there would be leisure to sort and pack away what was no longer needed, and by then Mani would have gone back north for good.

Most of the time India could ignore the confusion of the room. She spent her days teaching or working in the school office downstairs. She ate on the veranda, entertained on the mook. Gradually the office became only a storeroom and a place to sleep. Whenever the disorder seemed unendurable, she decided to take a day off and remedy it. Then something more important intervened, and she postponed the house cleaning until a more convenient season.

The night before, Angela had knocked on her door to ask if India had any pieces of lace, and had waited while India looked. She had hunted through her drawers, searched several shoe boxes of assorted odds and ends in her wardrobes, and two hatboxes on top of them.

"Never mind," Angela said after half an hour. "I can get along without it."

"But I know it's here somewhere."

Angela giggled. "So many things are!" she said.

"Yes, it's dreadful." India looked at the room ruefully.

There was too much of everything, too much furniture, too many books, and on the table catalogues, ledgers, maps, charts, textbooks. She felt an impulse to sweep them all together and burn them.

"Where did you get the mirrors?" Angela wanted to know.

"People gave them to me from time to time," India said. "And of course if I give them away the donors will find out, so there's nothing to do about them." There were five hung about the walls, several above eye level. The most offensive was the one Seng Liow had given her. It was painted with a garish boat scene and with big Chinese characters in red, wishing her happiness and a long life.

"Shall I throw something and smash it?" Angela inquired, following the direction of India's eyes.

"Not while I'm looking."

"What about a few of the pictures, then?"

"I'm planning to pack most of them away in the spring," India replied.

Angela walked along the walls, examining them. "They look like the collection from a third-rate photographer's window, if you don't mind my saying so. That one especially!"

It was the picture of a naked baby, as large as life, with the sex made inescapable.

"I agree," India said, "but it's Sawai's baby, and after six girls she was very proud of him."

"Well, surely no one is sentimental about these!" Angela pointed to a double row of Mission Meeting pictures beginning with one labeled 1905 and showing men with walrus mustaches and women wearing shoe-length skirts and pompadours.

"When I take them down I'll have to have the wall washed," India objected. "And there just isn't time."

Angela looked at the pictures closely. "It must have been hot wearing those long dresses in the tropics."

"It was," India admitted. "But I've always thought they were more graceful than the flour-sack dresses that came into style with the twenties."

Turning from the pictures, Angela confronted the room. "What about the books?" she asked. "Couldn't we put some of them into boxes?"

They had overflowed the one bookcase. Drifts of them were collected on the two almirahs that held India's clothes, on some of the chairs, on the red lacquer stool with gold claw feet the church had given India for Christmas, even beneath her bed.

"They could, if I could find a day to choose which." India sighed, exhausted at the mere prospect.

Angela was looking at the umbrella stand in the corner on which hung six or seven hats and a topee. India had considered removing this and bringing in another bookcase, but that would have left the problem of what to do with her hats. There was no one to give them to, and they were still quite good. She remembered meeting a ricksha coolie once wearing a pink felt she had thrown away. He had looked extraordinarily funny, and yet she had experienced a sharp unpleasant sense of shock, as if she herself were identified with the hat because it had once belonged to her. Besides, if she got rid of these familiar buckets and scoops, where would she find hats to replace them among the pancakes, lettuce leaves, and ice-cream cones that women were wearing?

She explained as much to Angela, but the explanation did not impress her.

"You never wear them," she said.

"Once in a while I do, to parties, you know."

Angela looked at the hats and said good night. The next afternoon when India returned, they were gone.

"I burned them all up," Angela explained brightly. "Now we're dusting your books. I've sorted them by kinds so you can choose the ones you need to use. Det will put the rest into the bookcase in Mani's room. That's one piece of furniture Mani won't have any use for. We've already moved one of the wardrobes in there, too, the one with your furlough clothes in it. Doesn't the room look better?"

"But my hats!" India wailed.

"Now don't be like that!" Angela was firm. "They were antiques." Her head was tied into a towel, and she was sitting on her heels beside a pile of books, looking up at India with a wickedly mischievous expression. "It was time someone took you in hand."

"Oh dear, I suppose it was." India sat down bleakly. Then in fairness she added, "The room does look better."

There were no more books on chairs or under the bed. The Mission Meeting pictures had been packed into a box, and the walls were washed so that only a faint row of checkers showed where they had hung.

Angela's square little chin was still up. "Now, what I want you to do next," she continued, "is to go downtown tomorrow and order a good Milan straw from Miss Rubinstein. That's all you need beside your topee. But you do need that. Really, you know, the thing you wear on your head to a party should look like a hat, India, not like a coal scuttle decorated with last year's roses."

And the next afternoon India went.

CHAPTER 23

DARUN, ANGELA, AND INDIA WERE ALL WORKING IN THE OFFICE ONE afternoon early in November when India looked up from her desk.

"What day was it you took Eng Siow home?" she asked Darun.

The teacher was copying the October attendance report, and before she answered marked her place carefully with a card.

"A week ago Sunday, mem *kha*."

"Was it as long ago as that?" India felt a twinge of annoyance with Darun. Eng Siow should never have been permitted to stay with her mother for ten days. India would not have allowed the child to remain overnight if she had been consulted. "Have you had any word from her?"

"Yes, mem, she wrote yesterday to tell me that her mother is very ill."

"I'd better go after her right away. I shouldn't have waited this long."

India stood up. "I think I'll go now," she said with decision.

The look on Darun's triangular face became remote, and India saw that the teacher had taken the words as a criticism of herself. Her next remark gave no hint of this, however.

"Do you want me to come with you?"

India considered a moment. It was unlike Darun to be careless about the welfare of a child. Of course she was busy. She was always busy. Even so, why hadn't she reminded India that the girl was staying with her mother, so that India could have brought her back to Jasmine Hall? The whole incident was strange. Was Darun's failure to do so mere chance, or was it, possibly, one of those subtle ways the Siamese had of expressing dissatisfaction? And if so, dissatisfaction with what, and with whom? Surely Darun would not endanger Eng Siow because she was annoyed with India!

"When is your attendance report due?" India asked the teacher.

"It was due yesterday."

"Then you'd better finish it. I'm sure I can find the house. Angela, do you think you can copy the treasurer's report for me tonight?"

"Of course, India, right away."

India could not have said why she was uneasy about Eng Siow, yet many times before she had known this swift enveloping concern for someone. It was as if God tapped her on the shoulder and said, "Go now." Whenever that happened, she had gone into the slums and back alleys without question and without fear, reminding herself of Christ's promise to his disciples, *Lo, I am with you alway, even unto the end of the world.*

Eng Siow's father was a Christian Chinese and a member of Second Church. When he had learned that he must return to China on business and that he would be away for a year, he had begged India to take his daughter.

"Please, mem," he pleaded, "please you take Eng Siow by you. She good girl. You teach her be Christian, not bad woman like her mama."

India had consented, knowing that he did not exaggerate his wife's character. She was a Siamese woman of low class and an inveterate gambler, with little interest in her only child. Every night, sometimes until dawn, she sat hunched over the cards with her friends.

Eng Siow was, as her father had said, a good girl. She was fourteen and beginning to be pretty, with the parchment skin and silky black hair of the Cantonese, and her mother's large dark eyes. Jasmine Hall had no class for her, so every morning she went to the eighth grade at the Jane Hayes School in a big double ricksha with Pastor Rasami's two older daughters. She was very bright and had moved up from fourth to first place in her class. The month before, her father had sent her twenty ticals as a reward and written that he would be home in December.

When a maid had come with news that Eng Siow's mother was seriously ill, Darun had taken the girl home. The mother had implored Darun to let her daughter stay. Darun had been unwilling to do so, but after talking with relatives who were taking care of the sick woman, had decided that it was impossible to refuse.

India was conscience-stricken to think that she had not called. She hurried to dress and, once on Bamrung Muang Road, found a taxi without delay. Eng Siow's home was in a small lane at the back of a row of shops belonging to her father, not far from the river. The lane was rutted and narrow, and the taxi driver refused to endanger his springs by driving down it. India paid him off and entered on foot.

Business was slack in the late afternoon. Scabrous pariah dogs lay dozing in patches of sunlight. Some children playing hopscotch halted as India passed, staring at her, round-eyed. A hawker selling noodles and sauce trotted ahead of her, with his stove on one end of the carrying pole and his table and wares on the other, shouting, "Kui tiow ba me O-O-O-O-O-O." A woman coming out of a shop to buy from him gawked at India. "Ang mau! Ang mau!" she shouted over her shoulder, and several other women joined her for a look. From the river came the incisive bleat of a steamer and the moan of a launch in reply.

Eng Siow's home stood at the end of the lane. Beyond it was a high board wall and, facing it, an even higher wall of brick, from which dingy paint, once yellow, was chipping. The front of the house—one of a row—was closed by a series of many-leaved doors. A panel stood slightly ajar. The adjoining houses were tightly closed and looked to India as if they were used as warehouses.

She knocked on the open panel, but no one answered. The room within was windowless and dark.

A gecko sounded its dragon call in sudden stentorian tones close to her ear. *"Tokae! Tokae! Tokae! Tokae!"* She looked around uneasily and was caught by the wicked little eyes of the lizard, motionless on the inside wall of the house, two feet from her head. Its green jaws were gaping, and its twelve-inch body was more horrid for red spots. Then it moved rapidly away.

She glanced doubtfully up the lane and knocked again. When there was no answer she stepped over the high sill into the room. It was sparsely furnished. There was a round table with a marble top in the middle of the floor, and on it several glasses. Flies buzzed through the odor of stale beer. Four wire-backed chairs, like those India had seen in drugstores when she was a little girl, had been pushed back unevenly from around the table. Two carved Chinese chairs were set against the far wall. A high altar table inlaid with mother-of-pearl stood between them. Over the table hung a mirror painted with lotus flowers and Chinese characters, and above it a red satin banner richly embroidered.

There was no one in the room or in the kitchen behind it. A few feet from where India stood, a crude staircase led to the sleeping rooms above.

"Eng Siow, are you there?" India called.

The silence was complete except for the muted shouts of the children at the head of the lane and the distant complaining of a river boat. There was something eerie about the house, as if an invisible presence waited but would not speak. India, listening, heard a slight sound like the whisper of movement when someone shifts position, then nothing more.

She called more loudly. "Eng Siow, are you up there?"

Still there was no reply.

India began to climb the stairs to the second story, cautiously, for there was no railing. When she emerged into the larger of the two sleeping rooms, it was tightly shuttered. For a moment her eyes discerned only the vague outline of a high bed in the corner. Then she saw the figure of a woman lying on a padded sleeping mat in the middle of the room.

The woman was dressed in a red calico camisole and a faded sarong of Javanese pattern. The feet at the end of the sarong were splayed. One hand was extended, open and empty. The other seemed to have relaxed its hold on a snuffbox only the second before. The mouth was slack and the eyes wide.

The house was very still. India took a step, and it reverberated through the stillness.

"It was death that I felt here in the house," she thought, kneeling quickly by the woman.

The body was still warm. India looked around the room. The bed had no sheets, but on a chest was a folded blanket. Now that her vision was adjusted to the twilight in the room, she became aware of Eng Siow huddled in the corner, her hands before her face. India shook out the blanket and covered the dead woman, then went to the girl and took her hand.

"Come downstairs, Eng Siow," she ordered.

The girl was trembling and her hands were icy. Shambling a little, she complied.

India made her sit down in a chair and went to the kitchen. She heated water on a charcoal brazier and found some tea. Eng Siow turned her head aside when India held it to her lips. As India insisted, there was a rush of feet. Six or seven people came through the door, relatives, apparently, no doubt summoned by the maid when she saw that her mistress was dying. They stopped short in surprise.

"She is already dead," India told them, and the women cried out sharply.

Still wailing, they clambered up the stairs, and a burst of fresh lamentations came as they found the body. The sound carried to adjacent shops, and in a few minutes other women appeared to join them.

Two men, who had come in with the first group of women, seated themselves at the table. Eng Siow immediately slid to the floor from her chair and salaamed them, then crouched beside India, unwilling to sit in a chair so long as her elders were present.

One of the men took a straw cigarette from behind his ear and began to smoke it. He was evil-looking, with bold eyes that were occupied now in a careful examination of India. His clothes were careless and too bright-colored for respectability. He wore a rose panung, badly soiled, and an orange plaid shirt in imitation of the cowboys in Western movies. There was tattooing on his chest where the shirt fell open.

When the cigarette was finished he spoke. "I am Mae Kluie's brother," he said, putting his palms down on his spread knees like an actor in a bad play. "What was the manner of my sister's death?"

"I don't know," India answered. "She was already dead when I found her. I'm the director of Jasmine Hall where Nai Po left Eng Siow while he was in China. I've come to fetch her."

"No," the man said with finality. "I can't let her go back now."

"But her father entrusted her to me."

"She must stay here until after the cremation. There will be services every day, and people coming and going who will have to be fed. It is fitting that she should help her relatives in this, since she is her mother's only child."

"How many days will that be?"

"Perhaps three, perhaps more."

"It isn't proper for her to stay here now that her mother's dead. Nai Po wouldn't approve. I can bring her back for the cremation."

"There will be women about. They can look after her."

He lighted a cheap cigarette from a packet tucked into the top of his panung and continued to study India boldly. The longer she sat opposite him, the less she liked him. *There was a Siamese word for men like this*, she thought, *men who made their living in the borderline areas of the law, sometimes on one side of it, sometimes the other. They were* hua mai *(wooden heads). What was the English equivalent? Gangsters? No, that implied organization. Toughs? That was closer. Rascals? Scoundrels? There wasn't enough opportunism in either word.*

The man's face was broad and dark, as if he worked on the river. His eyes were shifty but not servile, studying her with careful calculation. Eng Siow sat on the floor between them. Then the man's mouth curled into an unexpected smile that seemed to strive to be ingratiating.

"We are all poor people here," he said with whining humility, palms turned up, shoulders lifted in a deprecatory shrug. "Could the honorable mem lend us fifty ticals toward the expense of the funeral? When Nai Po gets back from China he will repay it."

India looked around the room. "You have all this furniture that you can sell," she answered quickly. "It should bring more than fifty ticals."

Upstairs the wailing continued. People were coming and going. A neighbor sidled through the door with incense and candles. One of the relatives hurried down the stairs and covered the mirror with a tattered square of cloth. India saw her go into the kitchen and heard the sound of kindling being broken up for a fire.

"True," the man agreed, "we will sell the furniture, but it won't be enough. We will have to have services for three days and make offerings to the priests. Then there is the coffin to buy and the undertaker to pay. Add to that a shadow play and an orchestra for three nights. Four hundred ticals will hardly pay for it all."

India's purse lay on the marble top of the table. What had she brought with her? Not more than ten or eleven ticals. If she said she would not lend them anything, how was she to get Eng Siow away? This was a clever rogue.

India made an alternative proposal. "Nai Po is a Christian," she said. "Why don't you let me arrange a funeral of the sort he would have if he were here? I'm sure he would oppose the kind of thing you plan."

The man ignored her proposition, and with the Siamese scorn of penuriousness said, "Surely fifty ticals is not a large sum for a farang."

"But it is," India objected. "I don't have anything like that with me."

"You could go home and get it."

"But why should I pay for spirit rites when neither Nai Po nor I have any confidence in them?"

The man's face soured. He lost interest in her. "Oh well," he said indifferently, "it doesn't matter anyway. Eng Siow will sell herself. It was all arranged yesterday. We're to have a hundred ticals for her."

"You can't do that!" India cried out sharply. "Her father will never let you!"

"He's in China."

"But he left her in my charge. I'll go to the police."

"Do you have papers to prove it?" And seeing by her consternation that she did not, he added, "She is willing." Then, to forestall any move India might make, he said peremptorily, "Go upstairs to your aunt, Eng Siow, and stay there."

The girl obeyed without a word. India looked around helplessly. The two men at the table smoked and watched her with laconic pleasure. Two more men had materialized as they talked and squatted on either side of the door. The servant girl brought a kerosene lamp and set it on the table. It made India conscious for the first time that darkness had crept down over the yellow wall opposite and filled the alley.

She stood up. She had been foolish to come alone, but even Darun would have been impotent here. She half expected one of the men to snatch at her purse as she went through the door, but no one stirred. In her anger she refused to say even the formal words of farewell, *La kon, kha* (I take leave of you), and none of them spoke as she left the house.

All down the dirty lane and out to the street she hurried. Whatever she did she must do quickly. Should she try the police? Was there any way to reach Nai Po by cable? Would anyone lend her fifty ticals until payday?

She was still walking rapidly, heedless of the rickshas that swirled around her, when the insistent honking of a motorcar horn penetrated her fog of concentration. A voice said, "Didn't anyone ever tell you that motorcars are dangerous?"

It was Mr. Denniscort's brown face leaning out of his car and grinning his gamin grin.

"I was lost in thought, to coin a phrase," she replied. "I didn't even hear you."

"You need a safer place for your thinking, then. Get in."

India sank into the wide seat gratefully. "I shouldn't have expected to meet you in this part of the city anyway."

"I have a boat anchored at the foot of the street."

Mr. Denniscort's fondness for boats was one of his most entertaining idiosyncrasies to the Siamese, who found almost everything

this unconventional diplomat did entertaining. Some of the wealth-
ier nobles owned big power launches, and when they learned of his
interest invited him to go on long cruises to the gulf. He preferred
the humble craft that plied the river, from the frail canoe of a
woman who sold betel, to a heavy freight barge with a great sweep
at the back. He had tried everything and had even made an effort
to persuade the master of a Chinese junk to let him take the loaded
junk down the river, but without success.

"I'm going up to Ayuthia tomorrow by boat," he said. "Wouldn't
you like to go along?"

"I can't, but thank you. I have something on my mind."

"You don't look as if all that thinking you were doing had
helped."

"It hasn't so far. I'm trying to rescue one of my girls who's being
sold into prostitution to pay for her mother's funeral."

"No!"

"I've just been offered the choice of paying fifty ticals to get her
back or letting the relatives sell her for a hundred."

"Why the bargain rate?"

"I suppose to avoid trouble with her father, who's in China on
business. She's a nice girl, too. That's what makes it such a tragedy.
She doesn't really understand what she's been persuaded to do."

"Then why is she willing? Surely they can't dispose of her against
her will."

"They've convinced her that her mother's chance of getting into
heaven depends on the rites they'll have performed, and that it's
her duty to provide them. The Siamese have a proverb that says,
The dead sell the living. It usually means that the living are so
encumbered by the cost of cremations that they spend their lives
paying for them, but this time it's literally true."

Mr. Denniscort leaned over and tapped his chauffeur on the
shoulder.

"Turn back!" he said. His eyes had begun to sparkle. "We'll rescue your maiden in distress right away."

"But, Mr. Denniscort——"

He wagged a lean brown finger at her. "Tut, tut! I'm the knight
on the white charger."

"But what are you going to do?"

"Look impressive and pay them off. I left my sword at home today."

"But fifty ticals! How can I let you——"

"Fair lady, you can't stop me. Show me the villains, forsooth."

India laughed and felt herself flooded by a kind of crazy relief. They came slowly back down the street, and she pointed out the opening of the lane. The chauffeur turned the car into it gingerly, protesting that it was bad for the springs and that he wouldn't be able to turn around. Mr. Denniscort ordered him on.

Their passage caused a sensation. People ran to the doors of shops to watch them go by. Children were scooped out of the way. Pariah dogs, caught in the glare from the headlights, yipped and fled.

As soon as the car stopped people collected around it. India and Mr. Denniscort climbed out. India heard the chauffeur and footman warning the people away, threatening them with dire punishment in the name of the American Government if they got finger marks on the shining black surface of the car.

Mr. Denniscort looked around at the squalid shops dimly lit, the leprous dogs, and the people, whose faces in the uneven light looked both vacant and sinister.

"Do you walk around alone in these slums?" he asked.

"In the daytime, yes. They're not nearly so frightening as West Madison Street in Chicago."

Everything was as she had left it. The two men sat at the table still. Their two henchmen squatted on either side of the entrance. Overhead the women moved about as before. Even the beer glasses in which the dead flies floated had not been removed from the table. No one stood or offered them chairs.

Mr. Denniscort looked around curiously. "You'll have to do the talking."

"Shall I tell them who you are?"

"No, let's rely on the power of money." He reached into his pocket and brought out his wallet.

India addressed the man at the table. "I have brought the money," she said. "Where is Eng Siow?"

Someone at the door whispered to someone else. The word

moved up the stairs to the mourning women and trickled through the room. "The American Minister. It's the American Minister."

Abruptly the wailing stopped. One by one the women came down and squatted in the shadows, Eng Siow among them.

The man at the table was playing his role with relish. He smoked a cigarette in a leisurely manner, savoring the rare chance that made it possible for him to be rude to people of importance.

All the eyes in the room were on him. He seemed to be deliberating with himself, ponderously, like a judge.

"I shall have to have a hundred for her," he said at length. "That is what we have been offered."

"You agreed to fifty," India answered firmly, not letting her voice rise, knowing that among the Siamese any sign of anger was evidence of weakness. "You told me that all you needed was fifty."

His eyes flickered at the American Minister, and then he smiled ingratiatingly at India. In the uncertain light of the kerosene lamp the smile was incredibly more evil than his previous truculence.

"We are very poor, and there's the orchestra and shadow play and food for the priests to pay for. A hundred is hardly enough, but we do not wish to be greedy."

"What's the matter?" Mr. Denniscort asked.

"Now that he's had a look at you he wants a hundred. The Siamese have a nice feeling for values. He assessed me at fifty, but he thinks you're worth at least twice that much."

"Shall we give it to him?"

"If you'll give me the fifty I'll try the effect of cash."

He counted it into her palm.

"Here's fifty ticals," she said, turning back to Eng Siow's uncle. "Will you take it and let the girl come with me or not?" She laid the money on the table.

There was a stirring in the room, low conversation. The man sat impassive, smoking, not glancing in the direction of the money. Then a woman squatting behind him spat, a red stream that lay along the floor like blood. She was an ancient crone, naked to the waist, her flaccid breasts hanging against her flanks. Her eyes were the bright cold eyes of a bird of prey.

"Take it, you fool, and let her go!" she said in a shrill, authoritative voice. "It will make less trouble in the end."

The man paid no attention. He lighted a fresh cigarette and sat for several minutes smoking. India stood motionless, waiting. Mr. Denniscort studied the people on the floor, and they stared back at him. This was a great event, something they would talk about for years—that the American Minister had come after Eng Siow. They looked at the girl covertly, wondering why one of the world's great should trouble himself about her. Or did he desire her himself?

Then, as of his own volition rather than because of the old woman's prompting, the man reached out slowly and took the money. He turned and looked at Eng Siow. With a slight movement of his head he indicated that she was to go. Dumbly the girl moved from her place on the floor, crouching to keep her head below those of her elders. India turned toward the door. The girl followed. Mr. Denniscort brought up the rear.

Out in the lane the chauffeur had somehow managed to turn the car. India told Eng Siow to climb in. She huddled into the far corner of the seat.

"Do you do this sort of thing every day?" the Minister asked.

"Hardly."

"But it does happen?"

"The knight on the white charger has never appeared before."

"By the way, I'm more than ever certain that I'm going to get that settlement for Miss Kane. I haven't told her, though. I remembered my orders."

"Mr. Denniscort, please. I didn't mean to give orders."

He laughed. "We do make a good pair of conspirators, though, judging by tonight. Maybe we can do as well for Miss Kane."

CHAPTER 24

THE ONLY CLOUD ACROSS THE FALL WAS THE COMING VISIT OF THE Board delegation. As the depression deepened in the United States and giving for missions fell off proportionately, it became apparent

that cuts in the budget were inevitable. This enhanced the significance of any report the three men might make. Everyone in the
Mission was infected with a feverish necessity to impress them with
the importance of his own work.

India could not escape the general disquietude. Her problem was
especially difficult. If the men had been going to stay in Bangkok
several months or even weeks, she would have been more hopeful.
She could have invited them to the school often, and if they were
not timorous she could have taken them with her into the slums.

There was nothing about the school plant itself that would impress them. It was just an old residence converted to a purpose for
which it was only half adequate. The house had not been painted
in three years. The furniture was what she had received from Wang
Lang long before. The garden was also the children's playground,
so that the grass was worn away by many small feet.

She could not help envying Grace the physical plant of Wattana.
There was the lovely approach by canal, slow and pleasant along
shady waterways. Then there were the broad green lawns leading
up to the buildings, clipped shrubs, neat flower beds, shady trees.
Everything would be freshly painted and immaculate, big and
adequate, businesslike and yet gracious.

The men would be impressed by the classrooms with their good
lighting and modern furniture, their maps and up-to-date equipment, the well-dressed and well-cared-for children in the school
uniform of dark red pasin and white blouse. They had the intelligent appearance of upper-class girls and the special charm of that
special class of Siamese child, which was a combination of physical
beauty, gracefulness, and punctilious manners. The teachers were
alert and well dressed, too, intelligent and able to speak English
with the visitors. There were the playgrounds, the big airy dining
room, the little hospital, the domestic science kitchen.

Buildings of brick and stone could be displayed. Big schools like
Wattana, hospitals, leper asylums had nothing to fear and much to
gain from an inspection, for the function of the eye insured them
a response. The kind of work India was trying to do was intangible.
There was no system of weights and measures to gauge the impact
of God on human hearts. She couldn't parade her successes of the

spirit, such as they were. She couldn't set up a runway or employ an announcer to say, "Gentlemen, Exhibit A. Here's a girl who was abandoned by her husband a month before the birth of their child. I took her in, saw her through her confinement, helped her keep the child, and now have trained her as a teacher." She couldn't display the long line of humble people who through her had come to a knowledge of God. It was not only impossible, it would be indecent.

She knew that Amery sometimes regaled dinner guests, even strangers passing through Bangkok, with her more spectacular failures. She hoped he would refrain from prejudicing the delegation with any of his deftly told stories. There was, for instance, the girl she had tried to help after she foolishly became the lesser wife of a prominent official against his wife's wishes. He finally sent the girl away, although not until she was pregnant. India had helped her, but as soon as she was well again she had gone to his home and tried to kill him with a cleaver. Of course the story got into the papers. The escapades of Dulcie's orphans sounded ludicrous, too, told in the right way.

If she had time to talk to the men, to know them, she thought she could make them see beyond the rackety-packety appearance of Jasmine Hall, with its assorted collection of child derelicts, to what she was trying to do. Why did the Board spend money to send out men on whose judgment they would depend, without giving them adequate time to form more than superficial judgments?

It was finally announced early in November that the delegation would reach Bangkok from Penang on Tuesday, December 16, and would leave for the north December 21. India was informed that she could expect them at Jasmine Hall between two and four on the afternoon of Thursday, December 18.

Kru Darun and the teachers conferred at once on a suitable program. School would be in session at two, and it was decided to take the men through the classrooms first, then seat them on the lawn for a short program of songs and perhaps a play, to be followed by tea. The Siamese teachers and the Bible school girls would prepare special delicacies, and India's kitchen was to provide sandwiches and a farang cake. A song was written for the occasion in Siamese and translated into English as well. The third pratome would sing the Siamese version and the fourth the English. Three garlands of jasmine and rose petals were to be woven in the traditional manner with which the Siamese honored those to whom honor was due.

At noon on December 16, India waited on the platform of Hua Lampong Station with the other missionaries for the arrival of the International Express, which came twice weekly from Penang. Comings and goings in Bangkok still had something of the festival character of the old days. People starting out on furlough could expect their friends to be at the station platform, some with gifts of fruit in neat baskets, some with flowers or garlands, some with presents that would be useful along the way. Often the necks of people who were leaving were so hung with garlands—more delicately made but otherwise similar to the Hawaiian leis—that only their eyes emerged above them. Arrivals, too, could look forward to seeing friends waiting for them. It was a pleasant experience to step off the express and find oneself surrounded by familiar faces. Someone always brought coolies to help with the luggage. Someone always said: "My car's waiting. You're coming home to lunch with me."

The three men who stepped down from the train were obviously pleased with their reception. An informal line on the station platform waited while they were introduced. They looked like ordinary men, India thought, not so formidable as they had become in people's minds. Dr. Howard James was the leader of the group. He was a big slow-moving man, a little stooped, with graying hair, ugly in a Lincolnesque way. Dr. John Ransome also had gray hair, but he was small and brisk. Mr. Silver was round and heavy, with thick black hair, and beads of perspiration across his forehead and upper lip. He looked less like the successful lawyer he was than like an aging actor who had been forced to relinquish romantic leads for character parts.

India saw them again at prayer meeting the next afternoon. Dr. James addressed the group, and everyone was there to hear him, listening intently for some clue to the men and their purpose. After a few preliminary remarks Dr. James defined their function.

"We have been sent more to strengthen your feeling of contact with home than for any ulterior purpose. It has seemed to some of us that in these days of rapid transportation it should not be necessary any longer for you to feel the sense of isolation which was such a heavy burden to pioneer missionaries.

"It is our hope that through us you will feel a more vital connection with the home church, and that we shall draw inspiration from you for them. It is this unity of the body of Christ that we consider important. The depression in America has forced us to many long thoughts. It has never been easy to find money for the missionary cause, and it is harder now. Part of this is due to the lack of knowledge, of intimate contact between field and church. It is that gap we hope to bridge.

"We are not here as judges to settle the disputes that may have arisen among you. Differences of opinion are inevitable among thinking people. You have been chosen for this work not only because of the living quality of your faith but also because of your known potentiality for leadership. It is not strange that in a collection of leaders there should be little inclination to follow, hence sharp differences in regard to the conduct of the work. It would not be fitting if we, in the short time we are to be with you, should be charged with the responsibility of settling these.

"Rather, it is our purpose to bring you inspiration for the task that lies ahead. Let us examine together the nature of that task and then dedicate ourselves anew to its greatness with a solemn sense of the power of Him whom we serve. . . ."

India lost the thread of the discourse at this point. In essence, Dr. James had served notice that the delegation had no intention of acting as a court of appeals or as a means of transmitting such appeals to the Board. That was going to make life pleasanter for them, certainly. Dr. James seemed to disclaim any purpose of passing judgment on what they saw, and yet that was ridiculous. The mind could not maintain any such blank. Since it was inevitable that, when they got back to New York, the Board would be guided by their judgment on controversial matters as having come freshly from the field, it would have been more honest of them to have probed the points of difference, listened to testimony on both sides, balanced charge with defense.

Money was short, as Dr. James had already pointed out. There was going to be less to work with. Everyone would try to retain his share of the appropriation. Some would fail. Probably not one of those present except Grace, who had nothing to worry about since Wattana was endowed, was listening to the address. Each one was asking, "Will it be I?"

She could almost see the men around a table in the Board rooms a few months hence, and someone asking: "Now you men are just back from the field. What do you think about Miss Severn's school? Is it worth the further outlay? Or is it one place where we could save?"

It isn't fair! she thought. *They ought to stay longer or not come at all. They ought to admit that they can't escape responsibility. It's cheap of them to talk about spreading inspiration! Inspiration! There's continuing inspiration in the work itself. All anyone needs is to be allowed to do the job waiting to be done. But then preachers have this disproportionate idea of the value of talk. How many people listen more than halfway through a sermon?*

Anne Howard was nudging her. "You look skeptical, India. Aren't you being inspired?"

"I need money, Anne, and I'm worried. You can't feed inspiration to children."

By two o'clock the next afternoon the schoolrooms had been carefully swept and all the blackboards were clean. The teachers were wearing their best clothes. Several of them even had on hose and shoes instead of the flat babouches they ordinarily wore. A series of tea tables had been set under the big rain tree in the front garden, and the Bible school girls had made five kinds of Siamese cakes. One of these was made of coconut shredded by hand and cooked with sugar. It was thought likely to please the farangs, since it was very sweet. One called *thong muan* was a tiny roll of light batter baked between irons, not unlike a superior ice-cream cone in flavor. One was made of rice flour, coconut milk, and sugar, a small round drop so delicate it melted on the tongue. Another, hardly bigger than a marble, was an edible leaf filled with spiced meat and cooked. And the fifth, called "golden mist," was a sweet vermicelli of egg yolks and sugar that the Siamese had learned to make from the

Portuguese several centuries before, and for that reason still considered foreign.

The making of them, since all were intricate, had taken the older girls two full days. Plo had supplied plates of sandwiches and a cake. The tables were beautifully decorated with bowls of roses, but the cakes would not be brought out until the last minute to keep them as long as possible from the hordes of ants. Bible school girls would serve. The teachers would sit down at the table with the Board delegation.

At two the men appeared in Amery Hillow's car. Amery was with them. India had hoped that the men would come alone. It would have given her at least a few minutes to talk with them.

She had another reason for wishing that Amery had not accompanied them. Two days before she had received an envelope from one of her friends in Lampang enclosing a letter from Amery, with the comment attached: "India, did you know that you were a lamb appointed to the slaughter? Please watch out! Love, Inez."

The letter, which was addressed to Inez' husband, read:

Dear John:

The Board delegation will get here the sixteenth and will leave for Chiengmai on the twenty-first. They'll have only one day with you, December 30, but I think that will be enough. I have good reason to believe that there will be further cuts after their visit, so do your best to impress them. I'll be traveling with them, according to present plans.

I think we'll come through all right here in Bangkok, with the possible exception of Jasmine Hall. Wattana and B.C.C. won't come into question, of course. The evangelistic work is hardly likely to be cut, and the Maternity Home is on a sound financial basis. I don't entirely approve of the project, as you know, but Catherine Darrow has a paying clientele, which makes her almost independent of Mission support.

But Jasmine Hall! India has a heart as big as the universe, but you know the rest without being told. I had to see her recently about this visit of the delegation and I must confess that her collection of second-rate girls, indifferent teachers, and feeble-minded children gave me a jolt. What the delegation will think, I don't know, or perhaps I do. Of course it was a mistake that she ever left Wattana.

If there's anything I can bring you, let me know. Please keep this letter confidential, since it's not generally known that the Board is definitely cutting next year's budget.

My fraternal regards,
Amery

The letter had brought into focus many things India had ignored —a slur here, a criticism there, a story Amery had spread. She had caught echoes of them in many people and knew that what had come to her could be only a small part of the total. Was it possible, she asked herself, that Amery was slowly and inexorably isolating her with ridicule? Deprecation had a cumulative effect that was hard to counter. Fighting it was like fighting shadows. But surely she was wrong to see the letter as part of a campaign directed against herself. That would imply a remorselessness of purpose which she could not attribute to any of her fellow missionaries.

The doubt once raised made it difficult for her to act entirely natural with Amery when he appeared with the Board delegation. She seemed to feel an answering unnaturalness in him. He was too effusive in his greeting. He pumped her hand a little too long. He made too many intimate remarks, as if to prove to the men of the delegation that he had been India's friend for years. It was tinny, and at the same time disturbing.

The men looked tired, as if the traveling they had already done had sapped their vitality, or as if they were not yet acclimated. They went through the classrooms perfunctorily. They had been at Wattana that morning. India felt her enthusiasm falter as she saw the school through their eyes. Half the children were not wearing the school uniform, and by two-thirty all were distinctly rumpled. The air was still, and there was a smell of perspiring small bodies. The classrooms seemed dingy and in need of paint. The desks, after having been used by several generations of school children, were scarred and stained. Why should they be impressed?

They looked at the church, and Dr. James remarked that it was too bad the congregation didn't build a more suitable sanctuary.

"They're saving money for it," India explained. "They have several thousand ticals, but of course it will take more than that."

Even as she spoke she realized how humble the shaky wooden benches looked, the plain pulpit, the old organ. These men either had no imagination or they were too weary to exert it. They could not see the ghosts of all the people this room had served.

With something like relief they went downstairs and into the garden, after the briefest of glances at the dormitories.

School was dismissed, and the program began. This went better. The men seemed to enjoy it, and clapped when it was over. Each of them was presented with an example of needlework done by the girls, a cutwork tablecloth for Dr. James, a pair of pillowcases with wide crocheted edges for Dr. Ransome, and an embroidered sofa cushion for Mr. Silver. Then the Bible school girls arrived with the tea.

India saw the men one after another refuse the cakes the girls had made.

"We have to be careful what we eat," Dr. James explained to India. "Mr. Silver had a bad attack of dysentery in Lahore, and we've been cautious ever since."

They took a few sandwiches and a piece of the cake Plo had made, but when they rose to go at four-thirty the untouched food was still on their plates. They shook hands with the teachers and with India, then with obvious alacrity climbed into Amery's car.

India went to her room and wept. It was the first time in years she had cried in this way, but she could not help it.

CHAPTER 25

BY THE NEXT MORNING INDIA KNEW A SENSE OF RELIEF THAT THE visit of the delegation was over. For better or for worse it was at least behind her. The whole school immediately plunged into the wonderful excitement of Christmas. In every grade children were preparing their parts in the Christmas program. There was much whispering about gifts, much planning and laughter.

The church was also busy with preparations. Few of the members had festivities in their own homes. Christmas was a communal affair. It was customary on Christmas Eve to have a picnic supper in the garden to which every family contributed. Then there was a pageant in the church and a community tree, hung with gifts that included pencils and notebooks, drinking glasses, lengths of cloth, crocheted lace, and even on occasion a chicken in a poke. The old house was full of gaiety and song, and in the joy of the Christmastide India put firmly away her last regrets for the fiasco of the delegation's visit.

One of the customs that had caught the imagination of the Siamese church was caroling. Few but the younger people attempted it, since by usage already inflexible caroling began only at midnight and lasted until dawn. Every house visited was expected to offer the carolers candy or cake or soda water, so the night was one long party.

India awoke about three to hear *Silent night, holy night* . . . rising toward the starlit sky beyond the veranda. She was tired from all that had gone before, so tired that she did not rouse fully, and through the dreamy half awareness in which she listened the beauty of the words and music was somehow real, as if it were once again the angels who sang to a weary world the promise of peace and good will—*It came upon the midnight clear, That glorious song of old* . . . The voices sounded happy. A thrill of happiness crept over India, and she lay quietly listening until the singing was finished. Others were taking care of the refreshments. Before the young people left she was asleep again.

When the pleasurable excitement of Christmas was over, India was immediately faced with the necessity of making a decision about Ploy. She had put it off from month to month, but the problem did not solve itself. Ploy had learned nothing except how to improve her own appearance. She now dressed neatly and brushed her new bob to a glistening black. Her calico panung, faded from many washings, had a pattern of small stars on a blue ground. Her white blouse was neater and far less flamboyant than the sleazy pink silk in which she had arrived.

Her work improved not at all. When Grace came for dinner New Year's Day the tablecloth was so badly spotted and rumpled that India thought it had been stuffed into the buffet drawer without folding. The silver was tarnished and indifferently laid, the forks not entirely clean.

India did the only thing she could. "I'm sorry, Grace, but will you stand up while I change this cloth? Ploy hasn't enough interest in her work to change a cloth without a specific order." Dulcie shot her a resentful look which India ignored. "Get a fresh cloth from the buffet, Angela, please, while I take the dishes off."

When the table was set Dulcie excused herself abruptly. India did not urge her to stay. She was tired of Dulcie's swollen sensitivity. If the older woman chose to regard criticism of her protégée as criticism of herself, she could. Certainly she had never fulfilled her promise to train Ploy.

The next morning India scolded Ploy severely, and the girl sulked for the rest of the day.

"You don't get anywhere with Siamese, talking like that," Dulcie remonstrated. "You've made Ploy lose face. Why did you have to rip the tablecloth off right in front of Grace?"

India was unsympathetic. "I have feelings too," she said, "and they were very much offended by that disgraceful table. There's no excuse for careless work, and I won't put up with it any longer. Either Ploy does better or she goes at the end of the month."

"But you can't send her away," Dulcie wailed incredulously. "Why, she's beginning to take an interest in the church."

"If her interest were sincere it should have had a good effect on her work," India answered unmoved. *"Do it heartily, as to the Lord,* you know, Dulcie."

The next evening Darun came to India with a crudely printed letter she had intercepted. The problem of amorous correspondence was constant in Siamese schools. One of the obstacles missionaries had met when they opened schools for girls in the previous century was the fear of Siamese parents that the ability to write would be used in the composition of love letters. Early schools had had to reassure the parents by taking the most elaborate precautions to protect girls entrusted to them. Knowledge was less valued than vigilance, and when the vigilance of the mems proved more effective than that of home, girls were left in schools for the protection given them. The one cardinal sin of such a school was not failure to instruct, but the loss of a girl through elopement. Jasmine Hall had a good record in this respect, and most of the credit belonged to Darun.

She had been standing on the upstairs veranda that afternoon when she saw Ploy in the yard below talking to a small schoolboy. Quickly and silently she slipped downstairs and out of the compound after him. He dallied by the canal to throw a few stones, and when he saw her standing beside him a look of utter terror came into his face. He ducked and tried to run around her, but she was too quick for him. With a deft movement she scooped his books out of his arms.

"Stand still!" she said, and his face worked as if he were going to cry, but he stood where he was.

Kru Darun untied the strap with which his books were fastened and flipped over the pages. It took her only a minute to find the letter she had known would be there.

"Who gave you this?" she demanded.

The small boy looked around helplessly, but it was no use. Justice had dropped from the sky and had its talons in him.

"Ploy," he said, in the smallest voice he could manage.

"Where were you to take it?"

He rubbed one bare foot up and down the other leg and hung his head.

"Perhaps it will help your memory if you come back into the school and stand in the corner for an hour."

An hour! It stretched out before him like eternity. His mother was very strict. When he got home he would be punished a second time if he were an hour late. He capitulated. "To the teashop at the corner, *krop*."

"And who were you to give it to?"

"She didn't tell me his name, *krop*."

"Who were you to give it to?"

"To the policeman at the first table."

"Give me the money she gave you."

The small hand went into the pocket of the black shorts. Slowly it came out with the money; slowly it dropped the silver coin in Kru Darun's hand.

"If you carry letters again, do you know what's going to happen to you?"

The dejected head moved a little.

"The head teacher is going home with you and tell your mother."

Tears welled up in the black eyes and ran down his cheeks. The little boy stood frozen at the thought of this new abyss. Kru Darun smiled in spite of herself. Elaborately casual, she unpinned the coins she wore at her waist and took off five coppers. The child watched her dully.

She leaned down. "Are you going to carry a letter again?"

He shook his head, more vigorously this time.

"All right, then. But you've done it several times already, haven't you?"

He nodded.

"You promise that this will be the last time?"

"I'll never do it again, *krop*." He raised his eyes to hers with a faint stirring of hope.

"Then I won't tell your mother or your room teacher this time. You did a very bad thing, and you thought the head teacher wouldn't catch you, but she did. And now you've promised her you'll never do it again, so she's going to give you these five satangs for a cake. Every time you take a bite you say to yourself that it's much better to obey your elders than to get into trouble."

The letter was a crude thing, printed on a sheet of paper torn from a notebook. Ploy had learned to write only recently, and her vocabulary was limited. It was addressed to "Pi Mian [Older Brother Mian], whom I honor." This was the usual form of moderately intimate address. The body of the letter began with no references to the flowers and birds, as it probably would have if the correspondence had been in its earlier stages. It plunged at once into Ploy's complaint against the mem. Ploy was ordered about from dawn to dark. The mem was *ju-jee* (picayunish, unreasonable, demanding). No one cared about poor Ploy except Pi Mian. She was terribly unhappy. Maybe she'd drown herself in the canal. Could Pi Mian do anything about it?

Kru Darun sent for Ploy and examined her in India's presence. The girl came sullenly and knelt before Darun, as did all the servants. She was a heavy girl, dark from years in the paddy fields. Kru Darun showed her the letter, but Ploy remained impassive.

"Why did you write it?" she asked to make a beginning.

The girl refused to say, keeping her eyes on the floor. She had transgressed one of the strictest school laws. She had been caught. She had no recourse except to stubborn silence.

In the end Kru Darun gave up. She sent Ploy to her room and told India that she would detail two of the Bible school girls to wait table until Ploy repented or India found a new maid.

"I think she'll run away the minute she isn't watched," Darun warned.

Dulcie came to the office as they were discussing the best course to follow, and Darun handed her the letter. For once Dulcie attempted no defense of her charge. The gravity of the situation was of the sort to impress her. She had no patience with sexual irregularity and little understanding of the normal impulses of a seventeen-year-old girl.

"I'll take care of this," she said.

In a few minutes she went past the office, with Ploy following meekly in the wake of her long black skirt and starched shirtwaist. At supper Dulcie explained that she had locked Ploy into her sleeping porch.

Ploy was confined there all the next day, while Dulcie neglected her other duties to spend hours with the girl, cajoling, arguing, scolding, pleading. Once in a while India would catch the sullen accents of Ploy's country voice, but most of the time it was Dulcie's prim soprano she heard.

"I've gotten the story out of her," Dulcie told India with satisfaction at the dinner table that night. "She met this Mian the first time she ran away. He was the policeman who brought her back, do you remember? It seems he's from a district near hers, north of Ayuthia. You know the contests the country people have, where villages send out canoes and the people engage in singing contests to see who can improvise the best and funniest lyrics? Sometimes a boatload of men and a boatload of women will get to throwing insults back and forth, all to music, you know, and in rhyme. It can be very funny in a vulgar way.

"Well, Ploy and Mian decided that he had been in the boat that had been singing at her boat the year before, so they thought it was fate that had brought them together again here. She's been sending little notes to him ever since she learned to write, and he sends notes in to her. It's a good thing Darun caught them or she might have eloped with him."

"You don't think she will then?"

"Not since I talked to her. She's promised me she won't."

"Maybe we ought to arrange a marriage for her. It would be better than an elopement."

"She's old enough, of course, but I think I've persuaded her to wait until she has more education. This man isn't a Christian. I've neglected the child with all I've had to do, but I'm going to start teaching her English tomorrow. She'll be back at work in the morning."

Dulcie was perhaps less confident than she seemed, for as she left the table she added, "I think I'll keep her locked up tonight."

About nine o'clock that same evening India was called to the house of an old Christian woman who was dying. It had been an hour before India could find Pastor Rasami after the messenger came to summon them, but they reached the old woman in time. She was lying quietly on a pallet in the upper room of the tenement where she lived with her son and his family. The son, his wife, their children, and many of the neighbors were gathered around her. She smiled weakly when they came in, and her face was peaceful as she heard for the last time the majestic words of the communion service:

"... *the same night in which He was betrayed* ... *the Lord Jesus took bread, and when He had blest it, He broke it, and gave it to His disciples, as I, ministering in His name, give this bread to you: saying, Take, eat; this is my body, broken for you: this do in remembrance of me.*"

She could not swallow the bread, but India had held her up for a sip of grape juice, then laid her down again gently. The dim eyes were fixed on Pastor Rasami's face as he concluded:

"Eternal Light, Immortal Love, we bless Thy Name for all Thy servants who have kept the faith and finished their course and are at rest with Thee. Help us to abide in their fellowship and to follow their example, that we with them may sit down at the marriage-supper of the Lamb, which is in heaven. Amen."

It was twelve o'clock before the old woman's breathing ceased, and she was at peace. A wind had risen and was blowing through the almost deserted streets, unseasonal in its suggestion of the monsoon.

"I really think we're going to have a shower," India said to Pastor Rasami as they hunted for a taxi, and he agreed, although rain in January was rare.

Before they could reach Jasmine Hall the rain had come, unrestrained and violent. India thought with exasperation, as it came through the torn curtains of the ancient taxi, that tropical rain and tropical sun were without decent moderation. Big drops struck across her face. Her only satisfaction was that the rain would fill the Ali Baba jars, which she had neglected to have stored.

The compound gate had been locked, and the honking of the taxi horn failed to bring Klee, who had probably taken refuge with Det when the storm began. Pastor Rasami got out to open it, since the taxi driver refused. Just for a moment the headlights seemed to illuminate a figure crouching against the inside of the gate.

There had been an epidemic of thievery in the neighborhood lately, and there were always thieves who prowled on a rainy night when the sound of their movements could not be heard. The week before, the Maternity Home had lost four blankets and a clock to a thief who fished them through the barred windows with a hook on the end of a bamboo pole.

India was on the porch and only a little wet when she heard someone screaming.

"Kru," she called to Pastor Rasami, and he put his head to the opening in the taxi curtains. "Don't you hear someone calling?"

There was a lull in the storm and they both heard it. He opened the door to jump out, telling the driver to wait, but the driver refused. If the honorable sir was not leaving at once he must have his money and be on his way. The fury of the storm had resumed, and they could hear nothing for a minute. Then in another lull they heard it again. It was a human voice screwed high with terror and no disembodied devil, as the frightened taxi driver had thought.

"It's in the back," Pastor Rasami said, and began to run.

India followed as fast as she could. There was no one on the back or side verandas. Pastor Rasami switched on the lights, and together they looked around. The teachers had rolled the moolies down and pulled the wicker chairs back against the walls. The double doors were all bolted. They thought for a minute, listening to the roll of the rain, that they must have been mistaken. Then once more they heard it, closer this time, but outside and nearer to the ground. To India's mind came a picture of someone beaten by robbers in the blackness of the lane and tossed into the compound for dead.

Pastor Rasami jerked up a moolie, admitting the rain. The flickering light of the single bulb seemed hardly to penetrate the darkness, but he ran down the side steps and out onto the lawn with India behind him. When the cry came again they could distinguish words.

"Help, help, help!" someone was calling.

They stumbled among the shrubs and then they found her. It was Ploy. She was wedged into one of the water jars up to her neck, clutching the edge of it with frantic fingers. The stream of water from the downspout poured over her head with the force of a fire hose. When she could catch her breath she screamed.

Pastor Rasami took her hands and tried to pull her out, but she was so tightly fitted in that he could not move her. Her shoulders refused to come through the opening at the top of the jar. There was no time to speculate on the bizarre circumstances of her being there.

"We'll have to break the jar," India shrieked in his ear, and he nodded.

He ran back up on the veranda to find something strong enough to use on the thick earthenware, could find nothing, and disappeared across the bridge in the direction of the coolie's cottage.

In two or three minutes he was back with Det and Klee. They had a hammer and were chattering with excitement. The girl's hysteria impressed them less than her ludicrous appearance. They were laughing as they began to chip away the lip of the jar, which was more than an inch thick. The rain continued to come down in torrents, and the stream from the downspout dashed against Ploy's head no matter how she tried to shift.

"Careful!" India called. "You'll hurt her."

In a minute the first big piece broke out of the neck, and Ploy lunged forward to free herself.

"No, no!" India shouted. "You'll cut yourself."

The frenzied girl was past reason. It took the combined strength of Pastor Rasami, India, and Klee to hold her until Det could break enough of the jar to make it safe for her to climb out. Then she collapsed on the ground, and they had to carry her into the house.

They laid her on the floor in the office, and India ordered Det to make a fire in the kitchen while she went for blankets. "Please watch her, Kru. Don't let her run away."

It was hardly necessary. The girl on the floor made no effort to move. India ran upstairs for towels, dry clothes, blankets. She put Pastor Rasami out of the office and rubbed the girl thoroughly with a rough towel, then rolled her up in blankets and forced hot tea between her chattering lips. As her chill subsided she seemed to slip into something like a faint or a coma. Her eyes rolled up so that only the whites showed, and her mouth hung slack. After a little, a second chill began.

Angela came running downstairs wearing a blue dressing gown, and when she saw India working over Ploy went after Kru Darun.

"But how did she get in the jar?" Angela asked, picking up a towel, beginning to rub Ploy's legs and feet. Darun was chafing her hands.

"I don't know," India answered, sitting back to get her breath. "She hasn't said anything yet."

"It's strange Miss Dulcie didn't hear her," Darun said. "Ploy was on her side of the house."

"I didn't hear her either," Angela admitted.

Det came with another cup of hot tea, and they forced it into Ploy's mouth. She still shivered occasionally under the blankets, but the gray look of her face had grown less. She had closed her mouth and eyes and was beginning to whimper.

India went up to Dulcie's room. The rain was abating. India called her at first softly, to avoid waking the dormitory full of children, and when she did not answer rattled the door.

"Yes?" Dulcie's voice was sleepy.

"Dulcie, please wake up."

"What's the matter?" Anxiety tinkled in the question. India heard her fumbling to loosen the mosquito net, then heard her feet coming across the floor. The light went on, and Dulcie's head, the puffy hair on end, came through the door.

"What do you want at this time of night, India?"

"May I come in?"

Dulcie stepped aside. She was wearing a long white nightgown with an embroidered yoke, edged with a ruffle of lace. Her bony feet showed beneath it.

India went across to the screened porch. The door was locked on the inside. She released the spring and snapped on the porch light. Dulcie followed her.

The porch was empty. In the middle of it lay a thin pallet, one side mattress, one side mat, of the sort common in Siamese homes. Dulcie's mouth fell open.

"Where's Ploy?" she demanded.

The porch was screened with copper wire from floor to ceiling. There was a railing with carved splats about two inches apart, and wire behind it. At the top of this railing near a post India found what she had expected—a big flap of netting that had been cut loose. A pair of scissors lay near it on the floor.

"My best scissors!" Dulcie wailed, picking them up.

India reflected, looking through the hole at the old downspout, that it was a miracle it had not given way under Ploy's weight. Evidently the speed of her descent had deposited her in the jar. She remembered the figure she had seen lurking near the gate and fitted the last piece into the puzzle. "Older Brother Mian" had been waiting.

Dulcie put on a wrapper and slippers to follow India downstairs, chattering in excitement and anger. When she saw Ploy lying on the office floor her high voice became abusive.

"Be still!" India told her sternly. "Ploy has been through enough tonight. You can talk to her tomorrow."

CHAPTER 26

THE NEXT MORNING, WHILE THE SCHOOL BUZZED WITH THIS NEW scandal, Ploy lay on a bed in Kru Darun's room, listlessly staring at the ceiling.

"She won't run away," Darun assured India.

Nor did she. By the second day she was up and around.

"Now what shall we do with her?" India wanted to know.

"She wants to go home," Darun answered.

"But she doesn't have any home!" India exclaimed.

Darun smiled a little, almost apologetically, as if she hesitated to disillusion India. "Only her father is dead, and she doesn't like her stepfather. That's why she was willing to come and live with her aunt."

"You don't mean Dulcie!" India said incredulously.

"Her second cousin really. Miss Dulcie doesn't acknowledge her Siamese relatives openly, but she keeps in touch with them just the same."

"And Dang?"

"She wants to go back too. She only came to keep Ploy company. Their mother lives in a little village near Ayuthia. Ploy ought to marry and settle down to country life. It's what she's fitted for. She'll never be happy here."

"Is Sanu a relative of Dulcie's too?"

"The daughter of another cousin."

"But is she an orphan?"

Darun shook her head, and they both laughed. Dulcie, with her self-righteousness, her religiosity, her insistence on the need of three homeless children for shelter and food, to have practiced this fraud!

It took several days to arrange the details of the children's return. By that time Ploy was again in high spirits. She told the schoolgirls that Pi Mian was going to send a go-between to ask for her hand in marriage. His father was a village elder, a man of consequence, and her family would not refuse. Dang was glad to go back with her sister, but in the end Sanu begged to stay.

For several nights India had found a miniature wreath of jasmine on her pillow when she went into her room to go to bed. Such wreaths were a common expression of gratitude or affection, so she was not surprised.

Then one night Sanu was kneeling beside her door.

"What are you doing here, child?" India asked. "It's past your bedtime."

The little girl bowed to the floor, bringing her joined palms up and over her hair in the most abject salute that country people know, as if she literally took the dust from under India's feet and placed it upon her own head. She said a few words in a frightened voice, so low that India could not catch them.

"Say it again, Sanu, I can't hear you."

"Don't send me away, *mem-chao-kha,*" the child whispered.

"Come out to the mook and let's talk about it," India said.

She took a chair and the child knelt beside her on the floor. She was a thin little girl with great dark eyes in a narrow, sensitive face. The fringe of her new bob was still uneven around her ears.

"Why don't you want to go home, Sanu? Ploy and Dang are going."

The child trembled and was apparently unable for the moment to speak what she had come to say. India, trying to help her, thought that it must have been a very strong emotion to conquer her fear of approaching so august a person as the mem.

"Please don't send me home, *mem-chao-kha,*" she pleaded in a quavering voice.

"You'll have to tell me more, child, if I'm to help you."

Bit by bit the story came out. The little girl kept her head bowed as she spoke, and her voice wobbled. Her mother was dead. She had been sent to live with an aunt who didn't like her. There were four younger children. She had to take care of them while her aunt sold cakes in the market. Jasmine Hall had seemed like heaven. She loved all the teachers and the other children, and she loved to study.

"I want to go to school, *mem-lord-of-thy-slave*," she said, her voice a little stronger. "I like it so very much. Dang is still in the first pratome, but I'm in the second already. I want to be the little girl of the mem-lord-of-thy-slave, and I'll study very hard. I can wait table instead of Ploy, and wash the dishes of the mem-lord-of-thy-slave. I do it better than Ploy already. And I want to belong to the God of the mem-lord-of-thy-slave, if she'll only let me stay . . ." The voice trailed off into silence with the effort of speaking.

India looked down at the black head and thought of Ruth. Naomi could not send Ruth back, and no more could she send Sanu.

"Very well, child, you may stay, but go to bed now."

The little girl looked up. She was plain, small for her eleven years, with shaggy hair hanging around a thin, intense face. The eyes, troubled and unbelieving, lifted to India's and then widened slowly with hope. The mouth turned up into a flashing smile, and the child threw herself down, laying her forehead on India's shoes in a gesture of utter devotion. Then she was up and running shyly back to the dormitory.

India went to her room and opened the Bible to read again the passage that Sanu had brought to mind:

. . . and Orpah kissed her mother in law; but Ruth clave unto her. And [Naomi] said, Behold, thy sister in law is gone back unto her people, and unto her gods: return thou after thy sister in law. And Ruth said, Intreat me not to leave thee, or to return from following after thee: for whither thou goest, I will go; and where thou lodgest, I will lodge: thy people shall be my people, and thy God my God.

India sat motionless for a long time, thinking. The child's eyes raised to hers had opened into her soul, and India had seen for that moment all the suffering of the unloved, unwanted, overworked little girl. Beyond that she had seen again what sometimes became dim with its familiarity—the hungriness for learning of such a child, and the wonder of the new world that had opened to her through the gateway of knowledge. Who would have thought that out of Dulcie's pseudo orphans should have come a child like this? Perhaps another Darun. The quality was there.

Dulcie was annoyed with India's decision.

She had been resentful of India's chiding.

"They *are* orphans!" she had insisted, when India took her to task for deceit. "An orphan is a child who lacks one or both parents. Look the word up in the dictionary, if you don't believe me."

"Is that what you did?"

Dulcie tossed her head, unwilling to admit any fault.

"No one likes to be deceived, and casuistry is intentional deceit," India said. "I'm surprised you'd stoop to employ it."

Dulcie's thin lips had compressed. Now, instead of being pleased that Sanu was to stay, she was angry, glad to find what she evidently considered a legitimate occasion to vent her spite.

"What am I to say to her aunt?" she asked the next morning as she stood on the veranda with Dang and Ploy and their bundles, waiting for a taxi. "You made me write her that the child was coming home."

"I don't see any need to feel apologetic," India remarked. "Just tell Sanu's father that she's the only one of the three that did well in school and that I'm assuming her care myself. Tell him I'm going to make a teacher of his daughter. That will please him."

Peace came to Jasmine Hall with the departure of Dulcie's orphans, but peace was only a relative term. At best such intervals were short.

Already in the second week of January the days were beginning to be warmer, a hint that the hot season was approaching. The school year would end in March, a few days before the Siamese calendar year. The fourth grade, which was required to take government examinations, was hard at work. Kru Prachum was beginning to press them, keeping the weaker ones after school, reviewing each day.

Mani had returned to Jasmine Hall on the last day of the year. India saw her installed in her old room with misgivings. She had hoped that something would happen to keep Mani from coming, but nothing had. She had even gone so far as to check with Dr. Crane, to be sure Mani was not pretending that she must see the doctor merely because she was bored with the remote country town where her husband was stationed.

"She can come down once a month for three or four months, if that's easier," he had said.

India had written this information to Mr. Soderstrom, but he had replied that he thought it was better for Mani to be in Bangkok, since he was going to be in the forests for most of that time.

India's conscience troubled her about Mani in more ways than one. She secretly agreed with Grace on the undesirability of having Mani in Jasmine Hall, where she epitomized a system of values that was at variance with everything the school taught. Then too, India recognized the fact that Mani was volatile and unstable and might at any moment plunge the school into scandal.

In addition, India felt a sense of guilt at her failure to influence Mani. She tried catching her at odd moments and talking to her.

"But I am a Christian, mem," Mani would protest when India broached the subject. "I've never been a Buddhist." She did not take offense at India's concern. She accepted it as natural and dealt with it patiently.

Actually Mani spent little time at Jasmine Hall. She had many friends in the city. Her mother and most of her relatives lived on the Thonburi side of the river. India wondered if she resented not being permitted to stay with them, but apparently she did not. At Jasmine Hall she was close to the center of town, and this seemed to compensate for any restrictions that living in a Mission school imposed.

A place was set for her at meals, but she seldom ate at Jasmine Hall. Since her husband was paying for board as well as room, India was troubled by this. She suspected that Mani preferred Siamese food and went where she could get it, unwilling to risk being considered socially inferior by asking that it be served to her instead of foreign food. India solved the problem of her own obligation by having a breakfast tray sent to Mani's room at nine o'clock every morning. Then if she was in at lunch or teatime, one of the servants asked whether she would come to the table or have a tray. She usually went out for dinner.

Meals when Mani did appear were hardly pleasant. Angela seemed to arouse in her some special resentment or jealousy. India could not decide why this should be. There had been nothing in Angela's attitude to provoke it, except perhaps indifference and that quiet assurance which would always be, for one so unstable as Mani, maddeningly unattainable. Or perhaps it was just that she was jealous of Angela's greater beauty.

Like all half-castes, Mani hated the darkness of her skin and longed above everything else to be thought white. Her dark hair and eyes were really very beautiful, but they could never seem so to her. It was gold hair and blue eyes like Angela's that she coveted. Whatever the reason, she obviously felt some obscure need to impress Angela. It made her affected in manner and ostentatious about her activities. When she could, she made slurring remarks or invidious comparisons, which Angela ignored.

Dulcie disliked Mani openly. The older woman's criterion was duty, and while she served it casually herself, she never overlooked the flouting of it in others. Mani's creed of joy infuriated her.

Mani would come sauntering from her room down the length of the church toward the veranda in the high-heeled slippers she liked to wear. As a child she had of course gone barefoot, and perhaps because of that she had never learned to move her feet in foreign shoes with a grace to match the rest of her body. They clumped as she walked.

Dulcie had only to hear the sound of them to stiffen. Her lips would set. Her head with the piled white hair would come up. Her eyes would glint. Sometimes she would sniff before she deliberately lowered her eyes to her plate, pretending to be engrossed in the food. On other occasions she would raise them and glare, so that the glittering black eyes were the first thing that struck Mani as she came around the corner.

"Good evening," Mani would say in the sultry voice that was like a wet kiss.

Dulcie would jerk her head up, if she had been looking down, and eye Mani frostily. Some evenings she made a point of ignoring the girl, as if by doing so she could impress Mani with her disapproval. Then India and Angela would have to make conversation with what help they could get from Mani. Or Dulcie would stop eating and watch Mani sternly for a full minute. Or again she would pick at Mani with little gibes and innuendoes. This was the most difficult of all for India, who tried to interpose herself between them and her guest.

So far as could be seen, Mani was impervious to anything Dulcie said or did, in fact was unaware of her intention. Dulcie was not part of the world that had meaning for Mani—the world of Hollywood, of beautiful clothes, of jewels, big cars, smart hairdressers, of clubs, and money, and fashion. The only real wish that India ever heard Mani express was connected with this world.

"How do you like Prae?" India had asked, to make conversation one evening when Dulcie was pecking at her food in frozen silence.

"I don't like it at all," Mani had answered frankly, raising her soft eyes which had still the simplicity of a child's, without a child's innocence. "But in five years Georg can retire, and then he's promised me that we can live in Paris."

She said *Paris* reverently, passing her tongue lingeringly over the sound of it, and her face glowed with warmth and the sparkle of excitement.

"Why Paris and not Copenhagen?"

Mani came out of a dream of dark sweet streets, of the Bois in spring, of perfumes and *couturiers* and the Comédie, and gave India a strangely muted look that said if she were one of the elite, one of those born to beauty and to joy, she would have had no need to ask.

"I've never been there, but I love Paris," she answered in her caressing voice.

She ate each course dreamily as it was served, with dainty little movements of her pretty hands. Her mind was far away on other things and other places; while her fingers did what was required of them. Her shining hair dropped heavily around her face. It was parted in the middle and fastened on either side with diamond clips. The oval of her face between the wings of hair had the petal softness of a gardenia in the candlelight. The long upturned lashes were shadowed on the cheeks. Her mouth reminded India of the words *beauty's ensign—crimson in thy lips*.

India sighed. For Mani, after all, life was very simple. She wanted only pretty clothes, jewels, amusement, and men. Nothing else touched her, India's concern least of all. As for Dulcie, Mani gave her exactly the amount of attention she would have bestowed on an ugly piece of furniture.

India broke the spell by asking, "What did you do today, Mani? Go shopping?"

She had been to a movie, and while she told the story of it her eyes glowed with animation. When she was through she lapsed into reverie again, breaking the connection with India's dull world.

Once in a while Mani's world invaded Jasmine Hall briefly and then retreated, abashed by its drab utilitarian aspects or bored by its earnestness. Perhaps a car would be parked in front of the school for an hour, and two or three smartly dressed women, usually Eurasians and young like Mani herself, would go upstairs to Mani's room. There would be the sound of their laughter and quick words; then in a little while they would come out and go down again to the car.

If India happened to pass them on the stairs, Mani would introduce them. They were not all as pretty as she was, but they were well groomed, and there arose from them a delicate odor of expensive perfume, of soap and bath salts and powder, that was very pleasing. The men who came with them were Europeans or Eurasians, never Siamese. Mani and her friends had chosen the half of themselves that was white and avoided consciously the half that was Asiatic. Nevertheless, Asia clung to them inescapably.

The men sat downstairs on the veranda or upstairs on the mook, looking uneasy and bored. The odor of their cigarettes would penetrate the classrooms. A teacher would look out to see if some parent had come on business, and then go back to her work, wondering perhaps what Mani did all day, while she taught thirty or forty small and wriggling children.

On one such afternoon India would have passed a young man sitting on the veranda with a perfunctory greeting, if he had not risen and spoken to her.

"Miss Severn?" he inquired. "I'm Kurt Jorgensen, Mr. Soderstrom's assistant. He asked me to bring a package to his wife. May I leave it with you?" He indicated a small square box he had set on the table.

"Has anyone called Madame Soderstrom for you?"

"One of the teachers said she wasn't in, and no one knew when she was expected."

"I'll see if I can't find out for you. Come upstairs and have some tea with me while you wait."

He hesitated, then accepted.

He was a nice-looking young man with a square, intelligent face and thick, light brown hair. He wasn't tall, but neither was he short, and his shoulders—in fact, his whole appearance—were solid and at the same time agile. Before they had reached the top of the stairs India came to the conclusion that he was not one of Mani's young men. The errand was genuine.

"You're with the Danish East Asiatic Company, then?" she asked.

"Yes, I've just been transferred to Bangkok."

"But your accent is American."

He laughed, pleased. "I grew up in New York. My father was in the export-import business there. I went to Columbia for three years."

India settled him on the mook while she went to find Angela.

"There's a young man from Prae here with a package for Mani," India told Angela. "I asked him to stay for tea."

"Oh, India, I don't want to meet him."

"He didn't come to see you. There's no reason to be alarmed."

"It isn't that. It's just too much effort to meet strangers. I won't come out to tea today, please, and you don't need to send me a tray."

"There's a time after every illness," India told her firmly, "when you have to take yourself by the scruff of the neck and go out to meet people again. Besides, I stopped on my way home and bought some cakes from the Worachak Road shop especially for you." The proprietor of this shop had once been a servant in the palace and knew many palace recipes. It was the only place in Bangkok where one could buy a dozen or more kinds of unusual Siamese cakes and pastries.

Angela agreed reluctantly. She had been lying on her bed, ready and dressed. A little color had come back into her face since the time at Nong Khae. Her eyes were clear, the same deep blue as before. A lot of her hair had fallen out during her illness, but a thick golden fuzz had grown in, and with the rest of her hair cut short around her ears it looked like a halo. She was thin still, but it was the thinness of fragility, not a matter of angles and bones.

India had warned Angela. It had not occurred to her that Kurt might need a warning. She had merely told him in passing that she would call a friend who was staying with her. Afterward she speculated on what the words had meant to him. He had probably drawn a mental picture of a woman who was the duplicate of herself, gray-haired, in her late forties, another missionary in undistinguished clothes.

Certainly Kurt was not prepared for Angela. He stood up as they came onto the mook, and India saw his eyes. In the second before she made the introduction unbelief became wonder, and wonder was driven out by awe and a quick flash of something else.

"Madame Suksamran, Mr. Jorgensen, who has just come down from Prae."

Angela smiled, and as always when she smiled her face took on the look of being lighted by candles from within. "How do you do?" she said.

He bowed deeply over her hand in the continental manner.

"How far away is Prae?" Angela asked as she sat down.

"Four hundred miles north of here in the teak country. I'm with the Danish East Asiatic Company."

"I thought you were an American," Angela remarked.

"That's just what I told him," India said. "He says he grew up in New York."

"Do you know New York?" Kurt asked Angela.

"Not really, I'm from Chicago—one of the suburbs, that is."

Plo brought the tea, and India poured. Kurt ate the egg sandwiches and the little cakes as if they were ambrosia. Angela only nibbled. India persuaded him to tell them about his life upcountry. He had been in charge of a timber camp under the direction of Georg Soderstrom. Much of the time he had lived alone in a bungalow with his servants, far from other Europeans.

"That must have been lonely," Angela remarked.

"I liked the work. I had a wireless, so I could get the B.B.C.

broadcasts every morning from London. Once in a while I could pick up San Francisco or Berlin. I subscribed to a lot of magazines, and I had a lot of records." He went on to tell them of the elephants that the company used to work the teak forests. "I've got some pictures of them," he said. "I'd like to show them to you, if you're interested, especially the movies."

It was all pleasant and commonplace enough. India was pleased to watch Angela drinking her tea and listening as if she were amused. This was a forward step, and better for being unplanned.

Then she turned to Kurt and was not so sure. His face was bronzed from working outdoors, and his eyes were a candid blue. The nose below them was well defined, and the mouth strong but somehow easy, as if laughter were as natural to it as command. But the eyes never left Angela's face. India spoke to him, and with the discipline of courtesy he turned to her for a moment; then the eyes turned back, apparently impelled to do so.

India could feel the surge of great excitement in him. He was falling in love with Angela, on first sight, quite simply, in a headlong manner, as if he had slipped over Niagara Falls and now rolled down with the water in blissful ignorance of the rocks below. India had an impulse to call out to him, "Stop! Look! Listen!" but even as she felt it knew the warning was too late, that his ears were stopped against reason. He had come out of the jungle after two years of solitude and on his first afternoon in Bangkok he had found Angela, like a dream, like a vision. Unwittingly and unthinkingly India had done this thing. She sat aghast, her tea growing cold in the cup.

If there were any slightest hope that Angela would return his interest it would not be so disturbing, but Angela was still entrenched behind a barrier of her own erecting. Kurt could not be expected to perceive it. Only India saw it clearly like a glass wall between them, invisible from his side, but tangible for all that.

When Kurt rose to go, he asked if he might bring his elephant pictures to show them some evening during the next week.

"Yes, do!" India said impulsively, and was surprised to find that she had gone over to the enemy.

Would Angela resent it? Or was Angela unaware of what was going on? She looked a little tired, but unruffled by emotion.

"I'll call you about a convenient time." Kurt was speaking to India.

"We have no telephone."

"Then I'll drop by in a day or so, after I unpack the film. And will you give this package to Madame Soderstrom?"

"Is there a message?"

"No. Her husband put a letter inside."

CHAPTER 27

KURT JORGENSEN RETURNED TO ARRANGE A SHOWING OF HIS PICtures two days later. India was out at the time. She learned of his call from Angela, who had been sitting on the mook waiting for India when Doe brought him up.

Angela seemed distrait, as if the visit had been in some way unpleasant. All she said was that Mr. Jorgensen had selected next Tuesday evening, unless it was inconvenient for India, and that the teachers and schoolgirls were to be included.

"Does he have a screen or shall we put up a sheet?" India asked.

"He'll bring his own screen."

India poured herself a cup of tea. "You've had yours, of course."

"No, I waited for you," Angela said.

"Oh, I'm sorry. I'm very late."

"I invited Mani to see the pictures too," Angela went on, choosing her words carefully for no apparent reason, "but she said she'd seen enough elephants working teak to last a lifetime."

"Mani can be very rude."

"Yes. She really unsheathed her claws today. Neither Mr. Jorgensen nor I quite knew what to do. That's why I suggested that the girls be included. After all, she——" Angela left the sentence suspended, and India looked up quizzically.

Catching the expression, Angela abandoned evasion. "Don't look so omniscient, India," she protested. "I was going to tell you about it, really. It was just silly, that's all."

Angela had been alone on the mook when Kurt Jorgensen arrived. He refused tea, saying that he was going on to a party and had dropped in only for a minute to ask whether Tuesday would be convenient for them all. They had been discussing this when Mani came out of her room and apparently heard their voices.

"As soon as she realized who it was she came to the mook," Angela said, laughing a little. "I know this sounds ridiculous, but she came in big bounds like a panther and gave me a look that should have killed me on the spot. Of course I know she doesn't like me, but still! Mr. Jorgensen stood up and said, 'Good afternoon,' which she didn't even bother to acknowledge. 'Why didn't you write me that you were coming, Kurt?' she asked instead. He made some perfectly ordinary rejoinder, and she invited him to sit down, pointedly ignoring me. Then she sat perched on the arm of his chair. 'I thought it wouldn't take you long to get your transfer after what I said to you at Christmas,' she whispered to him, but loud enough for me to hear.

"He jumped up, and his face turned brick red. 'I had nothing to do with arranging this transfer,' he told her. His anger seemed to please Mani. 'Well, it's certain Georg never arranged it,' she retorted. It was then that I tried to bring the situation back to normal by inviting her to see the pictures 'that Mr. Jorgensen has *so kindly* been offering to show *us all.*' It was easy to see what was in her mind, and I wanted to disabuse her quickly.

"When Mr. Jorgensen didn't sit down, Mani stood up too. She laid her hand on his arm, saying that how he happened to be in Bangkok didn't matter after all, and that she'd show him the town. There was a party at Pinkie Something-or-other's at five, and they could begin with that. He thanked her coldly and declined."

Angela took a sip of tea and set her cup down before she went on.

Mani had sent Angela a blistering look from under her eyelashes, holding her responsible for Kurt's refusal. Feeling very much like an innocent bystander involved without fault in someone else's quarrel, Angela had been at a loss to know what to do.

Mani refused to give up. "Madame Suksamran never goes out," she had said. "She won't mind if you come with me. You'll excuse him, won't you, Angela?"

Before Angela could open her mouth Mr. Jorgensen had answered for her. "I'm not asking her to excuse me. As a matter of fact, I have another engagement."

Mani changed her tactics then. Still standing in front of him, so that he could not in politeness sit down, her eyes widened and grew soft. She laid a hand on his coat sleeve.

"Please come with me, Kurt," she wheedled. "Pretty please. I want you to come."

Angela could see his face over Mani's head. The muscles around his jaw had tightened, and his eyes had seemed to turn a lighter blue. He had removed Mani's hand from his arm, but without roughness.

"Not today, nor tomorrow, nor any other day, Mani. If that sounds rude, well, don't forget, I told you once before, Georg is my friend."

Mani had stood looking at him a moment before turning and walking stiffly away. They could hear her heels clicking angrily down the length of the church.

"I looked at him," Angela continued, fixing her eyes on India's face a little anxiously, "and he looked at me, and after a minute we both laughed. It was such a ridiculous performance. 'I'm sorry,' he said, and I answered, 'What makes it funny is the automatic way she cast me in the role of *The Other Woman*.' And he said, 'That's the only part I liked. It would have been so flattering if it had been true.'

"India, you're going to laugh at me, but I blushed and couldn't think of anything to say. Still, I liked his not making explanations. It was obvious that he hadn't been having an affair with her from the fact that she tried so hard, but I think most people would have had to say so. He just stood there grinning at me, and then he said, 'If that had been a trial of strength, you see who would have won.' And I blushed again. What am I going to do about Mani, India? I don't want any trouble with her."

"Just ignore the whole thing," India answered. "What else can you do with a woman like Mani? All she understands is her own way of life."

The one reassuring thing about the incident was Angela's reaction to it. India would have expected her to avoid Mani and make excuses for not seeing Kurt's pictures. Angela did neither.

The next Tuesday evening Kurt Jorgensen arrived about seven-thirty.

India was contrite. "I'm sorry it didn't occur to me to ask you to dinner, Mr. Jorgensen."

"Call me *Kurt*, won't you, please? And next Tuesday would do just as well."

She laughed, liking the suggestion of impudence and the further suggestion that he intended to try to see Angela.

"Next Tuesday will be fine. At seven, then."

The projector and screen were set up in the chapel, and the children and teachers assembled. Angela came down wearing a white silk dress with a blue cashmere sweater over her arm. Just as Darun was about to switch off the lights Mani also appeared. She was wearing an evening dress of flame-colored jersey, cut low. Her languorous mouth was painted to match the dress, and she trailed a chiffon scarf in her hand but did not put it across the creamy smoothness of her shoulders. The school children stared, and there was a rash of whispering with a titter here and there.

"Hello, Kurt," Mani called, waving her hand. A big ruby flashed on one of her fingers. "I came to see your pictures after all. Say you're glad to see me!"

Without speaking to anyone else, she walked across and sat down on the end of the chapel bench nearest the projector, leaning her elbow on the table.

The pictures were very fine, almost professional. They showed the whole story of teak logging, from the ringing of the trees and the felling, to the work of the elephants in getting the logs out of the forest and into the water. They concluded with pictures of the logs arriving at the sawmill in Bangkok. The skill with which the elephants maneuvered the great logs was almost unbelievable. Some of the canniest worked without direction from mahouts. When a log was actually in the water a look of satisfaction seemed to come into the eyes of the great beast that had sent it there.

Teachers and pupils were entranced. Many of them had spent all their lives in Bangkok and knew little of their country outside the capital city. Kurt explained and Kru Darun interpreted for him. After the lights went on the teachers came individually to thank him, and the girls came too, not quite daring to speak, but salaaming him shyly as they slipped past.

"Did you like them?" he asked when India and Angela came up.

Mani was still sitting on the chapel bench. She had taken out a cigarette and was holding it between her fingers. Always before she had been careful to observe Jasmine Hall's no-smoking rule. Nor did she light it now, but put it between her carmined lips where it drooped, looking peculiarly insolent unlit.

"The pictures were grand," India said with enthusiasm. "The children will never forget them."

"Of course I took more and cut the parts that weren't clear. It's hard to get enough light in the forest. There's something about elephants working, though, isn't there? Each one has his own personality and his own way of handling logs."

Mani sat staring moodily ahead.

"I could almost see that biggest one studying his problem before he decided what to do," Angela remarked.

"I don't agree with people who say animals can't think," Kurt answered eagerly. "I've watched those beasts solve the most intricate problems, for instance when the logs jam, and as far as I'm concerned that's thinking."

Mani stood up with slow and studied grace. "Do you have a match, Kurt?"

India looked at her, annoyed at this flouting of a strict rule, and in the chapel, but withheld reproof until morning.

Kurt fumbled in his pockets, found some matches, and lit her cigarette.

"What are you doing the rest of the evening?" she asked.

"Staying here as long as they'll let me," he said, turning back to India and Angela.

Mani took his hand and tugged at it lightly. "Jelly and Bill are picking me up in a few minutes. Come along to the club with us." Her lips parted eagerly over white teeth.

"You've forgotten your lesson," he said, turning his head briefly and disengaging his hand.

Two of the teachers standing respectfully behind India looked at each other. Mani saw the look. She saw also the square set of Kurt's jaw and shoulders. She shrugged, but her eyes blazed for an instant at Angela before she turned and walked across the room toward the door, moving slowly and rolling her hips under the red jersey dress. The scarf still trailed from her hand. No one said anything during this progress. Mani demanded and got the tribute of their eyes, nor were they conscious of giving it.

India broke the silence. "Come upstairs and have a glass of ginger ale, everyone."

Kurt put his projector and film away, chatting of his life in the teak country. He talked easily and well, so that the loneliness and fascination of it were like something they had read once in a book.

When the teachers went back to their rooms he said, "I bought a car yesterday. I thought maybe we could sort of christen it with a ride tonight, if you're all agreeable."

"Couldn't we break a bottle of ginger ale over the hood for you?" Angela asked mischievously.

Kurt stood up and bowed from the waist. "The champagne of your presence will be more than adequate."

Angela colored and looked annoyed with herself for it. Nevertheless, she agreed to go when India expressed enthusiasm.

Dulcie and India sat in the back seat, and Angela was in front with Kurt. They rolled slowly through the evening streets, seeing the lights and the crowds. The shops on Jawarad Road were still open. Chinese clopped along the streets in wooden pattens, yielding only to the most insistent tooting and honking. The car passed through the business district to the residential, where the night air was fresh.

India's mind was busy with the problem of Mani. She would have to go somewhere else. Her obvious determination to take Kurt from Angela, who didn't want him, was creating an impossible situation. India had no intention of risking Angela's peace of mind, so hardly won. Kurt would have to understand that too.

But India had reckoned without Kurt. The campaign was his, and he was more astute than she would have expected. He never asked her co-operation and he never risked losing it. Evidently he had made inquiries about Angela. At least his cautious maneuvering suggested this, although he would hardly have needed to ask. The whole city knew her story. Not until Charoon's body was cremated and Angela herself had left would it die. Perhaps not even then.

India had also made inquiries. It was not difficult. Every foreigner, by his oddity, was under constant scrutiny. There were few secrets in Siam. What she learned about Kurt was good.

He came to dinner the next Tuesday, bringing identical bouquets of red roses for India, Dulcie, and Angela. Mani, as usual, had gone out long before the dinner hour. Dulcie was on the mook waiting to greet him. She had proved an easy conquest. When later in the evening he invited them for a drive, Dulcie asked him to go down New Road.

She knew a great deal about the city and its past. As the car moved slowly she pointed out landmarks and told them odd bits of history. Up to the middle of the nineteenth century, she explained, Bangkok was a city of canals with only muddy paths on land. King Mongkut had built New Road, which was really the oldest road in the city, and finished it with impressive ceremonies in 1864.

"My father had bought his property on the river ten years earlier," she said, filled again with the excitement the old futile story always stirred in her. "He was one of the first foreign pilots here. His land wasn't far from the British consulate, which is the post office now. The consulate was the finest building in Bangkok outside of the palace in those days. Of course my father's property was even more valuable for being near the consulate. After the road went through he was offered large sums of money for it."

"But what happened to your father's property, Miss Dulcie?" Angela asked when the older woman did not go on, half turning around to hear the answer.

They had passed the business district and were moving out along the broad tree-lined road that led to the Throne Hall.

"He left it to us, of course," Dulcie replied. "It was to be rented until we three children were grown. Then we were to do as we pleased with it, but the consul was a scoundrel." An angry surge came into her voice. "He'd been busy for years lining his pockets by selling American citizenship papers to Chinese so they could flout the Siamese liquor and opium laws. When he was ordered home to account for this he sold our property and gave two thousand ticals to the missionary family who were taking care of me. The other children were dead. It was a ridiculous sum, of course, not a fraction of what the property brought, and besides, the sale was contrary to the terms of the will."

"And if the property had been been left until you were of age, you'd be a very rich woman, is that it?" Angela was still turned toward the back seat.

"I'd be a very rich woman indeed." And Dulcie sank into bitter silence.

No one quite knew how Tuesday became Kurt's night at Jasmine Hall, any more than they could have said how he became *Kurt* to Dulcie and Angela as well as to India. There was something easy about his presence that disarmed them all. India had maintained her neutrality after her first guilty act of partisanship, unwilling to hazard Angela's tranquillity by supporting Kurt's wary siege.

India suspected that Angela was in a curious state of mind, where she enjoyed his coming but refused to recognize the significance of his visits. She did not or would not think of him other than as someone who made life pleasanter and asked nothing in return. She seemed content to drift, aware perhaps that the dreamy half-world in which she lived could not last, but happy in it, reluctant to shatter its spell by any action of her own. If she was aware of the ultimate necessity to come to terms with Kurt, she was for the moment passive, glad to float on the surface of the stream and postpone the inevitable.

India was content to let her. With each week Angela looked more like the girl of the year before. Her body was round again and her eyes were clear. Even her hair dropping over her eyes in a newly grown bang had regained the rich luster, the look of burnished and antique gold, that India remembered. Often now Angela ran downstairs with a quick tattoo of feet on wood. She continued to eat hungrily, and by nine o'clock in the evening she was ready to go to bed.

"I don't know what's the matter with me," she would apologize, yawning.

"Oh, go to bed," India would answer in mock disgust.

"But I never used to be like this."

"It's just your body knitting up *the ravell'd sleave of care.*"

Angela was part of Jasmine Hall's life process, and this was apparently a satisfactory substitute for a life of her own. At least it had brought healing of the spirit. She was on intimate terms with all the teachers, except Darun, who maintained her customary reserve.

One afternoon India found Angela cutting out identical blouses for the Bible school seniors. The pieces lay strewn about her room, and Angela, with her hair tied back in a blue ribbon and pins in her mouth, was fitting Bua Kham.

"For graduation," she explained through the pins. "All alike."

She often sat down at the piano with the girls, and the sound of "Swanee River" or "Down by the Old Mill Stream" would float out from the chapel. She had even taken over the task of helping with the church music, drilling the choir and playing the wheezy organ Sundays for service.

When Jim and Anne came to tea, as they did frequently, she joined them naturally, and this was true of all India's guests. Mr. Denniscort called twice to see how she was getting along, and on the second occasion invited India and Angela to come to the Legation for dinner.

The one young person of her own kind who had penetrated her enchanted garden was Kurt. Throughout the winter term he arrived every Tuesday for dinner promptly at seven. There was something very clean-looking about him. His thick hair would be carefully in place, his eyes would be full of anticipation as he came up the stairs. His white suit was always stiff and clean, and his brown shoes were shining. And into the old house with him came the one thing it lacked, something masculine and attractive and strong.

He always brought three identical gifts: three boxes of candy in crisp white wrappings, three bouquets of roses, three corsages of tiny yellow orchids, three boxes of linen handkerchiefs with *I*'s and *D*'s and *A*'s embroidered in the corners, three boxes of monogrammed stationery, three bottles of cologne.

When India protested, he argued: "But this is the grossest bribery. I'm just insuring next week's invitation." And before India could object further he had turned to Dulcie. "How's my favorite heiress this evening?" he asked, and Dulcie was bridling and laughing, completely enchanted.

So the Tuesday dinner and ride became a ritual, and no one told Mani. Tuesday was the evening of the club dance, which she never missed. She was rarely in Jasmine Hall any day after four o'clock, so she did not know that Kurt came often to play badminton or have tea.

In February he invited them on a picnic. They offered to bring the food, but he refused. This was his party. The trip up the river in a launch he had hired was very pleasant. They ate their supper in the pavilion of a temple courtyard. Two or three curious novices stood watching them a few minutes and then went away. From the temple they could hear the musical chanting of the bonzes at their evening devotions. Each stanza started low and rose toward a crescendo, then low again and again rising.

Coming back down the river after the moon was up, India said, "Sing, Angela!" and Angela sang for them.

Her clear soprano floated out over the river in "Always" and "Who." Then she sang "I'll Take You Home Again, Kathleen," "The Rosary," and "Danny Boy" for India and Dulcie.

At Kurt's request she sang the "Jewel Song" from *Faust* and "The Evening Star" from *Tannhäuser*.

"What's that thing that goes mmmm-mm-mm-mmmm-mm?" Kurt hummed a few bars.

Angela looked at him, stricken. "It's 'One Fine Day' from *Madame Butterfly*," she said in a small tight voice, and would sing no more.

Kurt flushed deeply but offered no apology, evidently thinking it would only make the situation worse. They were all silent the rest of the way home.

CHAPTER 28

IT WAS MANI WHO PUT AN END TO THE INTERVAL OF PEACE. THIS had not lasted more than five or six weeks, yet to all of them it seemed longer. India knew that Mani's pursuit of Kurt had continued, but she did not mention this to the others, and Kurt never spoke of it.

Vina kept her informed. "Far pastures are always greener, you know, and what you can't get is the thing you want most. If he goes out to the club, she follows him around, and they say she lies in wait for him at his house night and day. He never goes home until he telephones his boy to be sure she isn't there. It's awkward, you know, because of Georg. He ought to know better, but he still believes anything Mani tells him. I think Kurt would be justified in having the boy throw her out."

"Maybe he's read about Potiphar's wife," India remarked, "and remembers what happened to Joseph. I simply must send her away."

"Yes, you should. She's insanely jealous of Angela, you know."

"And there's no reason for it, either."

"Of course there's a reason. Angela is everything Mani wishes she were, and the one man Mani can't get is in love with Angela. The woman's dangerous, India. You'd better get rid of her."

"Oh, she's not that, Vina!" India protested.

Before the day was over India was less sure of this pronouncement.

It was Dulcie's birthday, and Kurt had brought red roses. Each woman was wearing one in her hair. There was a cake in the middle of the table with a dozen lighted candles on it, and Kurt was teasing Dulcie to tell him her age. They were all laughing. The light of the candles, the usual red altar candles, gave the table a glow of intimacy in the surrounding darkness.

When India became aware of Mani she was standing against the lattice wall that divided the mook from the veranda, staring in at them. The mook was unlighted and heavily shadowed so that except for the fact she was wearing a white dress she would have been invisible. India saw the movement of white and then eyes against the holes in the lattice. It was shocking to know that someone crouched there watching them, taking in the table, the familiarity of their laughter, Kurt's banter, and their acceptance of him. She pushed back her chair to investigate, and Mani came swiftly through the door.

The long white dress, like all her dresses, was fitted closely to her body. The diamond clips in her black hair flashed as the candle-light caught them. One hand lay against her throat, as if she had forgotten it there, and the other was clenched at her side. Her eyes halted the conversation at the table. They flamed, and their force brought Angela's head up first and then Kurt's. Dulcie, struck by the change in the expressions opposite her, turned around.

"Well," she said, stiffening, "I never! What do you mean, creeping up on me like that? I never in all my life——"

The word *never* hung suspended in the air. They had never, any of them, seen anything like Mani's eyes. They were primeval, out of the forest, out of a savage world that killed to possess.

No one at the table spoke. They were more shocked than they would have been if Mani had walked out onto the veranda naked.

The eyes never wavered. "Kurt," she said, and her voice pulsed, "what are you doing here? I've been hunting for you."

His hands gripped the edge of the table, the look of shock still on his face. He seemed at a loss, handicapped by the presence of three women or some mistaken concept of chivalry. Mani began to walk around the table toward him with the slow stalking movements of a jungle animal. None of them thought it strange then or later that he did not stand. There was nothing about her to merit this ordinary courtesy.

When she got to his chair she said in the same low, vibrant voice as before, "Why don't you stand up?"

There was a nightmare sense of paralysis on them all, as if the unreal horror of a dream had caught them, robbing them of the power to move or think. Kurt looked at India almost helplessly, but he did not stand.

Then Mani slapped him, drawing back her hand and striking the side of his face hard, putting into the blow all the humiliation she had ever felt, all her hatred for the white world that would not admit she belonged, all the fury of a woman scorned by a man.

He leaped out of his chair, kicking it backwards, and grabbed her arm as she raised it again, throwing it back at her so that it struck across her own face.

"You bitch!" he shouted. "Leave me alone!"

She laughed, a deep, exultant laugh, and, moving with incredible swiftness, threw her arms around him and kissed him on the mouth. He pushed her from him, and she fell back against the house wall, hands outspread, palms flattened against it. Her eyes moved slowly from Kurt to Angela, full of hate, but also full of triumph.

From below the mook there came the complaining *honk, honk, honk* of a car. With slow and sinuous arrogance, her ego restored, Mani leaned away from the wall, turned, and went out. There was a mumble of voices from below, a man's querulous, Mani's brief and indifferent, then the roar of a motor.

Kurt picked up the chair. He set it in its place and looked at India. "Perhaps I'd better go."

"Of course you're not going," India said, and the comfortable tone of her voice relaxed the tension. "You haven't had your ice cream and cake. We're not going to let Mani spoil Dulcie's party."

Nevertheless, after their drive Kurt asked to speak to India.

"Miss Severn, I can't go without offering some explanation and apology."

"It's I who must apologize for what happened to you in my house," India said. "There's nothing to explain."

"Not even to Angela?"

"I've never discussed you with Angela."

He took out his handkerchief and wiped his face. He looked young, hunched forward in the wide chair with his hands clasping the handkerchief between spread knees.

"I love Angela," he said simply. "I did from the first time I saw her. I haven't said this to her because I thought she wasn't ready to hear it. Now I'm afraid of what Mani has done, and I don't know what I should do. Can you tell me?"

"Kurt, I don't know."

He looked rebuffed. "I shouldn't have asked."

"Why not? I'm *in loco parentis,* and you're declaring that your intentions are honorable. There's nothing wrong with that. But I'm not sure. Angela's been ill, as you know, and obviously you also know that there's been other trouble. Now she's like a child who's learning to walk again. Step by step she's making her way back into life, but she isn't quite ready to run and play with the other children yet. I'm afraid of what the effect of Mani's violence may have been. Angela still flinches from strong emotion."

"I'd like to ask you one other thing. Are you for me or against me?" He tried to smile, but the muscles of his face were tensed.

"That isn't important, you know."

"I think it is."

"Then I'll answer by saying that I'm for Angela."

"And against me?"

"Not against anyone. But frankly, I don't want her to have to live out here after what's happened."

"I thought of that. I'd be willing to live in the United States."

"What about your career?" India questioned.

"I've always wanted to go back."

India considered this and was touched by it, and by a certain doggedness and humility in the slope of his shoulders.

"If I were choosing a husband for Angela," she said, "I shouldn't be concerned about money or prospects, but I'd look for strength and kindness. I've always believed that only the strong dare to be kind. Well, Kurt, you're both, and you have a rare perspicacity, if you'll excuse a long word. If you had rushed at Angela, she would have run. The fact that you controlled yourself means to me that you have the insight and courage to help her the rest of the way back, if she wants to let you.

"But something has happened to Angela here that you may not understand," India continued. "Her faith has changed under adversity from the superficial to the real. It will always be from now on the fountainhead of life to her. Unless the man she marries has a matching faith, Angela will never be completely happy. There's a fundamental weakness in a home where a man considers religion his wife's business. Do you even know what I'm talking about, Kurt? Be careful of your answer."

Without lowering his eyes from hers he began to quote:

"I believe in God the Father Almighty, Maker of heaven and earth: and in Jesus Christ his only Son our Lord: Who was conceived by the Holy Ghost, Born of the Virgin Mary: Suffered under Pontius Pilate, Was crucified, dead and buried: He descended into hell; The third day he rose again from the dead: He ascended into heaven, And sitteth on the right hand of God the Father Almighty: From thence he shall come to judge the quick and the dead. I believe in the Holy Ghost: The holy Catholic Church; The Communion of Saints: The Forgiveness of sins: The Resurrection of the body: And the Life everlasting."

"Are those anything more than words to you, Kurt?" she asked when he had finished.

"Yes, Miss Severn, they are, but I don't talk much about them. People don't any more, do they?"

"Perhaps they're ashamed to admit dependence on God in this age of science and reason."

"I think it's more a consciousness of—well, of imperfection, you know," Kurt said slowly. "If performance doesn't match profession, it's better not to talk too much."

"Maybe you're right."

"Do I pass, Miss Severn?"

India laughed at his persistence. "Kurt, I told you before that that's up to Angela."

"But I want you on my side."

"Not until it's her side too." She said it gently, but she was firm. She would put no pressure on Angela. "I couldn't come over ahead of her, you know. It would seem disloyal. But I like you, Kurt, and one thing I will promise. I'll send Mani away tomorrow."

Before India could act, Mani had acted.

India was combing her hair the next morning when she heard Mani's sullen voice saying, "I want to talk to you."

The answer came in Angela's voice, which was light, refusing the challenge. "Come along to breakfast, then. We don't have to stand here."

India heard a dull thud and Mani saying furiously, "Leave him alone! Do you understand? Or I'll kill you."

India dropped her comb and ran.

When Angela told her about it later she explained: "The frightening thing was not what she said. It was her eyes. I know now how people feel when they look into the eyes of a murderer and say to themselves that in another second it will be all over."

As India came through her door she saw Angela crumple, saw Mani step aside to let her fall. Then she took hold of Mani.

"What do you think you're doing?" she demanded, shaking Mani with uncontrollable anger.

Mani went limp but refused to answer. Silence had been her refuge against authority always. She did not raise her eyes even when India released her, but stood looking at the floor, defying India to produce any effect upon her.

"Get into your room and pack your bags. I'll give you until ten o'clock to get out of here, and then I'll call the police."

She knelt beside Angela, whose eyes were fluttering open. Sanu came running from the kitchen, and India sent her for Doe. She helped Angela back to bed.

"I'm all right," the girl said shakily, beginning to cry.

"I'll send your breakfast in to you," India told her, ignoring the tears. "Doe will sit with you."

India went in to see her again at ten-thirty. She had been mulling the problem over. She had hoped until now that Angela could wander a while along the paths of the dream country in which she had taken refuge and then come out of it on her own initiative, step by step and mile by mile. Coming voluntarily, she would be, if not unscathed, at least whole and prepared to begin again. Mani had shivered that never-never land to bits. Sending her away would not mend the splintered sky. Evasion was therefore futile and postponement equally so.

"Mani has gone, Angela," India told her, and added reflectively, "She's an evil woman, one of my failures. I hope what she did hasn't spoiled Kurt's friendship for you."

Angela broke a cookie she was holding into halves, into quarters, then crumbled it bit by bit onto her plate. "I'd rather not see him again."

If India was disappointed it did not show in her face. "Perhaps you'd better write him a note and explain."

"Couldn't you do it for me?"

"That wouldn't be quite fair."

"I don't suppose it's fair anyway. He hasn't done anything."

India poured a fresh cup of tea from the pot she had brought with her and took a sip. "I understand, Angela, but I still think you'd better do it yourself. If you'll analyze what's happened for a moment you'll see why. Mani has forced you to face an issue before you were ready, but the issue existed and couldn't have been evaded much longer. When we're well and strong problems are easily dealt with, but when we've been ill they assume proportions far beyond the compass of our wills to wrestle with them."

She looked at Angela kindly and saw in her troubled face perplexity and distress. "The simple fact at the base of all this is that Kurt has fallen in love with you, and you aren't in love with him. You don't really want to fall in love with anyone, because you're the scorched child who draws back from the fire. But Kurt, being a normal man and deeply in love, would have forced the problem on you eventually. That doesn't make Mani any less culpable, but it helps to explain what she did. She wants Kurt, therefore she's jealous of you."

"But why should she be when I don't love him?"

"Because he loves you, and that makes you her rival in spite of yourself."

Angela put her head down on the bed and began to cry. "I don't want to see either of them again," she wept. "Please write him for me, India, please, please."

India had expected Kurt to object so she was not surprised when she and Angela, returning from dinner with Anne and Jim, found him waiting on the mook. Angela colored, seeing him, and her "Good evening" was strained.

"Miss Severn," Kurt said without preamble, "I found your note when I got home an hour ago. You don't mean it, do you?"

India sighed. The prospect of another scene, however controlled, was almost more than she could face.

Angela turned quickly to leave.

"Don't go, Angela," Kurt pleaded.

"Sit down, both of you," India ordered resignedly.

She took a chair between them. Kurt sat on the edge of his, very straight, his jaw set, but Angela huddled down into hers. India thought a moment, considering how best to begin. If she was not to be evasive, she did not want to be blunt either.

"Kurt, you know that Angela is still not strong. You probably know that her illness was complicated by what had gone before it. Her husband had been killed in an ugly accident. Maybe you know also that her marriage wasn't happy, partly because Charoon's mother opposed it and partly because he had taken several lesser wives."

Angela said nothing but seemed to shrink deeper into the chair. Kurt was watching India steadily, trying to discern the angle from which he might expect attack.

"Since she came to Jasmine Hall," India went on, "Angela has refused to see any of her old friends. If you had been one of them, we should never have invited you here."

Kurt nodded.

"What I want you to understand"—India chose her words carefully —"is that, as a result of all that happened to her, strong emotions are in themselves repulsive to Angela. It's something she can't help. If what Mani did was merely put on an unpleasant act, sending her away would have closed the incident, and we could all have forgotten it. But she brought Angela face to face with the fact that you're in love with her, and that's what makes her unwilling to see you any more."

"Why, Angela?" Kurt looked directly at Angela, and his voice was gentle. "Why should that matter so much?"

She did not look up but sat miserable and shrinking in her chair, twisting her handkerchief with nervous fingers. The few words she finally summoned came with effort.

"Because I don't love you."

"I know that," Kurt said, and his voice was still gentle. "I hoped maybe you might learn to, but even if you never do I'd like to go on seeing you because it gives me pleasure. I won't be coming under false pretenses any more, and you won't need to be afraid that you're holding out any false hopes."

She shook her head miserably. The wretchedness in her white face had a finality more complete than words. It defeated Kurt's resolution.

"All right, then," he said, and India felt a pang of pity at the bleak look in his eyes. "Of course if you don't want me to come any more, I won't, but I'd like to ask one last favor. Come out with me in the car for half an hour and let me talk to you."

Angela looked at India, hoping for reprieve, but India was nodding.

"You ought to do that much, Angela."

The girl stood up listlessly. "I'll get a sweater," she said.

Neither Kurt nor India spoke while she was gone. The clock struck ten-thirty as they stood waiting on the mook. Jasmine Hall was quiet, but the noises of the city came in to them, and the sound of bullfrogs in the canal.

India watched Kurt and Angela go down the stairs together before she turned toward her room, profoundly depressed. They were back where they had been before, she and Angela.

She had turned on the light in her room when she heard a scream. The sound split the night, and India, without consciously moving, was running down the stairs. There was a single weak bulb burning on the veranda below. India could see Angela huddled at the foot of the steps to the porte-cochere. Kurt's car was parked fifteen feet farther down the drive. Between it and the steps she saw the white back of his coat. He was crouching.

Suddenly out of the night something leaped at him. He dodged and struck with his fists. India heard the sodden thud of flesh on flesh, and Kurt's adversary jumped backward with catlike speed. There was the deep panting of two people sucking air into labored lungs. Once more the attack was repeated, and once more fought off.

Then India screamed as Angela had screamed earlier. Kurt's slow retreat toward the light had shown her that the left shoulder of his coat was crimson. Neither of the contestants paid any attention to her. There was for the moment no other sound than their thick panting.

Kurt crouched and the other one leaped out of the dark, struck, was beaten off, and withdrew. As his assailant came in for another blow India saw with a sick constriction of her heart that it was Mani, but not any Mani she had known, not even the jungle Mani of the night before. The lips were drawn back over the teeth, the nostrils distended, the hair hanging dank, the eyes glittering. Mani was amok! Suddenly as she leaped there was the glint of light on metal, and India screamed again.

The sounds of assistance were agonizingly slow in coming. There was the rattle of doors and calls of "Det, come quickly!" "Klee, where are you?" More doors flew open, and more lights went on.

Mani crouched, oblivious, waiting her chance. Then behind her in the increased light India saw Dulcie approaching from the lane. Her white head advanced calmly until the tableau between her and the steps caused her to stop.

There was screaming on the verandas now, the running of bare feet, calls for Det and Klee, but India could not tear her eyes away to see if either man was coming. Again Mani attacked, retreated, and crouched, and as she did so Dulcie moved forward a few feet. After the next attack she moved forward again. Then with agility surprising in a woman of her years she raised her umbrella and brought the handle down on Mani's head.

Mani crumpled like a sack of old clothes. There was silence. Now that they were no longer needed, Det and Klee arrived chattering. Kurt and India rolled Mani over. Her palms had opened, and from them, into the grass, had fallen the razor blades she had fitted between her fingers. India picked them up, counting eight, and put them in her handkerchief. Some of them were bloodstained.

"Now you, Kurt," she said, and turned to find him sitting on the running board of his car with his head back against the door.

Dulcie took out her handkerchief silently, and silently they stanched the cuts along his face. His hands were bleeding, too, but in the half-light they could see no serious wounds.

"Hold this against his face, Dulcie," India directed, "while I send Det for Dr. Crane."

It took the doctor only half an hour to reach them, and in the meantime they had moved Kurt to the veranda. The teachers had brought a blanket and pillow, and one of them knelt beside him, holding a handkerchief to a wound that still bled. Kurt lay with his eyes closed.

"This one will have to be stitched," Dr. Crane said. "Can you take it without an anesthetic?"

Kurt nodded without opening his eyes. He winced during the process but said nothing. There were three stitches.

"You're a lucky man," Dr. Crane said. "Another inch and she'd have gotten your jugular."

He cleaned up the wounds on Kurt's hands, rolled him over, and cut off his coat. The razor blades had slashed it through across the left shoulder, but the heavy duck had been a protection. None of the cuts in the shoulder and upper arm needed stitches.

In the confusion and her concern for Kurt, India had forgotten Angela. She found her sitting on a bench in the dark with her head in her hands.

"Is he all right?" she asked weakly.

India sat down beside her. "He's just fine," she answered, " a few little scratches and one cut on his cheek."

Angela shuddered, and the shudder reminded India of Mani. She jumped up and ran over to where the girl had been lying, but she was gone.

India hurried to the veranda and drew Darun aside. "What happened to Mani?"

"I don't know, mem *kha*. I thought Miss Dulcie was watching her."

Dulcie knew no more than Darun. "She was lying there when I went up with you for medicine, India, and after that I was busy ordering coffee. Perhaps she got away then."

Dulcie was strutting, the center of attention, with all the girls grouped around her in awe. Rather cautiously Det and Klee explored the garden with flashlights, but Mani had gone.

"Let's get him upstairs and into bed," the doctor said to India when he was through, and India rushed up to have the sheets on her own bed changed.

Kurt protested that it wasn't necessary, that if the doctor would help him he could get home all right, but Dr. Crane was adamant. "In the morning will be time enough."

Kurt grinned at India a little crookedly as the doctor helped him upstairs.

"I'm a hard man to get rid of, Miss Severn," he said.

CHAPTER 29

ONLY GOOD LUCK AND THE LETHARGY OF THE BANGKOK PRESS KEPT the story out of the newspapers. It traveled quickly by word of mouth and was added to the legend which had grown up around Angela.

That part of Bangkok Station acknowledging Amery Hillow as leader censured India for endangering the good name of the Mission. The two ameliorating circumstances were that her friends stood with her and that Angela did not retreat into an impenetrable reserve as she would have done a few months earlier.

The girl went about her usual tasks very quietly. In this the other teachers helped her. When Dr. Crane found that Kurt was running a temperature and sent him to the Nursing Home for a few days, Angela went with India to call on him, indifferent to the covert glances of the sisters. The three of them said nothing of what had happened when they were last together, but in wordless agreement talked about things of no consequence. Angela even managed to laugh a little. She promised to write Kurt at Cameron Highlands, where the doctor was sending him for a week.

The whole affair subsided quickly, and India's attention returned to the problems of the school. There were many things to do, since the term was drawing to a close.

The teachers at Jasmine Hall were hired on a year-by-year basis.

This was for their convenience. Several of them were married and did not wish to commit themselves to a longer period of service. The new contracts were drawn immediately after the holidays, and it was customary for a teacher planning to resign to notify India of her decision by Christmas.

This year the pressure of events had been so great that India had neglected the matter until the end of February. She asked the teachers to return their signed contracts on March 1 and did not attach any importance to the fact that Darun's lay among the others unsigned. The next morning, when the head teacher came into the office with the attendance reports, India handed the contract to her with the remark, "You forgot to sign your own, Kru."

Darun put the contract back on the desk.

"I'm not returning next year, mem *kha*," she said quietly. "I have been offered the position of principal at Nakon Sritamarat, and I've accepted it."

India was aghast. She had taken it for granted that Darun's devotion to Jasmine Hall equaled her own, that for the Siamese girl as for herself the school was a life work. What had happened? What had gone wrong?

"Is there something the matter, Kru?" she asked.

"No, mem *kha*, nothing." Darun's face was without expression.

India searched her eyes, and the eyes did not evade this searching. Neither did they respond. India had the feeling that, without her having observed it, the doors of Darun's mind had closed against her, softly, stealthily, one by one. But why? And when? There was no defiance in the Siamese woman, no antagonism that India could detect, no resentment. Only a great finality.

Darun went on: "I have been here long enough, mem *kha*. It is time for a change. Besides, it will be better for David."

"Is your salary inadequate, Kru?"

"It is, yes, now that I have David, but that's only part of it."

"Suppose I raise it ten ticals a month. Will you consider staying?"

Darun declined, courteously, but with a patient determination against which India's arguments were useless. The matter was settled. *Ajan* Hillow had offered her the post. She felt ready and able to assume the greater responsibility of a principalship. She had been happy at Jasmine Hall, but she felt that her usefulness there was over. She was looking forward to having full charge of a large school, confident that after her long apprenticeship in Wang Lang and Jasmine Hall she would make a success of it.

The news left India dazed. It was more than the necessity for replacing Darun—difficult, even impossible as that would be—which disturbed her. It was the dissolution of an old association, one that had meant much to her—and, she had supposed, to Darun also. There was, too, a vague presentiment that Darun's abrupt decision to leave had a deeper meaning than the teacher's explanation supplied.

India could think of nothing else all day. In the evening she talked to Darun again, with the same result. The teacher's mind was made up. She listened to what India had to say but could not be deflected from her purpose. And India once again had the feeling that she was standing in a long corridor where all the doors were shut against her. Yet she could not accept Darun's decision, could not believe that it was final. The bond that joined them was of such long standing that it had seemed to her permanent, not subject to the wear and tear of ordinary relationships.

Darun had been her first ward, her first lame duck. That had been twenty-six years ago. India had just arrived at Wang Lang, and Darun was eleven. The child's mother had died when she was born. Her father, a journeyman carpenter employed by the school, had disappeared before the funeral, leaving the baby behind. No one knew his family or village, or even the name of his province, only that he was from the north. No one ever appeared to claim the child.

Wang Lang had been conceived on a pattern of strict equality. Edna Cole, its principal for almost forty years, had been a pupil of Helen Peabody, who had been a pupil of Mary Lyon at Mount Holyoke. Under her direction every girl was assigned domestic duties. Children who since birth had been bathed and dressed by servants and waited on constantly learned to sweep floors and wash dishes. But no system of regulations could defeat the ingrained feudalism of the Siamese.

In the hierarchy of the school, hidden behind its façade of democracy, the position of a girl's father largely determined her relative importance. This system was tacit but universally accepted. It was the reality against which the idealism of the farang mems beat ineffectually. Each daughter of a prince or noble had a retinue, self-constituted from among the daughters of less important families, who waited on her. Only when one of the mems was watching did the highly born perform the menial tasks assigned them.

Most of the charity pupils accepted their low rank in the caste system of the school without resentment or emotional disturbance. India was quick to discover that this was not true of Darun. She had neither great talent nor great physical beauty, either of which would have helped raise her to higher position. Her face was angular, her hair lank, her body too thin. Still she refused to accept the implications of her birth, choosing loneliness to companionship at the price of subservience.

India soon realized that Wang Lang had failed to give Darun the one thing she most needed. The school had named her, supplied her with food, clothing, shelter, affection, and the opportunity to get an education. But none of these could satisfy the yearning of a Siamese child for the rich and diverse life of a large family, and the security that its position in the community was able to confer. Where family was paramount, she had neither mother nor father, brothers nor sisters, uncles, aunts, nor cousins. She was alone in the world.

A trifling incident revealed Darun's sense of isolation to India. Early one evening, shortly after she had come to Wang Lang, she went down to the lower landing to make arrangements with the boatman for a trip to town. Darun was kneeling there, watching the upper landing where a private launch was being nudged in toward the school steps. The little girl's face was sharp with an angry longing that startled and puzzled India.

She followed the direction of Darun's eyes and saw a woman climb out of the launch and walk toward the school with the dignified steps of one who has been taught in childhood that a lady moves deliberately, like a duck or an elephant. By this time Darun had seen India, bobbed a salute, and scuttled back toward the dormitory.

India paused to observe the rest of the tableau, trying to discern its meaning to the child. She already knew Darun's story.

The slim white launch was tied to the wharf, and three uniformed boatmen squatted there, fending it off carefully to protect the paint. A maid with something in a napkin followed her mistress toward the school. India watched while the teacher on duty greeted the visitor obsequiously. A servant was summoned and dispatched. After a few minutes a little girl about Darun's age appeared and, salaaming both teacher and mother, settled down at her mother's feet on the veranda.

India walked back toward the school while her quick imagination finished the incident. She could almost see Darun, small and alone, watching unobserved as this more fortunate child came running into the dormitory with the gifts her mother had brought. Probably there were cakes in the napkin, to be shared with her intimates. Maybe her father had sent a tical. Perhaps, better than either, there was news that the family was having a tonsure ceremony or important cremation for which she was to be excused from school. Any and all of these things made her a person of consequence. By comparison, Darun was no one.

From the moment of this discovery, India made Darun her special concern. She was quite aware of the limitations on what she could do, but within these she was determined to do something. She took Darun with her on her own vacation to the seashore. When she was going to town she would ask Darun to go along and would buy her some trifling gift—a washcloth, a yard of lace, a jar of colored glass for her bath powder. It did not trouble India that in the tight little world of the school she was accused of favoritism. She had made up her mind to help Darun achieve some small bolstering importance. And in this she was successful. No child marked out by one of the mems for special attention was without position of a kind.

Darun had rewarded her with a deep and wordless affection that found outlet in the very services she had denied girls who considered themselves her social superiors. She was always inarticulate. Nothing altered that.

Darun had learned early a trick of drawing deeply into herself against the careless snobbery of the children which no schoolmistress could forestall. By the time she graduated first in a class of twenty she had developed an assurance that was, so far as anyone could see, impervious to slight. Although she never overcame her extreme reticence, her past difficulties had produced a tensile strength that gave her a certain distinction.

She had not grown any prettier. She was always too thin, her shoulders rounded, but she became one of the most skillful primary teachers Wang Lang ever had. *Honorable teacher,* the children called her, kneeling before her. She had many friends. If anyone remembered her origin, it had lost its importance. And if she was ever lonely, it was because loneliness can be a habit.

When India moved from Wang Lang to Jasmine Hall, Darun came with her.

"You're taking Darun, of course," Grace said at the time.

"I'd like to," India answered, "but I hate to rob you. And then, too, it doesn't seem fair to Darun. Wang Lang is more than a school to her. It's her home."

"My dear, you must take her." Grace was firm.

"But——"

"India, don't be a fool! She's your man Friday. I think you need her, anyway. Someone has to play Martha to your Mary, now that I shan't be around to do it."

"You don't mind?"

Grace was exasperated. "Of course I mind! But neither you nor I can change the system, so take her with my blessing."

Darun had been an integral part of the school ever since. She had found an additional teacher, hired a coolie, watchman, and cook, and helped secure two of the first five pupils who came to the school when it opened.

They were not even settled in Jasmine Hall before their problems began, problems arising out of the interaction of many people living together, and others more serious. India recalled those first weeks vividly, and especially an incident that had threatened to end the school before it began.

Second Church had accepted the invitation to share Jasmine Hall, and a group of the younger men had brought the school fur-

niture across the river in small boats to save India the expense of
professional movers.

After the furniture was in place, they decided to clear the compound of weeds and brush. The thick vegetation certainly harbored snakes, but India hesitated to hire the work done because
of the expense. For several weeks the young men worked in their
spare time, chopping bamboos and grubbing out weeds. Then one
Saturday morning they cut down a big rain tree to let sunlight
into the front garden, piled the limbs on their brush heap, and set
fire to it. India was arranging her upstairs office when she heard the
crackle of flames. Running to the veranda, she saw fire spreading
through uncut weeds to a half-concealed privy on the edge of the
canal, which went up in a puff.

An excited Chinese merchant ran out of the shop the privy
served, shouting and cursing, and threatened to call the police.

"I sue you plenty, plenty!" he screamed, shaking his fist at India,
who had raced down the front stairs and out into the garden. "I
make you go 'way this place quicker, quicker! You bad woman!
You damn, damn bad woman!" And he abandoned English curses
for Chinese, the blistering heat of which she could feel even
though the words were meaningless.

India had no time to mollify him. Tongues of flame were spreading from the brush heap. It was the end of the dry season, and
Jasmine Hall was tinder. Darun had come running with several
buckets and an old wool blanket. Everyone set to work fighting the
rivulets of flame that trickled through the garden toward the house.
No one paid any attention to the shopkeeper, except one of the
young men, who shouted, "Stop cursing, grampaw, and beat out
the sparks on your side of the canal!"

It was two hours before the fire was under control. Neither Jasmine Hall nor the row of shops had been touched, but there was
an angry buzz from across the canal where men, women, and children had been battling the shower of sparks. India delegated the
coolie to watch the smoldering brush and went back to her office.

Only then did she have time to consider the shopkeeper's threats.
The young men had followed her, protesting that what had happened was an accident. So far as the size of the fire was concerned,

she believed them. On the other hand, they had considered the privy in their front garden an insult and had wanted to force the shopkeeper to move it. As for the tree, there was no question about that. It was indubitably a violation of the lease to have cut it down. As householder, India was legally responsible.

She sat up suddenly. Suppose the shopkeeper went to the police and accused her of arson. Suppose the Privy Purse canceled her lease. She could almost hear the shopkeeper demanding her eviction as an irresponsible woman who casually started a brush fire in a congested area at the end of the dry season. Even without exaggeration it was quite a tale—the crash of the big tree, the flames leaping thirty feet into the air, the sparks showering down on the row of shops, the licking runnels of flame threatening Jasmine Hall. No one in Bangkok had to be reminded how disastrous carelessness could be where fire was concerned. Every year whole sections of the city were razed by flames that slithered through hundreds of flimsy houses in a night and lapped up a street of shops in an hour. She felt sick at the thought that her cherished dream of a school could be consumed no less easily than the shopkeeeper's outhouse.

There was a knock on the door and Darun came in. Her broad triangular face looked anxious.

"Mem *kha*," she said hesitantly. "I'm a little afraid——"

India jumped to her feet. "So am I, Kru. I'll get a bath, and then we'd better start."

They had found the official from whom Jasmine Hall had been rented alone at his desk and explained the accident apologetically. There was no sign of the shopkeeper. The official asked, and Darun answered. All the way in the ricksha India had been steeling herself to meet the force of his disapproval, determined not to justify herself for what the young men had done. It was anticlimax when he tipped back his head and laughed, then waved a plump hand at her, as if he found her predicament funny.

"The mem wants to cut down a tree?" His voice was courtly, his head inclined toward her, but the laughter in his face was undiminished. "Very well, she may cut down a tree, or if she likes, two trees, three trees, only she must fill in this blank."

"I'm afraid we haven't made ourselves clear," India said unhappily. "The truth is, we've already cut it down."

He had a globular face and eyes that were swallowed into it when he smiled. Now they were peering out at her with a kind of conspiratorial amusement, as if what had happened to her served to enliven an otherwise dull day.

"Ah, but on paper the tree stands," he explained, lifting his eyebrows, "and as far as as the Privy Purse is concerned it will continue to stand until you and I cut it down—on paper. Now, fill out this application. No, not there, here! Let me do it for you, and you can sign."

He picked up his pen and went to work. When he had finished, and India had added her name, he asked, "Where was the outhouse?"

"It was on the edge of the canal," Darun answered for India.

He studied the plot on his desk and the legend attached to it. "On which side?"

"On our side, with a log across."

"I'll pay for it, of course," India interpolated, "but I hope you can keep the shopkeeper from making trouble about the lease."

He bent frowning over the papers on his desk, then looked up once more as his eyes vanished into his face. "There is no outhouse," he announced delightedly.

"But——"

"The mem has nothing at all to worry about."

"But——"

He waved a fat forefinger at her, as if she were a dull child who had not learned her lesson. "There is no outhouse on this plot of the property, therefore none burned down." He was bland.

"What do you think, Kru?" India asked Darun on their way home. "Did the shopkeeper go to the police?"

"I'm sure he didn't. He was trespassing, after all."

"But don't you think I ought to pay for the damage?"

They were sitting on the white cushions of the small first-class section of the tram. It was just after noon, and the hot street was almost empty. The motorman was sending the tram hurtling along the rails, and they swayed to its rhythm.

"Oh no, mem, no!" Darun's voice was stiff with disapproval.

"What was it but a few atap fronds and some corrugated iron?"

"I hate to make enemies at our front door, though."

"If you pay him you admit your fault," Darun pointed out.

"But——"

"We'll patronize his shop, and after a few months he'll be glad to have a school near by."

They rode on several stops farther. The conductor came through in his bare feet to collect for another division of the line. The frown eased away from India's forehead.

"Well, Kru, that was our first battle for Jasmine Hall," she said. Then she laughed. "It's not the sort of thing that would interest my supporting church in America. Still, it was important, wasn't it?"

In the eleven years of the school's existence Darun had found the answer to so many problems! India thought of the number and variety of them and could not imagine the school without her.

There was the day a dog wandered into the compound and bit a first grader. Det would have killed the dog if Darun had not intervened, ordered it roped and taken to the Pasteur Institute, where it was found rabid. She had reassured the terrified parents, and herself had taken the little girl back and forth for the injections that followed.

And there was the time Darun found a packet of love letters written by the father of two primary children to their teacher. She prevented an elopement, too, and so adroitly that face was saved for everyone. The children even continued to come to school.

Then there was the time she discovered that one of the servants was stealing jewelry from the girls and selling it to a pawnbroker. She managed to get most of it back before the first complaint arrived from an irate parent.

Darun had such good sense, and she was so diplomatic! It was she, India remembered, who suggested the solution of the most difficult problem they faced in the first years of the school—how to secure suitable pupils. India might have had charity pupils in numbers, but this suited neither her budget nor her plans. Sometimes when she was discouraged, she reminded herself that early missionaries had been forced to hire pupils for their schools. When they began work during the middle of the nineteenth century there was a proverb in every mouth, *Teach a buffalo before a woman.*

Now girls were given an education as a matter of course. Her difficulty was that Siamese parents, who were eminently practical, hesitated to send their daughters to a Bible school for fear no positions would be open to them on graduation. The Protestant church was small and poor, hardly able to support its few pastors, to say nothing of lay workers. On the other hand, graduates of schools like Wattana were constantly in demand for secular positions. As a result, parents able to afford fees sent their daughters to schools whose diplomas could be expected to have a market value.

One afternoon during the second year of Jasmine Hall's existence, Darun looked up from her desk as she and India worked together in the office.

"Mem *kha*," she remarked, "the Apostle Paul supported himself by making tents, didn't he?"

India nodded.

"Then his churches must have been poor too. Why don't we give our girls a trade?"

They selected two, teaching and midwifery. From that time on all the girls in the school were required to take courses in methods of primary teaching. There were many openings for trained teachers in country schools, since the first grades were poorly taught. None of the girls ever had trouble finding a position.

Dr. Catherine Darrow agreed to accept a limited number of girls from Jasmine Hall in her three-year course of midwifery. A term in the provinces had filled her with a horror of the high infant and maternal death rate of rural Siam where doctors were rare. She had organized a small school on the English model to train girls for service in outcountry villages. She was pleased with the idea of having some of India's graduates. On the completion of both courses, they would be able to support themselves by the practice of midwifery in country districts at the same time they worked in the rural churches. Several girls had undertaken this dual career since the plan was initiated.

Other teachers came and went during the years. Darun had remained as constant as India herself. The details of administration had come to be Darun's special province. India organized the curriculum, found English-language textbooks to be translated, and taught the advanced classes. Darun continued to recruit the Siamese staff, run the school kitchen, and discipline the girls.

It was she who had assumed the tiresome but necessary chore of censoring the incoming and outgoing mail. It was she who had watched inconspicuously when men came to the compound for social occasions connected with the church, nipped off unsuitable romances, and acted as go-between for young men who were acceptable.

She had been only twenty-six when she came with India to Jasmine Hall, but already behind her was a lifetime of schools. She was wise in the ways of institutions and of her own people, aloof to the point where Anne had dubbed her *Madame Fu Manchu.* And yet the younger teachers always felt for her that special blend of fear, love, and respect, which is the ultimate tribute of Siamese to authority.

It had never occurred to India that Darun would leave Jasmine Hall. She could not sleep for thinking about it. Darun's denial of any dissatisfaction was false, as evidenced by her discourtesy in withholding information about her decision until the last possible moment. Or was that merely the usual Siamese preference for the *fait accompli?*

She had known, of course, that India would not willingly let her go. Perhaps she had resented having all the responsibility for the school during Angela's illness without the prerogatives of the principalship. No, surely not. Then what was at the bottom of all this? There was something. There must be something.

The next morning India learned what it was.

CHAPTER 30

WHEN INDIA CAME OUT FOR BREAKFAST, JIM HOWARD WAS STANDING on the mook with his topee in his hand. She knew that only the most urgent business would have brought him at that hour. As soon as she saw his face she knew that his errand was distasteful. It was a broad face under curly black hair carefully brushed smooth, and all the lines in it suggested laughter, those around his eyes and mouth particularly. Today he could not manage a smile even in greeting.

"I have bad news, India."

"What about breakfast?"

"I want to get this over first."

"We'll sit here then."

They took chairs on the mook as far from the veranda where Dulcie and Angela were already eating as was possible. Jim spoke in a low voice, and even before he began beads of perspiration started out on his forehead.

"Amery received a cable from the Board about ten days ago telling the Mission to cut its budget for the coming year by twenty per cent. It wasn't entirely unexpected, and at the Executive Committee meeting last week the allocations were made among the stations. Amery got back from Chiengmai day before yesterday and called an emergency meeting of the Station's Executive Committee last night."

"And my budget has been cut. How much, Jim?"

"They took your appropriation away entirely."

"You mean it's the end of Jasmine Hall?"

"Yes."

The shock was so great that India felt no pain. She found herself curiously detached, listening to Jim's recapitulation of the meeting. Amery had argued that it was a question of closing projects where the least harm would be done. He mentioned the recent scandals at Jasmine Hall and pointed out that they reflected on the whole Mission. He criticized the scholastic standards of the school, saying that India took in girls without good preparatory educations, and that this lowered the dignity of all Christian work. He told the committee that even Darun, who had been loyal for eleven years, was now dissatisfied and had asked for a change. He concluded that, as all of them knew, India would have difficulty running the school without Darun's practical administrative ability.

Jim had defended Jasmine Hall, saying that the work was comparatively young, and that it was unfair to measure it by the achievements of schools established decades before. He mentioned the names of several graduates who were doing excellent work, and added that in his opinion India was making a vital contribution to the future of the churches, which no one else was willing or qualified to make. As for Darun, he had been told that she had not sought the position at Sritamarat. Amery had offered it to her, which looked very much like subversion.

They had debated the subject for more than two hours. There were four men and one woman on the committee. Peter Brentwood had sided with Jim. Grace had sided with Amery. Only Dr. Baker had wavered.

"I suppose you know Grace's line of reasoning, India," Jim continued. "She told the committee she had warned you a year ago that you'd have to redeem the reputation of your school. She talked about Mani Soderstrom, and some others whose names I've forgotten, and said that in effect you had been diverting Mission funds from the purpose for which they had been given. She said she pointed out to you that this was essentially dishonest, but that you ignored her advice all along the line, even when she hinted that unofficially she spoke for the committee. She mentioned Dulcie's orphans, and Angela, and remarked that your championing of Angela had offended influential Siamese who had previously been friendly to the Mission.

"This was the thing that decided Baker. He's always been timid, you know. She went on to say she had regretfully come to the conclusion that, for your own sake, you ought to be prevented from wasting your talents, and that in her opinion the solution was to assign you to a position where you would have no other responsibility than to teach children selected for you by people with more discrimination. She said you lacked the administrative ability to manage an institution of your own, and therefore, since there had to be cuts anyway, she proposed a motion to close the Bible school and Jasmine Hall as of April 1, with the proviso that you be assigned to Wattana. She said she considered herself your best friend and would see that you had work more nearly worthy of your special abilities."

Jim paused and mopped his forehead.

"I lost my head then, India, and made an angry speech in your behalf, accusing Amery and Grace of personal bias, and threatened to carry the fight to the Station. Amery didn't even get excited. He told the committee he'd polled Station sentiment already and that a majority agreed with Grace and himself. When it was put to a vote, Baker voted with Grace, and that left the decision to Amery. I'm sorry, India. I did my best."

As yet India felt nothing but the absence of sensation and was glad that pain would delay its coming for several hours. She had had too much experience of Mission politics to hope. If Grace and Amery had spoken so unreservedly, it meant that the careful lobbying was finished, the vote in open meeting was assured. Words of doubt had been planted long ago. The seed of disparagement had grown to harvest. The sordid incident of the fight was merely the occasion Amery had been waiting for.

"I think I'll go out to Wattana and see Grace now," India told Jim.

"Shall I come with you?"

"No, this is between ourselves."

India was still calm when she faced Grace across the broad desk in her office. Everything in the room had a quality of cold clarity, as it might have had on a December morning at home when the temperature had dropped sharply during the night and rime had frosted the landscape. The coldness in her heart killed the last of her feeling for Grace, not only the vestiges of affection, but also the sense of intimacy, which was the product of long association and shared experience. They had both changed with the years, as was natural. In her new harsh understanding, India was aware for the first time of how far apart they had always been.

She remembered briefly, in the second or so she stood without speaking, a young teacher whom Grace had dismissed some years before. In a flash she saw the shattered face, the nervous twisting hands, the bruised eyes of that girl on the day Grace had told her she would not be asked to return to Wattana. Grace had been as self-possessed as she was now. India drew a sharp breath of relief. She had failed wretchedly, yes, and many times, but she had never done *that* to any other human being. It was terrible to be destroyed, but more terrible to destroy.

"I've just finished talking to Jim," India said.

Grace looked at her quickly. "I'm sorry you found out that way. I was coming to tell you myself."

"Were you?"

"Naturally I was."

"Courtesy didn't prompt you to inform me in advance of what you were going to do?"

"I should think any breach of courtesy was yours," Grace rejoined. "You talk to Jim, jump to a conclusion, and make an accusation. Couldn't you withhold judgment until you'd heard what I had to say?"

India saw with detachment how easily Grace took the offensive. Automatically she had tried to weaken India's sense of grievance by shifting the burden of proof. But there was no further apology to be wrung from India.

"What made you do it, Grace?" she asked, refusing to be diverted. "Do you know yourself?"

Grace picked up a pen on her desk, then put it down. She looked around to be sure her Siamese secretary was not in the room. "The action was taken by a majority of the committee. Why do you blame me alone?"

"Jim told me exactly how the meeting went."

"You're misrepresenting the whole thing, or Jim is."

"I don't suppose you'll be able to believe this, but I'd actually be glad if I could convince myself your motive was honorable."

"Kind words coming from a friend."

"We're not friends any more, Grace." The statement was simple and quite flat. It held no bitterness, but Grace's voice when she spoke was full of injury.

"You mean that anyone who serves your ambitions is a friend, and anyone who obstructs them is an enemy. And by that criterion you repudiate my friendship. But I've always refused to let myself be blinded by affection. I don't believe that love has to abdicate its powers of reasoning. To my way of thinking, love seeks the highest good."

"Of which you are the sole judge?"

"I'm a realist, India."

"I suppose you mean that your concern is for the immediate. I've always thought expediency a poor excuse for setting aside Christian standards of action."

"The cut in the budget is immediate."

"This isn't a question of money, Grace, and we both know it."

"India, I believe in you as a wonderful person, utterly selfless and completely devoted to your work, but these last eleven years have proved that you're not an administrator. To be blunt, you're a good employee, but you're not a good employer. Anyone with a story that appeals to your sympathies can take you in. I believe you're wasting your life, and I'm going to salvage the rest of it for you even at the price of your friendship. I thought you'd understand, at least when the sharp edge of your disappointment had worn off, and I still think you will, given time. Then you'll apologize for what you said today, because you'll be ready to acknowledge that what I've done I've done for your sake."

India stood leaning on the desk with her hands, and her clear blue eyes searched the other woman's relentlessly. Under the pitiless scrutiny Grace's florid skin grew redder and the birthmark began to show along the side of her neck.

"Grace," India said, and her voice was so quiet it was almost expressionless, "you lie."

Grace jumped to her feet. She had been sitting while India stood. Now from her greater height she looked down on India with blazing eyes. Before she could speak India said:

"You see, I never knew you until today, Grace. I only thought I did. I've had intimations of the truth several times this past year, but I've ignored them. I realize now that you've never known yourself. You've kept your ego swaddled in flannel petticoats against the slightest draft of truth. And it's this lack of self-knowledge that makes you so powerful and so cruel. All the gentleness of Christ has passed you by. You haven't the faintest comprehension of the meaning of Christian love. A year ago you warned me not to take in any more waifs and strays, do you remember?"

"I remember perfectly, India. You were being criticized by everyone, and I hoped I could prevent exactly what's happened."

"I'm sure you think you did, but then you've never looked under the lid of your own heart, have you?"

"Don't talk nonsense." Grace was impatient. "The fact of the matter is that as usual you paid not the slightest attention to my warning. You went right on filling Jasmine Hall with harlots and idiots."

India's voice was still quiet, almost patient, as if it devolved upon her to render one final service that any show of anger would inhibit.

"Unfortunately I didn't realize until today what you were really saying," she told Grace. "I was so conscious of the fact that the school was doing good work and gaining acceptance in the Mission at large that I failed to recognize the supreme significance of your growing love for power. Now, of course, I know that you were telling me to take orders from you or else."

Grace opened her mouth to speak, but India motioned with her hand and went on.

"If I'd sent Mani away when you told me to, and submitted my list of new pupils for your approval, and turned out my sad little boarders, and consulted you on everything, and deferred to your judgment, and if I'd come to you about Angela and sent her away when you advised it, none of this would have needed to happen to me."

Grace's heavy lip curled. "I suppose it gives you some sort of satisfaction to abuse me, but you're willfully and maliciously misconstruing what has happened."

India seemed not to have heard. Everything was now clear. She saw Grace as a kind of female Moloch consuming the egos of other people, and she wanted her to see herself so, if only for an instant. She made one last effort to hold the mirror up to the woman who had been her friend.

"I was vaguely conscious of the way everyone had begun genuflecting to you, Grace, but I'd known you so long I still held myself perpendicular in your presence as a matter of right. When I didn't agree with your dictums, I disobeyed orders, and for this *lèse-majesté* I'm being reduced to bondage. The important thing for you to remember is that my bondage is as nothing compared to your own. I'm to work here where I'll be compelled to take the directions I once flouted, but by comparison I shall be free. The kind of chains you've just forged on your own petty, grasping, power-hungry self will drag you farther and farther along the road to injustice. You'll find you can't endure me near you and you'll have to go about the dirty task of discrediting me completely, having me retired or dismissed. And I shan't make it easy for you by rebelling, because I accepted the discipline of the Mission once and for all when I joined it, and I'll make no attempt to mutiny now."

Grace's nostrils flared.

"I shan't lower myself to argue with you over your distorted interpretation of my actions," she said haughtily. "I'll simply repeat what I said before. I was trying to help you a year ago when I first warned you, and I'm trying to help you now. You've consistently barred my every effort with your stiff-necked pride."

India was tired. There was no opening through the porcelain surface of Grace's self-righteousness.

"You're probably right about my faults, Grace," she said resignedly, "with one exception. Pride had nothing to do with my refusal to take your advice. I was impelled to do certain things for reasons of conscience that had nothing to do with pride. I can see now that my stupidity was overwhelming. Believe me when I say that if I had known what I know now—if I had thought for a moment that the sacrifice of my pride was what you wanted—I should gladly, *gladly* have gotten down on my hands and knees and crawled to you across the city of Bangkok to save Jasmine Hall. Is that pride speaking, Grace?"

For several seconds India stood motionless, looking into the eyes of the woman who had been her friend. She saw the color drain away from the birthmark and then from the face. She saw the hands grasping the desk turn white at the knuckles. She saw the eyes drop.

Then she turned and went out of the room.

India had only one idea when she left Wattana, to reach her room in Jasmine Hall without having to talk to anyone. It was disconcerting to find Mr. Denniscort's car under the porte-cochere.

"Mr. Denniscort," she protested when she had climbed to the mook, "why don't you send for me when you want to see me?"

"Don't scold," he answered. "I thought you and I were the two people in the world who were unconcerned for our personal dignity. Besides, I had such good news I wanted to have the pleasure of telling it. I've arranged a settlement for Miss Kane."

"How wonderful! Have you told her?"

"I thought I'd better discuss it with you first."

"May I get you something to drink?" India asked.

"No, thank you. The story is this. I have a friend who's a lawyer. I won't name him, so if Miss Kane asks who he is you won't know. He acted for me, unofficially, of course. I haven't committed Miss Kane to anything. To be brief, the consul who sold her father's property came to Bangkok shortly after the Civil War, a poor man. When he left a few years later he was a rich one. Of course there's nothing to be recovered from his estate. We can prove that he received thirty thousand ticals for the Kane property, a big sum in those days, and that he gave only two thousand of it to the family who had adopted Miss Kane.

"Our one hope at this late date was to invalidate the title, and this now seems possible. Under the terms of the will, which I have at the Legation, the consul had no right to sell. I had my lawyer approach the Chinese *towkae* who owns the property, just informally, you know. I wanted to find out whether he'd fight the case or agree to a settlement. It's the sort of thing that might drag on for years, but the result is reasonably sure. He must have thought so, too, because yesterday his lawyer offered a settlement. If Miss Kane will sign away all claims, he'll pay her a lump sum of twenty thousand ticals and two hundred a month for life. The property is worth at least a million. On the other hand, it would be a slow hard business to collect, and Miss Kane isn't young."

The half of India's mind that was clear of the gray fog which had enveloped it with her departure from Wattana welcomed the news. She tried to rally herself to an adequate expression of gratitude. She had not yet had time to consider what would happen to Dulcie, and the problem was solved.

When Dulcie came, prim and self-important, Mr. Denniscort

told her what he had told India, changing subtly the manner of the telling to impress her both with what he had done and with its finality. The valuation of the property he withheld altogether.

"I think I'll get a lawyer and fight it," she said, darting suspicious glances at Mr. Denniscort and India.

He shrugged. "As you wish, of course, but it may take years." He cocked an eye at India to say, "Your turn now."

A vigor that was rootless but sure came to India, and she spoke with authority. "You'll do nothing of the kind, Dulcie. You'll follow Mr. Denniscort's advice, and you'll thank him for all he's done for you. You want the money now, not after you're dead."

The inflexible calm of her manner had an immediate effect. Dulcie yielded graciously.

"How long will it take?" she asked after she had thanked Mr. Denniscort.

"A week or two," he answered. "I'll let you know."

When Dulcie had gone they smiled at each other. Downstairs the clatter of dishes told India that it was lunchtime. Angela came running upstairs and waved at them gaily as she went to her room.

"At least you'll have one less problem with Miss Kane gone," he said.

"Yes," she agreed. "It was strange your coming this morning, of all mornings." Without volition she found herself telling him what had happened and all that had gone before. She had thought she could never discuss it with anyone, at least not for years, and within the hour she was telling it to a man who was hardly more than an acquaintance.

"Isn't there some court of appeal?" he asked when she had finished.

"Not any more," she answered, and told him about the visit of the Board delegation.

"I'm very sorry," he said.

The simple words that everyone would use to her from now on, if they cared at all or pretended to care, were not hard to endure. They had meaning, even comfort.

"I'm sorry too," India replied. "I thought Jasmine Hall was to be my life work. I'm hardly able to grasp the fact that in three weeks the school will close forever. Now I wonder if I've been a misfit all along and never knew it until today."

"You and I are alike in one thing then."

She had lost the thread of thought. "What do you mean?" she asked.

"Neither of us accepts the pattern. Society punishes failure to conform."

India considered this carefully, and in the end saw some truth and no oddness in it. They were indeed alike in that one thing. She would never have thought of it herself, but now that it had been said it was true. There were others of her kind, who would have done as she had done, reached the same end, felt the same despair, found the same difficulty in acceptance.

"I'm leaving Bangkok in July," he said.

India felt a sense of desolation out of all proportion. She had never known Mr. Denniscort with anything approaching intimacy. Their common interests had brought them together at only a few points, but those occasional meetings had yielded a savor of their own that she would miss. Like had spoken to like, and deep to deep. It had meant nothing more to either of them, could mean nothing more, than a sort of mutual recognition, and yet she would miss it.

> *Ships that pass in the night, and speak each other*
> *in passing,*
> *Only a signal shown and a distant voice in the*
> *darkness;*
> *So on the ocean of life we pass and speak*
> *one another,*
> *Only a look and a voice; then darkness again*
> *and a silence.*

What would it have been like, she wondered, if the boy she had loved once long ago had been a man like this? Would she have escaped the terrible isolation that enfolded her now?

His thoughts seemed to have been moving along a parallel course, for he said suddenly, "I'd like to have known you when we were both young."

They sat a moment sunk into quietness, a quietness that had laid aside its usual guards. Then India said, "I'm sorry you're leaving Bangkok. What made you decide to go?"

"I'm a misfit too. I'm going back to my farm."

"I should have said you were the first *fit* we'd had in a long time."

He smiled. "I'm restless," he said. "It's been like that ever since my wife died three years ago."

"I didn't know."

He began to tell her about his wife. She had been thrown from a horse the year after they were married. For twenty years until her death she was an invalid. They had lived on his farm in New Jersey and spent their summers at the shore, where she loved to lie in the sun. From the small intimate stories that he told, India could see it all—the beautiful young woman embittered by her accident, going from doctor to doctor, gradually losing hope and settling at last into despair. She could see the active man learning to be gentle, impatient at first of finding himself tied, yet too honorable to abandon his wife, even when in a sudden storm of self-pity and generosity she begged him to get a divorce, marry, have children, lead a normal life. He had filled in the emptiness with boats, all kinds of boats, and a passion for sailing.

She had died quietly in her sleep three summers before. They had been at the shore. It was a cold night, one of those nights that come sometimes in August to say that fall is just around the corner. They had had a fire. He had been reading *Tom Jones* to her. She had put her arms around his neck and said: "Shane, you've been awfully good to me. I don't know why. I never deserved it." Perhaps she had a premonition. Things like that happen. She never woke up at all.

On any other day it would have seemed strange to India to have Mr. Denniscort tell her these things as if she were someone he had known all his life. Today she did not even wonder that a man so little given to talking about himself, or to any kind of personal confidences, should have talked to her as he had. There was a mutuality in suffering that precluded the need for explanation or apology. The terrible urge to cover, to hide, to protect was not forced to operate. They sat a few minutes longer, each busy with his own grief, then Mr. Denniscort stood up abruptly and retrieved his topee.

"If there's anything I can do for you before I go, I hope you'll let me know."

"There is one thing. I want to send Angela back to the United States. If the Princess refuses to acknowledge her claim to part of the estate, will you help me?"

"What about the young Dane?"

"I'd hoped, of course, but now I think I'd better try to get some money."

His eyes looking at her were warm. They were eyes that usually formed a wall between the world and the man. She had seen them sardonic and remote, even mocking, but she had never seen them warm before. The twinkle that seemed always in them had blinked out.

"I'll consider it an honor to help you," he said, and the old-fashioned words seemed strangely kind.

Then without a formal good-by he stepped across the short space between them. Leaning down, he kissed the top of her head lightly.

"You're a very gallant woman," he said, "and *gallant* is a precious word. I'm glad to have known you."

Turning, he went down the stairs.

India did not move. She stood perfectly still, looking out into the trees, watching carefully the slow slight swaying of a branch. Then, like a somnambulist, she walked across the veranda to her room.

CHAPTER 31

THAT NIGHT INDIA COULD NOT SLEEP.

For some reason she did not analyze she delayed telling anyone at Jasmine Hall the news of the school's closing until the next morning. She lay beneath her mosquito net in utter exhaustion, but sleep would not come. Her thoughts rolled north, east, south, and west, and the functioning part of her mind had no will to control their vagaries. Scenes came back to her out of her early years in Siam, things she had not thought of since.

She remembered the clothes she had been wearing the day she arrived at Wang Lang, a white shirtwaist with rows of tiny hand-sewn tucks, and a black skirt that swept the floor. Her hair had been arranged in a pompadour.

She saw again the room in which she had first lived, the white walls, the big old teak bed, the almirah in which she had stored her clothes, the washstand with the flowered china bowl and pitcher that did not match. The bowl was decorated with roses, the pitcher with lilacs. Some earlier occupant of the room had broken the rose pitcher and bought the lilac. Or perhaps she had broken the lilac bowl and bought the rose one to replace it. India saw the shining dark boards of the floor and smelled the odor of kerosene and wax with which they were polished, saw also the whiteness of the veranda floors scrubbed weekly by the school coolies with half coconut shells.

She remembered the nights she had been unable to sleep because of the giggling and tiny shrieks as one of the girls in the dormitory whispered a ghost story. She had resisted the impulse to get up and quiet them, until she knew that the teacher on duty did not hear. Then she would find four or five little girls huddled together in one bed, shivering with fear. Once there had been ten squatting on a single bed. They swore they had seen a *phi*. When she insisted that they show her, they took her to a window, clinging to her hand, and pointed through the darkness to a place where dimly a white wraith danced just below the kitchen.

"I'm going out to see it, children," she said, and was suddenly a little afraid herself, touched by the contagion of their fear. She lighted a candle and went nevertheless. Five minutes later she was back. "Come on, girls, all of you."

She drove them out, shaking and protesting, to where, leaning against the posts of the kitchen, an ironing board stood with the cover flapping. Someone had forgotten to put it away. "There!" she said triumphantly. "Now you know what a phi is." But the next week on inspection she found them huddled together as before.

As India lay awake the noises of the night grew less. Still she could hear the hawkers on Bamrung Muang Road crying their wares.

"Kui tiow pa mi, OOOOOOOO!" The sound of the Chinese selling noodles and sauce floated up clearly, and the shrilling of another hawker whose trademark was a flute. What did the man with the flute sell? In all these years she had never noticed. The sound of the streetcar bells still came, though it must be late. The motorman liked to ring them ceaselessly. *Clang, clang, clang,* she could hear each tram as it passed the head of the lane. And there was the steady *honk, honk, honk* of motorcars. She had been startled by the silence of American cars on her last furlough. Her ears were long accustomed to the steady honking of Bangkok drivers. Over and under the stronger sounds ran the shuffle of feet, Chinese feet in wooden clogs, Siamese feet in leather babouches.

Gradually even these sounds grew less. The restless life of the city went on throughout the night, but it was quieter now. A party of late revelers went past in the street, singing lustily:

> *"O Moon, great Moon,*
> *Give us rice, give us fish . . ."*

Countrymen, probably. Come to the capital on business. To sell a few head of cattle, perhaps. She heard faintly the sound of scuffling from the shops, then a scream, then silence.

Those first years at Wang Lang had been hard, but they had been good years. Miss Cole set a relentless pace for her young teachers. In a way she was more Siamese than the Siamese. At a time when they were aping everything European, she set herself to make Wang Lang a Siamese school. She would introduce much from the West, but her pupils must remain Siamese. They must respect their own culture and their own language. When they spoke English they must use no Siamese with it. When they spoke Siamese they must incorporate no English words into the sentences.

They were not allowed to adopt European manners, as they understood them, which was imperfectly. They must abide by the dictates of their own, and she knew—that had been the amazing thing about her—she knew when they erred. Yet it was strange, looking back now, to remember that what they would have changed she refused to let them change, and what she wanted them to change they clung to tenaciously.

Few of them gave up their fear of ghosts. Few of them ever became Christians. None of them altered the basic feudalism of their thinking. Their loyalties continued to be personal, not ethical. "This is the day I must go and wait upon my Princess," a child would explain, and go she must. Her mother had put her under the protection of some person of high estate in babyhood, and her whole future depended upon the whim of her Princess.

The night wore on, and a thousand scenes passed before India's eyes. She was not thinking. Her mind was awash. Two blocks away across the sleeping city she heard the heavy boom of the gong at Wat Tepsirindra. It was a murmurous baritone, insistent and strong, waking the bonzes to a new day from where they slept on their hard pallets in the monastery building. Already women were up in the city, cooking the rice to be ladled into their bowls. The night was almost over.

India tried to push her thoughts toward the future, but for the first time in her life she could feel no future. There was nothing to hope for, nothing to plan, except the immediate process of dissolving the thing she had created. First of all, she must take care of Angela. Tomorrow. Today. It would be better to do it before telling her. By the sixth of April she must vacate these buildings, the day after Easter. Her rent was paid until then. It was a blank wall without a gate, beyond which lay nothingness and, yes, despair, the end of hope, the nullification of her dreams, grayness, years to fill in with no longer any reason for wanting to fill them.

"I'm too old to start again," she thought. "When you reach middle age you need something to work for even more than when you're young, because half of what you once thought important now seems to be tinsel."

A verse from Corinthians came to her:

For other foundation can no man lay than that is laid, which is Jesus Christ. Now if any man build upon this foundation gold, silver, precious stones, wood, hay, stubble; every man's work shall

*be made manifest: for the day shall declare it, because it shall be
revealed by fire; and the fire shall try every man's work of what
sort it is. If any man's work abide which he hath built thereupon,
he shall receive a reward.*

What, of all she had tried to do, would be left after this con-
flagration? Not much. Most of what she had begun would die back,
like a plant that had sprouted too soon and been struck down by
frost. Going over the girls in the school one by one, she grieved for
them individually, saddened by the thought that what she had
begun she could not finish.

Salee, Bua Kham, Kae, Pinyo, the seniors. They were the last.
They would finish their courses. She remembered the first time she
had seen Pinyo. Her father was an elder in a country church, and
the child had had little chance for education. Once on a trip to the
village India had called on the old elder and seen the child there.
She asked him if he would not dedicate one of his children to the
service of the church, and after some thought he gave her Pinyo,
his youngest and favorite child. She was handicapped by a poor
elementary education, but just this last year she had finally overcome that handicap. She was a girl of marked ability, and she had a
simplicity and integrity that were refreshing.

It was the middlers and the freshmen for whom India grieved
most. Sanan and Bua Thong, both girls of great promise. There
had been joy in watching them develop, the endless fascination of
working with human beings. So many times you lost your gamble.
But there was always the off-chance that this one or that one would
fulfill herself. Was there any tragedy equal to that of the person
who lived below the level of himself? Why did people classify themselves so low when they could reach so high? What would happen
to the girls now? Was life always like that? When one stood on the
brink of accomplishment at last, did one always make some misstep
and forfeit the future?

India had no consciousness of having slept when she awoke. It
was nine o'clock, and the schoolyard was full of shouting children.
Angela had disappeared downstairs, and Dulcie was finishing her
coffee. What would have been hard to do before was easy, now that

Dulcie's future was assured. India told her in a few words that Jasmine Hall was to be closed.

"So that's it," Dulcie said. "I'd been wondering."

"About what?"

"Well, I knew Darun was leaving. I thought it was just because of jealousy."

"What do you mean? Darun isn't jealous of anyone."

"Of course she is," Dulcie answered tartly. "She thinks Angela has taken her place with you, and she doesn't like it. Don't tell me you haven't noticed how strangely she's acted these last few months."

"I hadn't noticed, and I don't believe it."

India felt a pang of sharp disappointment in Darun. Or was her own failure to express appreciation often enough really to blame?

"Have you told anyone else about this yet?" Dulcie asked, her eyes glowing with a new idea.

"Not yet, but of course the news won't keep long."

"India, give me two days, will you?" Dulcie was full of eagerness. "I have something I want to arrange before anyone knows that Jasmine Hall is closing. Promise me you won't tell the rest yet."

"I can give you today and tomorrow. After that the news will have leaked from somewhere else, if it doesn't before."

Dulcie nodded, satisfied, and got up hastily. India heard her leave the house a few minutes later and thought that for the rest of the year Dulcie's classes would see little of her. She was free at last.

To the school children, India supposed, the news wouldn't mean much, really. They'd have to change schools. The teachers would have no trouble finding positions. Howard and Jeannie Ansel's father had written that he would be back in May. Of the small boarders she felt troubled only for Riap with his crooked back and Tui with her dull mind. Sanu she would somehow manage to keep at one of the provincial schools. It was the dread of having to tell Angela that troubled her this morning.

All day she moved in the gray haze of the day before. Her thoughts had lost their roots, and she felt herself rolling with them, ballooning across the grayness as she had yesterday, like a tumble-

weed blown about by the fitful movement of the wind over a desert
plain that had no boundaries and no meaning. The feeling was so
marked that it was physical.

At lunch Angela looked at her sharply and asked her if she was
ill.

"No, not ill, but I didn't sleep last night."

"It's beginning to be hot during the night," Angela said, not
quite satisfied. "Will you be in for tea?"

"No, I have an errand as soon as school is over."

The Tan Ying kept India waiting a full hour, and India had no
illusions about her reason for doing so. It was an expression of dis-
pleasure. When she came in she was carelessly dressed in an old
pasin and a camisole. The two women got through the desultory
civilities as quickly as possible. The Princess offered India nothing
to drink, nor did she pass her betel tray. India felt only a vast
indifference.

"As you know, Tan Ying, your daughter-in-law has been living
with me for several months. I have come now to ask you about the
settlement of your son's estate."

"You can tell her that she's had the last penny she'll get out of
me, *wah!*"

"She doesn't know I'm here. She would have forbidden me to
come."

A look of genuine surprise crossed the Princess' face. When she
spoke again her tone was more civil.

"I owe her nothing, mem. She married my son without my
consent, and her coming brought us all nothing but sorrow and
deep trouble. She will have to look after herself. She was a waitress
before. Let her become a waitress again."

India looked at the other woman with great deliberation, studying the small mouth with its lines of petulance, the tiny useless
hands, the heavy body, the sagging cheeks, the small, irascible eyes.
Then she spoke again out of the deep quietness of her own defeat,
feeling in herself a power she had never had before.

"Your daughter-in-law will not have to wait tables. She is a
teacher and a talented musician. When she gets back to the United

States she will have no difficulty finding a position. If you have made up your mind to humiliate her here in Bangkok by reducing her to destitution, remember that she bears your son's name. You cannot revenge yourself upon her without hurting your own reputation. If she had died here in your house, as she probably would have without my help, all Bangkok would have whispered that you murdered her. The only reason you have escaped criticism so far is that I have done what you should have done. I can't do anything more for her now because the Mission is closing my school. I think it will be to your advantage to have her leave Bangkok and go back to the United States, and I think it is very much to your advantage to make a generous settlement."

"And if I refuse?"

"You realize, of course, that the marriage is legal? And that there is a marriage certificate to prove it."

The Tan Ying frowned, and India continued: "You realize also that she is entitled by law to a third of Charoon's property, since he died intestate."

The Princess shot India a sharp look.

"But you've already told me that she doesn't want the money."

"Yes, I've been frank with you. I thought it would be better to follow the custom of your country and arrange the matter between ourselves. These things are for older heads to decide. It's true that Angela doesn't want the money. But something else is true also. Angela is like my own daughter now. She will do what I tell her to do. The American Minister has offered to act for her, so she will not have to act for herself in any case."

India saw that she was beginning to make an impression. The other woman's mood had turned from one of anger to one of careful calculation. She must have wondered many times whether Angela would sue to secure part of Charoon's estate.

"I think, Tan Ying, that it would be better for all concerned if you offered a settlement through your lawyer. If it's generous enough it would not be necessary to go to court."

"No!" The answer was short and harsh, not softened with *cha* or *kha*. "I have sworn to all my family and my friends that the woman will get nothing out of me."

India stood up. "I'm sorry. You leave me no choice then. I'd

hoped you'd agree to a quiet settlement, in which case I was planning to see that Angela left Bangkok by the middle of April."

She turned to go, turned back. "Tan Ying, I have known you a
very long time. You think I do not understand your point of view.
I do understand it. I want to urge you once more to be generous,
because your generosity will honor your son's memory as revenge
never could. Why don't you send her portion with her? Then you
will have the memory of having acted well."

The Tan Ying sat lost in thought. India looked around the oval
room with its marble statues, its gaudy rug, its carved tables and
chairs, and thought it tawdry.

"And if I refuse?" the Tan Ying asked spitefully.

"Morally and legally, part of Charoon's property belongs to his
wife. I'm only trying to persuade you to do voluntarily what you
are well aware you can be compelled to do."

The other woman made no move. Her sullen face continued
blank.

India felt herself defeated. "Good evening," she said coldly,
speaking in English.

"Wait!" The Tan Ying motioned with her hand, but India refused to sit down again. "How much will you take?"

India made no answer.

"I'll give you ten thousand ticals, but not a satang more."

Without a word India turned toward the door.

"Fifteen thousand."

"Mr. Denniscort will be glad to see your lawyer any day, Princess. I suggest you tell him to make an appointment. I shall leave
the sum to them. Good evening."

CHAPTER 32

WHEN INDIA REACHED JASMINE HALL SHE WAS SO UTTERLY WEARY
that she threw herself down on her bed without waiting for dinner
and fell at once into troubled sleep. She was still asleep, tossing

from side to side and muttering to herself, when Dulcie knocked on her door at nine o'clock.

India sat up, confused. "Who is it?"

"It's Dulcie. May I come in? I have some good news." She waited expectantly.

"Yes, come in," India answered dully.

Without turning on the light Dulcie edged carefully around the furniture to the bed and drew up a chair.

"India, what do you think has happened?" Her voice shrilled with triumph. "I've bought Jasmine Hall."

"What?"

"I finished making arrangements this afternoon. Mr. Denniscort helped me."

India tried to rally her confused senses. "I didn't know it was for sale."

"Oh, they've been trying to settle the estate for a year. I thought you knew. Then last month someone told me the Privy Purse would take fifteen thousand ticals for the house if they could get cash." Sensing an occasion for resentment, she justified herself quickly. "I knew you'd find out soon enough. *Sufficient unto the day is the evil thereof.* Last night it occurred to me I could buy it myself." She paused, waiting eagerly for India's comment.

Inside the mosquito net, India sat with her arms around her knees. It was like Dulcie to have known that the property was for sale and not to have mentioned it. Well, it didn't matter any more.

"Aren't you going to congratulate me?" Dulcie prodded her.

"Yes, of course." India roused. "You have my warmest congratulations. Now you can start your orphanage after all."

"Oh, that, I've given that up. Ever since I heard from Mr. Rockefeller, you know."

"I didn't know."

"Yes, they can't help me. I guess I forgot to tell you. But I want to keep the primary school, if you're willing." The school was registered in India's name and could not be turned over to anyone without her consent. "I don't want the Bible school, of course."

India could see Dulcie's spare figure against the veranda lights. It was tense, waiting, suspicious.

"You won't have Darun to help you," India reminded her.

"I know. She's being married. I found that out today."

"I can't believe it," India said heavily. There had been no court-ship. How strangely these things were arranged sometimes! "I thought she was going to Nakon Sritamarat to take charge of the girls' school."

"She is. They're both going. She's marrying Kru Chinda." Dulcie forgot business in her pleasure at exploding bits of gossip like a string of firecrackers under India's composure. "You mean she didn't tell *you?*"

"No."

In some mysterious way this knowledge enlarged Dulcie's sense of triumph. "She was in love with him before he married Wasana. Perhaps you didn't know that either. She's been dead only six months, so they're being married very quietly on April 12. At Amery's house. Darun's gotten very intimate with the Hillows lately."

India added no comment. She had worked with Siamese long enough to understand what had happened. She had taken Darun for granted. That had been a primary mistake. She had presumed on the limitlessness of the teacher's loyalty, forgetting that the human spirit needed to be refreshed by appreciation. It did not greatly matter whether Darun had turned to Amery—and to Grace, of course, for certainly the plan was as much hers as his—in search of what India had failed to give her; or whether the two of them had employed Darun's jealousy and dissatisfaction to weaken Jas-mine Hall.

Dulcie went back to her request when India showed no inclina-tion to discuss Darun. "You'll let me have the school, won't you?"

India, still engrossed in her thoughts, did not answer.

Dulcie added with a kind of worried defensiveness, "I'd ask you to stay, if I could, you know, but on my small income I can't afford it." Then, with dawning acquisitiveness, "Unless the Mission would leave you here. Do you think they would?"

India felt a thrust of bitter amusement. "I doubt it, Dulcie. I have a new assignment already."

Dulcie heard nothing but India's acceptance of her new suprem-acy. "Then you'll turn the school over to me?"

"Who'll act as head teacher? You'll have to find someone with a sixth *matyome* certificate."

"That's all arranged. Prachum's husband is being sent to the United States for graduate study. She'll bring the children and live here. I thought I'd put her in my room," she continued reflectively, "and I'll take yours. When do you plan to move?"

"I'm going to Petchaburi after Easter. I'll try to have everything out by then."

"You'll leave me the furniture, of course."

"I'm giving it to the church, if they want it."

"The church can stay on here," Dulcie interposed swiftly. "They can pay rent. Let me see, I should think twenty-five ticals a month. And their electricity and water."

"That will be their decision."

"But I need furniture. How can I run a school without it?"

"You'll have money left after you buy Jasmine Hall."

"Yes, but I want to keep it in reserve."

India pulled the net out. "I can't make any promises until I've talked with Pastor Rasami," she said by way of dismissal. "I think I'll get something to eat."

Half an hour later she knocked softly at Angela's door.

"May I come in?" she asked, and when Angela answered stepped into the room.

"Turn on the light, if you like," Angela said. "I'm just lying here watching the fireflies."

The end of the room that had been part of the original veranda was screened from floor to ceiling and overlooked the canal, where thousands of fireflies flashed on and off in unison, outlining the bushes on which they rested. Angela had her head propped on her arms and her legs crossed. She was wearing some pajamas she had made for herself, with the legs cut off above the knee, and sleeves and collar eliminated. "The bare essentials," she had giggled, pleased with her wobbly pun. Her soft hair was pushed up over the top of the pillow.

India pulled up a chair and sat down. She had put off telling Angela the news until she had seen the Princess, and found herself no more ready now. Patiently and cautiously she had fashioned this magic thing, this companionableness between herself and Angela. There would never again be anything quite like it in her life. Now she must take it into her hands and break it in two.

If she were actually my child, would I feel like this at having to thrust her out? she wondered. It was hard to sever by act of will a tie that had been woven so carefully.

"Angela," India began, unable to postpone the telling any longer.

The girl sat up quickly. "What is it? I've known something was wrong for two days, but nobody would tell me."

"The Station has voted not to appropriate any more funds for the school or for my rent. That means the end of Jasmine Hall. I'm being assigned to Wattana, and you'll have to go back to the United States sooner than we'd planned."

"Oh no, oh no!"

"Yes, it's all over but making the final arrangements."

Angela was sitting cross-legged within the net, her face toward India. The room was dark, and India could see only her silhouette against the faint light beyond the screens.

"The bastards!" she said. "The damn, damn, damn, dirty bastards!"

She began to cry, rocking back and forth with her knees clasped in her arms. India let her cry. She would be glad when she herself could.

After a while Angela asked, "Isn't there anything to do?"

"No, nothing."

"A whole lifetime of service, and this is your reward. I hate them! I hate them!" And she started to cry again.

India began to talk quietly, telling her of Dulcie's plans, of Darun's approaching marriage and transfer, and went on from that to Angela's own immediate problem. "I saw the Tan Ying this afternoon. Don't protest. Let me explain. By law you're entitled to a third of Charoon's estate."

"I don't want it. I'll get a job."

"No, Angela, listen. It takes money to go home, and I can't let you stay here. Remember Charoon the way he was when you first knew him. Remember how generous he liked to be. I want you to let him help you now. Mr. Denniscort will arrange the details. You won't have to do anything but sign some papers. I think the Tan Ying is going to agree to a settlement out of court."

"India, I can't, I can't."

"Yes, child, you can and you will."

They sat some time in silence. Once more India's thoughts went billowing across the gray plains, ballooning where they would, like tumbleweed.

But it was said, and Angela had accepted it. Her voice was small when she spoke. "India, please take the money and build another Jasmine Hall."

In the gray desert of her blasted hopes India's heart jumped for a moment with gratitude. This instant of feeling in the limitlessness of unfeeling that comprised the expanse through which she moved, lost and alone, gave her a new surge of strength.

"No, Angela, that's impossible, but I'm grateful for the sweetness of your offer. I'm under orders, you know. I can't refuse the discipline of the organization to which I've given my loyalty. I've seen people try it once or twice. It's never successful. I believe that what the group does is more important than any contribution I can make alone. And I can't let you stay on in Bangkok. It would have been only a matter of six or eight months anyway. You need to go home and start over."

"Yes," Angela said, and her voice was low and submissive.

India floundered on, feeling instinctively that all she had to say must be said tonight. Tomorrow there would be the slow-building wall that knowledge of their dividing ways would erect.

"I'd hoped for a while that you might learn to love Kurt. Perhaps it was too soon. What I want to say is that eventually the old wounds will heal, if you'll let them. Don't tell yourself there's any virtue in cherishing them. If you can love again, it's right to do so, not something to be ashamed of, or afraid of either, for that matter."

The sounds of the night came up to them, and the sweetness of some night-blooming flower. Angela pulled up the net and slipped from under it. She knelt at India's feet and laid her head on India's lap.

"India," she said, still in the small-child voice in which she had spoken before, "I haven't been honest with you or with myself.

The wound has healed, almost." India could feel Angela's body trembling against her legs. "I love Kurt," she whispered, and began to cry. "Only I didn't want to love him, and now I don't know what to do."

India felt a strange sense of peace. The death of everything she had lived for had some power to accomplish good for those she loved which her life had never had. It was a humbling thought.

"Does Kurt realize this?"

The soft head moved from side to side.

"Then you must tell him and ask him to wait until you're ready. It won't be as long as you think."

"I can't, India, I can't."

India put a hand under Angela's chin and tilted her face up. In the dim light she could see its pale oval and the dark wells of the eyes.

"Listen carefully, Angela. Kurt can't be allowed to see you go without knowing that you love him. If you refuse to tell him you'll force me to, and that will be bad for both of you. Remember that you and I do things the hard way, but we don't cheat. No, not a word! I won't listen. Come on now, get into bed, child." For the first time in their acquaintance she leaned over and kissed Angela on the cheek. "And don't name your first child for me, remember! *India* is a terrible name! Good night."

Two days later Kurt returned from Cameron Highlands. India was on the mook when he came running up the steps that first afternoon, and she was glad. She wanted to talk to him before he saw Angela. She had done little during the interval but hold imaginary conversations with him, searching for a way of saying what needed to be said. Did he understand that what had been written on Angela's heart had been written and could never be erased? That was a crucial question. If he was jealous of the past, it would not do.

What, after all, did he expect from love? Did he know? It was the great miracle, of course, the thing people sought all their lives and seldom found. Need of it drove the young to look into each new face and ask without words: "Are you the answer? Are you the other half of the torn paper that is myself? Can you fulfill this hunger of mine to be whole?"

But love was a question also, not just an answer. And it was never a cure-all. At best it was a moat and a wall and a castle. How could Kurt be expected to understand that? Would he understand that forgetting was a matter of the nerves and not the will, that time as well as love was needed to effect it? She couldn't very well say to him: "Kurt, sometimes you'll reach out for Angela and she'll run from you—yes, in terror. What will you do then? Will you be strong enough for kindness and waiting, or will you destroy her to appease your pride?"

She was oppressed with the conviction that however much this needed to be understood it could not be said. Kurt would imagine no situation for which his young man's strength was inadequate. To give an answer in advance of a question was futile, and to propound a question in order to supply the answer was also futile. There were difficulties that could best be met by unawareness of their existence. Wasn't ignorance the answer in this case?

But there was an urgency in her to protect, combined with a fear that anything she said might do harm rather than good, and a conviction that somewhere the words existed, adequate and right to her need. She wanted to help him understand Angela's difficulty. She wanted to find expression for the things Angela would not be able to say for years.

She wanted to cry out to him, "Remember that her wounds are very deep. They will reopen at a careless touch." She wanted to tell him something else he might discover too late. "Kurt," she would like to say, "when she holds your child in her arms, holds him to her breast and feels her strength and life flowing into him, then healing will be quick and complete, if you will let it. Be careful then for a while. Don't be jealous of the child. Remember that there is a need in her that the child alone can fill. She will come back to you."

When he stood before her all the words dried up on her lips.

"Hello, Kurt," she said, "you're looking fine."

The scar on his face still showed, but it was not going to be prominent. He had a present for her, a table cover in Javanese batik, and one for Dulcie, and something in a white package for Angela.

"I'll call her," India said when she had thanked him, and turned away.

There were no words for her purpose. The things she wanted to say couldn't be said unless they would be understood, in which case they didn't need saying. These two must blunder into each other's arms. Their love would effect some kind of union, however clumsily. Her heart contracted to know that it was beyond her power to save them pain.

Angela was in her short pajamas, hair tied into a tail, down on her knees, cutting out a blouse for one of the girls who was graduating.

"Kurt's here," India told her. "Take those pins out of your mouth."

Angela took them out obediently and stood up.

"No backing down now!"

"No-o-o." Her voice quavered over the monosyllable. "What shall I wear?"

They studied her wardrobe together. "I think that white linen would be nice," India suggested.

Angela giggled, a warm little chuckle deep in her throat. "But, India, it wrinkles so easily."

O God, thank you for that laugh! India thought.

"Angela," she said, pursing her lips in imitation of Dulcie, "you shock me!"

Angela giggled again. "I wish I could. You probably know exactly what I'm going to say."

"No, I don't."

"Neither do I. That's why I hoped you did."

"Why don't you wear the yellow silk?"

"All right."

"I'll go out and talk to Kurt. Don't take all afternoon. He already thinks you're beautiful."

The laughter faded out of Angela's eyes. "Will you tell him something for me?"

"It depends on what it is."

"Tell him I'm going home, will you?"

"Angela, how many times has he asked you to marry him?"

"Only once."

"Don't you think it would be fairer to tell him that you've changed your mind about the answer?"

Angela hung her head like a little girl. "I can't, India, I can't. I want him to ask me again."

India laughed with a gaiety that drove out for an instant all the sadness of the defeat in which she moved. "What a Cupid you chose! Well, here I go."

It was almost nine o'clock before Kurt and Angela came back to Jasmine Hall. Dinner was long over and India was in her room working on her accounts. Dulcie, as was her habit nowadays, had eaten early and gone out. For some reason of her own, she was avoiding India, going her own way busily, full of a new importance that had not yet shaken down into assurance.

India had been impatient to hear the sound of the car, but when it rolled into the drive and stopped she could not move from the chair in which she was sitting. The power of locomotion deserted her. All in the world she wanted was to be left in suspense without the necessity of knowing either the best or the worst. She had waited throughout the evening for this moment, and now she rejected it, but it came on regardless in the sound of feet crossing the veranda downstairs.

The footsteps halted a moment and Angela said, "Let's go up." India's heart began to pound. She could hear them coming, slowly, step by step. Then somehow she stood up, walked across the room and out the door. She searched her mind for any word of polite greeting it might contain and found it empty. She could only wait.

They were not smiling, but they came hand in hand, their faces turned up seriously, looking for her.

O God, thank you, thank you! she said in her heart, and aloud, "Hello, dears, congratulations and best wishes."

Angela ran up the last two steps and, throwing her arms around India's neck, burst into tears. India stroked the silken hair and her heart was full. She smiled at Kurt across Angela's shoulder, and his eyes looked wet as he smiled back.

"Now let's all get something to eat," India said, when Angela, still half laughing and half crying, borrowed Kurt's handkerchief. "There's one thing about people in love I discovered a long time ago. They're always hungry and they never know it. Come on, both of you."

CHAPTER 33

THE ACTUAL PROCESS OF CLOSING THE SCHOOL MOVED WITH IN-credible ease. After years of struggle, it seemed ironic to India that the termination of all her various activities should be by comparison so very simple that the few weeks in which she had to do it were ample.

The papers required by the government when one head teacher replaced another were prepared and submitted. India's own resignation as principal was even simpler. Dulcie's permission would come in plenty of time for the opening of the new school year, which she had set for May 7. Mr. Denniscort hurried the final arrangements of the payment to her and went with her to complete the purchase of Jasmine Hall.

Later the same day the two women registered Dulcie at the police station as householder of Jasmine Hall. The heat of March was already oppressive, and the officer to whom they explained their business had taken off his tunic and was working in a collarless muslin shirt. Several flies buzzed on the top of his desk. He spit into a brass spittoon beside it and began to write out the necessary forms with a pudgy fist and a good modern fountain pen, gold-mounted, of which he seemed proud.

"Sign here, please," he said, and India put her signature on the line he indicated.

"And you here, please." Dulcie wrote her name.

The transaction was complete. Dulcie was mistress of Jasmine Hall. The whole business had taken less than an hour.

Even Second Church, faced with the certainty that India, on

whom they had depended, was unable to help them further, solved their own problem with an expeditiousness she would not have believed possible. Pastor Rasami came to see her as soon as he learned that Jasmine Hall was being closed. His round parchment face that betokened a Chinese ancestry he would not have cared to admit gleamed a little with perspiration, and his eyes seeking hers were genuinely distressed.

"I am so sorry, mem *krop,*" he said in his careful English, "so very sorry."

India knew that he was aware of the crosscurrents that had brought her defeat. She did not want to discuss them with him. The last service she could do him was to prevent his taking sides. He must not be allowed even to make the offer.

"Sometimes it's hard to understand the will of God," she said, speaking quickly, "especially when it seems to us merely the will of man, and yet we must believe that *all things work together for good to them that love God, to them who are the called according to his purpose.*"

"But this is not good," he replied with simple directness.

"You know, Kru, I have thought more than once that the church is too dependent on me," she said, speaking almost at random to deflect his concern. "I've provided them with a place for worship, and supplied a whole corps of Sunday-school teachers, and helped in the pastoral calling. Maybe it's time the church walked alone."

She had begun without direction in order to turn Pastor Rasami's thoughts from herself to the dilemma of the church. Now she wondered whether there was not more wisdom in what she had said than she had intended.

"But what can we do?" he asked. "We are not rich."

"Churches rarely are, even in America. Why don't you call a joint meeting of the elders and deacons to discuss the situation?"

The meeting decided against renting from Dulcie, except as a temporary expedient. They voted instead to find and buy a site for the church. One of the elders knew of an old house on Phya Thai Road that had been vacant for years and had the reputation of being haunted. No one would rent it, and recently the owners had not been able even to keep a watchman. One after another they left, saying that a woman in a green sarong came every night to haunt them, walking down out of the house on soundless feet. The elder said that the house could be purchased for twelve thousand ticals. With a unanimity that they had never before shown on any issue the group voted to buy it, if it proved on examination to be suitable.

India went with them to see the house. It had been sturdily built of brick and masonry and had settled very little with the years. The lower floor, which according to custom was the least honorable, had been divided into eight rooms. They would make ideal Sunday-school rooms or classrooms for the primary school Pastor Rasami wanted to start. The second story had one large room, fifty feet long and thirty wide, as well as several smaller rooms.

The original Siamese owner had been educated in Europe. He had entertained a great deal, and the large room had once been filled with beautiful rugs, furniture, and pictures that he had brought from France. Perhaps in an effort to outshine the other returning students, who likewise built homes in the semi-foreign manner, he had installed a stained-glass window at the western end of the room. The effect of the light coming through it in the late afternoon was very lovely.

It was the window that decided the elders and deacons. There was not another house in all Bangkok with such a window. Excited and determined, they squatted in the middle of the drawing room to plan. India went on soberly to examine the dining room, the two bedrooms and bath that were also part of the second floor. There was even a fine outside stairway leading to the drawing room, evidently a concession to the prejudices of the previous generation.

The compound was walled and badly overgrown. India did not risk the snakes that long grass easily concealed but looked out over it from a window. It would make an admirable playground. The fact that it was separated from the road by a canal and approached by a bridge was good. This increased the privacy. Only the bad name the house had acquired explained its cheapness.

The church had taken eleven years to raise their first four thousand ticals. Now faced with the necessity of securing more than that quickly if they were to have their building by Easter, which was their objective, they set about it with an enthusiasm that swept obstacles out of the way. They formed committees, they canvassed. Mr. Denniscort headed their list with a thousand ticals. An American businessman added a second thousand. Vina Stout gave them five hundred. Even Dulcie proudly wrote a check for a hundred. When they saw that they were going to have enough, they arranged an initial payment with the balance due in ninety days.

"Why have I coddled them all this time?" India wondered to herself.

The school year ended officially on Friday, March 20. There were no commencement exercises for the primary school, only a chapel service with some singing and recitations. The children received their report cards and said good-by to their teachers, and that was all. A formal announcement was made of the change of principals and head teachers, but the children hardly listened.

By noon it was all over, and the primary pupils had gone, with their books and papers and a little final scuffling among the boys, who considered themselves free agents once they had taken ceremonious leave of their classroom teachers. Det, with two coolies hired for the occasion, began to clean the building for the commencement exercises of the Bible school, which were to be that evening.

The four girls who were to graduate—Pinyo, Salee, Bua Kham, and Kae—had pasins of heavy silk in a shade of robin's-egg blue with blouses of the same color. Angela had designed the blouses, and they were very smart. Kae had wanted a permanent wave for the occasion, but since the other girls could not afford waves India had refused her permission. Kae was still a little sulky with disappointment until the imminence of the ceremony took hold of her. The girls looked completely charming when they were dressed, with their smooth black hair, their dark shining eyes, and bouquets of coral roses for each one.

The pulpit had been removed from the church platform, which was decorated with palms and ferns. There were a great many flowers also. The edges of the doors were outlined with palm fronds split in half, then bent to form an arch, the foliage being trimmed to six inches in length. Even the knowledge that this was the end of Jasmine Hall did not dim the pleasurable excitement of the girls who were taking part in the ceremony.

The guests arrived early and loitered in the garden or on the verandas, talking and laughing. Jim Howard was to make the commencement address. He and Anne came in as it was time to begin, and his laugh boomed across the compound. *Khon sanuk*, the Siamese called him. It was a term of approbation—a jolly person, someone whom it was good to be near, someone who could be counted on to be pleasant. His buoyancy attracted them, and they admired his enthusiasm also. It was a proper American quality.

"How is it going?" he asked India, while his eyes searched her face for the answer he thought she might withhold.

"Fine, Jim," she said. "Give them something to remember, will you? You know how they love high-sounding words."

"When are you moving?"

"The day after Easter."

"I'll be here to help," he promised.

The old organ began to play and was joined by the piano in "Pomp and Circumstance." The teachers and pupils marched in, followed by the four graduates single file, their bouquets on their left arms. They were self-conscious but pretty, teetering a little on the heels of their first foreign-style shoes. They sat down on the front row. Salee played a solo on the piano. She had developed very well under Angela's teaching. There was a duet, the Scripture reading, the valedictory, a vocal solo.

Then Jim stood up to speak.

"Friends," he began, "we have met here this evening to dedicate four young women to the work of the church. The occasion has more than ordinary solemnity because while it is a commencement it is also a termination. Their lives of service are beginning as the school that prepared them for that service is ending. It is fitting that we should mention both of these things."

He went on, and the audience listened intently. A child cried, and his mother took him out. A little girl trotted up and down the aisle, but this was to be expected and bothered no one. The noises of the night came in as from another world. The group in the church was caught in the web of diffused light which separated them from the darkness outside. There was a spell over them that came from more than the speaker's words. The sense of finality the closing of the school gave contributed to it, but it was something beyond that. It was a feeling, momentary and yet real, of communality, with the girls who were graduating and the other girls for whom the school was ending too soon, with the teachers and India who had made the school, and the church, and the outer ring of parents and relatives, and beyond them, on the far side of the world, with others of like faith.

Jim felt the knitting together of his audience. As he finished, he said:

"The school is ending, and yet in another sense it is only changing form. It is no longer a building and a group of teachers. That phase of its existence is over. It has become these four young women and others like them who serve the church. In that sense it will go on as long and as well as their service. I charge you, graduates and students alike, to remember that you have become the repository of the hopes, the prayers, the efforts of your teachers. I charge you to remember that you do not live unto yourselves alone. As what has been is now a part of you, so what you are and what you have learned must be transmitted to those you teach. It is in this way the endless chain of service that binds the church universal is maintained. And it is a solemn obligation. *For unto whomsoever much is given, of him shall be much required.*"

He raised his arms and the audience bowed their heads.

"The peace of God, which passeth all understanding, keep your hearts and minds in the knowledge and love of God, and of His Son Jesus Christ our Lord; and the blessing of God Almighty, the Father, the Son, and the Holy Spirit, be amongst you, and remain with you always. Amen."

It was over. The school had ceased to exist.

There remained only the details of its physical dissolution. Dulcie, who had been absent on one or another of her mysterious errands for two weeks, was suddenly everywhere. She had made up her mind that the furniture in Jasmine Hall was hers by right, and she was determined to overrule India's decision to give it to the church.

India paid little attention to her. She moved still through the vast plains of unreality. The physical sensation of being freed from the pull of gravity, of being no longer rooted in the earth, of rolling before the wind, endlessly rolling on and on, continued. She was almost never hungry, and if she was tired she did not know it. What had to be done she did, but without emotion. She was glad for this lack of feeling. It made everything easier, so that she seemed to be anesthetized even against the pinpricks of Dulcie's acerbity.

No amount of patient explanation had any effect on Dulcie. The church was hurriedly cleaning their building and making a few essential repairs in preparation for Easter. As the time for the removal of the furniture grew closer, Dulcie pressed harder.

"You're acting out of spite," she said angrily to India. "I got Jasmine Hall and you have to go, and this is your revenge. But I won't let them take the furniture. You'll see."

Jim Howard, who was there at the time, replied, "Is that India's reward for giving you a home these past six years?"

Dulcie tossed her high-piled hair. "I've worked for everything I've had. I don't owe India a thing. And I'm going to keep the furniture."

"On the contrary, you've received a great deal for which you've returned neither work nor gratitude," Jim retorted. "But however that may be, Pastor Rasami and I are coming for the furniture next Wednesday morning so it can be in place for the Good Friday services."

"I won't let the trucks through the gate," Dulcie flared. "You can't trespass on my property. It's stealing, that's what it is, and I'll call the police if you try it."

Dulcie and India were on the mook the morning of April 1 when Jim's car turned into the lane. Dulcie had sent Det to bolt the gate earlier, and now she kept guard from her rocking chair. She started up, but Jim was alone. His car came to a stop. He stepped out and through the postern gate and unbolted the big gate. Then he walked back unhurriedly to his car.

He was a large man, but agile, and his movements were so sure they did not seem as quick as they were. When he had started his car he roared the motor. At the sound of the roar a big truck turned into the lane from the street and came through the gate behind him at high speed. Car and truck drew up at the front veranda.

Jim bounded upstairs cheerfully, as if there had been no duplicity in his action. Dulcie had jumped to her feet, but stood angry and confused by the speed of the truck's entry.

"Look, Dulcie," Jim said, "I've been thinking about you, living in this big house and I've been wondering if we couldn't make you a present or two for your room. Before we take the things out tell me what pieces you'd like to have for yourself. Will that be all right, India?"

"Why, yes, surely, with a few exceptions, of course."

Dulcie's eyes still sparkled with anger. "I want all the desks, blackboards, tables, chairs, and beds," she said waspishly.

"Oh, come now, Dulcie, you can't get them all into your room. Choose one or two pieces and we'll give them to you as a personal gift. You can have the finest piece in the house."

Dulcie faltered. The childlike side of her mind was caught by the pleasurableness of making a choice. She paused to consider, wondering what, after all, she liked most of the things in the house. These many years she had moved through a world in which she owned little but her own clothes. She had slept on other people's beds, sat on their chairs, eaten off their tables, kept her things in their chests and almirahs, used their cupboards and pianos. As long as India was mistress of Jasmine Hall, Dulcie had not even had the power to determine what went into her own room. She must ask for it. She was charmed now with the prospect of uninhibited ownership.

"I want India's big four-poster bed."

India and Jim had discussed their strategy in advance, but this was more than Jim had reckoned on, and he cocked his eye at India. She nodded. The bed was too large and unwieldy anyway. If it represented something special to Dulcie, let her have it. Downstairs the clatter of benches and desks being removed and piled into the truck sounded clearly, but Dulcie was oblivious.

"I want the desk in Angela's room, and that almirah too."

"All right. But not until Angela leaves."

Dulcie paused to consider, savoring the situation, pleased and diverted by the novelty of the game. If she heard the sounds of the furniture being removed she ignored it grandly, as beneath this new dignity that had come to her.

"I want some chairs, of course," she continued.

"Which chairs?"

She pointed them out, and Jim set them aside.

"Is that all?" he asked, eager to be off to supervise the coolies below.

She looked around carefully, determined not to miss anything she might later wish she had chosen, unwilling to let the charmed moment escape her.

"Well, the dining-room table and chairs, and the bedside table I already have, and the coir rug. And there's one more thing. I'd like the big curio cabinet that used to stand in the drawing room at Wang Lang. It belonged to my friend Miss Linwood."

The cabinet was a large one. It had come from the United States and had fared badly in the tropics. The varnish was chipped and peeling, as was some of the veneer. The joints had been reglued many times. The base had been eaten by termites and later filled with concrete. Jim looked at it dubiously where it stood against the wall of what had been the church.

"I'm not sure we can move it without having the base fall off."

Annoyance stormed over Dulcie's face at once, and Jim, seeing his good work undone, revised his opinion hastily.

"I'll tell you what I'll do, Dulcie. If you'll wait until I get back from my vacation I'll bring a cabinetmaker around and have him repair it for you. I'm afraid to move it the way it is. If the base falls out while we're carrying it, the glass may break, and we couldn't get a rounded glass like that anywhere in Bangkok."

Dulcie's face cleared. Then a crafty, calculating look came into it. "How much will it cost to have it fixed?"

"Oh, seven or eight ticals, I guess."

"I think it will take ten."

"All right, ten. I'll get it done for you." He was impatient to get away.

Dulcie was delighted. "If you'll just give me the ten ticals I'll spare you the trouble of getting it done. I know the very man."

"Not that she will, the old fox," Jim said later to India, but to Dulcie he said nothing.

He opened his billfold and took out the money. Dulcie accepted it with imperturbable dignity. Nor did she interfere with the removal of the rest of the furniture.

When it was all gone, except what Dulcie and India were keeping, Jim urged India to bring Angela and stay with Anne and himself, but she refused.

"I'd really rather stay here," she told him. "I'm very grateful for the invitation, but I don't want to accept it, Jim."

"You'll do too much thinking."

She shook her head. "There's been so much going on I haven't done any yet, and in the end it has to be done, you know."

"Later, then, when you're not so tired," he urged her.

"No, Jim, I have to pack my dreams in mothballs, and I want to do it here."

"India, that's futile," he said almost roughly. "I should think you'd know better."

"Maybe I should, but I won't have any peace of mind until I've thought everything out."

"This thing happened to you from outside. It wasn't your own doing."

"Perhaps, Jim, and yet somewhere there must have been a wrong turning that could have been avoided if it had been recognized."

"India, stop and think! There are a thousand possible turnings for every day in the week, and not all of them can be right. You remember how the Pharisees lay in wait for Christ, *seeking to catch something out of his mouth, that they might accuse him.* And in the end they got what they wanted at the price of their souls. If someone has laid a trap, well, none of us should blame ourselves for the result."

"It isn't as simple as that," she said slowly.

"But it is. India, listen to me! Grace and Amery have taken the work you wanted to do away from you. If you think that you could have appeased them, you're wrong. It was you yourself that challenged them and made them feel less by comparison, and it was you they struck at, not just Jasmine Hall. In the end nothing could have changed that. What I wish I could make you see is that there's something they can't take from you, the person you are and the things you've done and still can do. Not many of us have your ability to work with people, for instance. People trust you. They come to you, and you help them. And Bangkok is still full of people. I know this doesn't seem like much to you now. I'd only like to remind you that it's more than most of us have ever had."

He turned away in sudden annoyance with himself.

"I don't know why I'm preaching at you," he said. "I guess it's a habit. Excuse it, India. I'll see you later." He started down the stairs, then turned back. "I almost forgot. Here's something Anne told me to give you if I couldn't persuade you to come to us."

He handed India an envelope and left.

Anne had written on it in her firm hand with green ink:

A prescription for India, to be taken daily before breakfast, with the reminder that she has done a thousand times more than this and has no cause for regret. Love, Anne.

Inside the envelope were a few typed lines:

> *If I can stop one heart from breaking,*
> *I shall not live in vain;*
> *If I can ease one life the aching,*
> *Or cool one pain,*
> *Or help one fainting robin*
> *Unto his nest again,*
> *I shall not live in vain.*
>
> —Emily Dickinson

CHAPTER 34

ANGELA'S SHIP WAS SAILING WITH THE TIDE ON THE EVENING OF Saturday, April 4. It was intensely hot now that April had begun, with the dry heat that would continue until the monsoon broke.

That morning early the pigeon orchids bloomed. India was deeply glad. Their blooming was always unpredictable and welcome. From one end of the peninsula to the other, suddenly and without warning, they flowered on the same day and at the same hour everywhere. After the second day they were gone.

She caught a whiff of them as she was dressing, and went down into the garden before breakfast to gather some. On her way upstairs she stopped in the office to look for a quotation the orchids had suggested:

There often exhales from certain flowers something more and even better than perfume—I mean certain circumstances of life with which they are associated and with which they inseparably dwell in the mind, or rather in the heart, even as the hamadryads were not able to quit their oaks!

How very true, she thought. Because they had bloomed today they would always afterward be for her Angela's flower.

She set them loosely into a vase, where they looked like a flight of miniature doves, crystalline white, balancing along the slender gray stems that supported them. The blossoms were widely spaced, and there were no leaves, only the flowers an inch across, incredibly delicate and incredibly perfect.

Their light intoxicating scent sifted through the empty rooms of Jasmine Hall, and soon the whole house was spiced with the odor. It was a heady fragrance with none of the languor of other tropical flowers. Where the heavy-scented *jombi* and *jomba* gave forth a drugged perfume, the pigeon orchids were sparkling and piquant.

After breakfast Angela went off on a series of last-minute errands while India did her final packing. She wanted to do this, even argued when Angela protested that she would save time for it later. Emptying drawers, India thought to herself that she was old enough to indulge in a little sentimentality, while Angela was still too young to find it anything but maudlin. Well, she would not be there to pack Angela's clothes for her wedding journey, and this would have to suffice. Almost every dress stirred a memory. She would savor them while she could, folding her thoughts away as she folded the clothes.

She was glad that Angela was leaving Jasmine Hall before she

did. It was always better to go than to be left. And this approached
the pattern of normality: a child leaving home, going into a charted
future, taking the core of her being with her, intact and unafraid.
During the last few days something of feeling had crept back to
India's numbed heart, and she was content that it should be so, even
though what she felt was a bitter mixture of desolation and joy. She
would not have avoided it if she could. She had learned long ago
that to feel—regret, grief, sorrow, pain—as she did now, was better
than insensibility, which blotted out everything in a clammy fog of
unfeeling.

Here was the white dress Angela had been wearing the day Kurt
first came to the house. India held it up, half smiling, thinking of
how he had seemed just a stranger, someone to be greeted and forgotten. And here was the dress Angela had worn the first day she
came to Jasmine Hall. India remembered her face as it had been
that morning, white and pinched with suppressed fears and incipi-
ent illness. And here was the afternoon gown she had worn at the
Legation tea. India fingered the tissue thoughtfully, seeing Angela
once again in the late afternoon sun of the Legation veranda, like a
figure of carved gold. She sighed and put the dress carefully into a
bag with layers of tissue paper. Was it really less than a year ago?
The dresses had a faint fragrance from the sachets that had been
fastened to the hangers which held them. In the warm room they
made a bouquet.

The ship was not sailing until eight-thirty, when the tide would
be high. Angela's trunk was already on it. She was going to Singapore, where she would take a P. & O. steamer for London and there
change for New York.

She did not come in until late in the afternoon to bathe and dress
for dinner. India herself set the table since all the house servants
except Plo had gone. She put on a cloth of linen and lace that Eng
Siow's father had brought her from China, set the forks and knives
carefully straight, and brought out her best dishes of Chinese rice
ware. The china was a clear white with traceries of blue and a
pattern around and beneath them that the rice grains had left. She
had roses for the centerpiece and four fat new candles as red as the
roses, with the usual gold characters pasted around their bases.

Kurt arrived at six-thirty, and at seven they sat down. No one said much. There were little gusts of conversation, then silence, not strained but preoccupied. Each of the three at the table was moving away from the others on a stream of thought where one alone could go. None of them ate a great deal, but there was no sadness about this last meal that they would share in the old house. When they were through they went to Angela's room and closed her bags. Det carried them to the car, and Plo came down to see Angela off. She had a little tin of cakes as a going-away present. Angela thanked her gravely, then threw her arms around Plo's neck.

"Good-by, Plo," she said, and for the first time there were tears in her eyes. "You've been so good to me. Thank you."

Plo did not understand the English words, but she understood the emotion. She smiled and raised her joined palms in the Siamese salaam.

"God go with you and bless you," she said in Siamese.

Dusk was already thick over the harbor as they took the launch out to the ship. The lights were on in the cabins. Five or six Siamese students were leaving for Europe, and their relatives and friends were everywhere. The necks of the students were ringed with garlands. India felt a stab of annoyance with herself. She should have ordered a garland for Angela. It would have been the one perfect thing to do. Kurt had filled the cabin with fruit and flowers and books, but India wished that she had thought of the garland.

Then it was time to go. India disliked farewells. They were always inadequate to their purpose, anticlimax, the letdown, a kind of mockery of what had gone before. One pecked a friend on the cheek and murmured a few nothings. What, after all, was there to say at the end? Yet not to say good-by was to leave the sentence without its period. So under the goad of convention she turned and kissed Angela, when what she wanted to do was walk down the stairs to the landing stage and climb into the launch.

"Thank you, India," Angela whispered, putting her arms around her. "I—I—— Oh, India, thank you so much," and she burst into tears.

India disengaged herself gently. "God bless you, child," she said, and turned to the stairs.

In five minutes Kurt joined her. The launch moved away from the ship, which rocked easily on the river swell, with all its lights glittering across the darkness.

The house, when India reached it, seemed not so much dead as alive, alive with all that had happened in it. She had thought she might find returning to it unbearable, but she did not. The old stairs creaked as she climbed to the second story. The little ching-choks slithered above her head where the light Plo had turned on made a circle of yellow on the ceiling of the mook. The floor boards of the veranda creaked also, and the empty room that had been the church echoed to her steps, but she did not mind. The house was full of the people and things that had been, the comings and goings and beings and changings that had taken place there.

It was only nine-thirty, but she undressed and got ready for bed. Tomorrow was Easter. On Monday she would leave Jasmine Hall forever.

It was not until she pulled out the net from under the edge of the mattress that she saw the small white package on her pillow. She knew at once that it was from Angela and thought how like her it was to have put it there where it would be found only when she had gone.

India took it to the light and untied it. Inside the box was a second wrapping of tissue paper. She opened it carefully, and there in her palm lay a string of pearls. Angela's pearls!

"No, oh no!" India said, startled into speaking aloud.

They were like drops of moonlight, clear, unsullied, translucent, with a still beauty in which there was no chill. She sat for a long time looking at them before she read the card in Angela's hand—"To my mother-in-love, from Angela."

The tears that had not come all the long month of March, when her heart was parched as dry as the ground in the garden, came now, streaming down her face as she sat with the pearls in her hand. She did not try to stop them or even to wipe them away. She did not know what they meant or why they had come. It hardly mattered. They were like the rain which responded to laws one need not understand to know what it could do. At last the tears stopped of themselves, and she went to bed, placing the pearls in their box under her pillow.

CHAPTER 35

WHEN INDIA AWOKE THE TROPICAL MORNING WAS, IF NOT COOL, still clear. There was as yet no premonition of the pressing heat that would come later in the day.

After breakfast she sent Plo to church. She herself stayed home. It was the first time she could remember not going to church on Easter, but she wanted to be by herself for a while. In the afternoon there would be people coming and going as always. Now there was a little interval of quiet in which to think.

> *And peace I folded neatly*
> *And joy I hung to air—*
> *It took both arms to lift it*
> *Along the attic stair:*
> *Bliss I tied in lavender*
> *And comfort laid in rue . . .*

The garden was still. The gate was shut. India found a bench under the tree where the pigeon orchids had bloomed. Today the flowers resembled doves at rest. Wings that had been spread yesterday were tight against their bodies. Each small bird was balanced on a silvery stem, as if its flight were over at last and forever. The perfume of yesterday was gone also. Only a faint and occasional trace of it came to India, when a puff of breeze stirred the thickness of the morning air that was already warming toward noon.

The stillness surrounding her was complete. Even the faint and unmistakable clatter of the shops came as from far away. While she sat with her hands in her lap a great yellow butterfly danced lazily across the garden through the shimmering air. Her eyes followed it, back and forth and away, up and down and up again. In the shade of the rain tree on the old bench, the memories she had come into the garden to compose folded themselves away. What had been, had been and was. It had merged with the present. The need to go back dissolved. There was no room for bitterness in life. One was too small to know the purposes of God, too small even to measure the vastness of His plan or assay one's part in it.

The butterfly continued to dance through the hot bright air, smoothly, effortlessly, up and down, and its shining beauty engrossed her. The thinking she had believed she must do no longer seemed important. Let the dead past bury its dead. Let yesterday take care of yesterday, and tomorrow of tomorrow. She felt a sense of peace pervading her body. It was enough this Easter morning to watch the butterfly in flight. There was a long fluttering arc and then a pause on some flower where its wings moved slowly in the sun.

She sat entranced by the finality of its beauty. In the deep quiet that filled her the butterfly seemed part and symbol of Easter. Death, resurrection, life. They were all typified here. Bethlehem, Galilee, Jerusalem, Gethsemane, Golgotha, the sepulcher. And Easter, the great mystery, she thought.

In the end of the sabbath, as it began to dawn toward the first day of the week, came Mary Magdalene and the other Mary to see the sepulchre. . . . And when they looked, they saw that the stone was rolled away: for it was very great. And entering into the sepulchre, they saw a young man sitting on the right side, clothed in a long white garment; and they were affrighted. And he saith unto them . . . He is not here: for he is risen, as he said. Come, see the place where the Lord lay.

The butterfly was a soaring, a transcendent thing. It was not the fleshy worm it had once been. That state lay behind, as did the tomb of the chrysalis. It was the miracle of life after death displayed in microcosm. There was some lesson for her here, if she could find it. Yet she must not strive to understand. She must wait until the revelation came, in good time, now or later, it did not greatly matter.

For now we see through a glass, darkly; but then face to face: now I know in part; but then shall I know even as also I am known.

The meaning of defeat, the meaning of death, who could fathom either? They were too deep for the plummets of a human mind.

I die daily, the Apostle Paul had said. And that was true. There were a thousand deaths beside that final sleep of the body, perhaps each one a death of the earthly to make a resurrection of the spiritual. And who, knowing the death of self which was service, could doubt the continuing miracle of the resurrection, or predicate its form? That, too, belonged to God.

The future was no more her concern than the past. The sowing was finished now. The reaping had fallen to other hands. Perhaps she would not even see the harvest. Did that matter then?

Verily, verily, I say unto you, Except a corn of wheat fall into the ground and die, it abideth alone: but if it die, it bringeth forth much fruit.

The old words gleamed with an iridescence like the butterfly's wings. All she had hoped, all she had worked for, all she had planned and done, was dead. Eleven years of her life. Her corn of wheat.

It is sown in corruption: it is raised in incorruption: it is sown in dishonour: it is raised in glory.

Yes, defeat was often the seed of victory, waving its flag in the sprouting of the corn.

There would be days—who knew?—perhaps months of discouragement. One could not inter eleven years of oneself and everything one had hoped without grief. Sometimes she would lie awake nights asking: "How was I wrong?" or, "Where could I have done differently?" or again, "If I had made this turning instead of that, would the end have been other than it is?" Yet the clouds had opened for an instant, and she had seen life in the light of the glory of the purposes of God.

Now it came to pass . . . as I was among the captives by the river of Chebar, that the heavens were opened, and I saw visions of God.

Infinite calm filled her heart on a great tide of peace, and the old became new. She felt again the reach, and height, and depth of the grace of God, which is eternally new each time it is experienced by

groping human beings. On this Easter morning, as a fresh awareness of the meaning in life stirred her, India knelt beside the bench
with a feeling of awe like that of the two women in the garden
when they understood for the first time the significance of the empty
tomb.

The butterfly fluttered away across the garden hedge and was
gone. After a moment India's thoughts veered to another tomb, and
she remembered the bronze figure by Saint-Gaudens in Rock Creek
Cemetery in Washington. Someone had called it the most beautiful
thing fashioned by the hand of man on the North American con-
tinent. Did the statue have a name? She had heard it called *Grief,*
but that was wrong. The woman in bronze had left grief far behind.
Her face was enigmatic; withdrawn, perhaps; still, certainly; but
there was no grief in it, though there may have been grief long ago.
The face spoke rather of something that was beyond grief, beyond
pain. It spoke of something that was beyond the struggles of life,
beyond death, beyond sorrow, beyond earthliness. All those things it
had left behind on its progress into the realm of the spirit. What was
the word? Or was there a word for that face?

Not a single word, perhaps, or she could think of none, but there
were words. They came to her clearly like the sound of bells in the
distance.

> . . . *Ensured release,*
> *Imperishable peace,*
> *Have these for yours,*
> *While sky and sea and land*
> *And earth's foundations stand*
> *And heaven endures.*

There they were—*ensured release, imperishable peace.* The
woman in bronze had found them. She had passed the barrier of
ordinary sorrow and disappointment and despair and had entered
a garden of peace.

There remaineth therefore a rest to the people of God.

That was it. Not escape from despair and defeat and frustration
and the bitter death of hope, for there was no escape, but the thing
beyond. There was a state of rest that was life, not death, of acceptance that was not an end but a beginning.

Be still, and know that I am God.

Be still and know. Be still . . . Yes, the figure of bronze had been in the center of a great stillness. Somehow she knew, somehow she had learned the meaning of the resurrection.

This, then, this death in life, this rising up again of the spirit from the tomb of its despairs, this rolling away of the stone, was a foreshadowing of the greater resurrection, the life after death of self.

"I am not far from this knowledge myself," India thought with a great rushing influx of joy. "Perhaps I am already there."

She had paid for it with everything she had ever wanted or been or tried to accomplish. These were all dead, all of her that had been, but she was on the threshold of something beyond, of ensured release, of the great stillness, of imperishable peace, which came from God. It flooded in and in until there was room for nothing else in her heart, until her mind and body were full of it, until her hands tingled with it, until she felt as light as the butterfly that had danced before her in the air.

What was it that Booker T. Washington had said when someone asked him about the discourtesies he had endured? *No man can hurt my feelings.* She had never realized before how much the quiet statement meant. It wasn't arrogance. It was the state-of-being-beyond speaking, the thing that came after the slow and painful death of self, the endless knife wounds of insult and contempt, the bleeding of heart and mind. He had passed through the invisible veil into the sanctuary where the untouchable stillness was. *No man can hurt my feelings.* No, never again.

She knew with simple acceptance of her own limitations that she was not past caring. It was rather that she had experienced in the garden a moment of eternity, and in the light of the eternal had felt the span of her own years take on proportion and place. She had known with completeness that what she had been able to do could never be taken from her, and what had been taken from her was not to be.

It was Easter morning, and the stone had been rolled away. The grave clothes were still in their place, and the linen napkin also, but Christ had left them behind. He had met her on the road to Emmaus, and she was whole again, beyond pain, beyond death, beyond sorrow, beyond grief, beyond frustration, and beyond despair.

The words grew and swelled until they took on the accents of music, and the music became chords, and the chords a great chorale. It filled the reaches of the garden with its triumph like a cathedral organ.

> *Hallelujah! Hallelujah!*
> *For the Lord God Omnipotent reigneth!*
> *King of Kings and Lord of Lords!*
> *Hallelujah! Hallelujah! Hallelujah!*

"How strangely beautiful life is!" she thought, and closed her eyes to hear better the throbbing grandeur of the great magnificat that shook her soul.